To my wife Nedi

DESERT
PASSIONS
Wild Love in Sinai

ROBERT BETTELHEIM

DESERT
PASSIONS
Wild Love in Sinai

ROBERT BETTELHEIM

SAMUEL WACHTMAN'S SONS

DEKEL PUBLISHING HOUSE

ROBERT BETTELHEIM

DESERT PASSIONS
Wild Love in Sinai

Copyright © 2018

Dekel Publishing House
www.dekelpublishing.com

North American rights by
Samuel Wachtman's Sons, Inc.
ISBN 978-1-941905-19-7

English editing:	Richard Reinprecht
Graphic design:	Giulio Venturi
Proof reading:	Pnina Ophir

For information contact:

Dekel Publishing House	**Samuel Wachtman's Sons, Inc.**
P.O. Box 6430, Tel Aviv	2460 Garden Road, Suite C
6106301, ISRAEL	Monterey, CA 93940, U.S.A.
Tel: +972 3506-3235	Tel: 831 649-0669
Fax: +972 3604-4627	Fax: 831 649-8007
Email: info@dekelpublishing.com	Email: samuelwachtman@gmail.com

TABLE OF CONTENTS

SINAI 1967-1982

The desert can be a strange place to any citizen raised in an urban society, a harsh place where there may be no second chances. The conditions are inconsiderate and unforgiving to man and animal alike and mistakes can be costly. Here is nature at her very fiercest and the desert has conditioned and educated the people who live there to its inflexible realities. In modern times, the desert can also be a place for tourists seeking peace and quiet from a stressed and perhaps overactive, urban lifestyle. The eastern part of the Sinai desert bordering along the red sea had fast turned into a haven, a refuge and a place to relax and feel free. . . .

The Sinai desert is a peninsula, a wild triangle-shaped piece of land lying roughly between Egypt in the southwest and Israel to the northeast and has been a kind of no-men's land for centuries, inhabited by Bedouin tribes only. On its one-side lies an arm-like outlet of the Red Sea stretching out to Israel and on the other side are Egypt, the Suez Canal and the Mediterranean Sea. Any traveler traveling in the desert can well imagine the forty years of wandering by the Israelite tribes escaping their slavery from ancient Egypt, as related in the Bible.

With the coming of Israel's independence, the desert had turned into an asylum for smugglers and armed infiltrators. The Sinai desert usually lies in relative peace for large periods of time but in the twentieth century of our counting the serenity was shattered by skirmishes and two larger wars and in the six days war Sinai had passed over to Israel. Roads were built and many improvised tourist resorts had sprung up, mostly along the Red Sea coast, where in many places there are amazing underwater scenes. The coast has many areas of isolated sandy beaches with many hidden coves for privacy. Sinai is roughly two to three times the size of Israel and many Israelis rushed in to enjoy the vast expanses of empty space. Tourist agencies organized tours from all over the world and small villages and hamlet places began to flourish. The Bedouins living there, found their first real closer contact with Westerners. In many places, there is little or no water to be had and the army occupied it by dragging huge water tanks to wherever they might be needed.

We humans have a tendency to hypocrisy and the Bedouins are no exceptions. A two-faced code of behavior had developed. Theirs is a male dominated society and their women are kept on a short leash. Unmarried girls were seldom let out of the family compound and never without escorts. With the influx of Westerners to the Sinai resorts, nudity and sex were common. There were no tourist police, and the local males flirted and passed the time with female tourists of the other sex, both indifferent to race or creed, or a marriage license, it had become a free for all.

Traveling in the Sinai desert cannot but help to make the occasional nomadic itinerants, on jeep, car, bus, camel or donkey and especially pedestrian, wonder and speculate about the vast geologic periods of time that have passed and if comparing those with our own diminutive life span, will realize how short life really is. Even the most callous may be affected in some way. . . . They will put their daily issues behind and marvel at the forces of nature which hint at a clue to all existence and reality.

Robert Bettelheim,
Zikim, June 2018

THE THIEF

The term 'thief' is an ancient one in many languages, since thefts in one way or another are an integral part of our culture and history, probably from pre-recorded times. This tiny piece of information may draw attention to the fact that not a few words in our current Western world, are residue from Roman times, but the word 'thief' is not one of those. Each country and civilization has kept its own original and ancient idiom for stealing. Going further back in time, we can find mention of thievery in one of the Ten Commandments and before that even in ancient Egypt, which shows us one blunt label which has been around for a long while.

With the arrival of later civilizations and even more so in our modern times, we have created many additional expressions and terminology along the line for this very human act, adorning and disguising it with many high-sounding names, it has become sophisticated and complex, often involving highly organized participation, and the combined contribution of many institutes and individuals. We can call it to confiscate, or impound, commandeer or take over, take possession, requisition, annex, percentage . . . etc. . . . etc., we can even call it billing or sometimes taxes. All those are legal terms, as only too frequently the really big crooks are in charge and have legalized much of the act of grabbing and it is mostly the minor felons that are at odds with the law and keep the local police force occupied.

Gabi, not being aware of the former topic, would not have cared, or given much attention to it, even if he had. He had other occupations. As a youth, young and fast, he lived by his wits in one of the many sections in downtown Tel Aviv. Among the many other, of his not so legal, talents, he specialized in taking clandestine possession of articles not belonging to him. Being agile, alert and supple, few are the locked apartments which can withstand his endeavors to enter them when their occupants are away. He was not above handling drugs. If fortune turns against him, as it sometimes happens, then he would very enterprisingly create his own opportunities.

Fickle fate had not been kind to him lately and things had been getting very hot. Gabi, having stumbled upon a cheap source of drugs, borrowed as much money as his friends were willing to lend him and set about to peddle the stuff. Sadly, it turned out that the pills were weak and almost worthless. The ones they had given him to sample had been strong. They had cheated him! Those unfortunate circumstances had forced him to sell them at a loss. Desperate to get rid of his lousy wares, he had impinged on the local boss's industry and for once had not got away with it. His enterprising deals had clashed with the well-organized local, but not legal, activities in the area. There had also been complaints and threats and those induced him to move out of his territory into the neighboring one. There too, many people had been after him to demonstrate to him the error of his ways and he had twice narrowly escaped from some severe mauling. His name had been turned over to the police. Israel is a small country and hiding from the lengthy groping hand of justice is not feasible for too long a period. He might have to leave town for a while.

At this moment in time he happened to be 'laying low', not merely hiding from justice, that too of course, as a matter of routine, is only natural, but the main reasons for his concern and concealment were of a much more grim and somber nature.

Some of the bosses' family goons were after him and they meant business. He had hurriedly fled from his tiny shared room and crashed with one of his not so enthusiastic friends, when the latter said to him, "You can't stay here. You'll get us both in trouble."

"I don't have anywhere else to go."

"Get yourself to Sinai. They can't reach you over there."

"The desert? What shall I do over there?"

"It is full of tourists, Israeli and others, you'll get by."

It might be a good idea, but it did not take his fancy. Not having been away from Tel Aviv in years had made him uneasy to distance himself too far from the neighborhood that he and his contacts infested.

"I don't like it," came out of him.

"Yeah maybe being in jail is better," his friend mocked, "they'll get you in there."

Gabi, only too aware of the subject, knew that the inmates in jail had connections to the outside world and would make him suffer retribution for his misdeeds. They might cut or maim him, maybe even kill him as an example to warn others to keep their hands off the bosses' territory. There seemed not much choice involved, better leave and hide until things cooled off a bit. Gabi contemplated the matter with extreme aversion. The downtown section of the city used to be the place where Gabi had grown up to early manhood. There were his connections with their information; the tools of his survival, the area where he knew every alley, corner, passage and niche. The girls too knew him and on a slow night, their guys sometimes would let him have them at a discount or on a promise to deliver later.

Gabi, at the age of ten, been found himself an unwilling and terrified spectator as his dad, had killed his mom, striking her repeatedly with a knife and then pulling out a gun had shot himself. The horror of it would be a memory his soul rejected, but would come to him in dreams and nightmares, always disguised, making him unaware of its real meaning, but the emotions involved had been fierce and unmerciful and dealing with those by trying to ignore and reject them, did not help much. Growing up in a series of foster homes, he had been unmanageable, his mentors and overseers had moved him from one home to another, until he finally had run away. Gabi felt emotionally attached to the seedy downtown part of the city, but he could never admit this, considering emotions to be a sign of weakness.

At last he said, "Okay, I'll get going, but I need some cash." Knowing well enough that his buddy would dish out some money just to be rid of him; a liability and a risk to anyone who sheltered him. Gabi trusted no one, his friend might inform on him to find favor with the big guys.

Gabi left during the night taking the night bus. The next morning found him in Eilat, making his way to the tourist places. The town is north to an arm of the Red Sea and bordering the Sinai desert. In most seasons, there are many tourists there, local and international.

There were many five star hotels, shops and stalls by the seashore and the tourist centers. Numerous people were about enjoying the scene. Many were bathing in the red sea. Mats and blankets with clothes on them, dotted the beach. Further off cars were parked. Gabi had a good idea where people hide their money and soon found some wrapped in towels and under clothes, it was the one thing he did well, one might even term him gifted in that department. Gabi, having learned how car keys are often hidden in the exhaust pipes of cars, or under a stone nearby, while their owners are away, helped himself to some food and money, a lady's wrist watch and a tiny radio included while about it. 'Easy pickings,' the thought came to him, "this town is not so bad, why bother to go further south into the desert?'

Hitching a short ride, found him by an unguarded beach, not too far from the town. He saw tents stretched almost side by side. Large family tents besides smaller ones for couples. A few had been hastily constructed with blankets, all in all, a colorful spectacle, but Gabi was not interested in the view. Many of the people on vacation had gone shopping into the town or were bathing and had left their tents unoccupied.

'This is almost too easy' were his delighted thoughts, as he furtively helped himself to some more articles, including a bag to hold them. The sun had reached its zenith and the heat made itself felt. Looking around, he found a solitary shady place away from the beach, on the other side of the road to rest. Caching his loot there and being very tired from his exertions, he fell asleep in the shade.

The city council and hotel owners in Eilat had a strong interest in developing the tourist area, even more so, as many passed through on their way to the Sinai desert. There existed a running competition for the pockets of those visitors, inducing them to remain in the town for a few days before moving on southwards. An efficient strong police force had been formed to see that things run smoothly. There had been complaints. Money had been stolen and personal effects had disappeared, cars had been broken in somehow and valuables were missing. The police were set into motion.

The next morning, very early, before the sun arose, which Gabi knew by experience to be the best time for his exploits, found him exercising his talent in the dark. He did not enter the tents sprawling around. His technique was to lie down beside some of the smaller ones on the outside, then carefully and silently make a slit with a razor parallel to the ground and then downwards, inserting his hand and groping about cautiously, almost with surgical precision, so as not to awake any occupants. His searching hands would sometimes find a bag or purse or other articles of value. He had been thus occupied when two police cars appeared on the road running along the seashore. They were scrutinizing the area using a strong searchlight.

"I saw something move," one police officer exclaimed.

"A dog."

"Maybe a burglar."

"The Sergeant is driving us crazy. We'd better have a look."

A few Policemen got off and seemed to be coming Gabi's way, shining their flashlights. Gabi quickly realized that there would be no place for him to hide. Some of the tents might be unoccupied, as people sometimes remained in the town for the night. Raising himself from his supine position, Gabi gave the area a quick once over in the faint moonlight. Nearby stood a tent which appeared to be sealed and closed tightly, it looked deserted. Getting inside would be a risk, but there seemed no other choice. Moving fast, before the police approached any nearer crawling on his belly, Gabi quickly unfastened the opening and slid in, zipping it shut from the inside. Luck was with him this time; he found the tent vacant. It had been a close shave. He waited with a beating heart until the search ended, hoping that the owners of the tent would not arrive.

Late morning found him at his cache, emptying it and stuffing his filched loot into a bag. Hiking into the town, looking for a likely place to get rid of the articles with no questions asked would not be easy or to his liking. Having no connections in Eilat, made him feel exposed and defenseless. After much wandering around, he did find such a place, away from the tourist center. The shopkeeper had driven a hard bargain.

"The stuff here is worth five times as much," he complained.

"You'd better take the cash I offered. There is a police station nearby. You get my drift!"

It had not been a question. Gabi took the little money offered to him and fled. He had walked off with a less than a quarter of what his loot was worth. Eilat did not look so good to him anymore and if they caught him, it might go hard with him in a prison. Not the guards but the inmates were the focal point of his concern.

Gabi crossed into the Sinai desert in the afternoon. The spectacular scenery did not interest him. Quizzing his fellow travelers about the seaside resorts, big and small, he intended to get as far away from Tel Aviv as possible, while finding a prosperous place, compatible with his special talents. Hitching rides, caused him to end up in one of the smaller but more promising tourist centers; Dahab, which had once been a minor fishing village, a four-hour drive south from Eilat and nine or ten hours away from Tel Aviv; 'far enough' it seemed to him. Asking around and renting a cubicle-like room with a mattress for a few pounds, sleep came to him quickly.

The next day Gabi crisscrossed the place, taking notice of the many camps with rooms for rent and places where the tourists were concentrated. In the period of the Israeli jurisdiction, Dahab had been turned into a chaotic place, by the enormous numbers of people flocking there. All appeared very lax and easygoing and it happened to be this, as much as the beaches and the marvelous underwater scenes that the tourists loved. Here would be his new hunting ground and the more information gathered, the easier it would be. Some backpackers slept on the beach not bothering to put up a tent and tourists who rented rooms did not always bother to lock their doors when they left. The locks themselves were old and easy to open if need be. There were few real hotels and he did not bother with those.

Gabi had wisely developed a strategy: not to be greedy and to take only as much as could be got away with, so that no great fuss would be made. One of his favorite methods of relieving the tourists of some of their possessions was to wait until their last day in Dahab and then break into their places to see what could be taken and turned into cash. There were cameras and transistors; sometimes there were parts of diving gear and frequently some money to be found. People leaving were always in a hurry and complaints to the army authorities in charge took time and effort, so no complaints had been made yet to his knowledge. The pickings there might not make him rich, but they might be more than enough to get by. For the time being, it satisfied him. There were always other tourist resorts in Sinai waiting for him, if the going got too sticky.

In Sinai, at that time, people went about in bathing suits, mainly by the numerous shops and the market places, but by the beach and a little further off the center, many were nude. Clothes, among their many other functions, showed off a social status, and were mostly nonexistent in Dahab. Gabi in swimming trunks, or out of them, could well be a rich tourist and used this advantage to get acquainted with people and find out where they live and how long they would be staying. Trying hard to be careful and not taking too much while keeping a low profile had its difficulties, but finding a Bedouin who would be willing and eager to take the loot of his hands, often in exchange for hashish, turned out to be easy and effortless.

Gabi had noticed an old Bedouin with a camel giving rides around the place. He found him sitting in the shade. "Kif halak?" (How are you?)–a regular useful greeting.

He was answered in kind. Gabi showed him some watches. "How much?"

"Hashish," the Bedouin said.

"OK," Gabi agreed.

A deal had been made.

The next day the Bedouin brought a relative and for once, the actual transfer of goods proceeded with a minimum of verbal haggling. The hashish there happened to be good stuff, purer and unlike the diluted joints which were sold in Tel Aviv. Gabi managed to get good money for them. Things went smoothly for him, and, as time went on, he gradually synchronized with the leisurely pace of the desert routine.

Dahab has multiple coffee houses and restaurants, side by side with stalls and trinkets for the tourists in between, all very close to the sea; one, if so inclined, could take a dip between courses at mealtimes. Several eating places were in large tents, while others were under the open sky with only a piece of stretched fabric above for some shade from the very hot sun. All contain low tables with chairs or couches to lounge in and even mattresses to sprawl on. The waiters are mostly Bedouins and amateurs at their job. They are also very lenient and at times customers would have to chase a goat or a dog away. Cats too were plentiful and one could not leave food unguarded. Gabi spent much time reclining lazily on a couch in some of the places by the sea, sometimes indulging in smoking a nargilah and feeling at peace with the world.

Sex too did not take too much of an effort, being a handsome youth, there were willing females around, mostly in a holiday mood and being particular had never been his strong point as long as they were young and willing. Soon finding out that sex with tourists is different than sex with prostitutes, Gabi had learned fast. The girls there wanted some attention and foreplay and some semblance of romance. Having sex with a girl did not hinder him from pillaging her rented room before she left. He also found the Israeli girls more knowing, demanding, difficult, and so gravitated to American, English and European female tourists mainly. Not knowing much English did not pose a great problem, as language does not necessarily have to be a barrier when people do not want it to be so.

The weeks had easily turned into a month before he thought to telephone his buddy in Tel Aviv. 'Was the heat still on?' One of the places nearby had a phone. Dialing the number repeatedly got no answer. The next day a strange voice answered him.

"Who is this?" Gabi asked.

"Who are you?"

"Is Bergi around?"

"In a hospital."

"What happened?"

"Fell down the stairs."

Closing the connection, Gabi knew what that meant. His friend had been beaten up for sheltering him. It also meant that returning would not be feasible yet. 'Why hurry? What's the great rush?' His old haunts in Tel Aviv seemed far off to him. What had been there for him after all? This place was great.

A new career would be in store for him, though he could not be aware of it yet; that of part time gigolo.

As had become his habit lately, late morning found him lounging and reclining comfortably and drowsily on a couch in one of the many places by the sea, when an older woman sat down by a table near him. He had seen her around before, but had not paid her much attention. Lazily Gabi studied her. She had on a skimpy two-part bathing suit which seemed much too young for her, even though she had a good figure. She appeared the skinny athletic type and brown all over, but could not keep the folds and creases in her skin from showing. Dark blond hair, probably dyed. She pulled out a cigarette and leaned toward him, giving him a closer look at her breasts.

"Have you got a light?" She talked in Hebrew and so the affair began to move ahead on its bumpy journey. At first, Gabi felt somewhat unwilling to take up with an older woman. Politeness not being one of his traits, he snapped, "What the hell do you want?"

"A light please."

"I've got no matches."

"Then I won't smoke." A pause followed. "How long have you been here?"

"What is it to you."

She ignored that. "I arrived the day before yesterday. Where is the best place to dive?"

The woman, being an experienced conversationalist, had kept the talk from lagging. She told him her name, Yael, but did not give a family name. She lived in Ramat Aviv, a place of which Gabi had heard, a suburb of the big city. Wealthy people lived there. She kept the talk direct, sharp, and controlled what little conversation they had. After the preliminaries and talking about the hot weather, snorkeling, the food and other such platitudes, they talked about themselves. Gabi did not give away much and she did not exhibit a great deal curiosity. He looked very young and Yael asked him his age.

Gabi did not know his exact age, he had mentioned 'eighteen,' which she accepted at face value. She told him that she was recuperating from a nasty divorce and had come there to clear her head. Yael, incisive, came directly to the point: "I do not like being alone, I need a companion to show me around and I am willing to pay."

Gabi did not feel inclined to take up with an old bitch, distasteful to him, it would take a large sum to butter this up. "How much?"

"Three hundred per day. It's my third day here and I intend to stay another week at the least."

As things go, this constituted a large sum. Life in Dahab is cheap. Gabi paid rent with a few Egyptian pounds daily, which was the same as in Israeli money, around three USA dollars. Food might cost up to twenty to forty pounds or more daily, depending where and what one eats. A week of this would get him . . . two thousand one hundred, it seemed an enormous sum. Yes, it could be done. Did her offer include sex?

"What about the nights?"

"Twenty-four hours, till I leave . . . and I pay for all expenses." That settled it for him. "OK, done. How do I get paid?"

"Daily if you wish."

Yes, he wished and so began a new way of life for him. She wanted to do some snorkeling. Gabi, for all his time at the seashore, had actually been in the water only a few times and had not bothered to dive or snorkel. They rented gear, she showed him how to use it, and after a few trials, he took in the underwater scene and gaped, amazed by it all, never having given a thought on the abundance of life under the water. The sea resort had been a human hunting ground to him and nothing else. She being an excellent swimmer, did circles around him while he floundered about in the water. Toward midday, they got out of the water. "Let's get out of the heat to the hotel," she said.

"You live in a hotel?"

"It's air conditioned and cool there, we can have a meal after we wash up."

A taxi nearby had been hailed and brought them to the hotel. In her room, she shed her bikini unhesitatingly in two swift motions and stretched herself. Gabi stared at her small perky breasts and shaved pussy, naked she looked better and more appealing than in her bikini. He touched her.

"Not now. Later." She was firm.

They showered and had their meal in the hotel restaurant. Back in their room, they stripped, she turned to Gabi. "Now let's see what you can do."

Gabi began to fondle her, but she said, "I don't like much foreplay, let's get to it, shall we."

Yael had been too direct for Gabi, who felt the need to get himself into the mood for the old bitch, and for once had wanted some foreplay, not having a full erection.

"I have some cream, it should help." She opened a drawer and from a small tube, she smeared some lotion on his penis, it tickled and tingled, but not much else. She manipulated his penis, but that did not help either. Gabi was at a loss, this had never happened to him before and he said so.

Yael did have some experience with that problem in her past; her bravado and dominance had emasculated quite a few of her clandestine sexual cohorts and certainly had been one of the reasons for her divorce, but she did not want to admit that, it being easier to blame her partners. Now she mocked: "You men are all alike, bragging and boasting, but when a real woman comes along you are wimps."

"It is the first time this has happened to me," Gabi repeated.

"So now it is all my fault."

The old, bitch with her dominating ways, had castrated him. He became angry. "Why don't you shut up for a while?"

His anger had made her take notice. She could get rid of him, pay him off and maybe find another guy, but she reflected that she had invested too much already to give up easily. She lay down on the bed. "Come, lie down beside me."

They lay quietly beside each other not talking anymore. Time would be on their side for once, as life has schemed a plan for us humans. Members of the opposite sex will be attracted to each other indiscriminately, more so when lying naked side by side. Unless dire and exceptional circumstances are involved, nature will take its course. They touched each other, Gabi got a whopper, and things went well on their way.

After the deed had been done, they were both amazed at how good it had turned out to be. Yael congratulated herself on having found the right person and Gabi, excited by the prospect of easy unlimited sex (the old bitch was not so bad after all!), anticipated a great amount of cash coming his way. They hit it off.

Their deal had been a purely mercenary one, but spending time together with Yael, Gabi realized how in many ways she belonged to a world not familiar to him, one that had not existed for him and had not been too real to give it much of his attention. Gabi had a few years of basic schooling in his turbulent life and Yael appeared knowledgeable and educated. He studied her and asked her many questions. Learning from her and even copying her sometimes.

When she realized that, it made her want to give him more. She enjoyed playing the role of tutor with him. She showed him table manners and refined his speech. Yael, past forty, healthy and in her prime, had a voracious sexual appetite and this included getting her money's worth out of Gabi and in turn excited him to more and more efforts. They copulated like rabbits, often twice and more daily. They visited the nightclubs that had sprung up. The week flew by.

Two people intimate day and night, sleeping in the same bed, will in one way or another, learn about each other. Yael took a long time with her cosmetics in the shower, while Gabi searched around in her bag, as a matter of habit; copying any information that might, or might not, help him in the future. He found her I.D., a phone number, a membership card of a country club, and some addresses (one can never know when one might have to use those). Gabi had a plan: she trusted him. Most of her money had been placed in the hotel's safe, but there were cash and valuables in her room. He would on some pretext enter her room and rummage around in her place before she leaved, it would be rich pickings and she would never see him again. As the week came to its close, a new and strange feeling made itself felt, which caused him to feel progressively uneasy and reluctant to go through with his plan.

'What the hell!' he asked himself angrily, 'what is this? Am I getting soft or what?' but there were no real answers. All his life his emotions had dominated him and dictated his actions. 'What now?' Gabi had deliberated until the last moment, and then the opportunity slipped away. She had already collected all her stuff and packed her bags. Yael, noticing his moody appearance, wanted to think that their parting had caused it. A taxi had been ordered and they were waiting for it in the lobby.

"This is it then," Yael said fondly, "maybe we shall see each other again sometime." She had given him a handsome bonus.

"Come back soon."

"We'll see. I have to get back to take care of things."

The taxi arrived and Gabi helped her load on her bags. They kissed one last kiss and she was gone. It had all been so fast! Suddenly he felt alone and abandoned. She had been the boss and organized their days (and nights). Following her lead had made him content, not having to think or make decisions. She might have been his mother. Their affair had filled his day, keeping him fully occupied. 'What the hell! I cannot possibly be in love with the old bitch!' Her company had been stimulating. Now feeling aimless and at a loss with time on his hands, he halfheartedly returned to his former activities, but having enough cash stacked away to take it easy, made him listless and a few weeks later found him in a place by the sea, sprawled on a mattress, dazed in a drug-like coma. He was not the only one and the Bedouin waiters let him be.

Gabi unwillingly came out of his stupor, when someone tickled him into a partial awareness by using the tip of their sandal on his ribs. Grunting in annoyance, he turned over, not opening his eyes. Then some sharp object nudged him gently on his behind.

"Goddammit, leave me alone." His body twisted away, trying to return to its former comfortable stupor.

A giggle made itself heard, and that did more than all the prodding had done. He sat up and stared blearily at his tormentor. He saw a middle-aged female with black curly hair, and a heavy body with a round face. She spoke to him: "The Bedouin said that you are Gabi."

"What of it?"

"I am a friend of Yael from the country club."

"So?" remembering some manners, "Nice to meet you."

"I'm Dina. Yael said that you might be willing to be my guide and show me around. I will pay for your time of course."

That woke him up. "What did Yael tell you?"

"Let me buy you a cup of strong coffee first, go and wash your face, then we will talk."

There are few restrooms in Dahab, and no real running water, except for the hotels and some of the more expensive camps. Many places have small water tanks which have to be filled by hand. Gabi handled this by dipping into the sea. Returning to his place wet and cool, he listened to her account. Yael had come to the country club in Ramat Aviv, where they were both members, looking ten years younger, shining with a hallo of health and well-being. After they had done some exercises she and some friends were having coffee and light salads, they broached the subject:

"That must have been some vacation you had," Dina, remarked. They were all friends of long-standing and had confided to each other for years. Yael told them about her escapade, leaving nothing out.

Dina continued her story. "I too need a break from the crazy life in Tel Aviv. My husband is glad to be rid of me for a while," she mimicked him, "go, stay as long as you like, I'll manage." The cheating bastard, the minute I am gone some floozy will get his attentions."

Gabi did not care one way or another. He studied Dina, while she talked, speculating on possible sex with her. Ample breasts, thick legs and thighs, good, those were to his liking. Yes. Drooling of indulging in the expanse of her, aroused him: There seemed to be a lot of female flesh, just waiting for him to do his bidding. This might actually turn out to be good. Yael had refined him a little and shown him how to talk more politely. Gabi, a quick learner, said, "Ahem, I presume that the . . . financial arrangements will be the same as with . . . Yael?"

"Yes. I am also staying at the same hotel."

Dina remained for a whole month and Gabi stayed with her day and night lusting and wallowing in her body and surpassing her expectations. Dina, delighted, was a patron of the arts and spouted about museums, art galleries and theaters, films and concerts and Gabi listened intensely often asking questions, wanting to know more of this other world that appeared denied to him. Dina, as Yael, had been touched by his passion, and after the sex they had many discussions into the late hours of the night. Dina had been somewhat on the wrong track. Gabi did not thirst for knowledge; he longed to belong to another and better world. A kind of infatuation had erupted in him; he wanted to be a part of her world and sought information, not grasping that money, and not cultural issues, were the basis. His meager knowledge and absorption of the matters discussed might be second hand and superficial, but he tried to adopt them.

Phoning back to Tel Aviv a few times, got him nothing but indistinct information, as far as it was possible to find out from his contacts, that some guys might still be on the lookout for him.

After Dina left, there came Ronit, and later one more lady, Adi, younger and better looking than the others, but a miserly bitch (no bonus for him); then there came a recess. He had money now and did not feel the need to do any burglary, but it had become like a second nature to him. People were so careless, they deserved what they got. Cars and clothes were frequently left unguarded and helping himself to their contents, when in between ladies, was a simple matter of habit for him. By now, being used to middle-aged women, they did not seem elderly to him anymore and he had learned to appreciate them. They were more knowledgeable about life and had less illusions, they were practical and tolerant. Their expectations were realistic as were their anticipations and Gabi felt far more comfortable with them then with the young exuberant things who talked about romance, boyfriends, kicks, music and dancing mainly. Besides, older women had much more money than the chicks.

When the flow of Israeli women paused, he made contact with an English person, an older female that had been walking about nude, away from the center, by name of Daphne. She slept on the beach in a tiny tent and had little cash on her. She, being a regular nomad, living from day to day, seemed to have a screw loose somewhere. She was a colorful uninhibited character and a relief from the straight and narrow.

"I'm not from Earth," she would claim, "I come from another planet."

Gabi liked her and did not disrupt her fantasy, he did not know whether to take her seriously. He told her about his 'picking up' items from the tourists and about the women. They had some good laughs together.

Lying side by side nude by the beach, away from the center and exposed to the sea, they would cause people in boats and small yachts that were passing by to shout encouragements and sometimes sexual abuse, which Daphne enjoyed. She would get up and wiggle her breasts to tease them.

"This is what you do not have!" she would shout, "Come and get it."

As the reef prevented anyone on a boat from getting close to the shore, they had no fear of any encounters. Then Daphne had the idea of having sex in public, right in front of the passing yachts.

"Let them drool! They can't get to us." She was excited and strutted about jutting out her pelvis to the vessels.

Gabi, for all his illegal exploits, had always been a straight person, and this appeared too kinky. 'What a weirdo!' In addition, she had no money, he had enough of her and felt her to be a dead loss. Reluctantly he parted from her.

Gabi had been away from his home for over half a year now, and it had not turned out to be the kind of exile he had so feared. Time in Dahab had become very pleasant. However, he had phoned back home once too often. His former buddy had informed the bosses of his escaping to Sinai and an acquaintance of his, having the knowhow, had been able to trace one call to Dahab.

The bosses, well aware of the constant precariousness of their position at the top of the heap, knew that a show of strength was occasionally needed to keep things going their way and to show all what happens to anyone who messes with them. Two henchmen were sent to Dahab to find Gabi, beat him up and maim him, but not to kill him, and bring him back. They wanted him around as proof of their power.

Gabi, now thinking himself immune from any kind of retribution, went about his business totally unaware of the dark cloud which loomed over him. A day's drive found the two strong-arm guys in Dahab. There are many tourists mulling around in the area, and especially in the center, even as Dahab is not a very large place. The two goons threaded their way through on foot, their eyes popping out at the amount of skin exposed. They asked around, but no one seemed to know of Gabi. Away from the center, they saw a naked woman lying in front of her tent. It is always nice to talk to a naked woman, and one of the goons approached her about a youth; brown skin, black hair and of average size called Gabi?

He had got to Daphne. Yes, she knew the bastard, he had left her.

"Point him out to us, you'll get paid for your trouble."

"Sure, five hundred pounds."

"OK."

She pulled a T-shirt over her naked body. "He's in one of the places by the beach."

They followed her to the center. Gabi, loitering about the beach area, had been easily identified. The woman was ignored and when she became too insistent about her money, got a slap for her troubles, they pushed her away. The two swiftly picked Gabi up and force-marched him to a car. His hands were tied behind his back and when he tried to talk, they hit him and told him to shut up. The car moved away. Night had fallen and they tried to find their way in the dark. There were few roads signs in the area. Once outside the town they drove to a side path and forced him out of the car. They began to beat him up.

Gabi, despite the pain, tried to bargain with them, between blows, knowing from experience the only one thing which would work with them.

"Guys, I got money stacked away, it's yours! Let me go. Tell them you couldn't find me."

The blows paused. "How much money?"

He hesitated. "About twelve thou. In the hotel safe."

"Okay, let's go get it."

Gabi, when not with a woman, had rented a cheap room, but had kept the bulk of his money in the hotel safe, where he had formerly resided. Some money had also been hidden in his own tiny room, together with some papers. Near the hotel, they released his bonds. Sandwiched between the two hoodlums they entered. Having no choice but to ask for his money, he signed a receipt and the cash had been turned over to him in a bag. Once outside they snatched it from him and counted.

"You're short by a thousand."

"It's all I've got."

"Get in the car."

"You got the money, let me go."

"Sure."

He felt a blow on his head, then all blacked out.

In a strange way Gabi had been lucky. Those two goons had driven all day and were tired. One of the thugs had been fired by the naked woman they had met before and was impatient to get back and have some fun with her and this saved Gabi from being seriously hurt from the blows that he had received. They had thrown him in the back of their car. Now the one said, "We done our job, how about getting some nookie while we're about it?"

"You mean that woman?"

"Yeah, why not? An easy lay, we know where her tent is."

"I don't like old bitches, I'll get me some shuteye, you go, be quick."

"It'll be short and sweet."

He returned after ten minutes.

"How was it?"

"She didn't like it, wanted to be paid. I had to slap her around some to make her see the light."

A few hours later, Gabi awoke from his coma. The car had stopped. Gabi had somehow had managed to force himself into awareness. His body felt sore all over. Lying in the back of the car, his hands tied, stifling a groan and trying not to move, he overheard his captors talking.

"Where the hell are we?"

"You goddamned fool, you must have taken a wrong turn somewhere."

"What now?"

"It's so goddamned dark, we might be going in the wrong direction. The road's too narrow to turn around in the dark. We'd better stay here till morning."

"I'm bushed. Let's get some sleep."

Gabi continued to listen. Those guys were lost, having never been to Sinai before.

"That piece of shit is out and tied up. We lock the car and leave the front windows open for some air."

"Let's put him in the trunk."

"Right. A few hours inside won't kill him."

Emergency and desperation had sharpened Gabi's reflexes and wits. They had thrown him on the back seat of the car with a small bundle of old magazines. He managed to stuff one into the back of his trousers under his shirt, then faked unconsciousness. The thugs pulled him roughly out of the car and dumped him into the trunk. As the lid began to close on him he quickly turned and twisted, with his hands tied behind his back and exerting himself to the limit, managed to insert some pages of the magazine between the lock and the closing lid, so that with some luck they would prevent the trunk from locking properly.

The guys outside were too stressed and fagged out to notice anything. They had never been lost before and certainly not in a desert. "You stay awake for a couple of hours, then wake me," one said.

They killed the motor. The one awake tried to get some music on the car's radio, but there were only Arab stations to be heard. Cursing, he shut off the radio and fell asleep. All was quiet in the car.

In the trunk, Gabi waited for what seemed to him a long time. Cramped and not knowing whether the hoods in front were sleeping, he finally told himself that it was now or never. Nudging the lid softly with his head, did not make it move. He kept at it a few times more and the lid sprung open not having locked properly. The noise did not awake the exhausted sleepers.

Spurred on by his success, but groaning with pain the attempt had caused him, Gabi slid out, fell down and wiggled away unnoticed. Then, with some effort, got unsteadily to his feet, staggered and with his hands tied behind his back, started to limp away from the strip of road. Where to? He had to distance himself as much as possible from the car, taking care of his bonds came second, but Gabi knew he would not get far in his weak state. They would find him. Better hide first. It was not so dark now. A slice of moon had come out, but the main source of light were the stars. There were millions of them. Further off he saw some shadows and he made his way toward them.

Those shadows turned out to be a formation of rocks and boulders. Enormous geologic pressures had forced up mountains of molten rocks from deep beneath the surface of the Earth to its crust. In the coming centuries, they had cooled and dried and the weather had cracked and split them. Boulders, rocks, stones and gravel had come apart, fallen off and rolled about and were strewn around the area. Gabi had ducked into a small space in between huge adjoining boulders. It was cave-like, as some very large stones had fallen on top of them, it might be possible to wriggle his way still further in, but now releasing his bonds came first. Those bonds were straps of plastic handcuffs. He found a sharp-edged rock and by rubbing his bonds against it, soon got rid of them.

Realizing that his captors could not let things slide, made him crawl deeper inside the spaces between the rocks, hoping there were no snakes or scorpions about. They would have to search for him, even if it took all of the next day. The bosses do not like failures and they would be punished themselves if they did not bring him back. After resting for a while, Gabi got busy, first painfully turning around in a cramped space, then filling up the space behind him with loose rocks and stones. Anyone coming in after him would think it the end of the niche. Totally drained and beat by his exertions sleep overcame him.

The narrow desert road twisted and turned synchronizing with the lay of the land between the mountains. The boulders where Gabi had so painfully dragged himself to hide were very close to a bend in the road, but in his state he did not become aware of that, and strangely enough that would save him later.

One of Gabi's captors had awakened and thought to check the trunk of the car and found it open! Cursing he awoke his partner. "We are in deep shit, the goddam fucker escaped."

"What the hell . . .?"

"You were supposed to watch the guy."

"We locked him in."

"The fuck, if we don't find him, we get our asses kicked real bad."

They began to look for Gabi in the dark on foot. When the sun came up, they found themselves and their car on deserted side road twisting its way in between a mountain range. They drove the car in both directions getting out to search behind any large boulder, rightfully assuming that Gabi could not have climbed the steep slopes in his condition. The two goons were not in their element, the desert being a strange place to them.

Luck in its peculiar whim had again been with Gabi as the pile of rocks that were hiding him, were so close to the road that only a fool would hide there and his captors did not think to check it out thoroughly. If they had, they might have noticed that some of the stones piled up did not seem natural, but they had no food or drink in the car and were tired. They were also not too bright and had no idea in which direction Gabi might have gone. They searched all day and in all directions. The day grew very hot and they were exhausted, thirsty, hungry and footsore and as the evening approached, they gave it up as a futile job. They would have to retract and get back to the main road while there was still some light. A likable story would have to be fabricated. Gabi had not been found and no one knew where he had gone.

In his burrow-like hiding place, Gabi had awakened a few times and fallen back, groaning, to an exhausted sleep, once he had heard voices nearby and terror seized him. The strong sun at midday had not disturbed him much, as the rocks above him absorbed most of the heat. He had no idea of the time and did not dare to leave his shelter. When he finally did leave, it had become dark again and the car had gone. His cramped body hurt from toes to head and not having any food all day made him feel weak and dizzy.

What now? Having no idea in which direction to move, he remained stranded by the road, hoping that in time a car might come by. An hour passed, then another hour, with no car appearing. The road, which his erring captors had mistakenly entered, had branched out from a junction as a broad and well-kept one, but after a number of miles it had deteriorated into a small bumpy thoroughfare; a dead-end road unfinished. In one more mile it would decline into a pathway for army vehicles only, leading to a deserted Egyptian army camp. Gabi, disorientated and not knowing what else to do, began to walk, stumbling slowly alongside the road. However, he had chosen the wrong direction and did not make his way toward the junction and the main road, but slowly limped uphill, in the direction of the deserted camp.

He reached it in a few hours. In the distance remaining, the path climbed up steeply twisting and turning to reach the plateau-like top of a small mountain. Gabi caught a glimpse of light from a fire on top. The place might be inhabited! Knowing that he had to have help, made him brave the uphill climb.

The miserable outpost on top consisted of two wrecked bungalows that had remained standing with their roof partly fallen in, and some twisted shacks, which once had served some purpose. Now they were the temporary habitat of an aging Bedouin shepherd, two dogs and his flock of goats. The mountains of Sinai are infused with gorges, canyons and ravines; those are the arteries of the desert. Moisture is collected and concentrated there, and the tough goats and sheep are pastured in those areas

As Gabi approached, more dead than alive, the silence around him was broken by two snarling dogs which seemed to come out of nowhere and fiercely attacked him. Those were not like the dogs in Tel Aviv. They did not bark and they meant business. Gabi, in his weak condition, was pulled down and bitten and torn in several parts of his anatomy. He fought them off and shouted for help. The commotion had awakened the elderly Bedouin and he came running to call off his dogs.

Bedouins frequently consider outsiders as fair game and not as belonging to their rule of ethics. Before anything else could be done, the Bedouin searched Gabi's now inert body thoroughly for money and valuables. Gabi had none and this saved his life. Any cash found on him, would have been taken and he would be killed, either by the vicious dogs or by the Bedouin's knife and his body hidden in the desert where it would never be found. The shepherd dragged him, half-conscious, into his shack and tended to him. In the desert, many Bedouins are herbalists by necessity. He treated Gabi's wounds with desert herbs and fed him on bread (pitah), goat milk and cheese. Gabi had lost a lot of blood and felt very weak. The desert herbs had prevented an inflammation of his wounds. Some days passed and his wounds slowly began to heal.

Communication with the elderly Bedouin had to be at a minimum and in sign language, neither understanding the other's talk.

"Where am I?" Gabi would try to communicate with the help of his hands.

The shepherded would say something undecipherable.

"How long have I been out?" He made as if to sleep, would the man understand.

The Bedouin showed him four fingers.

"Four days?"

The Bedouin shrugged his shoulders.

During the day, the goats were grazing, the shepherd and his dogs guarding them left Gabi alone with some food and a jar of water by his side. Slowly getting better, he could move around a little. Now having much time for himself to mull things over, Gabi tried to figure out his options. Returning back to Dahab would be stupid and to get back to his old haunts in Tel Aviv, did not seem a likely choice. Lying low in some very minor sea side resort under a false name and hoping they would not send more guys to seek him out was not to his liking, needing more populated places to survive; living in fear and constantly have to look over his shoulder! No, not that. Getting to know some of the ladies from Ramat Aviv had unconsciously fired him with discontent. Gabi did not want to hide out in some God forsaken spot. He wanted to live! Action, people, parties and happenings. Having heard Dina speak of theaters and plays, museums, paintings, even attending a concert might be possible.

The Bedouin shepherd had a supply of bread and water with him and shared it with Gabi. They had a lot of goat milk and fresh meat as the Bedouin had slaughtered a goat. The dogs too shared their meal. When Gabi with signs asked him where the water came from, the shepherd pointed to a valley some distance away.

The goats had exhausted the grazing in the area and one morning the Bedouin motioned to him that they would be leaving and would not be back, showing him in sign language to walk back in the same direction he had come from and leaving him some food and water for one meal. Gabi had no idea how far away they were from any main road and did not feel strong enough to brave the unknown distance. The Bedouin tried to convey to him the information, by showing him five fingers. Did the Shepherd mean five kilometers or five hours? Gabi could not tell. Food and water were scarce and he should get started, but still feeling weak, decided to put it off until the next day.

When the Bedouin and his goats and dogs left, Gabi remained totally alone. Before, he too had been alone, but had not been well and most of the time had lain indoors on some goatskins and recuperated, knowing that the shepherd and his flock would return in the afternoon. They were human company, even if their communications were at a minimum. The Bedouin had a primitive fiddle and sometimes sung to it.

Now the desert closed in on him.

Sitting on a stone outside the shack, Gabi studied his surroundings. The camp had been placed on the top of a small mountain for strategic reasons. The spectacular view, with its chains of mountains and valleys between them, were to be seen as far as the horizon. Stones, rocks and boulders covered the uneven ground. There were so many of them! What a waste, if only all the land could have been put to some use. Did he believe in God? He supposed so, but had never been religious and had resisted all the attempts at religious schooling his mentors had forced on him in the past. Pondering on the scene before him, thoughts which never had occupied him before, now came to him; why should God create so much wasteland? The oceans too! They had taught him in school about them, why should there be so much saltwater no one needed? What the hell is going on in this world?

As midday passed, Gabi began to regret his decision to move out the following day, much of his meager supply of food had gone and the water bottle the Bedouin had left him appeared half empty. No food for him anymore today, and drinking must be sparse. Tomorrow would be rough. Night fell and he composed himself to sleep.

The desert is a place where life begins at night, animals become active in their search for food and for others of their kind. They have also learned to keep away from human habitat. Now that the shepherd and his dogs and goats were gone, a group of jackals came sniffing around, expecting to find some remains of nourishment in the refuse, which humans always leave behind. They began to howl and yelp.

Gabi could not sleep in the din. He got up and went out. The jackals, seeing him, reluctantly retreated. Gabi looked around and experienced the desert for the first time. There were millions of stars gleaming and sparkling, making the area glitter in a sheen of gold, silver, and hues of gray. The jackals had stopped their racket and a death-like silence made itself conspicuous by the total lack of any noise. Gabi felt something that had never been felt by him before in his life: Awe! What was all this? Why has it all been created? Sinking down on his favorite stone he looked up. Myriads of stars shined down upon him. In Tel Aviv and even inside Dahab there are not many stars to be seen. Gabi had learned that all those stars were like our own sun, not having given it much thought ever, being too occupied and busy with his own matters. The enormity of existence overcame him. What meaning does it all have? What importance do his own insignificant struggles have in this great scheme of things?

Feeling restless, he got up and wandered over to the other side of the deserted camp. The silent desert enveloped him like a blanket. Curiosity about nature had never been one of his qualities and had not motivated him to any contemplation. More mountains and chasms appeared in the strong starlight, there seemed no end of them. Behind a mountain range, a glimmer of light showed and spread as the moon came up, slowly and majestically flooding the area with its golden light and extending its radiance, revealing a spectacle Gabi had never seen before. Moonlight and shade had made the desert appear studied with fissures and cracks, arroyos and crevices. Stunned by the breathtaking beauty of it, he sat down on the ground watching the panoramic scene.

The clues of existence are not easy to unravel, but feelings which are stirred up by them, can sometimes do what logic does not get done. Gabi felt his life had been a sham and a waste. The heavenly bodies pressed down on him from above and the desert from below. By some process of osmosis, they absorbed him. Gabi felt immersed and totally consumed by the splendor all around. The mountains and ravines stretched out, until they disappeared in the dark horizon. His emotions were in turmoil. His own miserable activities seemed trivial and inconsequential. His deeds, or misdeeds, had never been questioned or criticized. *Was it for those that all this magnificence had been created?* A surge of disgust and bitter self-hate descended on him. 'I am no better than an animal, fighting and grabbing, deceitful, thieving and sneaking. I can do better.' Resolving to do better and feeling his lack of education keenly, the thought came to him, 'what is better?' He did not know and continued his new found self-disparagement: 'What a fool I have been in resisting the few chances of schooling which I had.' Being with Yael, Dina, and the others, had made him dimly glimpse and savor a taste of another kind of world, one which had remained unknown to him. Did they have a clue to this crazy world? Did they know of something he did not?

Gabi shook himself, those were futile thoughts and were not getting him anywhere. His soul had been stirred but he mostly unaware of it, feeling wide awake and realizing that sleep would evade him now, he came to a decision. Why not start on his journey now, instantly? The cold of the night would help him. All one had to do was follow the path and the road to a main one. What choice did he have? Remain there and starve? Waiting until morning would not make him any stronger and could not help him find his bearings.

He took the remains of the bread and the water bottle with him and started on his way.

It took him seven hours with a period of rest every half hour or so, but he made it to the junction, more dead than alive. The sun had risen a while back and the heat began to make itself felt. His small supply of food and water had been used up. A huge truck lumbered along and stopped for him. He climbed in heavily.

"Where to?"

"Dahab. Have you got something to eat and drink?"

"Here." The driver guy handed him a huge lunch box. "Help yourself."

Gabi thanked him and did so, gobbling up some of the food and drank thirstily.

"Where have you sprung from? The driver asked, noticing his condition and tattered clothes.

"My car got stuck, I had to walk, some jackals attacked me. I'll get someone from Dahab to tow me." The lie came to him without thinking.

"I can let you off by the junction."

A plan had formed in his mind. His own cabin in Dahab had not been searched by those guys and he had a tiny parcel with cash, well hidden behind a loose stone in a wall. Gabi calculated that the better part of two weeks must have past, the parcel might still be there. Getting the cash and moving to Tel Aviv, would be his next move, not to his old haunts, but to Ramat Aviv. Of all the ladies, Dina was his favorite. She might not have been beautiful, but she had a nice kind face and she had taken the most interest in him. He had paid her back by going through her bag while she had showered and copied her address from a letter, the same as with the others. Those notes had been left together with his hidden cash. Maybe they were all gone by now, but he could always wait for Dina and the others by the country club and if things got really bad, blackmail all of them, but the idea had become distasteful to him.

Gabi finally got to his place in Dahab, but found his former room padlocked. His key did not fit. Breaking in would be easy, but instead, he searched for the Bedouin in charge of the camp.

"My room is locked."

"No room, no pay."

"My bag inside."

"Other people rent."

"Where is my bag?"

"No bag."

"Open the door."

"Later, other people come."

Gabi, weak from his ordeals, did not argue. Waiting, lying in the shade, hungry and thirsty again but having no money to buy food, considered his next moves and possible scenarios. Luckily, the people who had rented his former place arrived and let him in. They watched suspiciously, as he removed a stone from the wall and revealed an envelope wrapped in plastic.

After a good meal, Gabi rented another room and went to sleep. He rested for some days, arguing futilely with the Bedouin about a sum for his filched belongings, bought more presentable clothes and the following day found him on his way north to Ramat Aviv.

* * *

Dina worked as a part time secretary to a lawyer and, being an enthusiastic patron of the arts, she had a busy routine. She started her morning with doing twenty laps in the country-club swimming pool before beginning her work. Dina, not being the typical housewife, with two growing children, had learned to be relatively independent. Her husband would occasionally accompany her to the country club in the mornings and have his breakfast there. As a building contractor, Amos earned much more money than needed to keep the whole family in luxury but Dina preferred to work and have a housekeeper at her home so that she could have her freedom. Sex with Amos had slowly deteriorated into a thing of the past, and now she and Amos were good friends and partners. Dina, aware that he had sex elsewhere, had become used to the idea. She did not mind and had accepted it as the routine of life. Many of her friends were in the same or in a similar situation. She too had had some minor affairs and this did not take up too much of her emotions or attentions.

On that particular day, Amos had come with her and they drove the short distance to the country club in his car. As they neared the entrance to the club, walking from their parking spot, she seemed to make out a vaguely familiar figure.

With some shock and dismay, she recognized Gabi.

'What is he doing here?!' In his new clothes, he looked fairly presentable, he had evidently found out where she lived and had been lying in wait for her. She froze in panic, her mind blank, but automatically continued her movements. As they passed him, she gave him a fierce terrified look, which, rightly interpreted, signaled her asking him not to acknowledge her here and now. Gabi kept silent and did not greet her, knowing that he had time on his side.

As Dina entered the club, her mind began to function. What could he want from her? Money? Would this turn out to be a blackmail of some kind? Amos had entered the restaurant and she adjourned to the changing room and put on her bathing suit. Ronit was there changing and they greeted each other, Dina, somewhat absent-minded and out of focus, could not concentrate on the social platitudes and Ronit guessed that she might be going through a bad time. They were old friends and had shared many secrets. Dina would let her know what bothered her in time.

Dina did not enter the swimming pool area. She knew that Gabi waited for her outside! Feeling very pressured, she pulled a robe over her costume and hurried out to meet him. Their greetings were abrupt and cool. Dina tried hard to be friendly.

"This is a surprise. What are you doing here?"

"I have come to see you."

"Me?" She would easily have added, 'Why me? What do you want from me?' but had thought better of it. She should not be too blunt.

Gabi had all the good cards in the game and knew it, but suddenly had felt shy and hesitated. "Dina, are you not glad to see me?"

"Of course I am happy to see you." The lack of conviction in her words had been obvious to both of them.

"I mean you no harm."

It cut no ice with her. "You are a long way from Sinai."

Gabi had given some thought as how to approach Dina. She would naturally be suspicious of him. How should he present his case? Gabi decided to play it by ear. He hungered for access into her world, knowing that without her and her friend's voluntary support, the only alternative left open to him, would have to be blackmail. Not being keen to pressure her, he rationalized; only if no other solution presented itself, then . . . as his last resort . . . how to put it? Well there would be no other choice left open to him.

"We need to talk. Is there any place where we can talk quietly?"

"This is so unexpected. My husband is here and I have a busy schedule."

"I've come all the way from Sinai for . . . this . . ." Gabi at first had intended to say 'for you' but that had sounded too passionate and unreal. The rest remained unsaid.

She gave in, as he knew she would. "I'll pick you up in an hour. Wait here. There is a kiosk nearby and you can get something to drink and eat. Do you have some money?"

Being after much more than a tiny sum for some goodies, he said shortly, "Enough for that."

She left him. Dina did not enter the pool, but fetched her things and changed into her clothes. She phoned the secretary in her office to tell her she would be late. She did not need the job and they all knew it, this enabled her a freer hand at work. She waited for Amos to finish his breakfast and drive them home.

Dina picked Gabi up an hour later in her own car and drove to the outskirts of the suburban area. She certainly did not want to be recognized by any of her many acquaintances. There was no more talk between them, each busy with thoughts. They arrived at the place she had in mind and ordered some food and drink. 'Time to get down to business,' she thought. Gabi's silence got on her nerves and the one sentence escaped her, which she did not want to say: "What do you want of me?" It gave the show away too soon.

Gabi kept silent, churning the subject in his mind and imagination many times, he now found it difficult to formulate. A fleeting image of the myriads of stars in the desert night passed through him. He cleared his throat. It did not come out as intended.

"I want to make something of myself and I need help. I do not know your world. I need advice and guidance. I will need some money too. . . ."

In spite of her concerns, Dina felt a twinge of sympathy. He wanted to better himself and it was only natural that he would need money and she had some prepared. She tried to keep the talk on a friendly basis. "How do you know about the country club here?"

"I also know where you live and the others too. I have my ways."

Being only too aware how easily he could blackmail her, she asked him, "In what way can I help you? . . . Besides the money," she added drily.

"I don't know! I need a place to stay. I need advice! Maybe you can hire me as the pool man, or gardener . . . or something."

"We have all those. This is all very sudden, let me find out what I can do. In the meantime, here is a sum, enough to tide you over for some days." She handed him the envelope she had prepared. "It is not much. Rent a room, but not here, find a less expansive area." Seeing his puzzled face, "Try Ramat Amidar. She gave him her number in the office. "From ten to two. Call me in a couple of days . . . at the office only."

So, in a strange way, Gabi became Dina's protégée. She helped him find a cheap one-room apartment and had inquired around, finding a course in the university which took in underprivileged students at a most basic level. Israel is a country of refugees and immigrants and the course itself would be subsidized, but there were many other expenses involved. It turned out he had never bothered to get any I.D., an important matter which would have to be seen to. No place would accept him without one. Gabi would have to work hard at keeping up, not knowing much English (or anything else for that matter), and most of the literature is in that language.

Dina paid his rent and the various necessities. She bought him clothes, took him to the theater and explained the plays to him. She took him to museums to see works of art and hugely enjoyed playing the role of tutor. He was like putty in her hands. She would visit his rented room and submit to his advances. It also cost her a tidy sum. It became too large an amount to keep from Amos for long. Dina had not worked at a lawyer's office for nothing. She had acquired a mind for business. She called in a meeting of her closer friends, Yael, Ronit, and another lady by name of Adi, who too had gone on a vacation to Dahab; and Gabi had 'shown her around.' The three older ladies were well on their way to fifty, but Adi had not yet reached forty. They were all involved and should help pay the price.

At first, they talked of many things that women talk about, then Dina led the talk to the good times they had in Sinai and the items they had found there and bought for almost nothing. In Israel, everything is much more expensive. . . . This chat introduced the subject Dina had in mind.

"Gabi is here, in Ramat Aviv."

"Here!?" The exclamations of the three were more of consternation and dismay than of surprise.

"Yes here . . . and seems to know our whereabouts. I found him at the country club. I had to rent him a room and pay for his expenses. He has enlisted in the university and is studying. We need to share the cost."

"What do you mean, *we!* Why us?" someone cried.

"Who else?" Dina pointed out the obvious. "Do you want him to contact our homes and husbands?"

Yael chuckled. "I wish that he would contact my ex. I'd like that."

"This is not funny. How does he know our addresses?" Ronit exclaimed.

"But this is like blackmail," Adi cried out.

"Don't I know it." Dina answered her. It is too large an amount for me to keep from Amos. We have to share it."

"Do you mean that we have to pay you for his keep!" Adi remarked outraged.

"Pay him, not me. Yes, there are four of us. If each of us pays one quarter of the expenses involved then we can make this work."

"It is not my business. I want nothing to do with him," Adi said.

"Me too," Ronit added.

"He knows all our addresses and might not be above a little blackmail," Dina reminded them.

"It is your doing!" Adi accused Dina. "You have given him our addresses."

"Are you crazy, of course not," Dina denied hotly. "You all know me. Would I throw our friendship down the drain? One morning he appeared by the club, frightening me out of my wits, and knew all he needed to know about us. Amos came with me to have breakfast and I had to exhibit a calm front. Gabi needs clothes, food and the rent has to be paid. I cannot continue alone . . ."

"How long has this been going on?"

"It's the second month now and I have paid all the costs, but I cannot keep it up."

No one seemed to know how to handle the problem, but they could not leave it be. The issue would not go away by itself. Dina had pointed it out repeatedly. Reluctantly they discussed the subject back and forth.

"Are you sleeping with him?" Yael, closer to Dina than the others, had dared to ask her point blank.

" . . . None of your business."

"I am answered."

"Then it is you who is blackmailing us," Adi accused Dina.

"Whatever you chose to call it. Blackmail is a harsh word. I cannot keep doing this alone. If you girls won't pitch in, then it will get out one way or another."

Adi turned to Ronit: "Dov is with the police, maybe he can do something about it?"

Dov was Ronit's husband. She said, "It would give the game away. Better not to involve him."

"Not necessarily," Adi argued. Dov had tried to hit on her, and she felt that she would be able to sway him.

They chewed on their issues for the better part of an hour, all realizing that they had little choice. Well-off as they all were, none had money to spare. One has to keep up appearances. To them those were not the futile superfluities and adornments of pampered women. In their world, social survival depended on the right clothes, in the right places, with the correct trimmings and trappings. First and foremost, necklaces, bracelets and other assorted jeweled articles, not all of which were presents from their husbands, were expensive. There were dresses and shoes, cosmetics and perfumes cost a fortune. Getting one's hair done periodically. Manicures and pedicures cost and an occasional peeling. Teeth needed checking and fixing. One could not walk about with a casual handbag, it had to be labeled and branded by one of the well-known designers and the same went for many other things as well. Then came household articles, curtains, pillowcases, lampshades, vases etc. . . . etc.. . . . Those were all expenditures which could be explained to their husbands, but they all protested against the outrage of additional expenses.

"He came to you, you are the one sleeping with him, so it's your problem, don't put it on us." Ronit remarked nastily.

"It is our problem!" Dina repeated emphatically. "You are in it as much as I am."

"I am divorced." Yael, her best friend, pointed out. "This cannot do me any harm. However, I am willing to donate something."

Adi and Ronit refused to participate in the funding of Gabi. Adi said, "You do what you like. I will not have any part of this." Ronit agreed with her. They appeared to mean it and as such left the whole burden on just two of them.

Yael grimaced, "I'll help as much as I can, but I'm afraid it won't be much. You know that I just had a difficult divorce."

"Thanks a lot, all of you," Dina said sarcastically.

Ronit added, "If he blackmails me, or threatens me in any way then I will tell him where to get off."

"That's right," Yael mocked. "What are good friends for."

It appeared hopeless. Dina had half expected this, but she had hoped. A rift had been torn between the four. With some help from Yael, Dina calculated she might be able to drag the money issue out for a couple of months. Then what? She would have to talk to Gabi, who–now studying hard–would have to get a job. A job would take time and energy away from his studies.

Gabi had enlisted in all the basic courses that his mentor from the university had advised him, but education is not only knowing, or studying. For Gabi, edification also happened to be in getting to know his fellow students and learning about their opinions and discussing ideas, in classes and out of them. New notions had assailed him, which would never have occurred to him before. Excited and happy, he tried to soak it all in. The world he had sought after was here. The bosses downtown might search for him in far off Sinai, but they would never dream of looking for him in the university in Ramat Aviv. Gabi liked Dina and sometimes they had sex. Afterwards some guilt about the emotional and financial load, which his studies had put on her, would appear. Finally, once after sex in his rented one-room apartment, Dina mentioned the subject, which now troubled them both.

"Gabi, I cannot keep this up. My husband will find out about it sooner or later, then it will have to stop, it is a no win situation for you too."

Gabi rightly understood it to mean the financial part of their liaison, not the sex part. A while back Gabi might have said, 'That's your problem.' Now he gave it some thought. "I have heard about a dormitory for students, I could move to there, they might have a place left. As a student, it is practically free."

"Then we would have no privacy."

"That too."

"Amos is not at home all the time. We could still find some time for ourselves." Then she asked the question which had been on her mind for some time. "Why did you seek me out and not one of the others? I am aware . . . that I don't have a figure like Yael or Adi."

"Should I get in touch with them?" He fenced with the question. "Yael is a bossy bitch." Dina giggled. "Ronit gives herself airs, she is too good for everybody and Adi is still a pampered girl. She is the youngest of your set, maybe I should call on her, as being nearest to my age?"

"No, I talked to all of them. They do not agree to pay for anything, except Yael."

"But you will."

"As much as I can, but it will not be enough."

He finally tackled the issue. "I could also get a student job at the university."

"It will take time off your studying."

"Dina, I like you. You have shown more interest in me than the others have. You are like a mother to me."

That had not been exactly what she had wanted to hear, but it touched her. She kissed him and effectively stopped the conversation.

Gabi applied, and eventually managed to get a place in the rooms which the university kept for needy students. They were three to a room, cramped in a tiny cubicle with room for three beds and a minimum of furniture. Being labeled as an underprivileged student had quite a few privileges in itself. Getting a job cleaning classes and offices, sometimes late in the evening or early mornings, together with his studies kept him busy all day long. There were his classes and assignments in the library to cope with. Much homework had to get done and Gabi put in a giant effort. To him it had become a survival issue. His roommates went to parties and discotheques. They were free and easygoing and he envied them. Dina and Gabi now spent less time together.

Gabi had four years of forced and hated schooling in his childhood and now that seemed by far too little to cope with his classes. Working day and night with a grim death-like determination and Dina helping him whenever she could, he felt himself slipping behind. In class, he did not always understand what the lecturer explained and often felt too embarrassed to ask, not willing to reveal his ignorance. Then a test failed and a week later another one. There were just too many subjects for him to deal with. Growing desperate, he quit his part time job, not mentioning it to Dina and studied in the additional hours, having no real idea of how much there would be to learn and how little knowledge he had to begin with. Another test returned failed.

Now having little money for real food, he lived on bread and milk for some weeks, before finally realizing it could not go on, something must be done.

Adi, coming out of her favorite beauty parlor, found Gabi lounging by her car. She had tried to ignore the fact that Gabi had anything to do with her.

She greeted him warily, "Hello there. Dina told us you were here."

"It's good to see you again," Gabi said, then coming straight to the point: "I am studying and I need some money."

"From me?"

"From all of you."

"What do you mean by *all of you*?"

"You know what I am talking about."

"I have no money to spare."

"Don't make me laugh."

"What does this have to do with me? Why me and not the others?"

"I intend to talk to the others too. Will you help out?"

"I'd really like to, but I can't help you."

"You know what will happen."

Adi considered carefully. "For how long a period are we talking about? This might take years!"

They were talking on the sidewalk by Adi's car and there was the occasional passerby. "We cannot talk here," Adi whispered fiercely.

"I have nothing to hide." Gabi pointed out.

Adi unlocked her car swiftly and got in. She motioned to Gabi to do likewise. "We'll go somewhere where we can talk quietly."

They drove to the outskirts of the neighborhood and entered the same place that Dina once had brought him to before. Smiling inwardly and feeling just a little sarcastic,

Gabi wondered. Did they all go to the same restaurants? The same country club? And maybe they had the same men too? . . . Like himself?

"What do you want from me?" Adi snapped, after they seated themselves.

"I am working now, but I cannot study and work at the same time. I need money."

"Don't we all," Adi snorted. "Others can work and learn at the same time, why not you?"

"I have too much to catch up with, and I don't know any English."

Adi took a firm tone: "Now you listen to me you young whippersnapper, I do not give in to blackmail of any kind. My good friend and neighbor and incidentally Ronit's husband, is in the police. I, we, can have you arrested any time. You leave us alone, you hear!"

Gabi had originated from a tough place and could not be easily intimidated. "Arrested or not, they can't stop me from talking."

"Nobody will listen to you. You won't be believed."

"Maybe not at first, but Ronit and Yael are in this too and so is Dina. The whole thing will fall apart."

"Go to hell you won't extract any cash from me."

"Adi, we were friends once and good together."

"Yes, before you came here to blackmail us."

"Dina gives me some money and Yael helps out too. I am struggling with my studies day and night. Does that mean nothing to you?"

"The first thing you have to learn is that there are no handouts in this world." She got up. "I'm leaving." She put some bills on the table. "For the drinks. If I ever see you again, I will inform the police." She left angrily. Gabi stranded, quickly pocketed the money she had left on the table and hurried away.

Adi phoned Ronit and told her the whole story. "I told him where to get off." She ended her narrative.

"What if he talks?" Ronit asked anxiously.

Ronit's husband, Dov, was an officer in the police force. Adi had turned to Ronit in the crisis for a reason. Dov had furtively indicated his wish for a romance, looks and veiled hints had passed between them. To Adi, he looked an older person, and she did not feel very attracted to him, but had remained undecided whether to take their budding affair a step further, she had led him on, not wishing to let go. Now she intended to use that.

"What is Dov in the police force for, if he cannot help out in a crisis. How high up in the hierarchy is he anyway?"

"A sergeant major, but what shall I tell him?"

"I'll come over, we'll tell him about a friend of ours, no name, who is being blackmailed. He should be able to do something."

The same evening the two ladies, with tears in their eyes, told Dov a sob story. A friend of theirs had erred and is being blackmailed by a former lover. Her marriage would be ruined, the children would be hurt. They implored him to use his rank and help them deal with it.

Dov felt reluctant at first. "What proof do you have? Is there a letter or any recording of him pressuring or blackmailing her?"

"Of course not!" Adi said. "This person is too clever to leave anything in writing behind."

"But what can I do? Will the lady reveal herself in court? It will be her word against his."

Ronit reproached her husband. "Dov, it cannot come to court! That would mess things up for her totally." Adi and Ronit continued to wear down Dov's resistance. Adi gave him some warm and promising eye contact, until finally he gave in. "Have you got a name, an address?"

Yes, they had both: Dina had told them and had mentioned the particulars. Adi handed them to Dov.

"I'll see what I can do," Dov said at last, which gained him hugs and kisses from his wife and Adi.

A few days later Gabi happened to be alone struggling with his studies. Two Policemen, not in uniform, entered. His roommates were out.

"We are looking for Gabi." One said. He showed a badge.

"I'm Gabi."

"We have reason to believe that there are drugs hidden in this place and have a warrant for a search."

Watching, somewhat amused, as they searched the place thoroughly, Gabi's smile receded from his face, as they extracted a small package of drugs from the locker by his bedside. They told him, "You'd better come with us quietly. You are being arrested for possessing and selling drugs."

He could not believe his ears, nor did he take it seriously at first. "Those are not mine! I don't know how they got there." His denials fell on deaf ears. They allowed him to phone and he called Dina, having her home number now. She had asked him not to call her at her home, but this was an emergency. A male voice answered him. "Yes?"

"Can I talk to Dina?"

Dina came to the phone, angry with him for calling her at her home.

"This is an emergency. The police found a packet of drugs in my locker. I am being hauled to jail!"

"My God. How did that happen?"

"I don't know."

"I thought you had finished with drugs!"

"They are not mine."

"Whose are they?"

"How should I know. Don't you believe me?"

"I don't know what to believe."

"I swear to you, on whatever is holy. I have never seen them before."

"I should certainly hope so."

"I need a lawyer."

"I'll see what I can do."

Dina worked in a lawyer's office and she explained the situation to her boss, also her very good friend. "I'm not a criminal lawyer," he reminded her, "but I will look into it. Tell me all about it."

Dina told him everything except the sex part. "What is your interest in this guy?" he asked her.

"We met in Sinai on my vacation. Having a deprived childhood made him an underprivileged student and deserves all the help he can get."

The lawyer got busy.

Trying to explain the drugs in Gabi's locker would be a near impossible feat. There must be a different approach. Finding out that Gabi had not known his own age and the age stated in the new identity card had been guesswork, the lawyer had a doctor check him and verify Gabi as being of under age, this together with being a first offender might get him off with a warning. In the meantime, Gabi remained under custody, the police claiming that, if set free, he might continue his trade. Dina visited him just once. Gabi, depressed and moody, came out with it: "This is Adi's doing, she threatened me. Ronit's husband is in the police."

"Ronit would never go along with framing someone," Dina replied.

"Those drugs were not mine!"

"Let's leave the subject alone. My lawyer will get you out."

"I will lose a whole year," he complained.

"You are still young," Dina reminded him.

"It's too much, I won't be able to catch up. It was hard enough before."

Dina said nothing for a short while. She too had her doubts and had formed a similar opinion. To catch up, Gabi would need private tutoring, lots of it, especially in English, but many other subjects too seemed to be beyond his reach. Studying all day long, nights too, with no other work to hinder him might help, but it did not seem possible or feasible to her. Where would the money come from? Dina reflected that she had her own life to live; her two teenage children were acting up and they were a handful to control. They came first naturally.

However, she said to him: "You still have many years before you. One year does not matter so much."

Gabi remained unconvinced. Having tasted of the world he had sought after so much, it now admittedly felt strange and foreign to him. He now remembered the predictions of the foster home people: "You will never amount to much." They had said to him more than once. What had all that studying to do with real life? Maybe this was not for him. He had felt unable to fit in and kept quiet. They parted morosely. Both full of doubts.

Dina's regular timetable began each morning with a swim and breakfast in the country club with her friends. Then she drove off to work and early afternoon would find her at home taking a short nap. After that came the evening with its many various activities. When Gabi appeared, he had created a rift between her friends and they did not breakfast together anymore. Ronit, with Adi, preferred a separate table. The four women had been lifelong friends, discussing and dissecting every part of their emotional lives, from children to husbands and lovers. They had chattered about fabrics and clothing, maids and hairstyles, cosmetics, shoes, handbags and whatever else useful to them in their lives. They had gossiped and even bickered among themselves, but they never had a fallout like the present one and it hurt them.

Eventually the habit of many years gradually began to assert itself. They greeted each other politely and exchanged a few words. When the police had arrested Gabi, Dina mentioned it to Ronit and Adi, who were seated at the other table, breakfasting in the country-club restaurant. Both Adi and Ronit had not wanted to feel guilty about what they had accomplished, but they did not feel too good about it either; it had been a survival issue for them and if need be, they would have done it again. However, they felt no need to mention it to anybody, especially to Dina.

Dina had felt a vague uneasiness, Gabi had accused Adi. He might be right, she knew how this worked and turned straight to Ronit: "Did Dov have anything to do with Gabi being arrested?"

Ronit turned red and at that moment she hated herself. "I know nothing of it." Which was true in a way? She had not questioned her husband or mentioned the subject anymore. She did not want to know.

Adi said, "Cannot we talk of something else? The guy took drugs, is that so hard to believe?"

Yael agreed. "We have fallen out because of him. Enough is enough."

"We were so stupid to let . . . that person, Gabi come between us," Ronit said.

"Come and sit with us, we've been apart long enough." Adi had voiced their own feelings.

"Right," Yael contributed. "It's high time we got together again."

"Yes, we should not fight," Dina put in lamely. Yael and Dina settled themselves around Ronit and Adi's table. They ordered breakfast.

"Tell us all about it," Adi said and Dina filled them in on what had happened.

Yael had to have her say: "I hate to say it Dina, but are you not getting over involved with the guy?"

Dina kept her silence, not sure how to react. She had had similar feelings herself on the subject.

Adi said firmly, "We owe him nothing."

Ronit stated: "He is someone we met in Sinai. That was then, this is now. He has no claims on any of us."

"This is not about claims," Dina protested weakly.

"Then what is it about?"

"I don't know . . . obligations? Doing some good."

"Don't be a fool Dina, let's not quibble about words. You should be able to let go, or has this become an obsession?"

"Actually, I haven't seen him for quite a time and I do feel some guilt."

"Maybe it is for the best," Yael said.

Their talk turned to other, more familiar topics.

Neither Dina nor Gabi's lawyer had known at the time that Gabi, young as he was, had been known to the police and had been listed as a felon and a drug dealer. His name had been turned over to the police by the local bosses downtown on whose territory he had impinged at a former time. The judge did not consider him a first offender and sentenced him to a year in a juvenile center. This seemed like a prison sentence to him.

Dinah's boss, as Gabi's pro bono lawyer, conveyed the news to Dina at the office.

"Can I visit him? Where are they keeping him now?" she asked, being conscious of not having visited for some time.

"I'm afraid not. He became violent and is kept in solitary confinement, or whatever they have over there." The lawyer looked at her strangely.

"What is it?" she asked him.

"Some papers have been found among his things, in his handwriting, with your address and other details on them, also the addresses and details of some of your friends in the country club. . . ." He named them. "What should this mean?"

"I have no idea." She lied. "Has Dov seen those?"

"No. I got them first, as his lawyer. Why do you ask?"

"I should not like him to get the wrong idea."

Her boss looked hard at her. "Amos is a good friend of mine," leaving the rest unsaid. They always had understood each other well.

"So am I, or am I mistaken?"

"Of course not."

"I appreciate that, hadn't you better leave it alone?"

He nodded in agreement. "I will get rid of them."

"Thank you. I owe you a big one."

The next morning, when the four ladies breakfasted together at the country club, Dina informed her friends of the sad news. They expressed some sympathy for Gabi.

"He is young, he'll get over it," Yael said.

"What will we do if he talks when they release him?" Ronit asked.

"He will have learned his lesson by then," Adi said.

Dina added reluctantly, "I did feel at times . . ."

Yael cut in: "The guy is a looser. I guess he just didn't have it in him."

Dina sighed.

THE END

AMIRAH

At the southern vertex of the triangular formed peninsular called Sinai, lies the town of Sharm el Sheikh, Sharem for short to most. To call the vicinity a town is to flatter the place somewhat; at the time, the civic area consisted of a large very loose collection of buildings placed far apart from each other and spread out for miles–in the desert space is cheap. With the influx of tourists and Westerners, new structures, shops, a diving center and small local travel agencies had sprung up and some buildings were occupied by the regional municipal offices. The improvised stripe of land straightened by one bulldozer for small planes to land would soon be turned into a regular airport and bring in thousands of tourists.

The whole area is a stony place and the road leading there, twists and turns between fields of huge boulders and rocks which have broken off from the surrounding mountains. Close to the seashore and at a distance of a mile or two north of the town, a kind of cove-like beach had formed beneath the cliffs overlooking the sea creating a protective area from the weather– be it the wind or the hot sun. A community of tents had sprung up there, mostly blankets and sheets strung together, with some colorful makeshift shacks among them. The inhabitants were all backpackers of both sexes–together or alone, saving their little money for other matters.

The desert had come under Israeli control in the Six-Day War of 1967 and remained as such, until handed over to the Egyptians after fifteen years, in exchange for a peace treaty. In that period, the whole eastern area had become a haven for people seeking sanctuary from the stresses of their civilizations. Tourist places sprung up like mushrooms after a rain, most of them by the Red Sea which escorts the desert along its eastern side; with vast expenses of beaches and mountains reaching right into the sea.

Not too far away from Sharm el Sheikh, at the very southern peak of the peninsula, there exists a very special diving site called the head of Muhamad, or Ras Muhamad, which had grown into major tourist attraction having pristine clear water with an enormous variety of marine life and bringing many tourists to Sharm el Sheikh.

Near the town, a small temporary Bedouin camp had settled down. Those Tribes were no more wanderers in the desert moving from to place but had their center up north in another village-town called Dahab and had come to Sharm el Sheikh to make some money of the tourists. They offered camel rides into the desert for ready money and the women baked their special kind of bread called pitah, over an open fire. For those who had the means, meals with roast lamb could be had together with strong coffee or tea in their tents and many tourists with families indulged in the desert gourmet.

The Bedouin soon learned who one of their best-selling agents of trinkets were; their girls up to the age of eleven or twelve. Those girls would wander about in small groups, dressed in colorful clothes and with their beautiful faces, raven black hair and flashing eyes could charm and captivate the tourists to induce them to buy beads and trinkets–or Pitahs baked by their mothers. Those fascinating girls had become very sure of their appealing and entrancing powers and could sometimes pester a not so unwilling tourist into buying a knick-knack, for which he had no need. When those girls became of age, they would not be allowed the same kind of freedom anymore and would only be able to leave their compound with an escort.

Amirah, a Bedouin girl, just under twelve years, and one of the eldest of one tiny group, was the one to decide where and when they should make their rounds and where the most money and tourists were likely to be. Amirah, being one of the more daring ones, would even flirt with a male tourist in a saucy childish bantering manner, just beginning to become aware of having special privileges, especially with men, not the males of her family, but others, and mostly tourists, female tourists too would be enchanted with her and fall under her spell.

"You buy." She would engage a male tourist holding out a string of beads.

"No thank you."

"I make, you buy," she insisted, flashing her eyes. The small group of girls around them giggled.

"I don't need any beads."

She had more in a loose pocket and pulled them out. "You like? Take."

"Did you make all those yourself?"

She nodded, not wanting to lie downright.

"All right how much for this one?"

"Very nice. Give to lady." Amirah enjoyed herself.

"I have no lady."

"Very bad." She smiled roguishly. The other girls tittered.

"You be my lady."

"OK, you buy."

They haggled about the price. Amirah always asked for five times as much as she expected to get.

Amirah (Mahmoud), in short, had many more ancestral names connected to her family and tribe and had worked in her homestead in Dahab since a small child. As a little girl, her duties had been to collect the eggs from the coop and sweep the sand away from the collection of bricks, metal sheets and stone, which made up their house. Growing up, she fetched water from the well, scrubbed the cooking pots and pans, and learned to milk the goats and sheep. Still later, Amirah would help her mother with the making of pitahs and learned to pluck chickens, skin and prepare mutton and to do the housework and when not selling trinkets to the tourists, would often relieve one of her brothers, guarding the family's flock of goats and sheep.

A busy girl, Amirah was eight when the Israelis came, opening the area to an invasion of tourists from all over the world. Her family, as well as others in the village, realized that easy money could be made from catering to the tourists. Her grandfather had a camel and gave rides to the tourist children inside Dahab. One of her older brothers had learned to drive a car and transported passengers from one place to another. The neighboring homestead had emptied itself of its family and additional cubicle-like rooms had been hurriedly built to rent to the throngs of invaders. Her own family had preferred to remain in their home. Amirah would often watch a series of new neighbors coming and going.

Her way of life seemed natural to her and she had never given any thought to anything else. Spying on the tourists at the neighboring homestead and seeing couples sleeping together in the open in one sleeping bag, kissing, hugging, and often walking about in skimpy bathing suits, and sometimes in the nude, had at first been a curiosity to laugh at. Living all her short life in a gender-segregated society where the women had a hierarchy of their own, independent of men, made her wonder and the seeds of a certain uneasiness were planted. Watching her neighbors, she saw men and women together and sometimes families with children, some of them her age; they laughed and listened to music and often played games with a ball, when not at the beach.

Amirah also knew about television, they had one on batteries in their home and listened to an Egyptian channel. Those were other worlds, they were not her world, nor her family's and all the antics and shows in the television seemed to have nothing to do with her, except for some vague and dubious entertainment.

Her unrest had grown when a family with two children, a boy her own age and his smaller sister, had rented some rooms in the homestead next to them. She could make out their features clearly. The boy with light hair used to wave to her. At first Amirah ignored his affable advances, but he being friendly, continued to wave at her on occasions and in time found his attentions acknowledged with a wave back.

Once, while Amirah tended to the sheep, they met by the fence bordering their homesteads. The boy smiled and pointed at himself: "Oren."

After a pause she did likewise, "Amirah."

They studied each other.

The language barrier did pose a problem, but a minor one. Amirah had been a fast learner in her dealings with the tourists, and had a smattering of English and Hebrew at her disposal. Oren too had learned English at school. Their communications were basic. "Israel," he pointed at himself again.

"You stay long?"

He showed her with his fingers, "Nine days."

The next time they met he had his younger sister with him. The girl made a face, "The sheep smell," and pinched her nose.

Amirah shrugged her shoulders, of course sheep smell. Why make a face.

"My sister Tami," Oren said. To her he had already mentioned the Bedouin girl he had met.

Tami had a two-part swimsuit on. "You naked?" Amirah asked her.

Tami giggled. "I'm not naked."

"All foreigners naked." She used the term 'abyath' (white person) but changed to strangers, in finding herself not understood.

Oren said, "We like it."

The notion sounded crazy to Amirah. One had to protect oneself from the sun, which can get very hot and dangerous, besides, Bedouins never showed skin in public.

Tami, fast losing interest, pulled out a game from a tiny bag and began to play. Amirah, curious, stretched out her hand.

"Mine." Tami moved away.

"Let her have a look," Oren told her.

"It's mine!" Tami resisted.

A short argument followed, in which Oren had his way. Tami fearfully handed the game through the fence.

The fence between the homesteads had been constructed as a barrier for straying sheep or donkeys, more like an enclosure. The children could easily cross both ways. Amirah took the game, a tiny tablet-like gadget including a doll which could be dressed with a variety of dresses. Amirah did not know what to make of it. Tami showed her, crossing the fence to do so. Oren followed suit. They played for a while. Oren, bored with the girl's game asked Amirah, "What do you do all day?"

His question made little sense to Amirah, busy all day with her chores and family, she had not considered this work, that was life.

"Nothing," she said.

"We have to go to school," he complained, "and then there is homework."

Amirah's older brother had gone to a regional school for some years. He learned to read and write. "You can read?" she asked them.

"Of course, but we have little free time to play," Oren complained.

"What you read?"

His sister giggled, "He took a book on sex from the library and showed me the pictures."

Amirah had little idea of what they were talking about. The words 'play' and 'sex' did not have the same meaning to her. Animals copulated; roosters, cats, dogs, sheep and even a donkey. Amirah, vaguely aware, from the talk which went on in the women's quarters, knew she would grow up to be a woman and would marry, copulate and bear children, but the future did not occupy her mind.

"What pictures?"

"Pictures. You know, of our . . . things . . . penis . . . vagina." Oren knew the words.

He smirked and so the subject became clearer to Amirah, "Genitals?" She used the blunt word they had. Oren understood. "Tami peeks at me when I undress."

"I do not."

"Yes, you do."

"Well so do you, I saw you looking."

"I will tell mom and dad on you." They continued their bickering not taking each other seriously.

Amirah had listened to their chit-chat amazed. A man entering the woman's quarters in their home, for whatever reason, is an exceptional event. A child might sound the alarm and the women would stop their gossip, a few women smoked cigarettes and would hide them. Some tension would be felt all around. Her new acquaintances talked freely of their mother and father! "I go," she said, reluctantly handing Tami her game back.

Amirah instinctively had felt her fraternization with the children of their neighbors would not be approved of by her mother and kept quiet. The Bedouin, and especially the women, have learned to be devious, as often the easiest way to achieve their aim in a harsh society, non-flexible mainly toward their females. The same rigidity did not extend to the males, who had learned to get on in the modern world. Amirah found ruses to meet with her stranger friends; a strayed sheep, or some chickens which had to be gathered into the coop, there were always some excuses handy. Sometimes they met, and Oren was alone or occasionally with Tami, always at the edge of their homesteads. Amirah had many questions.

"You write . . . all read?" used to be one of her often-repeated questions. Oren understood and once brought an old newspaper with him. "See? For all to read. Pictures too," he explained.

Oren had low grades in geography and had been encouraged by his dad to take an atlas with him and get some homework done. He hated geography. Once he brought his atlas along and explained to Amirah about the concept of proportions, countries, and oceans, even drawing with a stick in the sand. Amirah felt surprised: There were actually many other countries, all with different people and languages. Her tribe, the Bedouin, whom she had thoughtlessly taken for granted to be the center of all, were just tribes in one area of the world. She could grasp the concept, but emotionally it did not take. Oren, after explaining those subjects to Amirah, did not hate geography so much anymore.

Amirah, while peddling her wares with her peers, came in touch with tourists of many countries. To her they were all foreigners, but now she would ask them where they came from, then Oren would show her the place on the map.

Once Oren kissed her, on the cheek. She liked it, but remained still, not reacting. He kissed her again.

"No."

"Why not?"

There loomed unfamiliar, uncertain, and threatening ground ahead. She sensed danger. "No," she repeated, not being able to explain or say more.

"You like?" Oren asked her. Amirah hung her head, his kisses were strange, but felt nice.

Oren kissed her again and found no resistance. The girl kept quiet.

"Grown-ups kiss on their lips," he informed her and did so.

They met almost every evening, until Oren had to leave. They talked, sometimes kissed, and learned a little about each other and their families. Oren had learned to be devious in getting rid of his little sister on those occasions. On their last evening together, she flung her arms around him.

"When you come back?"

Oren had no real idea. His parents often took trips on holidays and he indulged in daydreaming.

"Soon," he said.

Oren bribed Tami into giving him her game with the doll. He would get into trouble later at home, but now he gave it to Amirah as a parting gift. "For you." They hugged and kissed and then Oren had to leave. Amirah hid her treasure under her blanket.

The Sinai desert, lying between Egypt and Israel, can have diverse significance to different people. To urban tourist denizens, the vast spaces can often mean some freedom from the strain of their daily habits and taboos and frequently is termed by them as relaxation. To others the desert can be a refuge, either from debts, or from a spouse, or alimony. There are numerous incidences in our society where, under certain circumstances, it might be prudent or even advisable to keep a distance.

For many Sinai can be a place where fantasies may come true. Lovers could consummate their love unhindered and in peace.

Married, or single and couples with children flocked there alike, some for clandestine encounters, and many were the young who came for a few weeks and remained for a month or two and some even longer. Life could be simple and easy along the east coast, southwards from Eilat and Israel. One did not need a hotel and could sleep on the beach and in the summer, even a sleeping bag might be superfluous. Food too could be had for little money and if the quality of the local cuisine is not always up to Western standards, the victuals were still nourishment and palatable, basic as they were. Many had fallen under the spell of the trouble-free daily routine of the desert. There might be occasional storms and strong winds in winter and autumn, but rain came seldom and cheap bare cubicle-like rooms for rent could be had for two dollars US per night if required.

In the coming years, members of Amirah's family had often periodically pitched tents near Sharem for some months and then returned home to Dahab. Amirah had many opportunities to get acquainted with Westerners in both places. Oren and Tami had been the first of her clandestine acquaintances. There had been many more. Amirah felt herself drawn to the tourists. To her they presented an open vast world of which she knew little. They encouraged her endeavors and treated her with esteem and praise.

Tourist people, when leaving their homes, are frequently freer and less restricted than is usual for them, having not only taken leave of their homes for a short while, but also of their daily life styles. In the coming years Amirah sought them out and learned much of the Western free ways. A few of her short-term Western acquaintances had shown her how to write a few words, sometimes even drawing letters in the sand, and she learned hungrily and quickly. A few tourist families, impressed by her will and search for knowledge, sent her first and second grade English grammar and spelling books, with friends coming to Sinai. One family coming from England, the Strunks, were particularly enchanted by her and periodically sent her books to the nearest hotel, where she picked them up. In time, this would become a routine. As Amirah advanced, she knew enough to ask for what she wanted and treasured her books, studied them and hid them carefully.

Many of us humans walk around with different and even opposing sets of notions and conflicts and are none the worse for them. We create separate compartments and Amirah did likewise, continuing with her daily life with a vague, but controlled uneasiness and mostly ignoring it, believing innocently that nothing much would change and not having fully understood her attraction to Western people; a fantasy remaining inside her, detached from her real daily life.

A few months after her twelve years, her period came and her mother told her: "Now you are a woman, and you have to undergo the women's ceremony. Tomorrow the old woman will come and we will have a feast with our neighbors and friends. It will not hurt much."

"What will not hurt much?"

"You will be made a woman, and then soon we will find a husband for you." Her mother explained to her, in general terms what would be done to her, but accentuating the honor and acceptance into grown-up womanhood and being a part of the female community.

Feeling anxious and fearful, Amirah went about her chores as usual. Family members and friends soon arrived, only women. They sat around celebrating and chanting songs, gossiping and partaking of the spread set out for them. They made much of Amirah, the women praised her and blessed her. Her mother and some other women led her to another room, gave her a drink, telling her to drink it all. The women sang more songs and her head swam. Her mother made her lie down on a mattress and some women held her feet. They removed her dress and her feet were spread. Amirah felt a sharp terrible pain which became almost unbearable! She shrieked, twisted, moaned, and screamed, but the women and her mother held her tightly and the ordeal was already over. An old woman, a professional, had been dexterous and quick, and had removed a part of her clitoris. The terrible pain, though dulled by the drug, continued to torture her. Crying in hurt she wailed bitterly, her body and person outraged at the invasion.

This ancient ritual, brutal and cruel, has an important social purpose and might easily be one of the main supports of the tribes who still practice female circumcision. The aim being to prevent females from having sexual pleasure and feeling during intercourse and so keeping them from straying. To the Bedouin, infidelities mean loss of face and honor with fights to the death of the offenders, or a payment of a huge substantial sum to appease the affronted family. In its own callous way, the ritual existed as a backbone of tribal society. Their girls and women paying the price. Primitive societies had found an easy way out.

"You are a woman now," her mother said to her proudly, "one of us!" She treated her daughter with herbs and drugs. The pain receded but lasted for a few days, then slowly faded away.

Amirah's life changed drastically. No more wandering around freely and selling trinkets to the tourists. Confined to her homestead, occupied with the housework, and tending to the livestock, there would be no more fraternizing for her. When leaving the compound for an errand, a younger member of the family would escort her. Amirah found some consolation comparing impressions with her peers in the same predicament. They talked about husbands and marriage, their future and main topic.

Amirah, mostly unaware, had emotionally internalized some of the Western views and had felt outraged at the intrusion on her body, but having no choice in the matter, accepted her fate. Now, when leaving the compound, a younger family member, would escort her. Vexed and resentful, she felt the constrain and became quiet and uncommunicative, doing her chores silently, mulishly and resisted her mother in plaiting her hair in a conventional Gebla style: plaits crossing over her forehead, which her mother had learned as a girl. Bedouin have close ties among their peers, but Amirah did not. The women in her clan considered her a queer one and waited for her to shape up.

Then Amirah met Hilda. Mutual curiosity had drawn two opposites together, Hilda an older ash-blonde girl from Sweden who informed Amirah about having sex with boys, condoms and love, they talked in broken English, her younger brother impatiently playing with a dog nearby.

Amirah had many questions. "A boy and girl can meet in your country and have sex?!"

"I had two boyfriends myself in the last year," Hilda giggled. "The last one had a big . . . you know what."

For Hilda, sex had emerged as a natural function, but, for Amirah, sex existed as one of the strongest taboos in her tribe, often stronger than life itself.

She persisted incredulous. "Your families do not fight over this?"

"Why should they?"

"But when you marry you are not virgin."

Hilda burst out laughing long and hard.

"Why you laugh?"

"There are no virgins in Sweden." She could not stop chortling.

Amirah learned of her future betrothal in four years' time to a member of her extended family, in fact a distant cousin of hers. She would be past sixteen then. The groom's family were already gathering camels and sheep for the bridal price. Not showing much interest in one's future groom is often an accepted mannerism and attitude, but to her mother's chagrin, in Amirah's case, the lack of enthusiasm might well have been genuine and her mother and aunts in the women's quarters considered her an ungrateful daughter. Amirah was not their favorite. One of her aunts who lived with them in the woman's quarters, a natural mimic, would strut around, wiggling her butt: "I am Amirah and I do not want a husband. I want to stay a virgin all my life." Then she sang an improvised song, sarcastic and funny. All the women laughed. Amirah hung her head.

Amirah, now considered a woman, wore an embroidered dress with blue as fitting for an unmarried woman. Amirah slowly blossomed from being a beautiful and daring vivacious child to a striking curvy young female with clear features. Her raven black hair and her flashing dark eyes could captivate any looking her way. A wide brow hinted at her hidden intelligence and full red lips stood out even on her brown complexion, exhibited a potential of passion stored in her, only waiting to be released.

We do not always know our motivations and if we do suspect notions and controversial ideas, then we often subdue and deny them. Amirah might have been unaware as to what propelled her, but some kind of a self-preservation made her seek to continue her clandestine contacts with Westerners. Those would be more difficult than before. She grew devious and often got her way with the help of many subterfuges. She felt shut in and imprisoned in the now small world of the women quarters in her homestead. Outside a whole world waited, and a large part of her wanted to participate in the action.

Bribing her smaller brother not to mention anything, she made friends with many of the neighboring tourists, always learning more words, composing sentences and secretly writing them down. Many tourists, Israeli and others, were touched by her avid hunger for learning and went out of their way to send her basic school books on grammar and spelling, which were hidden under her few belongings at home. Bedouins do not wash often, a leftover of former times when water was scarce. Amirah, imitating the Westerners, would solve the problem by dipping into the sea, without removing her clothes which would soon dry under the hot sun.

Amirah had a trick up her sleeve:

Sometimes a tourist family would come to one of the neighboring homesteads and remain for a while and Amirah would contact them and beg them in Hebrew or English to hire her for cleaning and housework. This being acceptable to her own family and brought in ready cash. She already knew much more English and Hebrew than the males of her tribe and could be very convincing. She would approach a likely tourist family: "Hello, my name is Amirah, do you need any help? I wash dishes, clean, do household work."

This would usually be answered with, "No thank you," and then, "How do you know English so well?"

"I learn from tourists."

"Are you a real Bedouin?"

"Yes. I live in Mahmoud homestead with family."

"Well we don't need a servant."

"No servant, madam, it is only way I learn English."

This would lead up to a long conversation and her charm induced many tourists to hire her. The woman hiring her always promising her mother to keep a sharp eye on her. Amirah did little housework, but studied hard and long, her current person in charge mostly backing up her alibis and even tutoring her and often passing her along from one tourist family to another.

Three more years passed with her clandestine activities, which spread out further from her home, brought in good cash, and made the women appreciate her more. At fifteen Amirah could speak English and Hebrew and write simple English sentences, and had more than a smattering knowledge of the outside world. In Amirah's mind and emotions, two different conflicting cultural concepts had developed and were for the time being kept in separate compartments. She would soon to be betrothed, but had not yet met her future groom.

In our Western civilizations, there are many young people who have not yet mapped out their life for themselves, and drift around the world, seeking, trying to make some sense of the miracle of life, but not knowing what to search for, and only too frequently hoping and believing their seeking to be something tangible which can be found. Many give up the fight to the inevitable as they grow older and only in later life may some of the braver spirits learn that the treasures of existence lie within themselves. The desert has always been a place for seekers and much of the jetsam and debris of our societies landed there in Sinai.

At the beginning of her sixteenth year, Amirah met Steve. He came from Holland tall and handsome. He had a guitar and a moderate singing voice and lived on the beach, earning just enough money to buy the most basic necessities. Women, drugs, booze, and debts had been his downfall in Amsterdam and now he enjoyed the rest and peace of an easy simple life.

Sitting by the entrance to one of the many eating places in Dahab, he noticed the Bedouin girl with the flashing eyes, the lower part of her face covered, always together with a sister or a young boy, who occasionally passed him by. A hopeful suspicion aroused in him: she appeared to be seeking him out. Steve had few inhibitions and once as Amirah came by he stared at her and made eye contact. She did not look away and for a fleeting second their eyes had met.

It was enough! A spark flew from one to the other.

He smiled at her, his heart beating fast. He tried to engage her in conversation.

"Hello there."

No answer, only two burning eyes.

"You don't talk?"

The pair of eyes seemed to show some warning signs.

"Shall I sing a song for you?"

Her eyes turned soft and deep, Steve felt that he could lose himself their depth. He began to play and sing but she soon distanced herself. Their small, modest adventure; but, for them, grand and encompassing, would repeat itself with small variations whenever she passed him on her way and Amirah fabricated errands which would allow her to do so.

They fell in love. A fantasy-like love of glances and hidden gestures. They had exchanged hot smoldering looks and he had tried to talk to her, beseeching, but had never been answered. They could not meet openly, but love, acute, poignant, and powerful would find a way. The Bedouin women have created a body of emotional oral poetry called Ghinnawa, which is passed along the generations. Amirah knew some and dreamt her heart away in the sleepless nights. Two different and opposing conceptions that until now had been kept apart, struggled within her: A strife knowing no quarter and never ceasing its poignant pressure, day and night, especially at nights. Love finally won the battle.

Passing Steve on her way to the market with her smaller brother, Amirah furtively dropped a tiny note. After she passed by, Steve read the one sentence written in English, with trembling hands.

'The Mahmoud homestead tonight, when the moon sets.'

Precise, short, and to the point.

Steve, electrified, did not know her name and set himself out to find the mentioned homestead. To him she appeared mysterious and exotic and he longed for her. The note had been written in English! He did not know what to make of that. Asking around he found the Mahmoud place, but when did the moon go down? He had no idea. He asked around, but none of his friends knew.

Night came and the moon arose in a silvery glow, a half moon. He did not sleep and watched it impatiently. The moon seemed in no hurry to set. He walked the half hour to the homestead of the girl. He would wait for her on the spot. Steve settled himself against a post and kept an eye on the moon. He had had a long day and allowed himself to daydream, eventually he dozed off.

He awoke with a shock. How could he have fallen asleep? He looked up, the starlit sky covered him and the world like a canopy of jewels. He could not see the moon. A sound repeated made itself heard and awakened him. He saw a shadowy figure moving away. "Pssst." He stood up. "Pssst," he repeated, his heart beating. "Here!" he whispered as loud as he dared.

The shadowy shape approached him. The girl! They recognized each other by the light of the stars. Now they could talk freely to each other, but both were tongue-tied. He stepped forward, she came closer, and Steve put his arms around her feeling no resistance. She clove to him with a passion equaling his own. Amirah, swept away by powerful emotions, felt like a leaf being pulled about in a flash flood. She seemed to have no control over herself. They sank down under the ceiling of stars.

They made love and then again, it had been late in the night when they had met and now they began to talk knowing only too soon the night would end.

They talked hurriedly, eagerly, beginning with each other's names.

"What is your name?" he gasped in English, which had become the daily international language among backpackers.

"Amirah, yours?"

"Steve, I'm from Holland."

"In Europe."

"You speak English!?"

"I learned."

"I have loved you from the time I saw you."

"But you never saw me."

"I saw your eyes. Tell me about yourself."

"I am Bedouin, we are a proud family, no one must know about us."

"Okay, but why the secret?"

"They might kill us if they find out."

"You're kidding." At the time, he had thought she exaggerated.

"I sneak out of the women's place. They all asleep."

During the night, a few women might have to get up for the call of nature. Amirah had done so, but had not returned yet. She had fallen in love with a Westerner and had indulged in many fantasies of another kind of life, unrestrained by Bedouin convention and traditions, which now sickened her. They had made her a woman and cut her so as not to feel pleasure in sex, she did not orgasm, but passion can be of the heart and mind, of the imagination and of hope. Steve symbolized an unhindered freedom to her and their covert meeting with nothing to hamper them had caused her to lose control in the amorous proceedings, recklessly and totally, giving herself to him in body and soul.

Steve had been charmed, enchanted and struck with her; for him her person signified the epitome of exotic, sexual mystery. Her image and her strangeness intrigued him. He did realize how Amirah had thrown all caution to the winds and if their affair would be revealed, it would go ill with her. However, he did not yet understand fully the seriousness of their position.

With the gradual returning of some vestiges of common sense, Amirah began to feel the seeds of some remorse for what had happened. She had crossed the point of no return. Bedouin families feel their honor tainted and degraded by any illicit sexual liaison and if not dealt with, they would be spurned and ridiculed by all the other clans and tribes. She had given up her virginity!! She could not be married. Pride, face and honor are paramount elements in Bedouin society. There were few ways to repair the damage done; one way is the death of the transgressors, but sometimes a large sum of money passing hands could do the job as well. Times were changing and she hoped their deed might not be as inflexible as it once used to be, even so things could not remain as they are.

Steve was surprised by Amirah's knowledge of English. He had learned English at school, but hers topped his easily. They conversed in whispers, between kisses and stroking, touching each other, trying to plan for the future.

Steve, aware of having a very special and unique person beside him, asked her, "Are there any more Bedouin girls like you?"

"I do not know."

"How do you know English so well?"

"I studied whenever I could."

"Without books?"

"I have some books. I can also talk Hebrew, but not write."

"You are amazing!"

That meant little to her. "We cannot stay here for long."

"Come with me."

"I cannot."

"Why not?"

"We Bedouins have strong rules, I am to be married soon."

"Do you love him?"

"I have not seen him yet."

"I will take you away from all this!"

They were not yet capable of any long-term plans; they would meet again the next night. Amirah had been tutored on sex by many Western girlfriends along the years and knew all about condoms, contraceptives and pills. The latter were not to be had and they would use condoms in the future. They would have to elope and Steve agreed. He had no money and few earning skills, however those seemed small obstacles for one in love. Something would turn up. Steve now checked the time on his watch; three thirty, they had been together for . . . over two hours. "I have to get back," Amirah said, "or they will miss me."

They met every night. A few more nights went by, and they were both aware of the danger of their affair. It could not last! The more time passing, the more chance of their concealed meetings being somehow revealed, and then they and especially Amirah, would be in real trouble. Steve had made some friends in Dahab and they banded the issue around. An idea had formed in Steve's head: they could seek refuge with the Israeli authorities, he knew Israel to be a Western democracy, surely something could be arranged. Once the knowledge of their meetings got out in the open, they would have to flee. Amirah and Steve discussed this back and forth amid the lovemaking and endearments.

At last they decided. Steve would go to the authorities for help. Sinai is under Israeli jurisdiction and a girl's life could be in danger, not to mention his own. Amirah would remain at her home for now and of course reveal nothing. Steve hitched a ride to the army post nearby and stopped by the gate. Steve, as many people in Sinai, dressed casually: loafers, short trousers, and a not too clean a shirt. He projected what he looked like, a backpacker tourist with no means. There were many like him around and he did not make the impression needed to get to see the senior commanding officer immediately.

He had to state his business and finally a soldier told him to wait. He waited an hour or two passing from one officer to another until a senior officer agreed to listen to him. He stated his business in his best English, knowing he had to come clean and be explicit, concluding with, "If the girl's family find out, they will kill her and probably me too."

"How old is your girlfriend?"

Steve knew that. "Sixteen."

"Then under our law she is still a minor. We cannot take her away from her family, unless severe harassment or abuse is shown beyond reasonable doubt."

Steve had not known about the operation Amirah had as a girl. "But her family might kill her."

"What citizenship do you have?"

"Dutch, Holland."

"Shouldn't you go to the Dutch Embassy?"

"There is none here."

"There is one in Tel Aviv, not too far, less than a day's travel."

"But we are Sinai, under your jurisdiction."

"The Bedouins are not easy to deal with and we try not to interfere too much with their way of life."

"But here is a matter of life and death!" Steve repeated.

"We enforce the law. Has any law been broken?"

Steve got angry. "Then you don't give a shit!"

"What do you expect us to do?" The Israeli officer, still a young man, did feel the passion and fears of the person before him. Officially he could do nothing, but he sympathized, having had a few love affairs of his own. He did not react angrily to Steve's outburst. "Be reasonable. Should we warn them? . . . Alert them and do more harm than good. There are civilian regional offices in Sharem, try those, you may be able to get a visa to Israel, are you Jewish? You might claim some kind of an asylum."

"I am not Jewish."

"Then try the Dutch Embassy," he repeated, "there is a bus going twice daily. Get her to Holland from there."

"Are you giving me the brush off?"

"Does your 'girlfriend' have any identity card or certification?" They both knew the answer. "Put yourself in my place. What would you like me to do? Go ahead, you tell me."

"Maybe take us to Israel"

"You are a Dutch citizen, not an Israeli one. Without identification, no passport . . . your friend would not be let in, even as a tourist. The best advice I can give you is to get to your country's Embassy and see how it goes."

Steve left the place with a sour expression. He had to do something, and fast, as time would not be on their side. He hesitated to return to Holland, not yet anyway, he had just come from there and under somewhat dubious circumstances, escaping from his debts. However, he did not have much choice. All the moves Steve had contemplated for Amirah and himself involved a bureaucracy that might take weeks, months. They did not have the time and he did not want to leave her for even a day. He should get to the Dutch Embassy by himself, but what could they do without her physical presence?

Amirah made him aware of the urgency of their position and after some discussions Steve took the bus coming from Sharem to Eilat and from there to Tel Aviv. Arriving late, he found the

Embassy closed. Tired and hungry he bought a falafel and a coke. What little money he had, needed to be saved for the trip back, so no hotel for him. He found deserted corridor and spent a sleepless night. The next morning, he reached the Embassy looking dirty and ragged. The guard did not want to let him in and only after showing his passport at the gate was he allowed inside. There were few people about. Another guard led him straight to the head of foreign affairs.

Steve unfolded his story, stressing the dangers and urgency of their position. After hearing him out, the head of foreign affairs lectured him about the precariousness of Dutch relations in the Israeli-Palestinian conflict ending with, "Those are perilous times, I am afraid we cannot afford to risk a diplomatic incident by smuggling a person into Israel. I am truly sorry. . . ." He left it hanging.

"But, sir, is it not possible to get some papers for her?"

"She will have to apply for citizenship."

Then the telephone rang and he had to leave. An aide had been present while Steve had unfolded his story. He had an idea. "Marry the girl, get a marriage license, then as the wife of a Dutch citizen we might be able to do something for you both."

"We are in the Sinai desert! There is no authority to marry us or give us a legitimate marriage license."

"Let me have a phone number, of your hotel. We might be able to send someone from the Embassy to marry you two legally, under Dutch law."

"I have no phone number."

The aide lost his patience: "Gotverdamt, what than do you want us to do?"

"Get me some papers, a visa for her, anything, please."

"Under those conditions? Impossible. You have to get her here in person in order to get a visa for her."

Steve's head swam; what kind of bureaucratic nonsense were those unconnected white-collar employees raving about? To get a visa one had to have one? However too much was at stake and he took hold of himself. "What should I do?"

"Apply for Dutch citizenship for her. I will give you some forms to fill out."

"How long will it take?"

"A few months, half a year."

"And if we get married under Dutch law?"

"The same."

The bureaucracy would take months. His last hope had gone. He took the bus to Eilat and hitched a ride to Dahab with an Israeli couple and they informed him of a colony of tents, fast growing and expanding a few miles from the outskirts of Sharm el Sheikh by the sea. They themselves had slummed there for a while last year, bathing and snorkeling. A dejected Steve returned to Amirah, admitting his defeat and they comforted each other by making love. Later he brought up the subject of the colony.

"There are hundreds of people there, maybe a thousand, so I've been told. No one will be able to find us."

"We must go," Amirah replied.

Both of them, each in his or her own way, underestimated the power of loss of face and dignity they would cause to her kin and tribe, not fully realizing the desperation and determination of the males in the family to put matters right and to regain their self-respect and honor. Amirah might have known better, but we all are efficient in deluding ourselves when we want to. They spent the night planning the details of their escape.

"I will come to the homestead at midnight to get you," Steve said.

"I have no watch for time," Amirah observed.

"Take mine, I have borrowed some money from friends, we can take a taxi."

"Drivers Bedouin, too dangerous, they might know me."

"We hike then. Make a bundle of whatever you want to take. I'll carry it."

The next day Amirah went about her daily chores as usual, but with a beating heart, realizing the last day in her home had come. She would never see her mother again, or her sisters and family, nor the place where she cooked, washed the pots and pans, or swept the floor. She knew every chink and fold in their place and silently took her leave of them. She had one minor problem: Amirah could not take much with her when she sneaked out during the night. Regretfully she would have to leave some clothes and her books behind.

All went as planned. They escaped in the dark of the night and got to Sharem late next morning. Their feat had turned out to be less difficult than they had anticipated.

In Amirah's homestead, the women missed her on the following day and were uneasy. After the first few hours had passed, her mother, worried and distressed, finally informed her father and the rest of the males. Against their will her parents and brothers suspected what might have happened, they became anxious, and as more time passed with no sign of Amirah, they grew frantic. All the younger members of the family had one time or another escorted her outside the compound. They were now thoroughly questioned; scraps of evidence were painstakingly scrutinized.

"Did you ever see Amirah stop to talk to anyone?" Her little brother was interrogated intensely by his parents.

He hung his head.

"Were you bribed?"

He kept mulishly silent.

"Speak, you have done enough harm to us."

"She stopped by the foreigner who sings with the music box."
"A guitar?"
"I don't know, but they did not talk."
"How many times did they meet?"
"Many times, on our way to the shops."
"Where is that place?"
He told them.

Her mother searched Amirah's leftover belongings and her books in English were found. A vague suspicion now became a reality: her partiality toward foreign tourists stood revealed. It became apparent that Amirah often passed a place where a tourist with a guitar sung for small cash, and sending one of the older brothers to look for him, they found the place unoccupied. Quickly searching the village and putting two and two together, the horrible and demeaning truth had eventually to be finally acknowledged: Amirah might have run away and they naturally assumed a man to be involved–and worse, not a Bedouin but a foreigner tourist! There seemed no other explanation: they now remembered how Amirah had shown no real interest in her future husband.

In dismay and some panic, another family meeting was quickly called, the women too, moaning and beating their breasts. Amirah's father insisted the calamity be hushed up tightly; not one word should get out or they would never live down the shame. Amirah's grandfather, the old patriarch should not be informed until the situation became clearer. The knowledge would kill him. A major disaster had occurred; not only had Amirah run away, but she might have absconded with a foreigner! They would never live down the shame! Amirah had to be found before anything gets out and her two older brothers should scout around to see what they could find out, but on the quiet.

Arriving at the colony, Steve and Amirah searched for an empty space to settle down. A dark-haired boy greeted them. "Hi guys, you new here?"

"Just arrived," Steve said.

"You got a tent?"

"No nothing."

"Walk with me. I'm Bondy, from Canada."

"Steve here, from Amsterdam, this is Amirah."

Bondy looked closely at her, "Where you from?"

"Indian." Steve said quickly.

"I can speak for myself," Amirah said.

"It gets real hot during the day, we'll get you some sheets or blankets from the guys. You must have shade," Bondy said.

For Amirah, the colony was bliss, they were immediately, unhesitatingly, and unconditionally accepted into the local community and quickly made friends. Her exotic dark beauty and her easy unassuming nature captivated all. A simple tent-like structure constructed of some sheets and a blanket or two, all donated to them by their neighbors and held up by a combination of sticks and some ropes, became their home. Their makeshift tent-like creation did not stand out among the few hundred similar ones. They ate when they liked, slept when they liked and made love when they liked and as they were close to the sea, they bathed when they felt like it.

Amirah, free from the constrains and taboos of her upbringing had, for the first time in her life, as much time as she wanted to satisfy her curiosity on Western lifestyles. Before leaving with Steve, all conversations, with others and with him, always had an urgent and hurried element in them. Now she had many questions, some awkward, others coming from misinformation and in her relative innocence caused much amusement with her friends of both sexes. Their friendly mirth encouraging her; like the laughing of elders seeing a child make its first steps.

New couples would arrive occasionally and others would leave, often relinquishing their unwanted belongings to their friends. Amirah and Steve soon accumulated all the stuff and gear they needed for a minimum of comfort. They were content.

Not all remained well in paradise. The food they ate, mostly conserves and bread or pitahs bought in nearby Sharem, did not go down too well at first, as Amirah had grown up mainly on a diet of rice with mutton or fowl, yogurt, pitah, and fish. She also had occasional bouts of anxiety and fear, having dared too much. Defying her family and her heritage had not been easy. Sometimes nightmares of her brothers catching up with her would awake her in fear. Steve, always loving and tender, consoled her, and Amirah slowly grew less disturbed.

The colony, not specifically a nudist one, had boys and girls bathing naked and often walking about in the nude. Amirah, more inhibited than most, had bathed in one of her dresses, but had felt ridiculous and had succeeded in borrowing and getting a two-piece bathing suit from one of the girls who claimed never to use it. Eventually she too bathed in the nude together with Steve and some others, rejoicing in the new found feeling of freedom on her body. Amirah had also exchanged most of her old dresses in the bundle they had brought with them, for more modern and stylish ones. The girls in the colony thought her clothes exotic and were happy to get them. Her nightmares were slowly receding, as the new way of life grew on her. Amirah had never been free before and now she rejoiced and basked in her independence. Every day seemed like a new blessing to her. Time passed quickly.

A more serious issue had reared its head: they had little money. Even in a primitive place like the colony, one had to have money to buy food and basics from a store in Sharem and that included bottled drinking water. They had scrounged off their friends as much as they dared. In Dahab, Steve had made some money by playing his guitar and sometimes singing.

"Amirah, I guess I'll have to go to Sharem, earn some cash," he told her one morning.

"No, don't leave me."

"We have no money I will hike to the center where there are hotels and regular tourists, sing some songs, buy food for us."

"I come with you."

"You know that you cannot leave here, in Sharem you might be recognized."

"I hate this . . ."

"I don't like it either."

They hated to part, even for a short time, but eventually Steve hiked to Sharem. The distance, only a few miles, had no regular traffic. However, Steve did manage to hike easily back and forth each day with some provisions and a little money. This almost ideal state of affairs lasted for some months. Amirah, left to her own devices for most of the day, in the free atmosphere of the backpackers' colony, had many proposals made to her. A girl invited her to a threesome with her boyfriend, offers of swapping mates, and generally all-around sex offers were plentiful. Some hinted at, but most of them were as straightforward as they could get. She told Steve about them and he shrugged his shoulders, "Sure why not?"

It is often in the nature of us human beings, that when we throw off our former notions and turn to another set of directives, be they logical or emotional, to go all the way and often swing, as the pendulum does, from one end to the other: Amirah being no exception. Together with Steve, and later separately, they had many indiscriminating sexual encounters. They had fun, exercising their persons, the exuberance of their youth, and their freedom.

Amirah had had a clitoridectomy at the age of twelve, but sexual stimulations can be in other parts of the body as well and also in the head, especially in the brain, and can be combined with many notions. Amirah enjoyed those encounters. Sex, frequently augmented with drugs, and mixed up with the idea of freedom, had caused them to throw off all restraints, but when there is little money there can be even less drugs. Amirah and Steve, when fortune smiled on them, did occasionally take some, but not enough to get addicted. Amirah had never been idle before, and now she had time on her hands and basked in the strange new luxury of having no chores. She chatted with her friends, bathed in the sea and went for strolls in the area.

Then one afternoon Steve did not return to the camp. Amirah felt anxious but not too worried. Possibly Steve had not managed to catch a hike back, though that had never happened before. Time went by, evening came and then night, it became apparent that Steve would not get back. Amirah slept alone for the first time since running away from her home, trying to keep away her tears.

The next morning came with no sign of Steve. Something felt very wrong. She went from tent to tent in tears begging some of her friends to search for Steve in Sharem.

"He has not returned since yesterday," she cried.

Not all took her seriously. "Maybe he's found a girl over there, or some rich tourist lady," one guy mocked.

"Some of us are going to Sharem today, we'll look for him," a couple promised. Bondi too promised to look for him.

"He usually hangs out by the hotels," Amirah told them.

"If he's there, we'll bring him back," Bondi promised.

Later in the day her friends returned, having found no sign of Steve. In desperation, Amirah herself went to Sharem. There were two food stores in Sharem and Amirah asked the Egyptian owners if they had seen a tall light haired European. One of them remembered him. Steve always bought food there, but had no idea of where he might be. Amirah remained in the area for some days and nights, passing the nights by sleeping in deserted corridors. Steve seemed to have vanished. Amirah did not believe he had deserted her, but at the time there appeared no clue as to what might have happened. She finally returned utterly miserable and alone to the camp.

Among Amirah's acquaintances was an Israeli boy called Rafi, a hidden same-sex person. He differed from the others and gave the impression of being more tender and sensitive. He lived further off in a tent-like makeshift shack, alone and did not mix much. Amirah had been drawn to him and now in her plight he comforted her. They talked through most of the night and he revealed his true nature to her. His buddy had left him before Amirah and Steve had arrived.

He added, "My folks live in Tel Aviv and I came here to get away from my parents and siblings, and the pressure they put on me to be normal like everyone else."

Amirah did not react.

"Don't remain alone," he said to her. "Come and stay with me till Steve returns. We'll have a platonic relationship."

He did not say 'if he comes back' and she felt grateful. Rafi, was one of the very few, who seemed to have as much money as he needed, and she moved in with him. Steve did not return, and Amirah, miserable, unhappy, often grew moody, waiting against reason for Steve to return. What could have happened? Did her family have anything to do with Steve missing? Her family would be looking for her, she knew, but they would not think of looking for her here. They did not know about Steve and had never seen him . . . or had they somehow found out?

A week later she discerned what probably might have happened. A boy came up to her. "Somebody may be looking for you. They asked me if I had seen a dark girl with a blond boy who may have arrived some months back."

"Who asked?" Amirah wanted to know.

"Two men, Arabs I think, but they were dressed in regular togs."

"What did you tell them?"

"Nothing of course."

"When was that?" Rafi asked.

The boy looked unsure. "Some days back, a week maybe . . ."

"Why didn't you tell me," Amirah cried, "What were you waiting for!"

"Is it important? I forgot." He left quickly.

Amirah, with a shock and a dreadful sinking feeling, realized that her past might be catching up with her. Those must be members of her clan, or someone hired by them. They had somehow recognized Steve and abducted him. Steve would never leave her willingly. One of her escorts from before might have guessed and revealed their romance. The chances were they had killed Steve. As a child, she had heard her brothers boast with stories of what they would do to regain their honor. They were looking for her! Steve had kept his mouth shut and not revealed anything, as they had not found her yet. Maybe they had tortured him. Amirah felt the certainty of his loss and hopelessness possess her. She began to mourn. Steve was no more!

Rafi saw her face. "What is it?"

"I have to go." She felt frightened and desperate.

"Go where?"

"Anywhere, away from here. My life may be in danger." With Steve gone, she did not really care anymore.

"What are you talking about?"

Rafi looked anxious and Amirah touched, poured out her story between sobs ending morosely. "They will find me and kill me sooner or later."

"You are one very brave person."

"That means nothing, you might be in danger too."

"I am also a brave person."

Amirah loved Steve and felt his loss acutely. He had not given her away and had loved her! Her appetite had gone. A feeling of guilt in having involved him in her life seeped through to her. Lying on her blanket, grieving, her face to the wall, Amirah understood herself to be an outcast. Anyone being exposed to her would be in danger! Rafi, naturally kind to her, made her drink some water.

After a day or two he said, "I may have an idea." He sank into thought for a while. "Come with me to Tel Aviv, no one will find you there."

"Are you crazy!"

"Not as crazy as you think. My folks are after me to get a girl and settle down. You be that girl."

"Being with me can be dangerous."

"Not in Tel Aviv."

"What shall I do in Tel Aviv? I don't know anything. There is no love lost between Jews and Arabs. Your parents will never accept me. This is a ridiculous idea."

"My parents will be delighted if I bring a girl home, any girl! They have always been left-wingers and are against racism in all its forms."

"We can't pull that off. Rafi, I really like you, but you are gay. It will never work. For one I have no papers of any kind."

"The passport problem can be fixed with money. We are friends, no sex, but who needs to know?"

"We will be acting out a sham."

"Maybe, but so is much of everything else. We could solve both our problems."

Amirah considered her choices: there was no way of repenting for what had been done to her family and kin. They would call her a whore. She had stained their honor and they would not rest until they had removed that blot. Reluctantly she fell in with Rafi's plan and they discussed the details. First a passport for her to get into Israel.

"I can probably get one from one of the girls, they can easily get another one." Rafi suggested. "They all need money, we can buy one, change the picture. They don't check much around here."

Getting a passport turned out not to be as simple as they had thought. A new passport generates an extended bureaucratic hassle and no one wanted to go through with the routine. They had exhausted the list of their friends, when a scruffy looking specimen came along.

"I heard you guys are looking for a passport?"

"Yes."

"I can get you a girl's passport." He leered at Amirah, "Indian like you, looks somewhat like you even. I want three hundred bucks and we make it," he nodded toward Amirah.

Rafi and Amirah studied each other. "I'm willing if you are," Rafi said to her. "I can get the money." Then, seeing Amirah's look of repulsion, he turned to the guy, "I'll give you the money but no girl. Let's see the passport first."

"Okay, I'm fetching it." He turned to go.

"You'll spend all that money on me? And you get nothing," Amirah wondered aloud.

"Who says I'm getting nothing!"

"We don't have sex."

"Amirah, I have the money, well . . . my folks have, so . . . no sweat, I get to feel good. We both win."

"The guy is going to steal his girlfriend's passport and get drugs with the money," Amirah pointed out.

"So . . . Maybe . . . their look out. What do you want to do?"

Amirah did not answer. The guy returned with a ragged looking passport which had seen many better days. Rafi checked the bedraggled item. "This is an old one, not worth a hundred bucks."

"The date's still good."

The document had, in fact, more than half a year to run and would do. The photo looked old and cracked, not much could be made out, the picture might as well be of Amirah and would not have to be changed.

"Two hundred bucks."

"Okay."

Rafi said to Amirah, "We have to get to Sharem for the money, tomorrow at bank opening time."

They planned. There was an airport in Sharem and they could fly straight from there to a minor airport next to Tel Aviv.

"I'm afraid," Amirah admitted.

"Nothing much can happen to us in the daylight. I intended to fly home anyway after Noam left me, but somehow I kept delaying, hoping he might return."

"Tell me about it."

"Sorry, I can't . . . yet."

When Amirah acknowledged her anxiety, she had not only feared flying, though she had never flown before. Knowing how all the international tourists had arrived by plane made flight plausible for her. Her real terror had not even been the fear of her kin redressing their honor, as much as of the big city! She would be without the tools and knowledge to deal with a strange life and would be totally helpless and dependent on Rafi. They had become good friends, but they were not lovers and to her that made a difference.

The next morning, they gave most of their belongings away to their friends and got to Sharem, the other boy and the passport with them. Everything went more or less as planned, with some inevitable delays. Rafi got money from the bank and they paid off the boy for the passport. Then they bought flight tickets to Sde Dov in Israel. The passport check had been speedy and casual and Amirah had been told to get a new passport as soon as possible. On the plane, Amirah, frigid with fright at first, held onto Rafi for dear life and felt incapable of acting independently. Later, with her nose glued to the little round porthole, she saw the world as never before, like in the maps. Then they flew above the clouds . . . knowing a thing and experiencing the same are different matters and she stared totally amazed.

They arrived in the afternoon and went through another nerve wrecking passport check and again Amirah was warned to renew her passport. Rafi phoned his folks. The change had been too abrupt for Amirah, her senses and instincts were numbed; in the morning, they were still been in the desert near her home!

The two older brothers of the Mahmoud clan had been busy searching for their sister, their first real and important task and they felt proud and honored with the trust placed in them. They would be the protectors of the reputation of their family. The desert is a large place and they had been told to keep quiet, which made their task doubly harder. Bedouins rely on each other and the spoken word can be passed on quickly from mouth to mouth, and turned into common knowledge. This could not be done now. The brothers moved around, visiting one settlement after another, eventually arriving at Sharem el Sheikh. Steve had been easily recognized in Sharem, due to the description of one of Amirah's former escorts. He was the only one singing with a guitar around.

"This is the foreigner," one of the brothers excited by their find said, "there is no other like him."

"We shall pick him up when he leaves and kill him," the other planned passionately, it would be their first kill and give them status with the clan.

Two overeager and hotheaded devotees picked Steve up, overpowered him, and dragged an unconscious Steve into the desert in their car, where they shot him in the head. As an outsider, they did not consider him very important, their honor would only be redeemed when they found Amirah. The two dedicated brothers had tasted partial success. Exited they returned to Dahab triumphant and came under heavy sarcastic criticism from their uncle.

"You two stupid goats!" he raved. "The foreigner could have led us to your sister, and in your impatience, you were too blind to see that. You had to kill him."

"We had to do so quickly, before anyone noticed," they defended themselves.

"Noticed what? Tell me what happened."

"We waited to see where he would go. He left the town and hiked a ride, but not alone. We stopped the car for him saying we can take only one person. We were seen."

"You should have made his acquaintance, driven him to his whore. Then we would have known where she is hiding. What have you done with the body?"

"We drove into the wadi and shot him. He is buried beneath a pile of stones. The jackals will not dig him out."

"I will not tell your grandfather of your stupidities. We must find your whoring sister and quick. I will see to it myself."

The same uncle had hired two Egyptians to scout the foreign colony in Sharm el Sheikh, giving them as few details as possible and promising them a huge reward. They would have to wear Western clothes, a thing not easy for some Bedouin.

Amirah had escaped just in time.

In the city, Amirah found, as feared, another different and almost totally new world. She did not easily get used to falling asleep at nights with the constant noise of traffic. The strange hectic ways and habits of a large city were foreign to her nature, but the most disconcerting matter of all, turned out to be the love and kindness Rafi's parents and brother too, doled out to her. They looked upon her as something of a symbol; Rafi at last had found a girl! He had been a source of desperate worry to them. They could not accept him being a one-sex person.

Rafi had run away to Sinai with Noam after many discussions, pleadings and even more than some emotional pressure from home. His parents were modern enlightened people, and they would have preferred their firstborn to fall in love with one of their own, but accepted Amirah and their son living together under their roof as second best. Amirah's modest ways and her exotic beauty had captivated them. Money too had not been a big issue. Rafi would be normal now, they hoped. Miriam wanted a grandson, the sooner the better.

Rafi's mother, Miriam, a second-generation Holocaust survivor, had suffered in her childhood and youth through her parents who had come to Israel beaten and depressed and totally at loss of what to do with their lives and their children. She knew what pain was like and had decided not to lay her past on her own children. She had emotionally sealed it tight. Miriam had never even hinted to Rafi and Tomer, her two sons, about the Holocaust and what their grandparents had to deal with. To her, Israel had been a new start. Her greatest fear had been that her firstborn Rafi might be a homosexual and it nearly killed her. She would do anything to keep Rafi and Amirah together.

Rafi's father had been disgusted by the thought of his son having sex with another boy or man. Love, adoration he could understand and maybe even accept, but sex?! The mere thought made him shiver in repugnance. He had broken away from a semi religious home and believed himself to be a man of the world. He believed in equality and in the curbing of the enormous profits of the banks and other multimillion concerns. The outrageous incomes of the top ten percent of the population had made him vote for a leftist party in the government, but homosexuality? No! That was going too far. Wisely, he had not forced or given his son any ultimatum yet, but he had certainly thought about it.

Then Rafi came home with Amirah, a beautiful Arab Bedouin! Rafi should have made a better choice, he thought, however he could accept her. A nice unassuming person and an exotic female who would soon learn their ways and all would be forgiven and forgotten. The children would be raised as Israeli.

Rafi told his parents all about Amirah, except for the one really important subject: they were not an item and he would remain gay all his life . . . the one thing his parents could not accept.

Miriam took Amirah to her heart. They went to shopping centers and Malls. Amirah learned about visas, credit cards, checks and coupons, among many other items of our technological and mercenary civilization. Miriam helped her to buy clothes and showed her how to dress. In the colony, no one had given much thought to dressing up. Entering a new life is never simple, especially in a big city. Naturally she made mistakes, but Rafi's parents laughed them away.

Amirah felt dreadfully uneasy. They slept in Rafi's room. They were good friends and Rafi probably had saved her from her own kin. Having sex with him would be a real treat and not only because of any gratitude. Rafi, naturally kind and sensitive, had shown no interest in her. They were living a lie and deceiving the people who were bestowing much kindness on them both. The subject irked at first, then bothered her and grew, developing into large proportions and frequently popped up when they were alone in Rafi's room. Amirah had never been able to feel at home in their room, though no fault of Rafi. The place and furniture and everything else there being his. Feeling a guest in his room with little to give to him, except her friendship and sympathy, did not seem sufficient.

Frustrated, she would begin, "Rafi we cannot go on like this."

"What do you want to do. Tell them the truth. Do you want to kill them?"

"How long can our . . . gambit last?"

"How long can anything last," he countered. "Noam and I were good together, but the sonofabitch had to run off with another guy," He said bitterly. Amirah realized he had not yet got over his last love. She herself could not understand how two males can love each other or have sex, and felt closer to his parents than to him on the subject. Between him and the other guy, Noam, there had been love, no doubt real love, and he still suffered, if only something could be done. Feeling exasperated and helpless, she mentioned to him on more than one occasion: "Rafi you know–we can have sex anytime you want. I want to, I really do."

"You're a good soul, Amirah and one day you will find the right guy," he retorted.

"And you are not him."

"I guess not."

She would have to come to terms with their contingency. Some evenings he went to gay clubs, frequently encouraging her to come along. Often, they were noisy, but nice. There were other girls around and they made her feel more at ease and accepted as a friend.

Miriam had never been one for much partying, or socializing, but now she proudly exhibited Amirah around to her friends as Rafi's future fiancée and also to quiet the hints and rumors which had been going around her son. Those ladies might have looked at Amirah strangely and privately thought their own thoughts, but they mentioned nothing aloud, not even hinting cattishly about a misfit liaison. Amirah, on being asked, revealed some parts of her former life. Miriam's friends saw her as a beautiful exotic flower. The holidays came and they sat with family and friends to feast. Amirah learned many strange ways and to eat strange food and began to feel accepted.

Rafi returned to finish his interrupted studies in law and his parents, mostly his mom, began to hint about a possible marriage and children, and they both felt very awkward. There were many bureaucratic formalities to get through which might take months. They had never dared to renew Amirah's passport. Their marriage could not be a Jewish one; they would have to go overseas to get legally married. To leave the country one needed a genuine passport and that would take some doing. The Ministry of the Interior is manned by many religious persons who create difficulties for non-Jews. The laws too, are not encouraging.

Rafi had put his parents off: "When I finish my studies." He had hinted back and this had bought them some time and a measure of liberty.

"I'm dying to be a grandmother, the sooner the better," his mom reminded him on occasions.

Amirah too intended to study, but did not yet know what. Maybe History. A coherent History of the Bedouins should be written, emphasizing the female's part for better and for worse. Having had much inside knowledge, her work could be her career. Rafi encouraged her. The university had grants for people just like her and would cost her little or nothing. They had actually applied to some offices and talked about enrolling her next year.

A small committee of teachers and lecturers had listened to parts of her amazing story and told her that with hard work, she could accomplish her aspirations, explaining what subjects needed to be studied, all to which Amirah enthusiastically agreed. The future looked bright. Rafi guided her to the university's main library and Amirah felt stunned by the enormous amount of books. Rafi helped her find books in English on the material to be studied and she applied herself. Involving herself with the intricate language in which introductions to sociology, anthropology and psychology are written, kept her occupied. Everyone had been very helpful. This state of affairs lasted over half a year and Amirah learned how to get along in the city, but Tel Aviv still felt strange and foreign to her.

Then it happened.

At one of the gay parties in which Amirah had participated as a guest, she noticed Rafi staring, emotionally engaged and aroused, at some person. The man turned out to be his former lover, Noam, who had come back from somewhere. Amirah had never seen Rafi so agitated. Noam, some years older than Rafi, with a short-trimmed beard, came up to him: "Hi kid. Long time no see."

"What are you doing here?" Rafi stammered.

"Where else would I be?"

"Why did you leave?"

"I made a mistake, I'm sorry."

"Sorry!! Goddammit, you sonofabitch. Sorry! That's all you can say now."

"People make mistakes. I made one. I came here looking for you." They continued to argue. Amirah stood aside, forgotten. Finally, Noam noticed her and more than willing to change the subject of his disappearance, he asked, "Who's the lady?"

"My very good friend, Amirah . . . from Sinai."

"Friend?"

"Yes friend . . . and a better one than you have been." Rafi wanted to get at him. He had an account to settle. "We sleep together."

"I don't believe this. What are you doing here then?"

"None of your business."

"Rafi, I feel like an idiot, I don't care who knows it. I deeply regret what I have done."

One thing quickly became obvious to Amirah: the Noam person wanted Rafi back. Where would that leave her? "Let's get out of here," she urged him.

"You go, I have some unfinished business here."

Amirah remained. Rafi and Noam continued their haggling and blaming. At last, Amirah had enough. "I'm going home."

They were too busy with each other to pay much attention to her. Leaving alone, gave her a bad feeling, which only grew worse when Rafi did not come home.

Rafi came late next morning with an apologetic look on his face and came straight to the point: "Amirah, I am going to live with Noam. Say what you like to my parents. I've had enough of our farce."

"But what about me? I can't stay here alone."

"Why not? My folks like you."

"Only as long as I am with you."

"I must be with Noam, Amirah, surely you can understand?"

"Yes, of course" But what about her? Rafi's folks were great people and they liked her, but they were focused on them being an item. What would happen now? How would they react? What will they say?

Rafi continued, "I cannot live my life according to my parents or anybody else. Haven't you done the same? You ran away from your folks too."

Everything he said rang true, but left her in the lurch. Amirah nodded glumly. There were too many matters left unsaid and she did not want to say them. Rafi seemed to feel a need to elaborate and they talked most of the morning. Rafi handed her a slip of paper. "Here is my new number. If you get into trouble of any sort phone me, no, phone me anyway."

Rafi left, also leaving a note to his folks explaining, excusing, and clarifying his position; he would continue with his studies, but would stay and live with Noam. He asked them to take good care of Amirah and to forgive him.

Rafi's parents were aghast at his return to homosexuality, they saw it as a disaster. They had been optimistic of Rafi going straight with this beautiful and exotic girl, who had naturally been the center of their expectations. Miriam questioned her profusely, even desperately, not omitting intimate details. Amirah felt extremely uneasy and guilty, as Miriam interrogated her about her connection to her son. At last all the misleading and deceiving came out. Both burst into tears.

Miriam blamed her, crying, "How could you have deceived us so?!"

"I'm so sorry." Amirah wept. "I had no choice but to go along with Rafi's proposal."

"You duped us! This is how you thank us for our kindness. We took you in. We gave you our love without reserve."

Miriam found it easier to blame her, than her firstborn. Frustrated and almost demented with grief, by the gigantic and catastrophic occurrence, she felt the affair might well be the girl's fault for somehow failing with her son. Amirah, understanding, kept silent. Miriam phoned Rafi with the number he had left and they had a few tearful talks. Rafi remained adamant and would not budge. Rafi's dad refused to talk to him. The parents quarreled, often hinting about blame and negligence. Tomer, the younger brother, stayed away.

The next few weeks were not easy for Amirah. Miriam, polite and kind to her, had little warmth to go with her demeanor and Amirah did feel guilty. Betraying Miriam's love with lies and deceit made her avoid eye contact. They went about their business, each within her own glass cage. Rafi's dad had not said much, but he had become more distant and aloof. He gave much thought to cutting Rafi off financially till he came to his senses.

At last Amirah could stand the strain no longer. Coming to grips with the situation, she phoned Rafi and came straight to the point: "I can't take it anymore, I'm going to leave."

"What are you going to do? How will you manage?"

"I can be a waitress."

"But where will you live? What about the university?"

"I'll find a place. There are still two months until the semester begins, then I can get a room in the students' quarters and find some work. Maybe the university will have to wait."

"I can let you have some money, my dad pays my tuition fees, but I will not take more money from him, so it's not going to be much."

"You don't owe me anything."

"I brought you here."

"I brought myself here, where else could I go? How are you and Noam getting along?"

"Fine just fine. I am at his rented place in Jerusalem, I will finish my studies in the university here."

They met at a coffee place and Rafi handed her a check. "The money should last you for two or three months' rent included. I'm sorry there's no more."

"I don't like taking your money."

"Noam's money, I don't have any. Please . . ."

"I don't know . . ."

"Isn't it an insult in your culture to refuse a present?"

Amirah looked at the check. "But your name is on the check. How come?"

"Noam hasn't got his checkbook yet. He will return the sum to me in cash, and I will send the money back home. I will not take any more money from my folks."

"Okay. Thanks, thank Noam for me, I do appreciate this, I will pay you back, but I am not going to run away. I will talk to your mother first."

"Tell her I love her."

"I think she knows."

"Tell her anyway."

Amirah did not look forward to the coming encounter, but she could not just leave the people who had been so kind to her and the two women sat down to talk. Miriam made few objections. "Stay here till you settle down somewhere." Then following with some bitter sarcasm: "Rafi won't be needing his room."

"Thank you, I will." Then on an impulse Amirah added, "You are very kind to me, I won't forget."

"How much money will you need?" Curt and to the point.

"I have found work. I shall have enough for my needs. Thank you for asking." Amirah lied to her, not having found work yet, but she did not want to take more money from Miriam.

Miriam just nodded, being still too upset about her son, for much else.

With that settled, Amirah prepared to leave. She searched and trying to save her money, found a tiny one-room apartment in the lower and cheaper part of Tel Aviv, near Jaffa, the Arab section. Later a better place might be possible, but for now the dump would have to do.

A bag with her things had already been moved to her new place. They would sign the contract when she cashed the check Rafi had given her. Amirah went to the bank to cash the check. There a calamity awaited her: Rafi's account had been closed by his dad since the morning. There would be no cashing in the check as it had been written in Rafi's name. After the dread and distress had worn off a bit, Amirah, a Bedouin and a proud person, calculated her options. First call Rafi for help. The phone rang and rang, obviously no one was at home. Crawling on her knees back to Miriam did not seem an agreeable alternative.

She had not yet looked for a job, but there would have to be an unpleasant talk with her new landlord, actually landlady. The proprietress, a hard-wary individual, in charge of that establishment, which consisted of a rundown building with rooms to let, had not let her have a room without a deposit. Amirah had left her bag with her, on the understanding that she would keep the room free for her. Now she accosted her, coming straight to the point.

"I cannot pay you yet, I shall have to land a job first."

"You promised to pay a month rent."

"I will pay you as soon as I get a job."

"You listen to me and listen carefully! I have enough trouble with tenants not paying their rent on time. I do not need another one. No rent, no room!"

"But I will pay you."

"Sorry."

"Then I will take my things and find another place."

"I have kept a room free for you for some days. Who pays me for that?"

"I will pay you as soon as I get my wages. I need a change of clothes."

"Once I let you have your bag, I will never see you again."

"You cannot keep my bag from me, I will go to the police!"

The woman burst out laughing. "Two of my cousins are in the force, I can call them myself."

Amirah realized the futility of their argument, the landlady would not let her have her room until the money was forthcoming and the woman would keep her bag as collateral. Amirah knew herself to be defenseless, what little money remained to her would have to be spent on daily expenses. She could not go to the police either.

In a matter of one day Amirah found herself practically homeless and almost destitute. Undaunted and resourceful she began looking for a job with the aid of a newspaper and a public phone booth. By now Amirah talked Hebrew fluently, but the tone of her voice and her inflection still retained their Bedouin heritage. Arab terrorists had planted explosive devices in public places and the persons on the other end of the line recognized her accent and did not want to hire Arabs. After exhausting most of her phone tokens, she had not yet landed a job. The night came, but Amirah remained undaunted; there would be a job for her in the Arab section, they had many restaurants and eating places, she only needed to persist.

In summer, the nights are hot and knowing herself to be rugged and tough, she intended to sleep in a park to save money, there were plenty of benches, and in the morning, continue to search for a job, anything would do: waitressing, working in the kitchen or even doing the dishes. Trying to phone Rafi a few times more did not help, no one answered. Rafi had no reason to inform her of his moves. He might be on a trip with his friend and not return for days. Amirah resisted a temptation to return to her former place, and took a bus to the more conservative area of the city where she knew of a nice park. The place appeared deserted. She settled down on an isolated bench and fell asleep.

A noise awoke her. Someone very excited called out in a voice agitated with lust and triumph. "Guys, we found us a girl!"

A light shined on her face. "An Arab, by God, she's an Arab!"

A group of wandering youths, looking for mischief and some fun, searching for drunks or homeless people to pester and fool around with, had found her. They were beside themselves with their luck. Fate had sent them a real bonus. They hated Arabs, to them, all Arabs were terrorists; a bus with innocent people had been blown up not so long ago. There had been many casualties. They had a good excuse as any.

"Grab her. Hold her tight."

Amirah struggled, shouting for help and fought her captors, giving them a hard time, but her screams went unheard. There were four attackers and her resisting only caused them to viciously beat her and kick her. They hit her on her head until she lay in a stupor. Then they tore off what remained of her clothes and raped her. When they finally left, Amirah remained half-conscious, too weak to move, then she sunk into oblivion.

A few hours later in the early morning found Amirah badly hurting all over her body, having bruises and cuts on her face. Her clothes were torn. The park was a public place. People would soon be about and they would notice her. Getting to a hospital meant informing the police. Her former passport had run out ages back and had never been renewed for fear of the authorities. She had had no other form of identification made available to her. A dread of being deported remained dominant in her mind.

She tried to get up miserably, but feeling giddy, sunk, groaning back to the ground. Amirah had suffered a concussion, she had been hit on her head and on her ears. After a while, recovering a little, a sparkle of reflected sunlight from the rising sun had made her take notice. Her purse had been flung nearby under some bushes, or fallen there in the struggle and had not been found in the dark. Pulling on her torn clothes, she crawled, fighting off her dizziness, and found her money with some remaining phone tokens.

Amirah had not eaten or had any drink properly since lunch the day before. Feeling very sick and retching, she got up laboriously, stumbling, staggered out of the park area and searched for a public phone. Maybe she would be able to reach Rafi at home now, he would help her. One or two people already about, looked at her strangely. Finally, a phone booth came in sight, only to reveal that it had been vandalized and did not work.

There should be a public restroom by the park somewhere. Returning to the park area and dragging herself around feeling wretched, she did stagger across a public restroom but found it still closed. Wiping the blood off her as best as possible under the circumstances and limping around aimlessly in a fog, she tried futilely to collect herself.

The very few early risers, bent on their business, might have thought her a drunk after a binge, and kept out of her way. Amirah stumbled upon another phone booth, a dialing sound confirmed it to function. Desperate and trying hard to concentrate, she dialed the number which Rafi had given her. The phone on the other side rang, but no one picked up. Had she misdialed? Repeatedly dialing the number did not help. At last giving it up, miserable and in pain, she shuffled, teetering unsteadily by a shop and studied herself in the mirror of its window, trying to take stock of her situation. Her face looked a mess, one eye swollen and the other discolored, her hair undone and messy, her body bruised and bleeding from cuts, could be covered up with what remained of her torn clothes. Amirah tried to put her hair in place.

Having erroneously thought that getting to the better part of the city to pass the night would be safer for her had landed her into real trouble. No one would give her a job now, it was paramount to get new clothes and clean up her face. The landlady had her bag with her clothes. Amirah, a Bedouin, could be proud and stubborn, not wanting to face Miriam for help made her search for a bus to the new place. Her head swam and with a great effort, controlling her dizziness, she took a bus, feeling very ill and ignoring the stares of the few passengers. In her fuzzy condition, Amirah had got on the wrong bus and found herself in strange unrecognizable surroundings.

Using the remains of her strength and will power she dragged herself from one bus to another until she recognized the correct bus stop. On the bus, again ignoring the looks of the passengers, she sunk into her seat. Exhausted and battered, her mind a blank, she missed her exit. From her bus stop to her new place, would, under normal conditions, be a five-minute walk, but dragging herself from one station to another took her much longer.

Laboring, faint, and wheezing over the uneven pavement, made her stumble frequently and almost fall. On her way, a lapse of memory caused her mind to wander and blank out. Oblivious to her surroundings and her intention to get to her things, she sank down on some stairs unfocussed. After a while, her memory returned. Her bag! . . . Her clothes. She must have them! Amirah forced herself to continue and finally arrived at her destination.

Hauling herself up the stairs with the help of her hands on the banister, to her rented room, she tried the door, but without much hope. The landlady had the door locked. That same woman lived in one of the rooms nearby, but which one? Knocking repeatedly on one door which seemed vaguely familiar got no answer. Amirah's body and soul had been severely abused. Her strength gave out and sinking down by the door to wait, she blacked out into a stupor.

A neighboring tenant, passing through the corridor found her. This person, Ezra, happened to be a cousin of the proprietress and had a discount, but as he never paid his rent on time, there had been trouble between them. He could not easily be evicted, as they both were members of the same very large family who supported his claims. There had been no love lost between him and his landlady. That seemed an opportunity to interfere with her affairs. The girl had obviously been beaten and her clothes were torn and partly revealed her body, making her look helpless. Being always on the make was like a second nature to him, and his instincts told him there might possibly be a potential source of money.

"Hello!" he addressed her. "What have we here?"

He received no answer.

"Are you okay?"

Seeing no reaction whatsoever, Ezra bent down to exam her face. Her eyes were closed. He then shoved her gently on her shoulder.

"Can you get up?"

Getting no response, he lifted her and carried her to his room.

Ezra had to pay a monthly alimony to his ex-wife and, being in debt for most of his adult life, had been jailed twice already for not paying. His large family had been brought to Israel from Iraq in their childhood. Being a despised minority there, they had stuck together, blood and family ties being strong in their culture. They were eight brothers and sisters, all with their children and some with grandchildren. The parents and elders too had brothers and sisters and there were many cousins with their children around. Some members of the clan were a part of the local Mafia, while two others were in the police force and occasionally shady deals would be made.

Ezra liked the cards and loved to gamble, as did most of the males in his family. Once a week they would gather at someone's home and spend all night playing cards and looking at porn (which was mostly ignored by their women who slept on mattresses with their children in a nearby room), and frequently losing great sums to each other. Ezra knew an Arab when he saw one. In Iraq, his family had suffered from the Arabs, he had heard stories from his parents and uncles and he hated Arabs with a racial hatred. In his youth, he had often sprayed the walls with inflating slogans like 'Death to the Arabs.'

He placed the unconscious Amirah in his bed and watched her coma-like sleep for most of the day, a healing sleep. The evening had almost arrived when Amirah came to herself, hurting all over and with a splitting headache. She turned on her side to retch and moan. After a while she found herself on a bed in an unfamiliar place, a strange man sitting on a mattress nearby on the floor.

She moaned in Arabic, not yet fully there, "Where am I?"

On hearing her, Ezra knew he had been right. He thought the girl might have run away from Jaffa, the Arab section in the city, or maybe be from one of the Arab villages. Ezra could still speak the Arabic of his childhood, but he sounded foreign to Amirah.

"You are in my place."

She painstakingly switched to Hebrew. "How did I get here? . . . Who are you?"

Ezra answered her questions shortly and gave food and drink to her famished and dehydrated body.

In the coming days he tended to her, not from love, but more like taking care of a costly commodity. He gave her drugs in the guise of painkillers. Keeping her drugged would be one way of controlling her. Their communication was minimal and he took care not to let her get away. A few days passed and Amirah did not yet fully understand her circumstances, but having nowhere else to go, had been content at first in her weak state to let things slide.

Ezra watched her day and night and locked the door securely for the few times he left for provisions. He also questioned her, trying to find out from where she had come from, but Amirah, evasive, refused to reveal anything. Ezra could be evasive too, answering her questions with, "Just get better and then we'll see." Such being the extent of their verbal communications.

Amirah, young and healthy, recuperated fast. Then one day, Ezra, without any fuss, climbed into her bed and had sex with her, Amirah felt too weak in soul and body other than to resist feebly. Later, he took her torn rags and threw them away. Eventually it did dawn on her, even in her drugged state, that he had imprisoned her, and once when Ezra left, she tried to find a way out in her underwear. Blindly, not thinking of where to go, or what would happen, if she did get out. They lived in a small one-room apartment with a kitchen and bathroom attached. The windows had bars and the door, a special strong one, had been adjusted as a precaution against burglars who infested the area, but those were also effective as an efficient prison. Ezra had done her no harm, except for having sex with her. Amirah, fuzzy from the drugs, finally confronted him:

"Why is the door always locked?"

"It is not safe for you outside."

"Where are my things?"

"What things?"

Amirah, concentrating, tried to explain the situation. "The landlady . . . has my bag."

"I see, you must rest."

Amirah sank gratefully back. A day or two passed but Amirah never saw her bag again. Eventually the subject faded from her drugged mind.

In her earlier years, Amirah had learned to be wily and crafty to get her way. Growing stronger made her think of overpowering him in his sleep. She searched the place when he went out. He had, with much foresight, cleverly locked up any sharp kitchen utensils, of which there had been very few, as he always ate out and he brought her food in disposable paper bags. He took great care in not leaving any plastic knives or forks around.

By now, Amirah had swallowed her pride, intending to contact Miriam any way possible. Naturally the room had no phone. When alone, she would frequently bang on the door until her arms hurt, but no one ever answered and she finally desisted the energetic futile activity. Does the proprietress know of her being locked up? Are there other tenants around? In her drugged state, nothing seemed certain anymore and all appeared hazy.

Ezra had sex with her on most nights. He was strong and there seemed no point in resisting him. One night, after they had sex and Ezra dozed off asleep, Amirah out of desperation, lifted up one of the small flimsy plastic chairs in the room to use as her weapon. She lifted it over the motionless Ezra. Then she wavered; never having had any reason to use brute physical force before, felt her energy seep away. The fragile plastic chair could not possibly incapacitate him. There must be another way. Ezra, as if he had guessed Amirah's intention, woke up and found another place to spend the nights.

Rafi, after returning from a trip with Noam, called home, his mom answered the phone, and after the inevitable tears, mutual accusations and pleadings, he asked to speak with Amirah.

"She left a while ago," his mother informed him.

"What! Mom, did you have a fight?"

"Nothing of the kind. She wanted to fend for herself."

"I don't believe this."

"Of course you don't believe your mother, I am lying to you, as always."

"I mean . . . it is hard for me to believe she left on her own will . . ."

"I told her she could remain until she gets on her feet. She left on her own initiative."

"I'll bet you did. Did you give her the cold treatment?"

"Rafi, do not talk to me so. Have you not done us enough harm."

He ignored her last words, they had churned the subject about enough, much too much for him. "Let me have her phone number."

"She did not leave one."

Rafi, having learned that Amirah had left of her own free will, still felt some guilt, maybe she did not want to be found, as she had left no number behind. He too felt hurt, they had been good friends, buddies. Not yet knowing his account in the bank had been closed by his father and being busy with his own life and Noam, he finally left off trying to contact her. She had his number.

One of Ezra's many cousins, Nuris, had some shady connections downtown and male family members visiting prostitutes there, often succeeded in getting a discount. Ezra phoned him. "Nuris, I've got a gold mine at home . . .," and he proceeded in telling him about Amirah. Nuris, just as excited as Ezra, said. "Keep her drugged. I will come and see for myself."

"Drugs are expensive." He had already begun his maneuvering to get a good price for her.

Amirah, not completely unaware of her plight, had been made apathetic by the drugs and did not care much one way or other. Nuris came over and checked her, had sex with her. Then they haggled about the price. Of course Nuris could not pay the enormous sum Ezra asked, so after much negotiating and haggling, a division of the percentage on roughly estimated future income was agreed on. Nuris had also commented: "Let the guys in the family in on her, it will help to launch her on her way."

Luck, which had deserted Amirah, returned to aid her in a roundabout way. Nuris bought his drugs from handlers. Those individuals did not always have the best intentions at heart and good business in the making had forced them to dilute their dubious wares, so as to get more cash for them. The drugs, which had been put into her food, had not had their usual potency. In her semi-drugged state Amirah, lying supine on her bed, heard them talking and understood; they intended to sell her to a brothel and were negotiating a price.

She must get out!

Ezra brought some food for her, leaving it on the table, he and Nuris left locking the door. Amirah got up, not touching the food, which she rightfully suspected of containing drugs, washed her face twice to clear her head, then she mercilessly poured water over herself. She had no clothes, but she knew where Ezra kept his own. She put them on. The she ransacked the place trying to find something that would help her escape. The few hangers in the cabinet where Ezra had his clothes were plastic ones, however she found one with wire. Quickly breaking the hangar and removing the wire she tried to spring the lock in the door. She twisted, turned, pulled and jabbed with the piece of wire without any results.

Amirah grew desperate, the cabinet had wooden legs, she overturned it, intending to pry one loose and pound on the door with it, maybe someone would hear. The ancient overturned piece of furniture broke and fell to pieces; some shelves flew out and spread their wares on the floor. Amirah succeeded in prying a leg loose with a strength she had not known she had. For a moment, her eyes rested on the mess she had made. A glint of metal in a crack caught her eye. She separated the shattered boards and saw a partly rusted key!

Her hopes had risen.

The key, a spare, had fallen between two adjoining loose boards. Not being able to fish or dig it out, Ezra had given up on it and forgot. With shaking hands, she applied the key to the lock. It fit and she turned the lock. The key, an old one broke with her unsteady motions. Disappointed and angry she twisted the handle in a fury: To her surprise, the door opened. She had managed to unlock it

She was free.

Amirah could be crafty, she closed the door, carefully jamming it so it would not lock again. Then she found one of Ezra's bags and filled it with his clothes and anything else she could find that might be worth some money. She found one phone token. Finally, she slammed the door behind her. Ezra would not be able to enter his own place with a broken key in the lock of his door, an amusing gratifying thought. Serve him right.

What now? Amirah had no money. Leaving the building she made for a telephone booth. Hearing a live sound, she put in her single token, she now remembered the number Rafi had given her. The phone rang and a strange voice answered her. "Who is this?"

Had she dialed the wrong number in her anxiety, "Is Rafi there?"

"Noam . . . are you Amirah?" He heard her accent.

"Yes, I am in trouble."

"Rafi is away on some learning mission. Can I help?"

"Noam."

"Yes."

He was a complete stranger, yet he had offered to help. She had no choice. "I need help. I have been beaten and kept a prisoner and drugged. I have just escaped . . ."

"I don't believe this," she heard on the other side, "You're not kidding?"

"I have no money."

"Are you calling from a public phone?"

"I have one token only."

He grasped the situation. "Quick, give me the number."

She did so. Then the phone switched off.

She waited until it rang again. "Where are you?" the voice said.

"Near Jaffa."

"I'm in Jerusalem." There came a pause. "Shall I come and get you? It will take an hour or more."

"Thank you, I am so desperate."

They quickly arraigned the details over the phone. Amirah, now ravenous, entered a nearby restaurant and felt self-conscious, as the waitress looked at her strange ill-fitting male outfit. She ordered food and lots of coffee. Noam would settle the bill when he came. For once, things went as planned. Noah picked her up, she had never felt so happy as when she saw him, all petty rivalry forgotten. She hugged and kissed him.

"You are so beautiful," he said. "I can see why Rafi was taken with you."

"We were never an item, no sex," she explained.

"I know that. Rafi told me all about you."

He paid her bill and they were off to Jerusalem. Rafi and Noam lived in a one-room apartment, in Netiv Yizchak. Rafi had cut himself off from his folks and Noam worked as an apprentice interior designer earning just enough money to pay the rent and live frugally with Rafi, they were in love and little things like money did not matter too much. They liked roughing it and enjoyed every moment together. Taking in Amirah would strain their resources to the limit.

Amirah had slept during the trip. Exhaustion together with the remains of her drugged state had set in. Noam did not bother her with questions. He led her up to their room, and she fell down on one side of the double bed and fell asleep as soon as she closed her eyes. She opened her eyes in the morning to find the place empty, the other side of the bed, crumpled, revealed that Noam had slept beside her, a note had been pinned to her trouser leg.

'I am off to work and Rafi should be back sometime soon. Make yourself at home.'

Rafi came in late morning, surprised and happy to see her. He noticed her tired face. "Tell me what happened."

Then Amirah burst into tears, she told him everything; about the check and how she had slept in a park, been gang raped and beaten, about Ezra holding her a drugged prisoner intending to sell her to a brothel and her escaping at last still in a semi-drugged state. Noam had rescued her.

"So my dad cancelled my account without telling me?" He felt a surge of anger. "I do not contact that bank anymore."

"I should not have spent the night in the park," Amirah said.

Rafi listened to her astounded. "All this in Tell Aviv?"

"They were teen-agers, four of them." Amirah referred to the night in the park.

"Not all of us are like that."

"Jews and Arabs do not like each other."

"Not true, not all of us," he insisted.

Amirah had taken stock of their place. "I cannot stay here, there is no room."

"We will make some."

"I will find work somewhere."

"We'll put a mattress on the floor for you and when you get better I want to show you something of Jerusalem."

"I have no money, no clothes, nothing . . . not a single agora."

Rafi chuckled. "That makes two of us. Noam's got some cash."

"I cannot take money from him."

"I can, Noam will do this for me."

Amirah, having no choice, moved in with Rafi and Noam. They were crowded in the tiny place, but luckily, one or the other was often out on an errand or studying or in Noam's case working. Amirah enjoyed the attention of two males. They spoiled her, they made her rest and recuperate from her ordeal and would not let her clean the place. The three found time and money to buy clothes for Amirah in second hand boutiques, both having impeccable taste but different, they loved to argue. Amirah flourished. The clothes they chose made her look like they had been bought in one of the most expansive shops. Rafi took her on tours in the old city, she saw the archeological excavations, the Wailing Wall and other sites and learned how Jerusalem is the center of the Jews from all over the world.

In the nights Rafi and Noam occasionally would have sex and they could not always keep it quiet. Amirah, no prude or novice to the proceedings, had participated in group sex with Steve in Sharem; however, she felt herself isolated from the two. They were a pair and she the outsider. As soon as she felt able, she intended to look for a job. In the morning, she began to circle the wanted ads, concentrating on restaurants in the area and knowing from experience that Jewish managers thought twice before hiring an Arab, unless it could be done for less money.

One ad caught her eye, 'The International: Cuisines and Recipes from All over the World.' The advertisement continued to promote the various wares. Dressed in her best clothes Amirah found her way to the edge of the Arab section and the restaurant. She entered the premises. A large place confronted her, tables with chairs on them.

"We're closed," a man sweeping said to her.

"I'm here to see the manager about a job."

"We have enough Arabs working here."

"Are you the manager?" She brushed past him and entered an office, a man set by a desk. "Are you the manager?"

"Yes, how can I help you."

"I need a job."

"We do not need any more Arabs."

She talked in Arabic. "I am a Bedouin."

"I thought your accent queer." He answered her in the same language. "Dress as a Bedouin and come in the evening, we'll see how it works out."

Amirah had given all her dresses away in the camp by Sharem, now she searched for Bedouin garb in the Arab market. She found only fake stuff, expansive flashier and made for the tourists. Having no other option, she bought a dress with the money Rafi had given her.

Amirah, coming back, found Rafi on the phone. From his distressed look she inferred that he was talking to his parents. He saw her and said into the phone, "Bye mom, here is someone who wants to talk to you." Ignoring Amirah's shaking head and denial motions, Rafi handed the phone to her, "Go on, she can't bite you."

"She can." However, she took the phone. "Miriam?"

"I'm so sorry about what happened to you, you should have called us right away. Rafi told me everything. Don't you know better than to sleep in a park . . . ."

Amirah flinched from the barrage and held the phone away from her ear. Rafi grinned. The voice finally ran down.

"We live in different worlds . . .," Amirah tried to say.

"What different worlds, we all breathe the same air. Tell me, are Rafi and his . . . friend sleeping in the same bed?"

Amirah looked at Rafi, who nodded, "Yes."

"Oh my dear God. . . ." The phone went dead.

"She is hurting."

"What can I do about it? Should I turn into a heterosexual for her?"

"I've landed a job at the International, there will be more money to go around."

"We've been there, they have waitresses from different countries . . . the food could be better though."

That evening Amirah began her work mostly running back and forth with dishes. Being good on her feet, and using her head as well, Amira soon learned the tricks of her new trade. She smiled at her customers, and by displaying an exquisite and exotic personality, earned many tips. The cliental were a mixture of Israelis, Arabs, and many tourists who gave the largest tips. The general atmosphere of fraternization and peace, in a very problematic zone, encouraged generosity. Pictures of the UN and UNESCO sites hung on the walls side by side with statesmen and politicians.

Amirah had been hired on a permanent basis, she could now pay for her keep. She went to work in the afternoon and remained in the restaurant till eleven or after the last customer had left. Waitressing had turned out not to be so difficult as she had supposed and she learned not to use up much energy on the job. Many customers enjoyed her dark fresh and exotic beauty. Tips rolled in. There were two Arab girls, a Russian, one Eastern European, one Philippine and one Israeli girl, all working together, exchanging phone numbers, talking about boyfriends and sometimes exchanging shifts. The girls also freely borrowed cosmetics and even articles of clothing from each other and swapped tales of the customer's often eccentric behaviorisms. The place felt like a sisterhood.

Nothing is perfect, occasional jealousies with fights and rivalries between the girls broke out, but no discrimination and their little skirmishes were soon forgotten. Amirah made many good friends in her place of work. Sometimes on slow days the girls just sat around and chatted. The Israeli girl, Malka, who worked part time only, grew curious: "To be a Bedouin sounds so strange and exotic."

Amirah snorted, "Ha, there is nothing exotic about it, mostly dull routine housework all day long, and one cannot go out."

"What do you mean?"

"It is like a prison, I only went outside with an escort."

"Male or female?" one of the other girls giggled.

"Mostly my younger brother or sister. . . ." Mentioning them had suddenly brought painful memories back. She had not thought about her folks for a long time. She thought of her mother. Tears came to her eyes. She sank into silence and the girls understanding, turned the talk turned to something else.

In a strange way, the camaraderie in the restaurant reminded Amirah of the colony in Sharem el Sheik. Both had people of many countries and the girls accepted her and made her feel good. Amirah had never really felt at home anywhere before. Growing up with her family had made her feel her chains, but now away from home she felt the ache of homesickness. She longed for the food at home, her mother and her little brother. The colony by Sharem had been okay, but the people there were temporary, the turnover had been great. In Rafi's place, she had been accepted as his girlfriend and future bride, but not for herself.

Amirah needed to belong and there at work they accepted her unconditionally. The girls were nice sympathetic and understanding, they treated her as an equal and were not judgmental. They helped her with advice and were supportive. Strangely enough the common assent and camaraderie facilitated to seep her will. It may well be a singular fact of nature that working together can unite and diminish those racial differences which plague people. Language seemed never a problem, they conversed in broken Hebrew and English.

Life was not so bad after all, she had friends and they confided in each other. Noam and Rafi too were good friends. Amirah had let herself be dragged about by the tide of circumstances. Her hopes of getting into the university receded and had slowly faded into the background. She felt her initiative and her will fade.

She had vague hopes and made plans. Soon she would have enough money to rent a room, maybe together with Vera, who had been drawn to Amirah's dark beauty. They had become very friendly.

"How old are you really?" Vera asked her once.

"Eighteen.

"It is not so bad here. Is it? We all help each other out."

"I intended to study." Amirah recalled. "A few more years here and I will do so."

"I came from Moldavia." Vera told her. "They promised me a well-paid job in housework. Here they kept me locked up with little to eat until I agreed to work as a prostitute. I do not regret anything. Later I ran away. At home, no one knows what I do and this is not such a bad place after all. I intend to return home with a load of money."

"How old are you Vera?"

"I am thirty-five, don't tell anybody, I have two children at home, my mother takes care of them, no husband, I send money home, it's our secret."

"Of course. How long have you not seen your children?"

"Too long. It's been two years since I last flew back."

"And you returned?!"

"There's good money to be made here, at home, no work, nothing!" She settled herself for a story. "I worked as a day and night nurse to a lady and when she died I found her passport, there is a man to whom we go to fix passports. I am an Israeli citizen now."

"Vera, I need an identity card."

"I will give you his number tomorrow at work."

The Mahmoud family clan in Sinai were not happy. Amirah, not being seen around anymore, made tongues wag. Insinuating questions were asked. Her two older brothers were now ridiculed by their peers, not openly, but veiled hinting about a girl, a whore running away with a man. Feeling insulted, the brothers refuted the allusions and reacted with violence. There were some fights, but they all knew the truth. The situation had become intolerable. The family of Amirah's future betrothed had heard some rumors and had become suspicious. They began to ask awkward questions and were informed that the wedding was off. Amirah's father finally initiated the old patriarch of what had happened, and he took charge of the proceedings.

The Mahmoud clan had sent hired friends to the shack camp near Sharem and found out that Amirah had run off to Israel. A furtive and relentless search began for her, which would last almost a year. Bedouin have friends and family ties in their villages in Israel. Those were recruited and induced with pledges of money, honor and tradition to contact the local Arab population and to find out what they can. Cash exchanged hands and spies had been found. Inquiries were made and questions asked. Time passed and more money followed. Finally, the knowledge seeped back to the Mahmoud family: Amirah was working as a waitress in Jerusalem at the 'International Coffee House.'

A family counsel had been called, only the males. The elder patriarch announced in no uncertain terms that they would willingly give up half of their assets to redeem their honor. His statement would be translated into action by the younger generation. The grapevine had been connected once again and more cash changed hands. Two Arabs in Israel were hired to do the job as the Bedouins in Sinai could not get there.

Being liked and accepted by the girls made Amirah content. Some of her friends, entertained vague dreams of bettering themselves or getting married. Amirah, being no exception, and possessing few other earning skills, fantasized; maybe some man would want to take care of her . . . sometime in the future. In the meantime, saving money was the important issue and would help to get her on her feet. Still young she would get her second wind. Possibly next year, or possibly the year after . . ., well the university would not run away. Some of her will and courage had returned to her. Her old plan of enlisting in the university engaged her conscious. Rafi and Noam were supportive. Malka, the Israeli girl, had told her; she was studying to be a nurse.

Arabs and Israelis can work well together when the profits are worthwhile. One evening two people in modern business suits entered the restaurant. They sat by one of Amirah's tables and ordered. They tipped her well. For the next two weeks, they–or one or the other–would come and order an expansive meal and they always tipped her abundantly. Amirah had progressed to first names with them both.

Amirah liked to walk on her way back from work, enjoying the streets, the shops and her freedom. A car stopped by invitingly. She recognized the driver as one of her steady customers. There seemed no reason not to take a ride. She opened the car door and sat down next to him. "Where to?"

"Netiv Yizchak."

They drove to a corner and another man appeared, he too had been her former customer and had been waiting. He got in and sat next to Amirah. They did not speak. She began to feel uneasy.

"Where are we going?"

"For a ride."

"I get out here," she said.

"In a minute."

The man next to her grabbed her and held her. She felt a knife at her throat.

"Don't move," he said in Arabic.

Amirah sat frozen with fear, not thinking, not daring to move. They drove to a deserted spot and forced her out of the car. They did not talk much, but were very rough, tearing off her clothes. She protested and got hit for her troubles. They had sex with her and then one tried to have anal intercourse.

"I don't do that," she gasped.

They paid no attention to her protests. One held her while the other had anal sex. When she resisted, they hit her. She felt a terrible pain and yelled. A blow on her head knocked her unconscious.

Amirah woke up, her head bursting, her body hurt. She lay on the backseat of a fast-moving car and found her hands tied behind her back. She groaned, but the two men in front paid no attention. The car sped on its way. An hour passed and the car sped on. They seemed to be going great distances. She had been kidnapped. Were they taking her to Dahab, to her family? She cried out but the two men in front turned on the volume and the radio blared. Having little control over her body functions she soiled herself, the smell eventually reaching her captors.

"Pig!" one shouted to the other. They talked in Arabic.

"Not me," the other denied. He turned to look at the backseat. "It's the whore."

"I can't drive with this stink," the driver complained.

"Open the window."

Amirah had been put into a car and driven southwards to her ancestral home in Dahab. Luckily, she was unconscious most of the time. The car took the smaller and less used roads. Arriving in Sinai, they came to a path leading from the road to the sea. The car took it. "Let the sea wash the filth of her," the driver said.

They pulled out a groaning Amirah and dragged her, torn clothes and all, into the shallow water by the shore. Amirah, lying with her hands tied behind her back, could not move much, the waves covered her and she coughed sea water. Her captors laughed amused. Amirah, almost drowning, gasped and choked and retched, but the water had cleared her brain. They dragged her back to the car.

"Where are you taking me?" Amirah had heard them talk and she too had said this in Arabic.

"Home."

"What home?"

"To your family whom you humiliated and degraded"

"They will kill me."

No answer.

"Please let me go."

The radio began its singsong. After a while, Amirah ceased her futile pleading and sank into herself. The car sped on avoiding the few villages and settlements and arrived at Dahab in the night. Four men were roused from their sleep and awaited her; her grandfather, her father and her two elder brothers. Their meeting was not amiable.

"You Whore." The patriarch spat on her.

"You shammed us," her father shouted. "Your parents, your loved ones!"

"We killed your foreign lover." Her elder brother slapped her.

"I want to see my mother, Mohamed and Aisha (her little brother and sister)."

"You have dishonored us all. They will not want to see you."

Amirah kept quiet. She had no more hope or expectations; she wanted it to be over quickly.

They forced her into another car and drove off into the night. Her older brother by the wheel and the younger next to him. They did not drive on the road, but on paths between the mountains. In an hour, they had reached their destination, an isolated spot. They pulled an unresisting Amirah out. "Now we walk." Amirah had long realized that it was useless to talk or beg for her life. She stumbled along drugged by the prospect of her coming death. Deep inside, her ingrained deep-seated cultural heritage had come to the fore. She had done a terrible thing, she had humiliated her family, all the people who had weaned her and she had loved. . . .

They arrived at a stony patch of ground. "Here," said the younger of her brothers. They stopped and for the first time faced her. Amirah looked her brothers in the eye. She saw two strangers. "Let me go. I will not return. No one will know."

Her older brother answered, "You shamed us and dishonored the whole family . . ."

She found nothing more to say. The brothers and sister starred at each other, energizing courage for the deed ahead.

"Do it quick then," she said.

Bedouins have a heritage of honor and bravery. Their sister's pluck touched them. They had intended to stab her mortally but the younger brother had just bought a gun; a bullet would be quicker. "I'll do it," he said. The older brother pushed his sister down to her knees, Amirah whimpered quietly while the other pulled out his gun and squeezed the trigger. The gun did not go off. Sweating with dread he pulled the trigger repeatedly.

"You fool," the elder one said. He pulled out his own gun and shot Amirah. He had aimed for her heart. She sunk to the ground and her movements slowly ceased.

With her last moments, there had come a measure of clarity. Her whole life did not pass her by, but bits and parts did. The intense acuteness and poignant pain of her childhood longings returned to her. She had wanted to be free, to be a part of the big outside world and, as consciousness faded, she regretted not having tried harder . . . having let herself slide and be swept away by the tide of events. She had wanted to study . . . become someone. . . . Her thoughts and feelings ceased, as a void enveloped her shrouding her into its emptiness.

Her assassins gently straightened her doubled-up body. Now that she was gone, they treated her with reverence. They untied her hands. Her younger brother kissed her. They covered her with layers of stones. They did not speak and the younger brother held back his tears.

The word came back to the Mahmoud family. At last they could lift up their heads proudly again. The deed had been done, and the stain on their honor removed! The patriarch called another family meeting.

He announced: "We are in debt but our honor has been redeemed."

THE END

Tattoo

Before his turn of three years in the army, Alex had worked as an apprentice at one of the very few tattoo parlors in Gush Dan, the populated center of Israel. His main tasks being to keep the place clean but sometimes he had been elevated to taking care of sterilizing the implements of the trade. He trained himself, practicing with a tattoo machine on various objects, grapefruits being one of those. He was quick and clever, and the master soon allowed him to help in the more serious work of applying the copying stencils and later some of the easier coloring and shading. He had a steady and firm hand and a pleasant 'bedside' manner, kidding and joking with the customer, especially if she is a pretty young female. His master had impressed on him the supreme importance to keep everything clean and sterile.

"If someone gets an infection later, you stand a good chance of being sued for negligence," he had said, "you don't want that, getting hauled to court can cost you your good name, not to mention paying the judicial and medical expenditures they hit you with . . . like the pain, suffering and mental aggravation caused to the plaintiff." He continued, "Believe me, never go to court."

"Have you ever been dragged there?"

"Yes, once . . . and once is enough." His boss had answered shortly. Then he added, "If anyone has problems with my work, I settle with him out of court." His grin had a sarcastic glint, he flexed his muscles.

Alex's parents originated from South Africa and Germany, but Alex considered himself a Sabra-Israeli born, as his mother had given birth to him on an Israeli ship. An only child, he grew up into fine youth and did his time in the army. Alex had come out of the army, weary, not wanting to work for a boss; he had enough of being told what to do. After his discharge he took it easy, wasting the most precious of all gifts: his life! Having no license, he dared not practice in the more populated areas and eventually gravitated to a distant aunt in Ashkelon, living in a spare room and with not much else to do, decided to open a tattoo parlor.

His decision had been an audacious one, as tattooing had not yet become popular and in the peripheries was almost unheard of. Much of the population in the South of Israel had been brought in from Middle Eastern countries; many were poverty stricken. The lines between religion and tradition had mixed and diminished. Tattoos and religion are not compatible. People as a rule were not excessively religious but unconsciously adhered to its customs. Getting tattooed had certainly not been on anyone's list of priorities.

The money from his discharge, together with some borrowing, enabled him to acquire a few basic necessary tools of his trade with their accessories: first a tattoo machine and disposable tubes, needles, ink, and a fair amount of stencils. He rented a smallish place with a large front window in the main street of the old town, put up a sign and felt ready for customers.

He spent much of his time in the parlor doing little, or listening to the radio. The few potential customers who came were curious young people, mostly without the means to pay him properly. He lowered his prices. His first real customer was the town prostitute, a youngish shabby lady by name of Rachel. Alex recognized her, he had heard guys talk of her being very compliant and not talking much. She studied his samples exhibited in the shop window and entered looking around curiously "How much does it cost?"

"Depends on what you want."

"Let me see."

He showed her his wares and the stencils of flash tattoos, readymade and simple: "Those are the regular ones, special custom ones cost more. I work by the hour."

"I like."

"You want me to go ahead?"

"I want three, one here." She chose a heart with an arrow and pointed to her breast, "and here" pointing to her bottom, "and this on here." She had chosen an anchor to place above her pussy.

"Do you want colors, or black and white?"

"Colors."

"Three tattoos will cost you." He named the sum.

"I pay."

"You shave down there."

"Yes." Without further ado, she lifted her dress and showed him. She had nothing on underneath.

The small parlor had two subdivisions curtained off. One for his work, holding a chair, a cupboard, and a small clinical bed. The other partition he used for sterilization which consisted of a pot of boiling water and his stores. He quickly led her to the tattooing chair. "This might take two hours or more."

"Okay I have time."

"We do your ass last, after I finish with your . . . front parts."

"Anything you say."

"The money . . ."

She smiled, more of a leer. "You want sex?"

He breathed heavily, yes why not? He did not have a regular girlfriend. She would do as well as any other. They haggled a little about her price and finally he began his work exercising a professional reserve. A few hours later, he put the final antiseptic touches to his job, explaining to her the follow up treatment.

Rachel turned out to be Alex's first solo and he felt satisfied with his work. Alex could not have known, but Rachel had inadvertently found him more customers. She had exhibited her new tattoos to her clients and some of them found their way to Alex's parlor. He would not get rich, but he made a living.

Life, for a virile young man in a small town, can be boring. Ashkelon at that time had no night life. An occasional tryst with Rachel, or a trip to the big city were Alex's only relaxations. He had no car, and getting back from Tel Aviv late at night posed a problem. He could have tried to find a job in his profession as an apprentice, but preferred to remain independent in Ashkelon.

Alex, not overly ambitious, and living from day to day, had a series of girlfriends whom he took in his stride, not losing too much emotional energy when they parted. The years passed him by. He and some friends banded together for trips to the bars and girls in the center. One month each year, the army called him up. Alex had enough of fighting and preferred to do his time in the kitchen or guarding army facilities, but he did not always have the luxury of a choice. The army sent him to Ophira, next to Sharem el Sheikh and he grew acquainted with the eastern coast of the Sinai desert.

The Sinai desert is not a homogeneous one; to most travelers its attractions are on the Eastern side bordering the Red Sea. The other side of the desert borders the Mediterranean and is mostly sandy with the main lure of the Suez Canal. The center is a mixture of mountain chains, rocks, and sand, weather-beaten by the winds of many years, with grotesque shapes carved by eons of nature, and some unbelievable oases where Bedouin tribes live, but few people get there. Alex remained unaware of their existence. The Red Sea and the settlements nearby had a strong appeal for him.

Time passed. Alex's parents died, a year between them, his mom claiming that after his dad died she had no more interest in life. Suddenly Alex felt very alone. He saw more of Rachel, appreciating the simple, easy, and effortless sex.

Once, after being released from the army, Alex returned to Ashkelon. Business as usual, was slow . . . almost nonexistent. He felt lonely. He did not see Rachel around anymore, and his friends could only speculate about her.

"She has joined the army" one kidded.

Another one said, "I know for a fact that she is in jail or in some institute for women. My father's younger sister works there."

"What did you hear?" Alex asked."

"Not much, I heard her name mentioned and that she's from Ashkelon."

"I'd like to be a guard in that place," someone snickered. "All those girls locked up . . ."

"Ha!"

"They only have women guards there . . . I guess."

In due time, Alex met Gila, they dated a few times and once when she came to see his tattoo place they had sex in the back. They began to date steadily. 'I guess this is love.' Alex thought to himself.

Alex and Gila took a holiday in Eilat. They remained for a while, and then, as many others, hiked south into Sinai along the coastline of the Red Sea. For many people, the desert can be a place to get away from the hectic dynamics of their society. Some, like Alex, hope for adventure and to escape the boredom of their humdrum life. In the present as in the past, seekers for another way to live, arrive to be alone and meditate, or in modern times, to have fun, free from authorities or relatives. The desert can also be a place where issues finally resolve themselves, a place for decisions and resolutions. Alex and Gila visited a few days at each place.

"Let's return to Dahab," Alex suggested.

"One place is as dirty as another," Gila complained.

At the time, Dahab was a small fishing village, crammed in between palm trees, and overflowing with tourists, Israeli and international, with no real accommodation and toilets. Most people slept in tents or on the beach. Human feces could be found in all corners and crannies, and still more people came to enjoy the desert places.

The Bedouins, sharp and clever, realizing the bonus which had fallen into their hands, hurriedly constructed cubicle-like rooms, each with one door and window to rent to the influx of tourists. Some had beds, others did not. Communal toilets were outside–a hole and a bucket of water in most places. Eating places were hurriedly put up and stalls with merchandise and trinkets competed with each other for tourist cash. Egyptian pounds, Jordan dinars, Israel money, and American dollars all were all accepted. There is a great reef brimming with marine life running parallel to the shoreline and has an easy entrance from the center of the village. The water is pristine clear. Scuba divers and snorkelers used it almost exclusively, and the area around is filled with makeshift restaurants and shops.

The way along the beach is narrow in some places, and often crowded. One has to give way to porters, asses with wares and even the occasional camel or car. Many people stroll about nude along the beaches or recline in a state of undress on the couches and deckchairs by the sea. Alex noticed how not a few foreign tourists had tattoos on their bodies. An idea struck him: 'Why not open shop here, in Dahab?' He wandered around and did not find one single tattoo place. He would be the only one!

The idea excited him and he brought it up with Gila.

She was not delighted. "Are you crazy? There aren't even normal toilets in this place. No way!"

"I've had it in Ashkelon, there's nothing going on. The place is for losers."

"And here?'

"Here tourists will come from all over the world. I can make a lot of money in this place."

There is one so-called 'main street' in Dahab, parallel and close to the seashore, it is not a real street but a way, and the ground is packed earth. The shops and stands are on one side and the sea with the many lounging places side by side, is on the other. Most of the shops packed tightly together, sell clothes, trinkets, or are eating places. Fresh caught fish (or maybe not so fresh) are displayed openly on the 'street' with no ice on them, as ice is not available, to the great delight of the flies buzzing around.

"One of those shops can be mine. Hundreds, maybe a thousand people pass by daily." Alex needed to convince Gila, who had become silent.

Alex found out that some of the shop owners were not Bedouin but Egyptians and appeared to cater to a higher standard. Their shops and restaurants were more pretentious and could jar the sensitive with the vulgarity of shiny appliances, shop windows and plastic designs, all out of place in the naturally simple surroundings.

"I can do better than they," Alex said.

They had a long argument and at last Gila, half-heartedly agreed to accompany him in his enterprise.

Alex felt enthusiastic. For once, he did not dawdle.

Packing the tools of his trade in two large suitcases, they rented a place from a Bedouin in between the stalls and restaurants along the beach and put up a large sign with 'tattoo Alex' painted on it. Most places in Dahab are one-story houses built with fabricated blocks and shack-like in shape. In the center and on the periphery of Dahab, there are simple sheds of wood or combined metal sheets.

Alex's tattoo parlor had a mud packed floor. Two large boards on the sides of his entrance exhibited his designs with pictures of body parts. Inside he adorned the dab unpainted walls with more designs and pictures of tattooed body parts. He bought some cheap carpets and covered most of the floor. A curtain separated his working place from the rest where he sterilized his tools of trade by boiling them in water aware of the irregular procedure, but having no other means.

At first, they slept on mattresses; once they found a centipede and another time a spider in bed, under the sheets. Sometimes, Gila would wake him at night, in fright, when she felt the tickle of mice running over her body. Most people feel the magic of the desert to some degree; however, some will move through the miracles of nature, unaware of their existence, or use them for their own purposes. The last straw was a tiny lizard that had found his way into their bed.

"I can't stand this place," Gila moaned. "I'm going back to Ashkelon. You can come with me or not!"

"I've just started, I cannot leave now," he stated.

"Then I shall wait for you in Ashkelon . . . I will not wait forever."

Alex spent the next day searching for beds, when he returned, Gila had already left.

Now two adjoining beds stood with their legs in cans filled with water to prevent the desert creatures from climbing up and joining them.

Almost immediately, he had customers. People in a reckless holiday mood will allow themselves to things they would never have done at home, and perhaps would later regret, but Alex was not the one to tell them so. There are no property, income, or municipal taxes in Dahab, and Alex made money. His main customers were foreign tourists, but a few Israelis also took part in utilizing his talents.

Tattooing is as old as recorded humanity and is a distinctive activity of our kind. Tattoos can be a sign of belonging to a group, same as cuts, incisions, and inflicting ornaments to one's body or changing parts of it to fit an aesthetic viewpoint. They can show one to belong to an elite class or to an inferior one. Tattoos can also be a status symbol, and in our own time, a way to impress others, to show off and maybe get the girls. However, at the time, this same decorative enterprise had not yet reached the height of its popularity and a tattooed person remained the exception, arousing curiosity and sometimes admiration.

Every month or two, he would make the exhausting trip to Tel Aviv and back for supplies. He saw Gila, but she had turned aloof and cold.

"I'm seeing someone," she informed him.

"Who?"

"Someone who doesn't drag me into a desert."

Time passed. If Alex's methods were not as sterile as they should have been, his clients made up for the slack by their enthusiasm. He would meet the occasional girl tourist and they would have sex in his parlor and sometimes she would get a tattoo. Alex learned more English and some Arabic. He made some friends on a non-permanent basis, as people come, remain for a few days, weeks or months, and then leave. The Bedouin too were curious and some males peeped into his place, skeptic and distant. Bedouin come from an Islamic culture and mutilating the skin is not done. To them, all foreigners were different and crazy, but as much money is to be made from the invaders, they held their peace and remained silent.

Occasionally, the word would get around of a party going on somewhere, either in a restaurant or a shop, and the young and not so young would assemble there for entertainment and kicks. There were few chairs and they would lounge around with their backs leaning against the walls. Alcoholic beverages are forbidden in Islam but drugs are not. At parties the tourists would bring their own drinks and the Bedouin would supply the hashish. Seeing the painful lack of drinks, Alex adopted a side venture: Together with his supplies, he transferred bottles of vodka, whisky, and wines to Dahab and sold drinks for an extortionate price at parties. He would buy his special inks and needles and other accessories in Tel Aviv and the liquor in Ashkelon. With his two large suitcases, he would get to Eilat and a taxi would take him to Dahab. His wares were always snapped up and no party was deemed a success without his attendance.

At one of those occasions he saw a familiar female and approached her. "Hi there, do I know you from somewhere?"

She looked up in the dim light. "Alex! From Ashkelon, right?"

"You know me?"

"Damn right I do."

"You are?"

"Your tattoo burned my ass."

"Sorry. Did you apply the salve?"

"I couldn't get butt fucked for a month."

"Rachel! . . . I didn't recognize you at first."

"Yeah."

She seemed different somehow. "What are you doing here?" he chuckled, "There's too much amatory competing going around for good business."

"I get my share."

"Right, okay, see you around."

"Wait you goddam fucker. I need a place to stay."

"Why, the beach not good enough for you?"

"I got to lay low."

"Why me?" Alex studied her, she looked younger. He remembered a shopworn babe. She had turned into a saucy bitch with a zest for life. He wondered how she did it. "What happened?"

"A long story. Come outside."

She got up and took his hand and dragged him, somewhat reluctant to the light by the entrance. Desert life and air had agreed with Rachel, her skin clear and aglow with a healthy olive brown color. Once she had slinked about furtive and defeated, ashamed of her sexual activities, but now she strutted proudly, accepting her femininity. She had changed; her hair, more stylish, and had been colored to a henna red tinge, which suited her complexion. She had earrings and makeup; she had lost weight and, in jeans and a blouse, she looked almost a girl.

She saw his look. "You get it for free."

"Okay."

The party ended late at night, all the members pleasantly intoxicated, Rachel had managed a customer and they all dispersed. Alex, somewhat disgruntled, walked home with Rachel. She carried a small bag.

"Is that all your luggage?" he asked.

"I don't need much here."

"How do you manage?" Gila had two small suitcases with her.

"I wash, stuff dries fast."

"There's water outside to wash," he said curtly.

Sometimes later, she slid into his bed. He felt her smooth body. She whispered into his ear." My pussy is ready for you."

Excited he entered her without much foreplay, she moaned. 'Faking it probably.' He thought.

"Kiss me, hold me tight."

To his surprise, he encountered a new and different Rachel, in Ashkelon she had remained passive, lying there like a limp doll. He kissed her and she opened her mouth for him. Suddenly the magic was there. She helped him with her body.

Afterwards they talked. Thrilled and delighted, Alex wanted to know more. "Where did you learn all that stuff?"

"What stuff?"

"The sex things."

"What are you talking about?"

"You know . . . participating . . . doing things . . . helping out."

"I don't know, I never learned anything . . . not at school."

They both laughed. "You are different," Alex said.

"I feel good. Here all different."

The next morning, he heard her story:

Rachel had run away from a violent and temperamental husband, they had no children and he wanted her back. She found herself pregnant and wanted to get rid of the child. She went to a clinic and they refused her, as she was legally married, healthy and young. She tried another clinic and they refused her too. She found an abortionist but he asked for a great deal of money. She ran from home, borrowed, did the streets and had her abortion with the money she earned. Shlomo, her husband, had involved the social workers.

Ashkelon is an out of the way place where under cover gangs made dirty money, either by laundering, or by juggling real estate properties and coercing garages and the open market owners to pay for protection. Some people in the Municipality took it into their heads to clean up and make the town more decent. They augmented the police force that naturally attacked the weakest and smallest group first: the prostitutes on the street. The social workers had informed the police about Rachel and they dragged Rachel home.

"I tried to be a good wife," Rachel told Alex in spurts and jerks. "But living with the guy is hell . . . I felt bored to death and got the . . . what's the word . . . stuck-up bastard mad . . . so he would beat me . . . to kill the boredom." Rachel paused, her rousing passion causing an uncharacteristic outburst of her usual short sentences. She continued in bursts: "I don't like to cook . . . I don't like to clean . . . so I am not good woman . . . the guy treated me like shit . . . finished in a second . . . even a client is better than him . . . and I make money. The miserly sonofabitch . . . smug bastard. I never had enough cash . . . except what I got on the side."

Rachel ran away again and got picked up, but this time the social workers put her into an institute, in fact a prison for women. "Shlomo was behind it . . . I know," she said. She attended educational courses to lessen her year in prison. In her own inarticulate words, she told Alex how they filled her head full of nonsense and shit, except for learning how to dress better and use makeup she learned nothing of consequence. "We had religion . . . a good wife is dutiful . . . keeps the house . . . raises proper children . . . all that crap . . .from old farts . . .who would not know a woman . . . if she sat on their faces . . .well not for me. They made me see a shrink . . . I agreed to all the crap . . . just so they leave me be."

Rachel had returned to Shlomo, chastised and more than halfway determined to make good. She tried; she really tried hard, "I just couldn't do it," she told Alex, "The guy's impossible. I hated him . . . for this . . . torture, I would kill the . . . bastard, what is the word?"

"Sonofabitch . . . Egoistic, uptight, take your pick," Alex said amused. "How about snotty?"

"Asshole, he is a real asshole . . . if I remained we would end badly."

She ran away again, this time to Eilat, and then whored her way to Dahab–having heard of disco and parties there. "I like it here . . . and I'm rid of the fucking dickhead," she concluded her story. Rachel, not being too verbal, had told her tale with pauses and groping for words, but had succeeded in conveying to Alex her utmost disgust and hate for her husband. Alex, detached, shrugged his shoulders. He did not mind Rachel staying with him, easy good sex, she earned her keep and made no demands, the place appeared livelier with her about.

With Rachel there, Alex's place became a kind of meeting place, with some guys and gals always hanging about. Drinks could be had, and Rachel served them, and if a guy had enough money, they had sex in the back. When she felt in a good mood, she would make coffee. His parlor being too small to hold more than a few, the bunch around would lounge in the shade of a nearby palm. Alex enjoyed the attention his new status gave him.

The shop next to his had developed financial troubles; its owner came to him and asked him if he wanted to buy him out; his proposal: break the adjoining wall between them and have a larger place. Alex did not. His parlor appeared large enough for his work and he would not pay good money for more room so the guys could hang out, besides breaking down the wall might cause the ceiling to cave in. The neighboring shop went to another person.

One morning a van parked beside the neighboring shop, unloading packages which were dragged inside by a youth and a man in an orthodox black coat and a hat, both external religious symbols. Not having much to do Alex went up to them.

"Need help?" Alex asked.

"Thank you. We manage."

"I'm Alex we're neighbors."

The man turned from his task. "Akiva, the boy is Moshe." They shook hands and Akiva returned to his work. Alex soon found out why Akiva had been curt: He was a Chabad follower and his shop in Jerusalem sold religious articles and books. Bibles in many languages were stored by the shop window together with prayer books. Candlesticks and other pious artifacts were displayed under a strong light. Akiva had not wanted the Chabad house to be next to a tattoo place, but there had been no choice.

Akiva belonged to the Chabad-Lubavitch movement whose aim, among others, is to reunite Jews back to religion. His superiors had long deliberated whether to send a representative to Sinai. Sinai appeared as a place of chaos and unleashed sexual promiscuity, profanity and a waste of time and energy for sending a husband and wife team with children. Akiva, a shop owner and widower with a grown son, had been sounded out and he agreed to undertake the assignment for a year. Most of his funds came from his mission, but try as he would, he found all the central places in Dahab already taken and he had rented the place next to Alex's parlor as a last resort. As all Chabad establishments, he kept open house, inducing Jews to partake of his hospitality (and if the occasion came up, reminding non-Jews of the so-called Noahide laws derived from the biblical Noah). He had also brought with him embellished artifacts from his former shop to exhibit and sell.

To orthodox Jews, being a Jew is being religious, not differencing between religion and Judaism. Akiva had a strain of the zealot in him which would hinder him in his work. As a rule, the Chabad people are cordial and behave with amenity towards outsiders, accepting rather than criticizing the secular ways of modern Jews too harshly. Akiva found this difficult. He could not understand the ease with which the young group nearby ignored all the rules of their religion. Were they not afraid of the Almighty? They ate seafood, which is unclean and not allowed, they went about almost naked, especially Rachel, they did not observe any of the Mitzvoth and acted as if the holy one, blessed be he, did not exist. There were non-Jews among them and he could not always tell them apart.

People visited the Chabad house in a sense of curiosity, looked at the artifacts, and remained for a few minutes to listen to him, but did not come twice. The group around Alex's parlor ignored him. Alex had tried to be neighborly but had sensed some animosity and so had left him alone. The posters of naked bodies with tattoos on them, which adorned both sides of his parlor irritated Akiva almost beyond control, finally he confronted Alex:

"Those pictures before your shop are an abomination, an insult to our religion!"

"They are the tools of my trade."

"Tattooing is not done by Jews."

"It is now."

"I insist you take those pictures down."

"You have some nerve coming here and telling me what to do. Go find another place if you don't like it here."

They continued to argue with no results except for a mutual aversion for each other.

Rachel and Akiva took an instant dislike to each other. "He reminds me of my husband," she said shortly after Akiva had left. "A know all." She paused. "He is always right." Akiva had not yet known of Rachel's occupation, as no one had told him, he would find out later, but her lack of attire irritated him, as did that of all females in the area. He had made a mistake in coming to this hellish place with his son, and as soon as his contracted year passed, he intended to leave. Moshe, over fifteen now, saw

Rachel differently. He drooled and fantasized at nights over her, sometimes ejaculating in his sleep to his utmost embarrassment. He washed his pajamas so his dad wouldn't see his nocturnal emissions and in Dahab wet clothes dry quickly.

The tattoo parlor and the neighboring shop had large backyards divided by a fence, as space in the desert is cheap. Those had once been used to keep sheep and goats. Moshe, whenever he could escape his dad's vigilant eyes, could not keep away and easily crossed the backyards to spy on Rachel.

Alex kept a curtained part in the back of his parlor for his privacy where he slept and had sex with Rachel. The wall leading to the backyard had been made to keep an eye on the livestock and reached three feet down from the ceiling. The rest were boards, which could be put up to close the gap, but in the desert heat it is advisable to have as much air circulating as possible. Moshe, from a distance, could observe their activities undisturbed and this became his favorite pastime.

When Passover arrived, Akiva approached the group by the tattoo parlor and invited them to dine with him. "We have good food, brought especially from Israel in containers and lots of wine. Tell all your friends, there is place for all who come." A free meal and wine is always welcome and many said they would. A young Bedouin among the group, said, "I come also."

"Of course," Akiva said with tight lips. He thought, 'We Jews are not missionaries and have enough trouble keeping our own flock together.' Akiva felt that his energy was wasted on outsiders and there were too many around for his taste.

The time had come and the Chabad house filled with people. One dresses for the Passover feast, but Akiva noticed how not a few had come with flip-flops and shorts. The women wore trousers, but at least they had blouses or shirts on. He gritted his teeth. He and Moshe had worked all day to arrange the feast.

He greeted all politely, knowing that there were gentiles among his guests. Moshe handed out yarmulkes to all the males. Akiva addressed his congregation: "Please find seats, the ladies over there," he pointed to a separate table.

A woman asked him in English, "Don't we get to sit with our friends?" Alex translated.

"Men do not sit together with women."

"How quaint," she said disappointed.

When they were all seated, the Hagada before them with an English translation, Akiva began his recitations, Moshe too doing his part. Akiva asked Alex to read a part but he begged off, so did a few others. The recitations were long and Akiva read fast, mumbling the words. Soon all got bored. A few tasted the goodies on the table. Akiva noticed and read on, an angry note creeping into his voice at times. The Seder continued with its ritual dipping and tasting of food. The guests were hungry and thirsty. They motioned and whispered to each other and nibbled at the food. There was no air-conditioning and the place grew humid and sweltering hot. Some people left for the rest room and escaped, while the rest sweating, waited grimly for the chanting to stop. The noise grew louder. Even the occasional ceremonial drink of wine did not help. After the meal, most guests left, excusing themselves with various white lies.

Akiva chanted on with only a few guests remaining, determined to stick it out. The feast had not been a pleasant experience, and Akiva felt that the evening had not been a success. He pinpointed the blame on Alex and the tattoo parlor–an outrage, the source of all the transgressions.

Some of the eye-catching scenes in Dahab are the groups of little Bedouin girls in their colorful dresses wandering about and selling trinkets to the tourists. Many are the people captivated by their beautiful faces and naïve charms, and are induced to pay cash for items they don't need and perhaps later will throw away. Late next morning Akiva saw some Bedouin girls selling their pitahs to the group by Alex's place. He hurried out. "Those are not allowed on Pesach!"

A boy said something and they all laughed. Not understanding, Akiva returned angrily to his shop. The relations between the two neighboring places had become strained. Alex, trying to be polite to a non-responsive neighbor, followed him and entered the gift shop. "Why fight? We are all from Israel."

"Then why do you not behave like a Jew?"

"Not everyone is religious."

"But you are a Jew. Don't you believe in God?!"

"I'm not sure . . . no I don't. Not the Bible fellow."

"How can you be a Jew and not believe in your God?"

"Well I am. The country was built by Zionists all nonbelievers."

"They believed, in their hearts."

"Of course you know what they believed, as you know everything. Know this then: After the Holocaust very few Jews believed in religion, my father came from Germany, I should know. Why force it?"

"One cannot know the ways of God and one cannot be a Jew without religion. Without God there is nothing. You should accept your God, then you would find wisdom, knowledge and love. Your soul will be filled."

"Your brand of it of course. It keeps you in business."

"There is no other!"

"I saw no love in you, when you shouted to us not to buy the pitahs, only bitter anger."

"I am outraged at your transgressions."

"Maybe you should tolerate them with love and understanding."

"Young man, are you mocking me?"

"No sir, you live a holy life, but we are different. I believe that one can be a decent good Jew and person without religion."

Alex left. Later in the day Akiva came into Alex's parlor, he had been too abrupt and wanted to straighten things out. Alex, busy tattooing the breast of a girl who lay exposed on a massage bed with only the lower part of a bikini on, could not stop his work. The girl smiled at Akiva, not at all mortified.

"I'll be back later." Akiva left quickly.

Eventually, Alex found his way to Akiva's shop. They talked politely for a while, then Alex asked him: "We people are human like you. Why not let us choose to live as we like?"

"We are Jews, not like other people, we have an obligation. The covenant of Abraham with God."

"Yes . . . in the Bible . . . but someone wrote the Bible."

"God dictated the Torah to Moses."

"Now how would you know?"

"It is written . . ." Akiva quoted verses and paragraphs from various authorities and Alex listened patiently until he finished.

"But those are all opinions and commentaries, someone wrote them."

"Our Lubavitch Rabi has the ear of God!"

"You know that too? . . . God broke that covenant when he killed six million Jews, women and children . . . not to mention over one hundred million people in two big wars."

"This is sacrilege!"

"Now you are going to say that we cannot understand the ways of God."

Akiva lost his temper. "You are an Epicurus, you will never amount to anything."

Alex, perturbed, said, "There is no talking to you."

"You must take down those abominations in front of your place."

"Why is the human body an abomination, if God created it?"
"There is a moral code dictated to us, we have to follow it."
They continued to argue, but finally Alex grew tired: "Those posters advertise my trade, I will try to modify them."
Those sentences would turn out to be their last exchange of ideas. They existed side by side in a cold ominous truth, mostly ignoring each other. Alex did little in the way of modifying his posters, covering the genitals with a strip of tape, which made them look unnatural and vulgar. After some deliberations, he removed the tape.
Life does not sustain a status quo; change is the name of the game. Had their shops not been side by side, things might have turned out differently. Rachel, going to their backyard, had noticed a litter of tracks bunched together in the sand–someone might be spying on them. Her first thought had been of Akiva, but to her amusement, she saw the boy sneaking around. She did not mention the subject, keeping it in her mind for possible later use.
The same evening she initiated the sex, wanting to give Alex a good time. Alex sensed her emotions and reciprocated. To her great surprise, Rachel had an orgasm.
"That was good," Alex gasped when they ended.
"Amen," Rachel admitted.
Lying beside her, Alex did not find their liaison strange; they had an open, free, and unrestricted rapport, which suited them both; and he had had other girls sometimes. If Rachel came during the night and found the other bed occupied, she might do two things; join them and sometimes frighten the other girl (but all in good fun) or sleep on one of the couches by the beach. However, Alex had not had another girl for some weeks, having Rachel cost him little effort, and she had grown on him.
"I'm beginning to really like you," he told her in bed.
"Only like?"

He gave the subject some thought. She gave him no trouble whatsoever, she was independent, maybe too independent, and, with her natural compliance, they had sex whenever he felt like it. He felt a surge of thankful passion for her. "More, much more than like," he blurted out.

She molded her body to his. "Because we fuck?"

Suddenly he realized that she had become a fixture in his life. He did not want her to leave . . . not now, possibly ever. "Rachel, goddammit, am I falling in love with you?"

"Maybe."

"How about you?"

"I think so."

"You love me?"

" . . . Yes."

"But you fuck around."

"Easy money."

They kept silent for a while, the enormity of their disclosures hitting them, each occupied with their thoughts.

Alex had second thoughts: 'Rachel is a slut, a whore, in her years of sex she might have had more than a thousand men'; the thought made him wonder at himself . . . what they had, loose as their affair was, felt special and good. As long as they remained there, she would be good for him, but if they ever got back to 'civilization' . . . he did not know what might happen. They would cross that bridge when they came to it.

Rachel too had her thoughts: 'Alex is undemanding and lets me do as I like. He does not boss me around.' Lately, she had given him more and more of herself. Just now she had had a tremendous surge of emotion which had engulfed her totally–she had wanted to give him all of her being. The feeling, a new one to her, made her recall her husband–she never had anything so powerful and real happen with him.

"Alex."

"Yes"

"I stop . . . you know . . . fucking around?"

"Don't lie to me."

"I will . . ."

"Do you want to?"

"Don't know."

"Whatever," he said surprised at himself. What the hell did he want? Then he knew; he wanted things to remain the same, not change. What about all the guys she slept with? Alex searched himself; did he care? Does he feel jealous? He felt nothing . . . but how can that be?! "You enjoy sleeping around?" he asked her.

"Make money. I am boss. I like guys. Feel good."

"Good for you."

"You not mad."

"Not today."

Rachel, having had a jealous and demanding husband, who laid down the law, could not easily grasp Alex's way. "You do not love me."

"If I am jealous and hit you, then will you call it love?"

"Promise you will never hit me."

"I promise."

"Alex, no more condoms"

"You want kids?" unbelievingly.

"Just you, I cannot have kids."

"How come?"

"My abortion did something inside."

Alex remembered she had told him about prostituting to pay an abortionist, probably some kind of a butcher. He found it hard to reconcile his notions with his feelings about Rachel. A part of him saw her as a free soul with no inhibitions–she did what she liked and when she liked–on the other hand, she was a slut and a whore. What the hell, he also used to sleep around, and maybe still would, why not? Rachel had slept with a thousand guys, but she preferred him . . . Number one. She had chosen him from all the rest and now they would have sex without condoms. He felt special. The whole affair with Rachel did not make much sense to him. Life is a puzzle and he accepted it as such. He acknowledged his indecisions; let things be. He made enough money for them both but she never took money from him.

Rachel now found herself picking and choosing her guys far more than before and had no more than two or three in a week. She made less money but did not care. Alex began to buy her clothes and they had most of their meals together. Rachel remained much of the day hanging around the tattoo parlor.

Akiva would at times sit in front of his shop, trying to make eye contact with passing people he thought were Jewish and entice them to enter his shop with offers of cool drinks, but as most passersby wore trunks, shorts and sometimes t-shirts, he had a difficult time in figuring them out. Talking first often helped. Naturally he made a few awkward mistakes. Now that Rachel hung around by the group near the place, he saw more of her.

Rachel had few talents, but sex and men were among those. She had changed from a shabby slut to a healthy vibrant female. She dipped into the sea twice daily, mornings and evenings. She felt loved and she loved her man and moving about half naked only augmented to make her virile presence felt. Akiva could not keep his eyes off her. He knew he was falling into sin, but could not help himself. He studied, but found it hard to concentrate. He tried prayer which helped him, but only for a short time. Then he tried to rationalize and use logic: By now he knew Rachel to be a prostitute, she had never hidden her trade and he reasoned: 'better to engage her then not to function.' He had a mission: to encourage Jews to return to the Torah, and he could not accomplish anything in his state. Some of his acquaintances visited prostitutes. He had now been a widower for two years now, too long.

Reason and logic can be the biggest whores of all and will bed with any project. Akiva waited for an opportune moment, when she passed by his shop. He gave her a big smile. "Come in, come in. I have something to interest you."

They had not spoken to each other for some time. Rachel felt naturally wary. "What is it?"

"An artifact, made of white gold and dusted with diamonds and can be turned into a bracelet."

Rachel could not resist, curious she followed him inside. Once inside, he quickly locked the entrance. Rachel, a veteran of many such similar incidents, saw him coming. Once she would have cowed and begged . . . or complied. She had been raped, one way or another, not a few times, but now she waited apprehensive but unafraid. She could handle the pious bastard. Akiva hurried to the other end of the place and locked the door to Moshe's room.

He took a glittering object from a shelf. "Nice?"

Rachel studied the artifact. Not her style at all, an arrogant haughty piece of work much too hoity-toity for her. "Costs much money," she said.

"Gold plated." He returned the piece.

Rachel had never been inside his shop. She looked around. There were religious items all over the place, candlesticks, mezuzahs, megaliths adorned and coated with silver filigree, yarmulkes, prayer shawls, and ornamented defiling bags; but more than all: books. Stacks of them. The place had a musty smell of an unaired library.

Akiva did not know how to talk to women and prostitutes were the lowest. He might have approached the subject slowly with tact, catering to Rachel's self-esteem and eventually building up to some of the standard clichés, but his frustrated, passionate desire had made him impervious to those fine distinctions. He was crude, and he had not supplemented Rachel at an opportune time. He did not play his cards right.

Akiva's tensions burst out of him uncontrolled. Turning to her, he gasped, "I will pay you," he wheezed . . . "for . . . sex."

Rachel had found love and she recognized Akiva as being against all that she stood for: a free unrestrained lifestyle. She had had her fill of his kind in prison: religious women claiming to know it all . . .'how a woman should behave and how she should not' (reminding her of her husband). Streetwise, Rachel knew the fragile vanities of men, and let him down easy.

"You are a nice person, but no. Sorry."

Akiva had not expected a refusal, since when do prostitutes pick and choose. "I pay you," he repeated, "how much?"

"I said no."

"Name your price."

"Let me out please!"

"I have money. I will give you this!" He took a Sabbath candlestick from one of the shelves, gold plated and shiny and showed it to her.

"Open the door!"

He grew desperate. "Why not, don't you want money? You are a prostitute."

True or not, Rachel now thought of herself as a free woman who does as she likes, if some guys give her money . . . well that's okay with her. Akiva had mentioned the one taboo word for Rachel. No one had ever called her a prostitute to her face. She kept quiet, not daring to give reign to her feelings. Akiva had insulted her where it hurt, and Rachel knew how to deal with insults: she would bide her time and would find a way to make him regret his words.

"What is it? Am I not as good as the others?"

"I choose my guys."

He closed in. "I will pay you double, what they pay."

"No."

He touched her.

"Don't touch me!"

Akiva grabbed her. Rachel had learned a few dirty tricks in her time–a necessary addition to her resume. She did not resist and let him embrace her, then she kneed him with all her strength. Akiva doubled up in pain moaning. Rachel took the keys from his pocket and let herself out. She did not mention the episode to Alex.

The next few days passed as if nothing had happened and Rachel kept out of Akiva's way, but her repugnance of him had turned into hate. What right had he to think of her as a low whore! Abhorrence can be passive, but hate, coupled with insult, can be active, vindictive and motivating ingredients. Rachel did not have a set of regular moral rulings, she felt triggered by her emotions. Her life in Ashkelon had not been something to boast about; raised by her granddad until puberty, he had made her feel an unwanted burden.

She had finally left home at fifteen and begun her career as an underpaid waitress with sex on the side. She had felt insecure and self-doubting, unsure of what her real needs were. The big world frightened her and she felt permanently inadequate. Shlomo had been knowledgeable, secure and she had felt protected and trusted him, at eighteen they married. Her husband had exploited her diffidence and lack of assurance and used her unscrupulously; he had acted as if she were his property–a house slave. Rachel had told Alex little about her past and when Alex questioned her she had one answer:

"I am what I am now." And if he insisted, she would come out with, "You know me," or "What is there to tell."

Rachel had one weapon to face the world: herself; and she would use it.

Moshe did not study all the time as his father would have liked, spying on Rachel and Alex occupied but a part of his attentions. He felt drawn to the beach and took short excursions to the shore, only a few minutes away from their place, claiming to want a dip, and his dad would reluctantly allow him some leverage. However, the main attractions to him were not the miracles of nature around, or under the sea. Another kind of miracle, definitely also of nature, had caught his undivided attentions. His father had forbidden him to look at women, but look he did. He drooled futilely imagining what it would be like to have a delicious piece in his arms.

Fantasies have no limits . . . Moshe, a conscientious youth, assiduous and determined to rid himself of those thoughts, not realizing the impossibility of his task, tried hard, but all he managed was to feel guilty. Wearing shorts, a t-shirt, sandals and a cap, he would enter the water to cool off. He did not swim, but lounged in the shallow places in search for the other sex.

Coming out of the water he would pass by one of the so-called 'restaurants' or eating places. People reclined on couches, some eating or drinking out in the open with only a canvas tent-like roof stretched above. On one of those couches, Rachel stretched out in a bikini. She knew that the boy had sneaked into their backyard hoping to catch them in sex. She had waited for her chance.

"Hello there," when he didn't react. "Say hello."

"Hello." He stopped.

"Sit down and cool off."

"I'm wet."

"So, get dry." Rachel moved to make place for him. She was irresistible. Moshe sat gingerly on the edge of her couch.

"Towel?"

A towel is not of much use in the desert, as the dry air and heat will quickly relieve one of any external moisture. Rachel took a towel from under her and handed it to him. He wiped his face and hair, taking off his cap to do so and replacing it. The towel soaked up some of Rachel's sweat together with her perfume. Moshe smelled the intoxicating elixirs.

"Take your shirt off." When he didn't move, she set up and took the towel from him and dried him under his shirt, her movements necessarily touching him with her body, her face close to his. Moshe riveted to his seat did not move. Then she moved her hand with the towel under his shorts and dried him there, the towel touched his genitals and he got a huge straining erection.

"What is that?" Rachel kidded, but Moshe, red in the face, could not speak. Without another word, Rachel masturbated him and in a few seconds he ejaculated, stifling his groans. Some of the sperm ran down his leg. Moshe felt he would die of shame, while Rachel amused, kidded him. "Now you are a real man." Moshe sat paralyzed. Rachel got up and wrapped the towel over his shorts. "Come." She helped him get up and led him woodenly to the sea. "Wash yourself."

When Moshe returned from his short dip, he still would not talk. They sat on the couch, Rachel joked, "Sperm good for fish."

Moshe did not react. Rachel said, "Sex is not bad."

"I have sinned," burst out from Moshe.

"No sin," Rachel said, "sex is life."

"Maybe for you, my father will punish me."

"Don't tell him."

"I must go."

"Say thank you?"

"Thank you." He fled.

The next few days Moshe had a hard time, he had sinned. Naturally, he had had small misdemeanors before, but he had now achieved a big one, a real transgression and it had felt so good. He wondered: 'does sin always feel good?' Why should that be? However, his guilty feeling did not keep him from hurrying to the seaside when he could make it, but he found no Rachel. He felt relieved and disappointed at the same time. Rachel, knowing she had her hooks in him, kept away on purpose. Two days passed, then once again Moshe saw her sprawled full length on a couch in her bikini. They made eye contact but she did not greet him. He stopped by her side.

She looked up, "What do you want?"

"I . . ." He remembered; she had wanted him to thank her. "Thank you."

"For what?"

"The last time . . ."

"No big deal."

"Well . . . thank you," he said lamely.

Rachel turned on her stomach showing her back to him, her bikini a thong on her behind revealing a set of full buttocks, a narrow waist and the thin string of fabric holding her bra. Moshe went out of his mind. Rachel handed him a tube of lotion. "Do me."

"What?"

"Rub cream on my back."

With trembling hands, he squeezed the tube forgetting to unscrew the cap first, when he did, a stream of lotion squirted on Rachel's back. He spread the cream out with his fingertips.

"Use your whole hand."

He massaged her tentatively, shivering inside with excitement. For one moment he looked around guiltily, his occupation was not exceptional for the place, two more persons were being treated with lotion. He felt a sense of unreality.

"Harder, use some strength," Rachel ordered him, getting him out of his revere. He applied himself.

"My arms." Moshe did those too.

"Now my feet."

Moshe did her feet but stopped above her knees.

"All the way up."

Moshe continued, his heart beating, he stopped by her buttocks.

"Higher, don't be shy."

He kneaded her round globes and felt the excitement and tinge of an approaching emission. He panicked and desisted bending over as in pain. The feeling receded slowly.

"What is it?" Rachel asked him, turning around.

"Nothing."

"Hadn't you better go?"

He looked at her with pleading eyes. "Please . . ."

Rachel understood him perfectly; she had intended to let him suffer and through him to get back at his father, but seeing his contorted face she relented. "Come here." She grabbed his head and kissed him, a real kiss.

She put her hand under his shorts.

Rachel still stung from Akiva's insult. She had not finished with him yet. After their incident, she avoided him, but a week later she loitered by his shop. Akiva came out curious but aware of a potential enemy. His balls had hurt all day. "Do you want something?"

"Your son is stalking me."

"You are lying." He did not want to believe her.

"We had sex twice. He is not like you."

"You are crazy!" he exclaimed in Yiddish (Bist meschuge).

Rachel thought he had cursed her. She shrugged her shoulders. "Ask him." Her mission ended, she turned and left.

Akiva accosted his son and soon forced the truth out of him, but, to his great relief, understood from–Moshe's stammering and protestations–that no real sex had transpired, real sex being interpreted as coitus only. Dahab, with all the half-clad nude females about, was no place for Moshe, and his father–reluctantly–decided to take him to live with his sister, Moshe's aunt. Akiva knew his sister to be notoriously lax and he did not want to lose control over Moshe, but he felt he had no choice. He would have to reside the remains of the year in Dahab alone. Akiva closed his shop and they left for Israel.

Rachel had not anticipated the result of her actions; however, seeing the shop next door closed, she guessed what might have happened. She still smoldered from being called a prostitute. Among the small group loitering around the tattoo parlor were a few young Bedouins who were attracted to the easy ways of the westerners. They came and went as they pleased, knew enough Hebrew to get by and ogled the girls hoping for some success. Rachel had gently repulsed some of their advances. Bedouins were Arabs and she did not care for Arabs. One of the nicer looking ones, Hamid, had been pestering her, carefully aware not to step over the line. Rachel took him aside. "Hamid, the man with the beard."

"Yes."

"His gift shop is closed."

"Yes . . ."

"The owner is in Israel now."

"What you want?"

"You take his things."

"No."

"You sell, make money."

He looked at her, their eyes met. She smiled at him, her message clear.

"You come . . . to me?" he panted.

"Later, afterwards."

Akiva returned to find his shop pillaged, many of his most valuable artifacts had been removed, but the books remained untouched. Luckily, most of his valuables where in Jerusalem, locked in a vault beneath his shop. His first thought was of Alex. He accosted him angrily: "Someone broke into my place!" he looked at him accusingly. "Much was stolen."

"I heard nothing," Alex said feeling defensive.

"Next door to your place and you heard nothing?"

"Are you accusing me?"

Akiva relented. "I don't know what to think."

"There is no lack of robbers here."

"I will inform the authorities."

"Ha," Alex barked cynically.

Alex told Rachel about the burglary and Akiva's veiled hints. "Have you heard anything?" he asked her.

"No, nothing." Rachel loved Alex but he did not have to become involved in her private feud.

"Would the Bedouin know?"

"They won't talk."

Both Rachel and Alex felt they had nothing in Israel to return to. They lived a free uninhibited and unobligated lifestyle which suited them both, apart when they felt like it and together at meals or in the nights. Sometimes Rachel helped keep the place clean and sterilize the non-dispensable tattoo implements. They were content. Many people do not know when they are happy, being too busy with their daily lives to give the subject much thought. Month after month passed in the leisurely routine of Sinai which they now took for granted. The group around the parlor might change, the turnout being weekly or monthly, but the guys and gals remained the same, as if created on an assembly line: Kicks, freedom, pleasure and sex as their main motives.

Alex did not take the trip for supplies to Israel anymore; he made arrangements. One shop in Tel Aviv supplied him monthly with his tools and another with booze. A hired car would fetch the wares together with others and bring them to Sinai.

Akiva, alone now without his son, found himself at a loss, with much time on his hands. He studied the commentaries, books were his only companions, but one can only study for so long. His frosty lack of affinity with his neighbors kept him from company. On his other side was a stall, with an Arab owner selling beach-clothes, from shorts, sandals, t- shirts, hats cheap sunglasses, semitransparent scarves, flippers, masks and snorkels and assorted trinkets, beads–one of the many boutique shops which had sprung up with the bonanza in the area. Somewhat to his surprise, Akiva found himself friendlier with the Arab than with his own kind.

Providence and chance do play a larger part in our lives than we realize, but only together with our own blueprints, which help motivate our feelings and actions. Rachel had run away from her husband not once, but three times. Shlomo missed her. She had kept house for him and the sex needed little effort.

After she left, Shlomo, a handsome hunk, had little trouble making contact with the other sex, but his overbearing nature never got him past the first few sessions. He needed Rachel like one needs a useful tool, and had mistaken his feelings for her as love. She had hurt his pride by repeatedly running away, and his cronies would sometimes tease him, for not being able to hold a woman, but carefully–as he was known to have a short fuse. He searched for her in Ashkelon, but no one had seen her. He visited her grandfather's home but the latter had no idea of where she might be.

Shlomo had a taxi and worked independently in Ashkelon, but occasionally had customers for the Ben Gurion Airport and even to Eilat. On one of his trips, to Eilat his passengers enthusiastically praised the new hotel in Taba, just beyond the Gulf of Aqaba and the casino, which appeared to be a great attraction, as gambling is not legal in Israel. He thought he deserved a holiday and intended to make a trip to Sinai, he could take his taxi with him and drive to wherever the road leads him.

The next day he found an army summons for one month mandatory service in his mailbox. He cursed. Shlomo drove a truck in the army and was sent to Ophira, a new Israeli town being built next to Sharem el Sheikh. Building supplies had to be brought from Eilat. He drove long days and nights on the Ophira-Eilat route and often took on hitchhikers to lessen the boredom of a lengthy trip. In Eilat, he sometimes spent a whole day waiting for his truck to be loaded and used the opportunity to get to nearby Taba and gamble. Having lost much of his money in Roulette and Blackjack, he would return to his truck and get to work.

As fate would have it, his truck broke down while unloading his wares in Ophira. There were no spare parts to be had and would have to be brought to Eilat from an army garage further away. His superior officer said to him, "Here is your chance, take your holiday now, this will take some time, come back in two days."

Forty-eight hours off is the official norm for a month's service, but in most places the soldiers received double the amount. "I need at least three days to get home, rest and get back," he argued.

"Don't go to Israel, why not stay here or go to Dahab, or Nueba and take it easy by the sea?"

"Three days," Shlomo insisted.

"Alright, you have three days. I will arrange your pass."

Shlomo did not go home, He had no one waiting for him there. He rode with one of his army buddies to Nueba. He found a small group of huts by the sandy beach, he bathed in the sea and lay in the shade of a hut. There were only couples and families around and he felt alone. After some hours, he grew bored and hiked to Dahab arriving late afternoon. Dahab comes alive when the heat recedes and Shlomo saw tourists and Israelis all bent on enjoying themselves. Music blared and people rushed about in the mad dance of life. Shops and stalls displayed their wares. The Red Sea in full view shined like silver turning into gold by the sunset. The mountains on the other side glowed with a shady red sheen.

Shlomo strolled past the restaurants and ogled the many half-clad females. He passed a tattoo shop and saw a boy getting a tattoo on his shoulder. Maybe he should get one for himself, he thought; a naked girl on his inner arm or a skull with crossbones on the back of his shoulder–like the tough guys. He had little money having lost much at the casino in Taba. He still had enough for a meal and some place to sleep.

He sat down at one of the open seashore places and ordered chips and fried eggs, the cheapest items on the menu, being amazed at the low price. Then he strolled back the way he had come and again passed the tattoo place, some guys and girls were hanging out and chewing the rag, one of them in army clothes. He addressed them; "Hi guys where can I find a place to sleep?"

"On the beach," one said.

The other, more serious, told him: "Try the Lighthouse, a big camp, this way." He pointed north, "They may have a free place left."

"Thanks."

"Where you from?"

He told them. They began to chat.

Alex, having finished with a customer, came out to join them. Talking with us humans is the same as dogs sniffing each other or monkeys grooming. We socialize, and what is said can be less important than how it is said and who says so. The group chatting contained a boy and a girl, one soldier, one Israeli couple, a lone English girl, a Bedouin and an American couple and they all had to say their piece and exchange information–the subjects being Sinai, Dahab, other places, the food, surfing, sex, parties and the amazing marine life under the sea.

Rachel, coming to join them, got the shock of her life and stopped in her tracks.

Shlomo!

She saw her husband, Shlomo, whom she had passionately wanted to forget, with a group talking to Alex. Had he searched for her and found her? How could he have known where she now lived?

Stunned she escaped from the place before anyone could see her.

Later in the evening, she returned and cornered Alex. "The guy you talked to before?"

"What guy?"

"The soldier."

"There were two. The one who just came?"

"Yes, him."

"I don't know him, he is on leave and went to the lighthouse camp."

"Alex, he is Shlomo . . . my husband."

"You're kidding." He saw her face, "No you're not. Great God . . . your husband! What is he doing here?"

"Looking for me."

"I don't think so . . . you were not mentioned. He is stationed in Ophira, his truck broke down and he is on leave, he will soon depart."

"I won't be around."

"You can sleep in peace; he won't appear in the middle of the night."

Rachel slept uneasily beside Alex. She felt wary of coincidences and did not like the idea of her husband being so near. The next two days she kept her distance from the center and the tattoo parlor. Shlomo did not, he lounged lazily on couches and dipped into the sea when he felt too hot. He had made eye contact with a Norwegian girl and one thing had led to another as is often the way with us humans. She found his domineering ways a quaint novelty and enjoyed them. He took her back with him to Ophira after his leave, his army buddies wisecracked knowingly. The army would not let her into the camp and she claimed to have to leave anyway. Shlomo finished his term in the army resolving to get back to Dahab as soon as possible. Taba and the casino had lost their charms for him.

Back in Ashkelon he settled some minor affairs and a month later found him and his taxi in Dahab. He planned on taking a long holiday.

He returned to his former haunts, renting a cheap hut on the far side, as Dahab was overfilled with tourists, some sleeping on the beach, he lounged sleepily by the seashore with an eye to the girls around, the tattoo parlor not far away. One day later, on his way to his favorite place he saw a familiar shape! He blinked and rubbed his eyes, she reminded him of his missing wife. Could that be Rachel? Here in Sinai!? She did look like his wife, he should know . . .

Did Rachel have a younger sister?

No, impossible.

She looked more appealing and desirable than when she had left. She had changed her hair . . .

He studied her from a distance, not exposing himself but hiding at the entrance of a nearby gift shop. He remembered her stooped and slinking about furtively, cowering, always on the defensive, this female stood straight, her body language different, a real dish. She had been at his beck and call; anytime he had felt like it, he had grabbed her by her hair and flung her on their bed. Sometimes she had whined and complained, but he had soon shown her the futility of resisting him—from sex to keeping the place clean. She had been a filthy pig when they first married . . . he had taught her everything she knew and now she had had the gall to run away from him! He could not believe his eyes.

The woman was his! His wife and he lusted for her.

Akiva saw a person standing by the entrance of his shop, he seemed to be watching someone. "Come in, come inside and look round. This is a Jewish place we have here."

Shlomo looked dazed. "What?"

Akiva easily recognized Shlomo as Jewish. "Can I make you something to drink? Tea? Coffee?"

"Yes."

"Yes tea or yes coffee?"

"What? Coffee please."

Shlomo pulled himself together, he had found her, he had found his missing wife. Now he needed a plan. He entered the Chabad shop.

Akiva brought him some biscuits and a cup of coffee. "My wife, blessed be her memory, used to bake, but now all I can serve you, comes from packages."

"Thanks." Shlomo, still a little befuddled, did not comment. He sipped the coffee gratefully. Rachel had not seen him. She appeared so changed . . . he had never seen her so sexy, a real peach. She had been his to do with as he pleased . . . his loins ached for her.

"You are looking for someone?"

Shlomo had a reverence for all things religious. He had never given the subject much thought or asked questions. Akiva, being a religious person, presented an indisputable authority to him. He answered naively, "My wife."

Akiva did not understand. "You are looking for your wife?"

"That woman is my wife!"

"Who?"

"In short cut jeans, up to her ass, sorry . . . showing all her legs . . ."

Akiva knew whom he meant. "You mean . . . the one called Rachel. She is your wife?!"

"Rachel, you know her?"

"We are acquainted. Are you legally married?"

"Yes. She ran away, I haven't seen her in a year."

Akiva needed to let all the new information sink in. "Come into the back. We have to talk." He led a hesitant Shlomo into the other room where they sat down comfortably to talk.

Akiva let him have it with both barrels, "Your wife is shameless, she is with another man and . . . has men for money."

Shlomo knew about the prostitution. "What other man?"

"The tattoo person, Alex."

"I've met him."

"She sleeps there in his place, with him."

"I want her back."

"You are well rid of her."

"I want her back! . . . What can you do for us? Arrange a meeting in your place?"

Akiva wanted nothing better; getting a husband and wife together is considered a great mitzvah, a good deed that would gain him esteem in the world to come, but he knew he could never get Rachel to enter his shop again. Naturally, he did not mention his part in the past sordid affair. He stalled.

"Where are you from? Tell me a little about yourselves."

Shlomo told him, he let himself go, confessing and complaining about his many grievances. Rachel had been a bad wife, she did not clean or cook properly . . . he had much to tell and Akiva listened silently not interrupting. When Shlomo ended, he asked him, "Why do you want her back? You can divorce."

Akiva had hit a sore spot. Shlomo needed someone he could control and dominate, but he could not admit this to himself, or to others. Seeing his wife there had spurted his desire for her. She was *his* and did not belong to anyone else.

"She is my wife," he said simply.

Akiva said, "Let me think it over, I'll see what I can do."

Shlomo barely controlled his impatience. "I will go and talk to her myself."

"Wait, you have waited a year, you can wait some more. I will talk to her." He got up. "You stay here. Drink your coffee." He pointed to the untouched cup, then he left.

Akiva approached Rachel cautiously, knowing her aversion to him. Rachel, together with some young people, were hanging about by the shade of a palm tree, some lying others sitting. She saw him approaching without pleasure.

"We have to talk," he said without any pretense at preliminaries.

Rachel wanted nothing more to do with him, but he was an elderly person and she made an effort to remain tactful. "Sorry, maybe later," she said shortly.

"We have an important matter to discuss."

She had enough of his subterfuges and lost her temper. "Get lost."

Akiva quickly relinquished his scheme of approaching the subject carefully. "Does the name Shlomo mean anything to you?"

"What? What did you say?" she cried upset.

"Shlomo."

One of the gang asked, "Who is Shlomo?"

"Someone I once knew." She said quickly.

"Come," Akiva motioned to her.

Rachel got up. They moved to a distance and talked in low voices. "Your husband is here in my place. He wants to see you."

"Here!? Has he come back?"

"What? Was he here before?"

"How do you know about my husband?"

"He told me everything."

"How did you find him?"

"Not important. He wants to talk to you, perhaps a reconciliation."

"I have nothing to say to him."

"He wants you back."

Rachel would say the longest sentence of her life: "I do not want to speak to him" . . . a pause, "not hear of him" . . . another short pause, "or have anything to do with him."

"You are still husband and wife."

"I want to be left alone."

"Is that your final word?"

"I do not want him near me."

"Why did you run away?"

"None of your goddam business." Rachel turned away and left.

Rachel did not return to her group by the palm. She felt dismayed and upset and had to think. She found a free couch by the shore and felt herself close to tears. Her husband had found her and he wanted her back. She knew how violent he could be when crossed. The right move for her would be to flee to another place. Rachel felt a pang of anger. Why could not she be left alone! She liked Dahab, she and Alex were doing just fine, they had drifted into a live-and-let-live lifestyle which suited her perfectly. Alex had his tattoo business and could not leave easily; besides, she did not want to involve him, if she left, she would have to flee alone and undercover . . . like before. No! She would not give up what they had, . . . have. For once, she would take a stand. Did she not have a right to live her life as she pleased? To hell with Shlomo! She would remain and continue with her life. Should she tell Alex about the new turn of events? She did not want to, and put telling Alex off, hoping Shlomo would accept her answer and leave, but she knew her husband; he was not the one to take no for an answer.

Akiva returned to his place deep in thought. He now disliked Rachel even more; a gross vulgar slut. Returning to Shlomo, he said, "There is no talking to her. She is determined to remain a loose woman. Whatever I said to her made no difference. She does not want a reunion."

Shlomo grew angry. "I will show her what's what." He got up.

Akiva held him back. "I have a better idea. Do not confront her yet, you cannot force her and fighting will not help you."

"She is my legal wife; I will make her come back to me."

"I have a free room, my son lived here, but I had to send him away because . . . that Jezebel seduced him. You stay here with me, next door to them. Let her see you . . . as often as possible . . . woo her, bring her flowers (a metaphor, there were no flowers in Dahab) wear her down, appeal to her, make her think of you and show her that you want her back, but don't fight and we shall see where you go from there."

"I have a rented hut further away, at the other end of the village."
"It is better you stay here, nearby."

Both Akiva and Shlomo knew little about women, except for their own stereotypes. However, the notion grew on Shlomo. Rachel deserved punishment and once she was his again, he would be only too happy to dish out some retribution. Remaining around nearby would make her vulnerable and exposed to him, what could she do . . . except leave.

"She might run away again," he argued. "Then I would have to look for her. She could be anywhere."

"She won't leave."

"Because of the tattoo guy?"

"She has it good here, she can be a harlot and admired as nowhere else."

"Please, she is my wife . . ."

"Those are the facts."

"I will soon change that," Shlomo said.

They did not waste time. Akiva cleared the remains of Moshe's things out and Shlomo moved in, but kept some of his belongings in the former hut he had rented. He could now get back at Rachel, but there had been a price. Akiva, a devout individual, said his prayers, and Shlomo had to follow suit: In the morning, at meal times, in the afternoon and evening. . . . At home, Shlomo might, on very few occasions, go to the synagogue on Sabbath and remain for half an hour or so but never longer. He preferred to work on Sabbath, as he could make more money with his taxi.

The next morning when Rachel came out of the tattoo parlor, she found Shlomo sitting on a chair before the Chabad place. She could not ignore him, but she tried not to meet his eyes. There were no greetings. "What are you doing here?"

"I live here now." Shlomo began to enjoy himself.

"With the old lecher?"

"He is a venerable person."

"He tried to rape me."

"Did you let him?"

"None of your business."

"You are a slut."

He had called her a slut many times before, she felt immune to his insults. "Are you following me?"

"Should I . . . maybe."

"Leave me alone!"

"I am not doing anything."

"Go to hell."

She had never dared to talk to him so before and left quickly before he could retort. Shlomo's presence caused Rachel a series of problems. She feared and hated him and did not want to be reminded of the old days with him. She felt afraid of his potential violence. She cringed inside and hated herself for it. What did he want? She had made it clear to him through Akiva that she does not want anything to do with him.

'I'm free of him,' she thought. 'How long will he remain here?'

Shlomo did not know how to court or flatter a woman and had made Rachel nervous. He felt pleased; she had run away from him and he would make her pay. He did not believe that the old religious person had tried to rape her, he knew his wife, she had probably tried to get money from him for her favors and had been misunderstood. Time was on his side and he controlled his impatience.

Shlomo now spent many hours sitting in front of the Chabad house listening to music. Rachel had no choice but to pass nearby, she did not greet him and tried to ignore his presence, but he would not let her and would greet her with a 'Good morning.' Or later in the day, 'How are you' and 'You look nice today.' He bombarded her with platitudes and commonplaces sounding innocent enough, but with cynical overtones meant to annoy her.

Their place had a backyard, and Rachel, so as not to meet Shlomo, found herself entering the parlor from its other side, just so she would not see her husband. She grew indignant and angry. Why did she have to enter her own place like a thief in the night? The last degradation made her finally confide in Alex. She told him what little she knew. She had no idea how her husband had found her–not that it mattered. Shlomo now lived in the Chabad house next to them, which could not be accidental; he must entertain some idea of getting her back.

"But what can we do?" Alex commented. "Akiva doesn't like us and probably is helping him. We cannot ask him to move–he will laugh at us. You should try to ignore him."

"I know, I try."

"But you cannot?"

"Impossible."

"Right come with me." Alex had an idea. "We can turn the tables on him." He looked at Rachel, "Put on your sexiest outfit."

Rachel had developed a faint sense of humor lately. "Take off your clothes."

Alex laughed. "We're going out."

They exited the tattoo parlor, Rachel in flip-flops, wearing the lower part of a skimpy bikini and a semitransparent short vest, her nipples protruding. Her long naked legs and the folds of her behind revealed. Shlomo, sitting on his chair outside the Chabad house, looked up, he had been listening to music. Alex and Rachel walked past him their arms around each other. No greetings were made. Shlomo gaped, he had never seen Rachel so attractive. Goddammit, she was his wife! She belonged to him only! No one else had a right to her! Alex and Rachel had passed him, and stopped further off by a palm. They embraced and kissed, Rachel's back turned towards Shlomo. Alex put his hands on her buttocks and kneaded them, Rachel cleaved to him, gyrating her pelvis. Shlomo, red and agitated, stood up, undecided. Akiva came out and held him.

"Let them, your time will come."

Still embracing, Rachel whispered into Alex's ear: "This is best I ever had."

Alex grinned, "You made me hard."

People passed by and Alex turned her towards the tree. Hiding their activities from all with his back. Passersby saw a couple kissing and some whistled encouragingly and flung a few ribald wisecracks at them, but all gave them space.

"I'll kill the sonofabitch," Shlomo raged.

Akiva held him back. "Don't you see? They are making a special show for you; do not play into their hands." He held him back forcibly. "He is not the culprit, your wife is!" Akiva began to pull Shlomo inside. "Do not watch anymore, they want you to."

Rachel and Alex entered a seashore place, chased a goat away and had a good meal.

They had won a round.

On their way back, the Chabad house appeared closed.

The next morning found Shlomo sitting on his chair in front of the Chabad house. Eventually Rachel passed by looking her sexiest. Shlomo did not speak but looked ominous. Rachel hated him for following her and not leaving her in peace. Hate and vindictiveness get along well together, and Rachel had developed more than a streak of the later. She now teased him provocatively, passing him more then she actually had to and changing her attire occasionally, just to provoke him. She needed to assert herself and get back to him. She would show him that she was her own woman!

With Alex busy in his tattoo parlor, Rachel would sometimes take one of her friends or former customers with her and walk by Shlomo, embracing them. Her abhorrence for him had few limits; she would make him pay for the many long years she had suffered with him.

Goading Shlomo could be a dangerous business, but in the heat of her victories, Rachel ignored the warning signs. She flaunted herself in front of him—'this is what I am and what you do not get.' Rachel would stroll by with her arms around two boys, sometimes kissing one or the other. Akiva realized how his scheme had backfired and had tried to keep Shlomo from sitting outside waiting for Rachel to pass. "Don't you see? It is exactly what she wants you to do," he would repeat, but with no avail. Shlomo could not keep himself from watching her.

Then Rachel, in her zeal, crossed the line. She had made a Bedouin friend, Hamid, and one fine day she took him and another Bedouin with her on some fabricated errand. Passing by the Chabad house, she put her arms around them. They were delighted. When they passed by Shlomo, she let them kiss her. Shlomo had been goaded beyond his limits. He acted. Leaving his place, he trailed her all day following her activities with interest, he spied on her. Rachel, not seeing him anymore by his usual place, had hopefully thought he had finally given up and left.

Rachel loved to have an hour alone by herself occasionally, especially at dusk after her dip. She would choose an isolated spot away from the center and sprawl on a couch or a mat by the seashore and if those were not available then the soft sand would do. She liked to watch the sea and the sun set over the mountains on the other side and congratulate herself on her achievements. She felt good about herself, she did not identify, analyze, or define her personal issues, but she liked to bask, feeling an inner glow of satisfaction. The sun set in an orange rosy glow, which reflected a dark brown red on the opposite mountain range as the view grew darker. The stars came out myriads of them.

Her reverie was rudely interrupted by someone lifting and overturning her mat. She rolled on the sand. "What the . . ." Then she saw Shlomo, his face a fierce scowl. He pulled her up by her hair, hurting her terribly. She opened her mouth to scream. He slapped and shook her. "Not a peep out of you or you'll get it where it hurts."

Even in her terror, she knew when to comply. The surprise confrontation face to face with a violent Shlomo had sapped all her confidence and self-esteem which had built up in the last year. Within a few seconds, Rachel had reverted to her former cowering associations with her husband. "Please don't hurt me," she begged.

"Shut your trap. You're coming with me." He pulled her along.

"Where are we . . ."

He slapped her. "I said to shut up!"

Rachel began to sob. Shlomo dragged her away from the shore. Despite the last year of freedom, Rachel now regressed to feeling a kind of déjà vu. She had been in the same situation before. This year had been but a fantasy and faded away. Shlomo would always be her husband no matter what. She tried to resist the feeling: Alex would search for her and find her.

Shlomo dragged her to the hut he had rented before meeting Akiva. He had to let go of her while unlocking the padlock. Rachel sprinted away, but he caught her arm easily. He dragged her into a small room, unpainted walls, one tiny window and one bed. He threw her on the bed.

"You are my wife!" He tore off her clothes, ignoring her pleadings.

"You filthy whore!" He slapped her and had sex with an unresisting Rachel. She waited him out, used to passive sex from before, knowing he would be quick.

The same evening, when Rachel did not return home, Alex had not been unduly worried. Rachel came and went as she pleased and often arrived late. Sometimes he would fall asleep, and occasionally they had sex. Rachel always willing.

Alex fell asleep.

Rachel's greatest danger was not only her husband, but her own mind and feelings. She halfway accepted her fate, complaining and crying out. In another part of her being, she felt that being dominated would always be a true and familiar destiny. Shlomo, together with his temper and violence, would be a part of her life forever. She felt like she had never left him and their former habitual dealings took over. She pleaded with him, whining, "Please let me go," repeating the same over and over automatically.

"You are my wife," he retorted. "You stay with me."

Rachel had hoped he would be satisfied with having her and that would be the end of it. "What do you want from me?"

"We're going back to Ashkelon."

Her hopes crushed, she sunk into a dejected silence.

"It is high time you stop fooling around and came to your senses."

Rachel knew from past experiences not to get into an argument with him.

The hut where Rachel now lay imprisoned had been hastily constructed like many others of their kind. There were no professionals among the builders, and Bedouins had executed the various building projects haphazardly. The small windows were made of wood and could be opened for air and light. The door, not fitting too well, had a large crack underneath. There being no safety regulations, the electric wiring for the one fly speckled bulb hanging from the ceiling, also the work of an amateur, had been spliced in parts and clamped loosely to the wall.

Shlomo copulated with Rachel once more during the night. He had locked the door and the key hung around his neck. Rachel checked the window, it appeared too small for her to wiggle through. They slept until late morning and Shlomo had her again. This time doggy style. On her elbows and knees, Rachel felt a burst of indignation and then a strange and new powerful emotion joined the turmoil of the awakening passions in her: Outrage!

A surge of revolt invaded her person. 'Did she have to suffer him?' With outrage, her former hatred of him, bitter and strong, returned. 'Anything is better than remaining with him!' She must resist.

Looking around for a weapon, Rachel noticed the spliced wire just above her head, leading to the ceiling. In desperation, she easily pulled the wire away from the wall, the isolation band having been ripped off left the naked wires exposed. This might be her chance! The tiny window and the door being closed, the room plunged into almost total darkness. Shlomo finished with a groan of satisfaction and pulled out. Rachel turned quickly and made as if to touch him, they stumbled on the bed and she pushed an unaware and surprised Shlomo against the wall. His back touched the naked wires and he began to convulse. Rachel too got a shock but she quickly released him and found a towel by the bed. She pushed the dazed unresisting Shlomo with a folded towel against the wall, pressing him hard against the wires and electrocuting him–the towel insulating her.

The voltage in the place was the normal household one and not enough to damage a person seriously, but Rachel, with desperate strength, had pressed him to the source for much longer than a few seconds and made Shlomo helpless and black out. Sobbing from exhausted emotions, Rachel let go and Shlomo sunk from his sitting position on the bed.

'What now?' Rachel panicked in the dark. Should she escape? She had no clothes. She searched for something to cover her. Shlomo had ripped her clothes off and thrown them about. In the dark, Rachel heard Shlomo moan and the rustling of some movement. She frantically searched for her clothes, before he should revive. Her groping hands found a heavy object, Rachel recognized the object from former times. Shlomo, a former amateur body builder, had brought a set of dumbbells with him. Again, she heard some movement coming from the bed. Full of blind fear and aversion she moved towards the closed door, forgetting in her terror that it is locked. A groping hand grabbed her arm in the dark and held her like a vice. She stretched out her other hand and found the dumbbell and struck at him blindly with all her strength, she felt it strike, all her frustrations fear and hatred were in her blows; once, twice . . . a third time . . . till he let go.

Suddenly all became deathly quiet, no more moans or movement. Rachel dropped the dumbbell and found the window. She opened it and light came in from outside. Leaving the tiny window open to see better she looked at Shlomo. He lay on his side, sprawled on the floor. She saw his back, red and raw from the contact with electricity. His head lay in a shadow and a pool of blood. She gasped in horror and almost fainted. What had she got herself into! Was Shlomo dead? Had she killed him?

Rachel spent some time moaning in self-pity. Eventually she took hold of herself and found her torn clothes. She put them on, whimpering, her hands shaking. She rushed to the door and found it locked.

The key!

She now remembered: The key hung around Shlomo's neck. She could not possibly undo the knot, she must cut the thong. Gingerly she approached the inert naked body, making a detour around the pool of blood. Shlomo, as many others, had brought sheets and kitchen utensils with him to Sinai. Rachel finally found a knife and released the key. Once outside she had the presence of mind to padlock the door. Then she remembered the open window. She entered again, shuddering and closed the window with its bolt. Locking the door for the second time, she ran all the way to the tattoo parlor.

Alex, waking up alone in the morning, felt not too concerned. Rachel, as well as himself, had an open relationship, but the nights she stayed away were few and far apart. A Bedouin waiter brought him breakfast from the nearby restaurant and Alex opened shop. He had no customers and idled the time away. Later, looking around, he did not see Shlomo sitting at his usual place in front of the Chabad house. Alex and Akiva did not speak to one another or Alex might have asked him about Shlomo.

Alex's relative peace shattered when Rachel arrived in tears and tattered clothing, her face swollen and discolored from the blows she had received. She sobbed and could not speak. "What happened?" But she appeared hysterical.

"Rachel, what happened?" He got no answer. Alex closed his shop and led Rachel to their place in the back. He made her a cup of coffee. Sipping the hot drink calmed her. Eventually she grew more cohesive.

"Alex, I'm in shit trouble."

"Did some sick bastard attack you?" He had already guessed so from her appearance.

"My fucking husband, Shlomo."

Outraged, Alex burst out. "How dare he?! This is the limit. I'll show him a thing or two."

"Ha!"

"What?"

"He is dead."

"What!!"

"I killed him."

He almost exclaimed 'what' again but stopped himself just in time. Rachel was not kidding, she looked like hell. "Talk to me, what happened?"

She told him, between sobs and gasps ending her story, "I could not stop . . . I hit him again and again . . . when he did not move . . ."

He held her in his arms tightly, and felt the stirrings of dismay. Rachel was in deep trouble, maybe they both would be. "He might have killed you, you had to defend yourself."

"He would never . . ."

"What are you saying?"

"What use am I to him . . . dead!"

Alex collected himself, he must help her, whatever the cost. "Where is he now?"

"In his place."

He controlled his impatience. "Right, and where would that be?"

"On other side."

"We have to go there and clean up."

"Never!"

"Rachel, a death is something no one overlooks. The authorities will find his body, he is your legal husband and they will find you and get the story out of you. You might be charged with murder . . . or maybe manslaughter. Do you understand!"

Rachel began to sob heavily. She understood.

Alex took control, he realized that only firm decisiveness would get them anywhere. "Rachel, clean up, take a shower and change your clothes! Eat, drink. We are going there, you have to show me the place."

"Not your business, Alex . . . I go . . .l eave . . . You never see me again."

"Rachel!"

"I go away."

Alex did not want to be a hero. Why should he to get involved with her troubles, best she should leave. Rachel would land on her feet, she always did. Embarrassed of his feelings he subdued them. They were lovers and buddies, he owed it to her . . . he owed this to himself.

"Don't talk nonsense. We will get out of this."

"We?"

"Yes we!" He made Rachel drink and eat a pitah with humus; she showered and changed her torn clothes. "Let's go," Alex said, "time may not be on our side."

"I can't go inside," Rachel moaned.

"We'll see."

Rachel showed him the area, but she was not sure of the exact location; Shlomo had dragged her to the place and she had not looked around. Later escaping, she ran away as fast as she could, not paying attention to her surroundings. There were rows of hastily built cabins all looking alike. They wandered around. There were some people about and one fellow chuckled amused, "Can't find your place eh."

"They look all the same to us," Alex retorted.

Then Rachel saw the taxi. She knew the car from before. "There!" she pointed. Shlomo would naturally park his car next to his place. They approached; Rachel had locked the door to Shlomo's cabin, but had forgotten the key in her former torn clothes, which she had left in the tattoo place. Alex barely controlled himself; frustrations, anxiety, and apprehension played their part in him. "Goddammit." He ejaculated. They would have to return for the key. They walked silently back, they might have had much to talk about, but were occupied with their thoughts.

Rachel regretted her actions, she should have escaped while he lay dazed and not diddled around. He had kidnapped her and raped her, and she had killed him in hatred and fear of him, but her life had not been in danger. Now she would be charged with murder. Could they maybe get rid of the body? How? Sink him in the sea or bury him. She shivered at her own thoughts. Then she remembered his car. How could they get rid of it? What a mess.

Alex had similar feelings and almost identical thoughts. He certainly did not feel happy in being involved, but he felt determined to solve the problem one way or another, as an accessory to the crime he too would be implicated.

They arrived at their destination. Rachel did not enter. Alex unlocked the door. In the dark he switched on the light, an instinctive motion. No light. He opened the window to let some light in, as he did so he heard a weak groan. Alex froze, horror and terror played amok with his feelings, a tremor passed through his whole body. Then the sound repeated itself, the open window had moved on its hinges. Alex's eyes not yet used to the dim light inside made out a shape lying on the floor. Had he moved? Shaking, he approached the man on the floor, putting his ear close to Shlomo's mouth. He could not be sure, but Shlomo may still be breathing.

Alex placed his ear on the fallen man's chest, he heard no heartbeat. Just then Shlomo seemed to groan again, but so weak, that if Alex had not been near he would not have heard him.

Had it been a groan, or some kind of a bodily function? Alex did not know. His eyes had accustomed themselves to the indoors by now. He looked around for the first time noticing the pool of blood from Shlomo's head, then he stared: Shlomo's head looked bashed in, the top a mess of broken skull and brain. The man would not live. No way. He ran out to Rachel, pale in the face and almost retching. "He is still alive!"

"Oh my God!"

Alex sucked in the air, "Not for long."

"What shall we do? Hospital?"

The nearest hospital was in Eilat, a four to five hours' drive. "Rachel, I saw him, nothing can save him. His brains are leaking out."

"Oh, my dear God!" Rachel began to sob heavily. "What have I done," she repeated, "What have I done!!"

Alex had considered their options, but due to the horrifying circumstances, his thinking processes were not functioning at their best. He made a giant effort: "We have to bury him, far in the desert where he won't be found and remove every trace of him from his room."

"Where?"

"We'll look at the map, I'll find a place."

"But he is not dead."

A family group with two children passed by, making eye contact greeted them shortly. The outside world continued on its way as usual, Alex and Rachel felt isolated. "We cannot remain outside for so long," Alex said promptly.

"I cannot go inside."

"I will cover him up."

"But he may still be alive!"

Alex lost his cool, "Well what do you want me to do, kill him?"

They entered, bolting the door. Rachel tried not to look at her inert former husband. Alex, crouching above him, could not make out any breathing or heartbeat, but felt too shaky to be sure. They began their work of cleaning up and packing all of Shlomo's possessions some of which she remembered from their life together. Even with the small window open, the inside of the room remained too dark to do a proper job, and they dared not open the door. They had to step around the pool of blood and they took care not to touch the open wire that had electrocuted Shlomo. Alex checked Shlomo again and covered him with one of his sheets, saying a silent prayer. 'God forgive me for what I do'–forgetting that he did not believe in a deity

"There must be a fuse somewhere," he said aloud to Rachel and went outside. The light blinded him at first. He found the cable which led him to an old-fashioned fuse–of the kind which is pulled apart to disconnect. Inside again he touched the live wire carefully, then connected the wires, covering each with the torn insulation and plugged in the fuse. Back inside, he turned on the switch. "Bingo," he emitted . . . trying to lighten the atmosphere, "And there was light."

They found Shlomo's car keys.

"The car? What do we do?"

"I don't know, if we sell the car to the Bedouins it will be found and we cannot hide a car in the desert for long . . . I know! We just leave the car somewhere; some Bedouin will take it . . . the car cannot be connected to us."

"That taxi is worth a lot of money."

"Our lives are worth more."

With extreme distaste, Alex wrapped Shlomo's bashed head in a plastic bag. They took turns in fetching water from a tank nearby, but, after the first time, Rachel refused to remain alone with the dead man. She fetched the water and poured the bloody rosy water out, away from their place. In time, Rachel escaped to a shop, got them pitahs with humus, and bottled mineral water. They had little appetite and worked all day.

When they finished, Shlomo had been rolled in a sheet and put in the trunk of his car, the place emptied of his belongings and packed into two of his suitcases also in his car. Night had fallen and they were emotionally and physically exhausted. They forced themselves to continue with their program. They wiped the room clean of fingerprints and left the door padlocked behind them, leaving the car by its place locked.

They were about to enter their tattoo parlor when Akiva accosted them, forgetting they were not on speaking terms.

"Have you seen Shlomo? He has not been here all day."

Rachel hid from him, she did not want him to see her face.

Alex answered him, "No, we are taking some days off."

Once in their beds, they could not sleep, the two discussed what they would have to get done. "It's best we bury him during the day, we use his car. Car lights are a dead giveaway in the night," Alex said.

"Tomorrow?"

"Of course."

"With his bags?"

"Yes . . . no! We should sink them in the sea."

"Why?"

"The desert preserves things, in the sea they disappear."

"Dump him in the sea then,"

"We would be seen carrying a body, bags are different."

"Alex, you've been good to me."

"Who else have I got. We are together in this."

"You want sex?"

"Are you kidding? Rachel, you're wasted. Can you even mention sex?"

"Men can always fuck." She touched him and soon had him erect. "Fuck me."

Alex felt some guilt. "Not in your state."

"I don't mind . . . for you." She pulled him into her.

Worn out as they both were, they had quick sex, Rachel, in giving herself to him, had an emotional upheaval; Alex really and truly loved her, he would risk his future for her. She found herself gasping in the throes of an orgasm. Alex poured himself into her. "I don't believe this." He panted when they finished. Finally, they fell asleep. They did not sleep soundly, the horror of the past event, inflicting itself on them. Rachel whimpered in an interrupted sleep, Alex put his arms around her and their total exhaustion finally caused them to get some rest.

The morning awoke them with its difficulties and quandaries. They had a crisis situation to deal with. Alex studied a map. "We should get to St, Catherine and from there take the Abu Rudies road, a lonely narrow road and far enough, there seem to be side paths which we can use as far as the car can go. Then we have to carry him to an isolated place and bury him. The whole thing will probably take us all day."

"His bags?"

"We take them with us in the car, but we won't bury them."

They were amateurs and forgot about shovels to dig with. Asking around in Dahab would cause suspicion to fall on them. However, there were many building sites, as new rooms were being constructed daily. Alex remembered seeing those around. The workers at the end of the day simply left their tools on the spot, as they were of no use to anybody else. "We will have to wait for night and steal at least one shovel," Alex said.

"Waste a whole day?"

"A change of plans, we dump his bags today, tomorrow we make the trip to bury him."

For once they planned well, forcing Shlomo's smaller bags into Alex's bigger ones, another bag held some large stones–three bags in all. They hired a boat with a small motor and headed straight east in the direction of Saudi Arabia. The Bedouin asked no questions, assuming the bags contained diving gear, cameras and food. The sea appeared calm.

The Red Sea is a part of the Syrian-African rift and they were afloat in the broadest and deepest part. About three kilometers out, they took out the inner bags, added stones to them and dropped them into the sea. They returned with the same three, now empty, bags. Emotionally strained, they rested. Late at night, they took a shovel from a building site and went to the car with the body inside, still standing untouched by Shlomo's hut. During the day, the hot desert sun had heated the car. The body in the trunk had already begun to decompose and smelled. A few dogs, lured by the scent slunk around, scratching the trunk trying to get in. The shovel chased them away.

"We cannot leave the car like this," Alex said.

"We should start now."

"It will soon be morning anyway."

Taking food and much water with them they set about to execute their plan, leaving the key of the empty room in the padlock for the Bedouin owner to think that Shlomo had left normally. Shlomo had kept his taxi full of fuel.

Inside the car the smell of the corpse made itself felt, but driving with the windows open let the cool night air flow in. Rachel tied a handkerchief to her face. They drove for some hours and it grew light when they reached St. Catherine and entered the Ras Abu Rudies road. The found a passable track leading into the mountains and took it. Alex drove very carefully, the last thing he wanted was to get stuck in nowhere with a dead body in the car. At a suitable distance from the road, Alex stopped the car.

"Here is where the fun begins," he joked trying to make them feel better. Rachel carried the shovel and some water while Alex with a grimace of distaste shouldered Shlomo's dead body. They had already entered the Western side of Sinai and there were patches of sand in between the boulders. Alex began to dig. Morning had passed quickly and the sun grew hot. Alex encountered stones under the top soil and had to shift the area of his dig accordingly. Rachel helped to dig. Finally, a grave had been dug. Alex rolled Shlomo in.

They closed the grave and rested after the strenuous work. While they had been digging they had not paid attention to their surroundings. They were enveloped by a sudden eerie silence. The ragged mountains nearby looming to great heights towered over them as if ready to fall down. They did not speak, staring at the grave. Alex tried to hide the signs of their digging.

Silence.

"Shouldn't we say a few words?" Alex broke the quiet talking in a low tone.

"You do it."

I didn't know him well."

"Kadish?"

"I'm not the praying kind, I don't know any words."

Rachel stood by the mound. She said, "I'm sorry, I killed you."

Silence.

"You were a real asshole."

"Say something nice," Alex encouraged her.

Rachel tried, "He worked long hours . . ."

"Go on."

"He was a tightfisted mean bastard."

"Something nice," Alex reminded her.

"Well he was. Who are we talking to anyway?"

"To ourselves. Let me try."

Alex cleared his throat and gulped a drink of water. "Yisgadal veyiskadesh shmey rabo . . ." He could not remember more and paused. "He was a man born of woman, a human being . . . good or bad, he was a . . . man," Alex ran down, "God in heaven have mercy on him." He said quickly: "Let's get out of here."

Returning, they got rid of the shovel at the same building site where they had got it from and cleaned the car thoroughly, even wiping it for fingerprints. They left it on the outskirts of the village, locked. Whoever took the car would have to break in, which suited them fine. Later they would throw the keys into the sea. They had done all that could possibly be done, and they felt the satisfaction of a well-done job. The following days continued as usual, Alex opened his parlor and Rachel remained inside their room more than she did before. They both felt that they lived at the edge of a precipice which might crumble under their feet at any moment. A week passed with nothing much happening.

Akiva, their neighbor, came over again. "Have you seen Shlomo?"

"We are not the ones to seek him," Alex pointed the obvious out.

"He did not leave, some of his belongings are in his room. He intended to return here." Akiva appeared suspicious.

"Why ask us?" Rachel said.

He did not answer.

"Maybe he went for a trip and will return," Alex suggested.

"Without saying a word?"

Alex dared, "You should find the authorities and inform them." Akiva might do so anyway.

Another week passed and then another. The routine and habits of their daily life asserted themselves slowly but surely.

Shlomo had a large family, four sisters and five brothers, all except one married with children. After a month of no communication from him, they went to the police and put him down as missing. They learned that the Eilat police had been informed of the fact by one Akiva. "Then why has nothing been done?" his sister asked angrily. "The police person doing the filing, had not been sure, your brother might have simply left."

Shlomo's clan were all fierce and aggressive personalities and succeeded in badgering the police authorities to send an Inspector to Sinai and find him. Inspector Frankel, all called him Frankel by his surname, a sandy haired individual with glasses and a pale complexion first interviewed Shlomo's large family. Then he arrived at Dahab and interrogated Akiva, checked Shlomo's room and his belongings. He came to Rachel and Alex with many questions.

"We want nothing to do with him." Alex had instilled in Rachel the importance of not talking in the past tense.

"When did you see him last?"

"I don't really remember, a month or two maybe, he sat on his chair by the Chabad house, annoying Rachel."

"Why would he want to do that?"

"He wanted her back."

Frankel turned to Rachel. "Do you know where he lived?"

"In the Chabad house."

"Did he have another rented place from before?"

"What did Akiva say?"

"I'm asking you."

"I have no idea."

"Did he come in a car?"

Rachel volunteered, "We had a car in Ashkelon. The taxi."

"Did you see his car here?"

"No."

"There were bad feelings between you and your husband."

"Very bad."

"In fact, you ran away from home a few times."

"Yes, common knowledge."

"Did he accost you at any time?"

"He sat and stared at me."

Frankel had got similar answers from Akiva. As Frankel very well knew, the best lies are close to the truth, but try as he would he got nowhere. He then used up much energy in trying to find out where Shlomo had rented a room, Akiva did not know, except that it must have been on the other side of the village. Frankel, walking from place to place, questioned the Bedouin owners. Shlomo's room had been rented since a few times, and no one remembered him or his room. He dug up zilch. Tourists come and go. The car too seemed to have vanished into the desert. There is no registration in Sinai. Frankel then searched in Israel, but the man had disappeared.

The year passed and Akiva ended his contract, packed his things, and left. The Chabad house had not been a success and it had been decided not to renew the place. Alex and Rachel were not sorry to see him leave. A candy store opened instead. The memory of Shlomo faded slowly from their minds, as time passed, and it was business as usual.

Akiva had been a year in Sinai, but had not been aware of the miracles of nature around him. The broad, open, and almost endless spaces, the ragged mountains forced and torn from the depth of the earth by its pressure; the sea and its unique wonderful marine life . . . all those meant little to him. Akiva loved his books, their contents a miracle of knowledge, wisdom and insight . . . what more does a person need? Returning to his place in Jerusalem, he reopened his shop, but he felt restless and grew easily irritated.

Many tourists visit Jerusalem, Jews and non-Jews alike. One stormy day a woman entered his shop; she had a fresh vitality about her. Clothed from head to foot, her head covered by a wig, showed her to be of religious persuasion. Suddenly, Akiva remembered the nude females in Dahab. He looked at her fingers–no wedding ring. Outside the rain poured and the wind howled. The shop felt warm and cozy. Akiva led her to the heating and helped her with her coat. He made her a cup of herb tea. The lady remained, waiting for the rain to cease. They talked getting acquainted.

In the Abu Rudies area, a group of permanent hungry desert jackals prowled, their sharp sense of smell had identified a whiff of carrion and followed the trace to its source; a buried corps in a shallow wind eroded grave. They dug in the sand with their paws and pulled a decaying carcass out. Their gnawing hunger soon made quick work of it, tearing a few rotting rags away and leaving the bones to bleach in the desert sand. Months passed, the seasons changed. It can rain in the desert. A flash-flood in the area washed any remains away. More time passed and a shepherd, led by his dogs, came upon the bones. Sometime later, he informed the authorities.

The local army bulletin in Ophira contained a news item of some interest. The remains of a dead body had been found, the skull bashed in. The sun-bleached bones left no means of available identification. Forensic science had it that the bones were two years old and might be connected to a person said to have been missing for those years. The police had been notified and Inspector Frankel renewed his old case. He learned that Akiva had married an American lady tourist and was living with her, his son and their daughter in Miami, in the United States. He wrote him a letter and received a polite letter in return. Akiva had no new information to give him and he wanted nothing more to do with the affair.

Neither Alex nor Rachel had seen the army dispatch. Again, Frankel drove to Dahab to talk to the couple. "Yes, of course they remembered Shlomo."

He came to the point: "Bones have been found in the desert, two years old."

"Two years?"

Frankel gave Rachel a sharp look. "I understand that your husband is missing for that same period?"

"Are they . . . my husband's?"

"Probably."

Alex interfered. "You should send them to his family for proper burial."

"Have you two ever been to Abu Rudies?"

"We have taken three or more trips in the last years, we might have passed there."

"Do you have a car?"

"No, we hired a taxi."

"Can I talk to the man who rented it to you?"

"You mean the taxi driver. Which one? The last one? I have no idea, some Bedouin. I do not know his name."

Frankel surrendered this line of investigation. "The bones were buried near Abu Rudies, and the skull broken by blows to the head. He was murdered and buried." Frankel studied their faces, but saw no sign of any guilt-like disturbance, it had been two years.

"My God!" Rachel exclaimed.

"Bedouins?" Alex asked.

"Shlomo might have gone on a trip," Rachel observed.

"Alone and without mentioning it to anyone? Very unlikely. What can you tell me about the last time that you saw him?"

"Well it's been some time . . ." They repeated their former story.

Frankel left, he had not expected to find any new information, but he had done his duty and tried. Alex and Rachel did not seem the kind of people to commit a murder, he thought, but who could tell? In the course of his investigations, he had met many unlikely incidents and he felt only too aware that the heart has few rules.

A human had been killed, murder, manslaughter, or self-defense. Life is not divided into categories. The broad wide desert can ingest anything in its stride. The winds will blow and the sun will rise and set, the seasons arrive and depart, but the greatest secrets of all are those in our hearts.

THE END

THE CALL OF THE DESERT

The Jewish community in Alexandria, Egypt, is an ancient one. This same society had been around and isolated for centuries, with a dwindling genetic pool which had caused some of Rita's older cousins to have poor eyesight and a weaker immune system and had forced them to spend more time with doctors than they all would have liked.

Rita's mom had fallen for a foreigner, an Englishmen, and eloped with him. Rita remembered her parents quarreling from her early childhood: her dad being more broadminded and much easier going than her mother. Eventually, he had returned to England. Rita's mother, not wanting to face the accusations and ridicule of her family, had left with her daughter for Israel. A distant relative had found them a moderately cheap apartment in south Tel Aviv. They lived on the second floor in above a row of shops. "Mom, why isn't father with us?" Rita would ask about her dad.

"You might have your dad to thank for your health, but not for much more," her mother would often–somewhat sarcastically–mention to her, but did not answer her question.

Rita's mom, notwithstanding her own romance and elopement, wanted her daughter to grow up in a strict environment and sent her to a religious school where girls and boys were taught separately. The school, and others of its kind, being the result of political coalition pressures, were conservative vestiges of former periods, and as Rita would much later admit, amounted to an educational outrage. The basic subjects were taught, but the real emotional emphasis had been given to religion and its literature and dogma, which would influence Rita's later life. Religion takes its notions from a much higher source than democracy or governments with their laws, and is not as flexible–but eternal and irrevocable. The same uncompromising attitude can worm its way into the souls of people who have been subjugated to the doctrines and may be expressed in matters of daily life, whether they are aware or not. Her future husband would turn out to be such a person.

In her class, Rita had been the first to develop breasts and have her period, and she became the envy of her mates. But in later years she had grown to be one of the tallest and largest in her class and had learned to face and ignore the unmerciful jibes and ridicule of her peers about her person. Soon, finding out that what had made the girls mock, often caused the boys to drool, she had many clashes with her mom over her attire, which her mother often thought too revealing.

"Rita, pull down your shirt, your belly button is showing."

"But mom, all the girls go like that now."

"This is disgusting. I won't have you walk around like . . ." She did not want to say prostitute. "Like a low person, a slut."

"Why can't I dress like the rest?"

"Because you can get pregnant before you know it."

Her mother, remembering her own mistakes, tried hard to make sure her daughter would not repeat them.

At eighteen, Rita had been wooed ardently and had married early to enable her to escape her mom and the mandatory army service. She had large features; each, when taken separately, may have seemed huge in size, but when put together accentuated her personality and made her comely and almost beautiful. She did not know what Gabai–her husband–saw in her and would often ask him, "What do you see in me?"

"A good wife. Large enough for two." He could be boisterous at times, with a rough humor.

"Is that all?" She needed love, affection, respect.

"Now don't start that all over again."

She knew herself to be a large woman and detested the words *big* and *large* with all their many shades of meanings and synonyms. Friends and relatives (but not Gabai) wanting to be tactful, had frequently applied those to her, and as such, life had dealt out its share of minor and not so minor troubles. Clothes which fit and looked nice were much harder to procure, and when a sale was in progress, her size appeared to have vanished from the shelves or hangars.

If Rita, perhaps not as fully aware as she should have been, had looked forward to finding more measure of personal liberty in her marriage. . . . She soon found out otherwise.

Her husband, Gabai, a schoolteacher, later to become the principal, had arrived from Iraq as a baby with his parents and had firm ideas and opinions, together with a chip on his shoulder. A woman's place is in her home. He feared and hated intellectuals of any kind and would often berate them.

Being himself born in a community which had escaped from daily persecution in an Arab country, Gabai hated all Arabs and wanted them out of Israel, but did not like the Europeans either (Ashkenazi as they were called), and in derision, at home, he would call them so, emphasizing the Nazi part of the term. They gave themselves airs and were snobs. They thought themselves better than others. In his home, he laid down the law as an overriding despot, often finding fault with his wife's way of running things, and when his will was not done would shout, rave, and occasionally turn to violence. The food had to be ready exactly on time and the place had to be kept spic and clean. At first, she tried to point out to him how his behavior was Levantine, just like the Arabs he so hated and would goad him to extremes. Gabai often found fault, hurting her by his sarcastic choice of words.

Her mother had badgered her, but Rita had never been hit since early childhood. She felt upset, insulted and then livid with anger, but had learned in her youth to control herself from jeers and abuse and kept her anger bottled up inside. She used the public library frequently as an outlet for her frustrations, and she read romances and poetry, while Gabai mocked her preferences.

"Do you have to read that romantic trash?" he would begin.

"I happen to like them."

He tore the book from her hands. "This is translated, is your own language not good enough for you?"

"I read what I can get from the library."

"Don't they have any books for women? Why not find a treatise on running a household?"

"I had to read those at school."

He tried to tear the book in half. "This is garbage." The book would not tear, so he tore some pages out in anger. "Are you trying to be an intellectual?!"

Rita knew better than to answer his question. She too raised her voice, "We shall have to pay the library for your action."

He slapped her." You are not to go to that library. I will not have it."

The argument continued into the night.

A child had been born to them, a girl, named Aliza, after his grandmother, and Rita totally occupied herself with nursing.

When Aliza grew older, her parents found an even larger stage for conflict. Gabai, being a disciplinarian, believed in molding characters from an early age, while Rita, much more lenient, tended to let her daughter's character develop with much less interference. Rita had secretly begun to use contraceptives to prevent herself from having any more children.

This state of affairs dragged itself on, mainly by inertia, for almost two decades. Rita's mother had died and she had never heard from her father. Feeling too weak and impotent to alter her situation, she had become resigned as the years passed by. When her daughter grew up, Rita confided in her and they joined forces. Eventually, Aliza escaped from an unhappy home to marry. Rita, after some more years, with her daughter's support and help, had at last gathered the courage to finally confront her husband about wanting a divorce.

Gabai had been surprised and infuriated, still not able to perceive her as an independent person, apart and free from his will. He had shouted and raved, then he argued and even complained: "How dare you make such an important decision by yourself?

"I want to live my own life!" would be her constant retort.

"Divorce will affect us both, not to mention our daughter and grandchild."

"I want a divorce, it is my life," she repeated stubbornly, "Aliza supports me."

"You have turned her against her father."

"You yourself have done so."

"If you leave, you will get nothing from me."

"We'll see about that."

They had been in the middle of a bitter struggle over their common property and had almost come to blows, but Rita had been advised by her daughter and had a defensive spray ready. She took it out of her bag and shakily threatened him: "If you touch me I will use that spray."

He cursed her bitterly: "You fat pig, I should be glad to be rid of you."

He backed off edgy and irritable. Rita had never stood up to him before. He left angrily, slamming the door.

Half an hour later, he was killed in a car crash. Rita had known him to be an impudent and rash driver, sometimes overtaking and dangerously bypassing vehicles on the road. She sustained some guilt but felt more relieved than sorry and went through the motions of mourning.

At the age of forty-five, she finally tasted the pungent taste of liberty, and at first, had been at a loss. Having a voluptuous figure and a narrow waist, she liked to emphasize those by dressing up. Rita, the mother of a married daughter with a child, did not think of herself as a grandmother yet. Not being in her first bloom anymore, she felt it imperative to find the right kind of clothes and show off her good points. She encountered just one store with large measures in her area, and it did not have a great selection. When looking at herself in the bathroom mirror, she would frequently gaze at her breasts with some degree of pride, they were pear shaped and not too large, and they sagged much less than what might be expected from a woman her age

Altering her choice of clothes to less severe and more modern ones had been daringly satisfying, but the years of her marriage had worn and eroded her will and self-image, which had never been much in the first place. Religious convictions had been hammered into her, and those helped and kept her from sinking into a sea of indecisions and despair.

A new plague awaited her. One morning she awoke from a nasty unthinkable dream in a cold sweat: She had found herself in a strange place with a strong need to relieve herself and there were no toilets around. Searching, she had come to some public ones with no doors. The toilets were grimy and had no seats, the floor disgustingly wet and filthy. Finding it difficult to choose the least soiled, but having no choice, she squatted to defecate, and, to her great shame, a group of people passed by, looked at her, and left derogatory comments.

Awaking, she pushed the dreadful horrid dream away. A few weeks later, the dream returned and so began a series of reoccurring similar nightmares to disturb her sleep. Burning with shame from one of those nasty dreams, she would mentally shudder in disgust mortification and indignity, upset and infuriated: 'What in God's heaven were those dreams? Everyone goes to the toilet to do their business. Why should I have to put with them, this is outrageous!' However, those dreams were not frequent enough to trouble her at her daily routines.

Gabai's timely death had saved her from a divorce settlement and from losing more than half their assets. Rita had enough for her needs without having to find work. Visiting her daughter and granddaughter once a week and not having a car or driver's license, Rita would take the bus to the main station. Some waiting and one hour's drive would get her to Ashkelon, the town where her daughter, grandchild, and husband where living, then another change to a local bus would get her to their home.

Rita always had a minor problem finding a place to sit on the long-distance bus. Knowing herself to be a large person, the seats being economy size, she could not but crowd the person sitting next to her. Passengers often will put their bags and luggage on the empty seat next to theirs and it irked her to ask a passenger to remove his or her bag.

Walking along the center of the bus searching for a likable place, as all the seats beside the windows were taken, she saw an empty space, apparently larger than the usual, next to a man looking out of the window. She sat down and they acknowledged each other with a nod. Evening had fallen. The bus started on its way and the lights dimmed. There were no reading lights and one hour can be a long time to keep silent. The person next to her smiled, and a controlled and polite conversation began. Rita mentioned visiting her daughter and family, and he admitted to being on his way to meet his girlfriend. In the dim light of the bus he looked an older person, and her curiosity got the better of her.

"You are not married?"

"Divorced."

Their conversation lagged somewhat at first, they mentioned their families briefly, but as the talk progressed, Rita found it comforting to talk to a stranger in the dark. Her unhappy marriage and divorce were brought up in very general terms. He too revealed having three children and one grandchild already . . . and claimed to be on very good terms with his ex-wife. To her, a strange notion, and she had wanted to ask him about it, but the bus had reached its destination and ended their talk.

The next week they met again. A whim of providence made them travel frequently on the same day and time. Being now acquainted, they sat next to each other. Their talk became more intimate, and she mentioned her shyness when taking a seat in the bus: "I feel uncomfortable on forcing myself into a seat next to someone else."

"Let me tell you my little secret," he said. "When I see a likable person approaching, I always move to make extra room."

"Am I a likable person?"

"I hope so."

"But I take up more than my share of the space."

"I don't mind, in actual fact I enjoy the closeness." His hand touched her thigh, which pressed into his own, and he revealed unashamed. "I moved aside and compressed myself on purpose, to induce you to sit down beside me."

"You shouldn't." Meaning his hand on her thigh.

"Why not?" He did not remove his hand.

"Are you making a pass at me?" The man, a stranger, made her bold. She would never have dared to talk so bluntly to any acquaintance of hers.

"What is so wrong with making a pass?"

She did not answer immediately, not having thought about sex in years. When Gabai had been alive, sex had become a habit and a duty. He used to do his thing and never took too long. Rita had almost forgotten what the sex had been like in their early days and hedged, "It is not done. I don't even know your name!"

"Gil."

"My grandson is named Gil," she said surprised. "I am Rita."

"Good, so we have something in common already." His hand remained on her thigh and felt nice and comforting, but threatening in a strange unfamiliar way. In the dark inside the bus no one would notice and she felt relieved. Not wanting any unpleasantness, she let his hand remain.

"You are going to your lady friend," she reminded him.

"I know . . . life is meant to live and to live fully, not to diddle around. I shall do my best not to regret anything when I die."

"What do you mean?"

"I have had affairs, some lasting, others not and I regret nothing."

Rita listened amazed as he told her about his female friends and the sex they had. There seemed to be more than a few in his past. Not knowing how much to believe of his tales, a part of her wanted to tell him to stop his boasting, but Gil did not seem the bragging type. The person beside her appeared to be gentle, considerate and polite, and claimed persistently that she had missed out on life. A strange foreign notion to her: is not life meant to be lived according to rules and duty? Mainly, living had become a long haul. Rita had a religious upbringing; one obeyed the laws. She changed the subject, "Tell me more about yourself."

"I was born in Europe, my grandparents and aunt were exterminated by the Nazis. My parents escaped with me. They called me 'Goldchen' Gold. When I grew up I changed to Gil."

"What do you do?"

"I write for a weekly, appraisals, criticism. . . ."

He came from the very race her husband had despised. His hand had stroked her thigh as they talked. She resisted an impulse to spread her legs in the dark. A former discussion repeated itself with minor variations. "Don't," she said.

"Why not?"

"You make me uneasy."

"Sorry." Gil left off and Rita felt a tinge of disappointment. 'Did he have to be so compliant?' Automatically she subdued her feelings. No one forced her to sit next to him. Arriving earlier the next time might solve the problem, or not, an empty double seat might be available and he would probably choose to sit next to her. . . . What did all this nonsense matter? She thought irritably. "Why did you get divorced?"

He turned sideways to study her face in the very dim night-lights of the moving bus. "I could just say we were not compatible and would be correct . . . in general, but to get at specifics, I felt suffocated and constrained in my marriage. Life went on all around me and I felt as if I had retired at an early age . . . I felt something is missing and I did not want to give up so soon, I had to do more . . . live my life."

"Is that a reason for a divorce and ruining a family?"

"I had to regain my independence. I could do nothing else, I did not ruin my family, I still am a father to my children . . . and grandchild. Remaining together in marriage might have done us more harm than good."

"Was there another woman?"

"Yes."

"And you left her too?"

"I am not a bad person and please don't make me out to be one."

"My husband and I quarreled bitterly about our divorce, but you are on good terms with your ex."

"Not at first, but as the time passed we became friends, knowing and understanding each other better than our friends do, also we still had to take care of the children and all sorts of problems which cropped up from time to time. When my sons wanted to buy her a present for her birthday, they consulted me. I knew and told them what their mother liked. She married again, but I remained single."

The bus arrived at its destination and they parted.

The next time they traveled together Rita took care to be early. Arriving later, Gil stopped by her seat. "May I?"

People may sit wherever they chose on a bus. Making a place for him in silence, her face resolutely unresponsive, she could not deny him and maybe did not want to. The bus eventually began its journey. The lights dimmed. Undaunted by her attitude, he said.

"I have brought some pictures of my girlfriends," and pulled out a small package. He had even thought of bringing a tiny flashlight.

Curiosity did get the better of her and she looked at the pictures by its light. God in Heaven, they were all stark naked! No decent woman would let herself be photographed unclothed. They must be a sham. Then one of the pictures revealed Gil, unashamed in the nude, his penis visible and his arms around a woman as naked as she had been born. So, all his boasting had really been true! Rita flushed all over her body and felt her spine tingle. She covered the pictures with her hand and looked away.

"I don't want to see them." She handed him the pictures

"Those too are a part of life," he said taking the pictures. "Life is not meant to be held back."

Some of the women in the pictures were smiling. How could they expose themselves? Rita, puzzled and shocked, asked him. "Were you not ashamed?"

"Should I be? What is so wrong? God created us. Should we hide his work?"

Their conversation appeared to be in danger of turning into a philosophic discourse, which neither of them wanted. Rita remained silent for a while feeling puzzled and perplexed: The fact that there are actually people who did as they liked and threw off all reigns was beyond her imagination. All her life, others had told her what to do and how to behave, from mother and teachers to husband, all under the canopy of religion and tradition. What about herself? What were her rights as a human being?

Then Rita remembered her nasty dreams, could she confide in Gil who, after all was a brief, short-lived acquaintance, but an educated knowing person? An intellectual, the kind her husband had always criticized. He had shown himself to be kind and considerate, even with his strange different notions. After seeing those intimate pictures, she felt an urge to unburden herself. 'What is there to lose? If the worst came to the worst, there is always an earlier bus available.' Having a strong need to talk to someone, she began hesitatingly:

"I have those dreams . . ." She stopped.

"Bad ones?"

"Very."

"I have my share. Probably all of us do."

"No, I cannot talk about them."

"Shameful, embarrassing?"

"Extremely so."

"I must have had similar dreams once or twice. I find myself in a crowd . . . naked."

"What do they mean?"

"I can only tell you what I feel myself, alone and isolated . . . an outsider with special needs. You are not the only one, but you deny them in yourself and probably are ashamed. Most likely you are suppressing your own feelings . . . feelings everyone has and you are rejecting yourself in the process."

Rita did feel some truth in his words. "I have had a hard, difficult life," she explained, and told him more about her married life and husband, ending with, "I shouldn't be, but I am happy he is gone."

"You are not at ease with yourself and those dreams have brought it up."

"Then why are they unclear?'

"Because, you do not admit them, a part of yourself is tricking you."

Farfetched as his words sounded to her, she would remember them later. "What do you see in me?"

"I don't know. Yes, I do. A nice-looking woman being overlooked by herself . . . I see a life wasting away."

"I am a nice-looking woman?"

"Yes, definitely, hot passionate stuff."

"I am a large person."

"So?"

"I have trouble finding clothes."

"Who gives a shit?"

A chuckle escaped her. Of course, a man would say so. "You did move aside, creating a larger space for me to sit . . . when we first met."

"Yes."

They were silent for a while, and then he came out with it. "Next week, can we meet, get a motel or something?"

"What do you see in me?" she repeated.

"I see life, acting out our stuff, being ourselves."

"And afterwards? The consequences?"

"I don't know everything. Whatever happens. Are we not two adults? We should be able to do whatever we like."

His answers had not been wholly satisfactory to her. She had wanted him to talk about herself, her person, but he had talked generally about his views of life. However, she felt flattered, the man wanted her, no doubt, he wanted her badly. Somewhat reluctant and with many misgivings, she agreed to his proposal and they decided to meet, quickly arranging the details.

Later at home Rita deliberated . . . what had she let herself in for? Illicit relations were a sin in the eyes of God! What does one call them? An affair? No, never . . . not yet. A date, a meeting? Those terms sounded too silly. Would they have a onetime fling? The French word 'rendezvous' which seemed more apt, came to her mind, but there had been no romance; mainly curiosity, sex, and some excitement. Two elderly people meeting on a bus. She was a widow now, and could do as she liked. Still, an affair smelled to her of cheating. Having never been 'unfaithful' to her husband, she asked herself, 'Who am I cheating?' but had no answer, 'then why do I feel so ambivalent and upset?'

Blaming and second-guessing herself became her main course in the coming days. Rita had never indulged in her urges and passions. What on earth had made her agree to his proposal? Having an affair was not like her and not like her in character. Not a day passed in which the subject did not come up in her mind. What of future involvement and possible implications? Standing him up, too went against her nature, having promised to be at the selected place at the prearranged time, she intended to be there.

They met at the appointed time and spot. Rita appeared quiet and perturbed. To smooth things over they sat down to a cup of coffee in a nearby place. Gil began to talk, but she interrupted him with an outburst: "I cannot do this!"

"What? Why? I thought we had all settled." In his dismay, he stumbled over some words.

Rita herself did not have any answers. Having sex with him appeared too much trouble and strange for her, not being able to imagine or see herself in such a position, while not feeling too good about herself, she firmly repeated her former sentence. A kind of argument ensued, but Rita desperately clung to her statement. Gil, realizing a lost cause, finally backed off. "Okay, shall we still see each other?"

"Maybe."

"On the bus?"

"Probably."

"Can I kiss you?"

Hesitatingly, "Alright."

He sought her lips, but she gave him her cheek.

They parted. Rita, with mixed feelings, felt relieved, but also at a loss and miserable. Life suddenly seemed dreary. The next week Rita took an earlier bus and they did not see each other anymore.

The loss of her husband made her realize just how much of her life had depended on him and as a regular housewife she had taken him for granted. Gabai had taken care of all the finances and given her an ample weekly allowance. He had been an insufferable tyrant, but at least had not been a miser and had enabled her to put money aside for a rainy day. Feeling alone and abandoned, Rita actually found herself on occasions wishing for her departed husband, it came to her slowly and ironic how even a despot and a dominant depressing personality like his, might be better than none at all. Gabai had been a part of her life, for better and for worse and she missed him - something Rita would not have believed possible a few months ago.

When her daughter told her of a trip to the Sinai desert for a week and invited her to come along, she accepted eagerly. Aliza said to her, "In the evenings we want to spend some time alone, go to some discotheques and bars maybe, do some dancing, you won't mind babysitting?"

"Of course not."

"We leave in two days for Dahab."

"I'll come the night before then and sleep over."

"Right we can pack for the trip."

They had a station wagon with ample space for the three of them and her grandson Gil. The desert begins in Israel's south and continues all the way through Sinai to Egypt. At first looking out of the car's windows, Rita saw unending open spaces, in monotonous shades of gray or light brown, with little relief in color or shape, and occupied herself with her grandchild. As they advanced further south, mountain ranges began to appear and the road twisted and turned. They stopped at an observation point to rest and refresh. The view stunned them. The forces of nature had created raw deep gaps and peaks, jagged and ragged pinnacles and crevasses, fissures with crack like gorges, they projected and demonstrated brutal power, indifferent to humans.

Her son-in-law had been taking pictures of the scene. "God has created all this," she observed, "I wonder what we humans can mean to it."

"What it can mean to us seems more likely." He had thrown out a careless remark on the spur of the moment, but had made her reflect.

After some more hours driving they rested and crossed Eilat, the most southern point in Israel. Entering the Sinai desert Rita found the general contour had changed from gray to a dominant dark brown, the color of magma forced from the belly of the earth. The wild scenes were even more ragged then before and the red sea glittering like a jewel on their left could be seen at times. They rented two rooms at a hotel in Dahab, a former fishermen village at the edge of the Red sea, already grown into a tourist resort.

After they had settled down, Rita found herself with time on her hands. The change of scenery and the free atmosphere prevailing, encouraged her out of the hotel to wander and shop for trinkets, all much cheaper than at home. Wearing her new modest one-piece bathing suit under a thin dress (which, in a spirit of adventure, she had bought especially for the trip, but later had regretted as too revealing) she chose some hand–embroidered pillow cases and some painted tricot shirts and assorted knickknacks. Her eyes popped out as some people passed by, the women topless! Rita gaped, stunned.

The seashore at the center of the village was dotted almost side by side with restaurant places and folding chairs, mattresses couches and sofas to recline on or bake in the hot sun, if one so wished. Rita strolled along the beach and stared. Many of the women were topless, unashamed and chatting or laughing with some men. Some females and some men were lying on their front, backs to the sun, on spread out folding chairs with a throng as their only attire. They might as well be totally naked, had been her thought, their buttocks gleaming in the sun, and she had not even dared to take off her dress and walk around in her bathing suit. Hesitating, she pulled off her dress, feeling exposed and naked, but nobody knew her here. Relieved by the thought, she intended to enjoy the sun before it grew too hot.

They sat down to eat. "Let's have some local cuisine," her son-in-law said and ordered shrimps and seafood.

"I can't eat that," Rita said.

"There's not much else on the menu," Aliza observed. "Mutton, chicken, rice, eggs and chips . . . and of course salad and pitahs."

Rita chose eggs, chips, and vegetables. She would not touch the meat.

Unless one participates actively in one of the various water sports, which include games, bathing, snorkeling, or scuba diving and surfing, there is not much to do in Dahab except to get into the water or loaf on the beach. One can always shop, but shopping in Dahab has its limitations. If one is so inclined, a camel and its rider can be hired for a limited time, and there are small boats of all sorts for hire. Many people hang around in the coffee shops or bars–or sunbathe–and Rita found herself with time on her hands. The evenings were occupied with babysitting her grandchild, while the young parents spent time in the various nightclubs and bars, but the days were mostly hers.

She found herself wandering further and further past the outskirts of the small village. On the south side, a little arroyo-like pass spread out and led to a sandy hidden beach, tiny and totally deserted, but just large enough for a small group of people to bathe in and she had it all to herself. She visited the place daily and once or twice, in the spirit of the place, feeling very brave and daring, took off her bathing suit for a short while, the air and water on her bare skin made her feel renovated.

Her daughter and son-in-law had decided to take an overnight trip to the Saint Catharine monastery together with her grandson. Did she want to come along? The monastery lay in the center of the desert surrounded by mountains. Jebel Musa the mountain named after Moses, were many claim Moses to have received the

Ten Commandments, is nearby. They would be driving in their own car, as fuel was cheaper there.

Her son-in-law said, "Rita, the trip is a lengthy one, probably, four or five hours one way," he kidded, "if we don't get lost." Getting lost could always be a possibility even with maps.

'Not for me' Rita thought, she sensed they wanted to be by themselves and begged off. They would also have to drive back and the trip would be a long and exhausting one for her.

They left early morning so as to escape the later desert heat and Rita found herself alone. The morning had not yet heated up and her secret cove called out to her. She put a thin gown over her bathing suit and left. It did not take her long to reach her destination. As she approached, the noise of many voices calling out made themselves heard and reaching the place, she found two tents pitched there. To her dismay, a group of tourists had arrived and their guide had led them to 'her place' as she had thought of it. There were people about and they jabbered staccato in a foreign language.

Rita advanced and watched them nonplussed, undecided whether to retreat.

There were many other places on the way back to the village where she could bath.

She saw some of the people began to take off their clothes, quite a few were young, but others seemed her own age. Bellies and sagging breasts were revealed as she watched transfixed, amazed still deliberating undecided.

One person approached her, nude, his penis dangling, causing her to freeze on the spot, unable to move or think. The man spoke to her. It sounded like Spanish. He said, "Senhora" and something intelligible. Not seeing her react, the man repeated a sentence with some funny pantomiming, a real humorist, broad, with stocky legs and a mat of hair on his chest. Thick eyebrows and his features projecting good will. His clowning calmed her and Rita finally understood him to mean: 'Why are you not getting undressed, they were all going into the water.' His body language signaled to her an invitation to join them.

Suddenly and totally unexpected, a strange reckless feeling arose in her. Those were all complete strangers from another country. They could not even speak her language and she would never see them again. Why not? Nobody knew her here! Yes! Why, on earth not? Shivering with suppressed excitement, not thinking too much, her mind a blank, she found herself taking off her dress, then without too much hesitation, pulled off her bathing suit and placed her clothes on a nearby rock. Turning around, fully naked, hiding her genitals with her hands, while her arms covered her breasts, she half crouched, not daring to stand up straight.

"Magnífico. Bonito!" The funny man exclaimed, repeating himself a few times and jumping up and down on alternating legs, his penis swinging. It was impossible not to laugh. Rita, used to being taller than others, felt unsure of herself, but the man did not seem to mind. He stretched out his hand for her. Bashfully with beating heart and feeling revealed, she allowed him to take her hand, exposing her breasts, and they followed the group of people into the water. Rita hurried into the deeper sea until the tiny waves covered her up to her shoulders. There was safety in numbers and the many naked people in the water made her feel more at ease. Some swam around in goggles and snorkels, but most of the group of Spaniards frolicked in the water with each other.

The man with her pointed to himself. "Eduardo."

"Rita," she said and then blamed herself for not using her brains. There had been no reason to reveal her true name. Eduardo showed no inclination to leave her side. Another person seemed to have attached himself to her, a taller man with a mustache. They exchanged some sharp long sentences. They were actually arguing over her. Large as she felt herself to be, those men wanted her!

The other person pointed to himself and said to her, "Felipe." Rita nodded, being too shy to answer. Rita had a smattering of French and English and tried to converse, but by the looks on their faces, they did not comprehend. After some more futile efforts at verbal communication, they communicated basics with hand signs, pantomime and with much laughter. Rita understood. They admired her, their eyes were shining as they mimicked admiration and desire. The smaller one, Eduardo pressed his heart and made to give it to her, he made her feel secure.

"Israel," she said and pointed to herself.

"Lisbon, Portuguese," they said.

So those people were Portuguese, which made no difference. The rest of the group, all nude, were all flirting with one another in various ways. They played games, some of the women were on the men's backs and wrestled with each other, they fell in a heap into the water laughing and squealing.

Felipe touched her breast and said something very soft sounding. Rita pulled his hand away, but gently. The message seemed to be understood by both parties. When they got out of the water Rita felt exposed and hurried to her clothes. They all dressed and some of the people began to prepare food. Eduardo and Felipe motioned her passionately to remain and eat with them. They both stuck to her and would not let her go. Some of the other men and women studied her.

The group of tourists had not known each other from before and made her feel less of an outsider. Sitting down between her two new friends, they tried to teach each other words in their various languages. After the meal, the hot desert sun began to make itself felt. Her cool room in the hotel, with the possibility of a nap, had invitingly called out to her. As she got up to leave, Felipe and Eduardo too got up and Rita realized they did not want to let her get away. What now? The free and loose ways of the place seemed to affect her. Confused and having done the unbelievable today, the pictures Gil had shown her passed fleetingly through her mind.

A daring impulsive suggestion struck her. Why not?! It would be her first time not with her husband. 'What is so wrong in being natural? If sex is not natural than what is?' Her daughter and family would not be back till tomorrow and probably in the late evening. They would be alone until then and could do as pleased. In her befuddled state, Rita had not been capable of thinking much further. The hotel where she stayed had people coming and going all the time and they would not be noticed. Her urges and impulses took over. She nodded to her two men. "Come," she said in French, and repeated it in English.

They did not need to be told twice.

The three spent the afternoon and a large part of the night in her place, the men leaving only very early next morning, as their group would be moving on. Only then, still in bed, did Rita take stock of what had occurred. STD's did not seem a problem. They had all been family men. In the time they had spent together, they had talked and pantomimed about their children, their wives too. The smaller one mimicked a sour funny face one could not help but laugh at. The room was in shambles, they had not slept much. She had been voracious and the two guys had been swept up by their mutual passion. The smaller guy Eduardo had been insatiable and tireless. They had gone and would never be seen again. Good. Very good. Totally and happily exhausted, a tiny pucker of satisfaction came over her features. Late morning still found her asleep.

The rest of the trip passed uneventfully for Rita, her daughter, grandson and son-in-law returned enthusiastic and excited from the trip.

Her son-in-law cried. "We saw sights not often seen by mortal eyes. The view is unbelievable. . . ."

They continued telling her about their trip thrilled and eager. Rita nodded silently, smiling contently to herself. Later in the day doubts crept in. Had she transgressed in some way? Telling herself repeatedly they had harmed no one, did not do much to diminish a feeling of guilt. Her fling with those two had been against her religion, but why should this be so? Had they harmed anybody? The matter remained a puzzle to her.

Back at home, life went on its dreary routine. Once a week she would travel to see her family and grandchild, having changed the day so as not to meet Gil on the bus. After her rampage with the two Portuguese tourists, life seemed tame to her. Marriage had no appeal for her, she did not need another boss. Never again! Would the only alternative be loneliness?

Aliza had suggested, "Maybe you could find some work?"

"What can I do? I stay at home, mom. Who would hire me?"

" . . . Well you could watch over children."

"I have had enough of housework. I need to do something new."

Rita's life had changed, her inner dialogue with herself had altered whether to her liking or not, but Rita drifted along, day after day, the conflicts in her, effervescent and fermenting. Should she take a lover? She felt shocked to her core at the thought . . . unthinkable, out of the question! A lover? Would anyone want her? Yes, Gil had wanted her. A lover might be right for a short time fling, like with those two Portuguese, but would a lover fill her needs for a real long-term companionship? Rita had a lot of questions, many of them unacknowledged and none too well formulated.

On one of her visits, Aliza, for reasons of her own, had asked her to change her weekly visit back to her former day. Rita complied reluctantly, not wanting to meet Gil on the bus and took an earlier one. There had been no sign of Gil and a pang of regret together with some relief made themselves felt. What in heaven did she want? Not feeling sure of anything anymore, but annoyed and angry at herself, she firmly forced herself to think of other matters.

Then one night Rita found herself in a strange place under the open sky and a burning sun. She urgently needed to have bowel movement and wandered around searching for a place, there seemed to be no toilets or people anywhere near. Partly hiding between two boulders on sandy ground, she crouched to do her business when a group of tourists passed by with ribald shouts of encouragement. . . . The shame and embarrassment caused her to wake up in a sweat. Her former reoccurring dream had appeared again, but with a new twist. God, how those hateful dreams annoyed her!

Later in the day, her unpleasant dream wormed itself into her thoughts–recalling the sand, the heat and the boulders; it came to her that her dream had occurred in the desert! Rita had never been a great nature lover but she felt an unexplained and enigma-like longing to return to her secret cove. The thought came to her, 'Why not take another holiday?' Not having had much of those in her life. This time she would be alone, with no one telling her what to do. Did she not need to recuperate from her husband's death? Living in Sinai was cheap and she had the means. . . .

Thinking about a matter and actually doing something were different issues, and Rita dawdled. There had been some medical tests to get through, then an appointment with her dentist. The bank had also called her for some financial arrangements and her hair had to be done and etc. . . . . etc. Those were daily matters, but they kept her going and two whole months passed before she finally gathered the courage to act.

We do not always understand why or what we do. On one of her trips to her daughter's home, she told her, "I think of going north, to Tiberia, maybe for a holiday . . . two weeks or a month to have a good rest . . ."

"Are you ill?" Aliza asked concerned.

"I need a change. I do not feel so good. Your father's death has depressed me."

"But there was no love lost between you and dad. Where will you stay?"

"I don't know yet. I'll send you a postcard, or maybe phone."

"Have a good time, you deserve it," Aliza agreed.

Why had she lied? Never having done so before, she berated herself. Not being truthful to her own kin and family was not like her. She felt like a thief sneaking away on the bus southwards to the Sinai desert. Feeling some guilt, she prepared for the trip.

The trip to Dahab took the better part of a day. In Sinai, the busses are erratic, most people switching over to taxis, and as her cab reached its destination, Rita felt a surge of excitement and adventure. In Dahab, the span in the price range of rooms for rent is great. From two US dollars daily for four walls and a ceiling to a luxury four-star place, costing up to a hundred dollars a night. Rita chose less expensive accommodations somewhere in the middle of the price range. Again, she found herself alone, but keyed up and eager to meet and experience whatever might come her way.

The next morning, her impatience made her rush to her secret place and found it deserted. She bathed there and as once before, briefly took off her bathing suit and reminisced fondly. On the way back, a meal at one of the better restaurants satisfied her appetite, then off to her room for a nap. She spent the afternoon in another stroll among the many tiny shops and stalls. The evening found her in a disco, but there were only young people there and they looked at her curiously. She felt an outsider. The next few days grew into a replica of the first one.

Rita did not want to admit, but some boredom had set in. Nature did not interest her much, nor did snorkeling and the other water sports. Disenchanted and feeling let down had made her somewhat listless, spending much of her time in some of the many coffee places by the seaside, reclining on a low couch, nursing a drink and sometimes dozing off (a common sight in Dahab's seaside places).

"Have you been to the blue hole?"

Rita lifted her head. Two scuba divers with some gear were talking nearby.

"Too deep for me," the other said.

"Fantastic scenery. You do not have to dive the whole way down."

Rita addressed them. "Where is that place?"

"Not far, the Bedouins drive one there."

With nothing much else on her hands, she visited the place and sat in one of the many open huts listening to the scuba divers talking their lingo which she did not wholly understand. The blue hole turned out to be a cavern reaching deep under sea level and seemed a very dangerous spot to dive in. Bored, she paddled along the beach in the shallow parts of the Red sea.

A few more days and nights passed in the hot lazy routine of the desert. Rita could not know, but a youth much less than half her age had stalked her. He was one of three young delinquents who had got themselves to Sinai for some easy pickings of the tourists. They had run from Israel where they had taken some heat from the police and other authorities. One of the three had noticed her being always alone and elderly, he considered her a possible easy prey.

He said so to his buddies, "There is this old bitch, we should get to her place and find some real cash. She must be loaded."

"How do you know; did you make it with her?"

They all laughed. "Very funny. All old bitches have money. I've seen her around a few times, always single, she has three rings on her on each hand. The stuff around her neck alone should be a thousand at least."

"Where's her place?"

"She lives in a hotel, second floor. We can get in easily to her porch from outside." Then came a series of details and planning, ending with, "A piece of cake."

A heat wave had struck the area and the night had been a hot one. The air conditioner in Rita's room, which had never been at its best at all times, had broken down. Phoning the reception got only apologies in bad English. Finally, a man came up to her room, but could not fix the problem. The heat had not only been the only matter which prevented her from falling asleep.

Rita, a woman at her prime, now discontent and easily irritated, vent her frustrations on the reception, giving them hell, and finally two electric fans were brought up to her. She had rinsed herself with water twice already and the towels were moist. Fresh ones would arrive only in the morning when the cleaning people came. She hung them out to dry. Her nightgown stuck to her and pulling the flimsy fabric off, felt the fans distributing the tepid air on her skin, which did cool her a little. She touched herself, trying to overcome a guilty feeling. Rita had masturbated only very few times in her life and always unsuccessfully. Touching oneself was a taboo! Stubbornly she continued until she grew tired. At last she desisted and feeling uncomfortable naked, pulled her nightgown back on. At last she fell asleep.

A scraping sound awoke her, it came from the door leading to the porch, then stopped. After a while the noise started again.

"Who's there?" she cried.

The door jerked open and quickly shut, as three shadowy figures sprinted inside. Rita had just woken up from a sleep and felt terrified. Her futile struggles did not amount to much. Her nightgown tore. Her hands were held and a bag had been pulled over her head. She tried to shout for help, but the hotel night person, if there was one, probably slept by his desk. Then a piece of cold sharp metal pressed into her neck. "One more peep out of you and we cut you." She ceased her yelling. They manhandled her and tied her to a chair. Rita, terrified, tried to overcome her fear and think.

"I can see a boob!" someone snickered in Hebrew.

"Shut up. Let's find the stuff and get out of here."

They talked in Hebrew. Those were burglars! Plain thieves. Experiencing some relief, Rita struggled almost overturning her chair, but desisted, aware there was not much of value in her room, as the bulk of her money had been put in the hotel safe. 'Nothing is worth getting cut up for.' Her heart beat fast. Two guys ransacked her room, totally and ruthlessly breaking anything breakable, messing and overturning the furniture in their nervous endeavors to find articles of some value. The one holding a knife to her, fondled her breasts with one hand. Rita sat motionless. "Nice titties," he said.

"Fuck. This is hardly worth our trouble," one of them complained on finding little cash and not much else of value. They pulled the rings off her fingers and tore off her necklace. "Shit!"

"We got practically zilch." Someone kicked her chair viciously upsetting it. The chair broke and Rita fell to the floor. "Please don't hurt me," she begged them under her mask.

"Where is the rest of your goddam money?"

"In the hotel safe."

"Fuck."

Rita lay sprawled among the shambles of the chair, not daring to move. Her torn nightgown had been twisted up by the fall and her struggles. Battered from the fall, but feeling unhurt except for the jolt, she pleaded with them not to harm her. They paid no attention to her mumblings under the bag. "Shut up!" Someone kicked her.

Then she felt her nightgown being pulled up even more. "Look at her snatch. Let's fuck the bitch. We get something out of her."

"She's an old hag."

"What the hell, a pussy is a pussy."

"All that flesh going to waste . . ."

"What a bush."

They studied her like a piece of prime meat. Rita did not shave her pubic hair, but had thought about it sometimes. Shaving, or even trimming down there, had smelled of sexual promiscuity.

"Anyway, her face is covered," one jibed.

She felt hands on her genitals, someone brushed her pubic hair. She squirmed.

"Hold her legs."

Her bonds had prevented her nightgown from being pulled up further, someone cut what remained of her gown above with a knife. She lay revealed, breasts and all.

"Wow, what titties!" Someone squeezed and fondled them.

"Guys, we don't do that," a new voice said.

"What the hell, now is our chance."

"No, we got what we wanted, let's move."

"Not before I have some fun."

Rita felt someone climbing on her. Were they going to rape her? She tried to move, but could not. Then there appeared to be a struggle and the one on her had been pulled off. Her captors argued violently, fighting among themselves. Someone took hold of her nightgown and she resisted futilely, but he pulled the torn cloth down as far as possible under the circumstances, covering her. Her fear diminished somewhat, those were kids, delinquents, teenagers by their voices, maybe younger than her daughter, but she knew better then to resist. Having found some courage, she pleaded with them from under her mask: "Give me one ring back . . . please."

"Are you kidding?"

"The one with the red ruby is my dead mother's."

"Go to hell."

"Please."

"Lady, we got to have something for our troubles."

"We're all from Israel. Can we not come to some understanding?"

"Lady shut up or we'll muzzle you."

Another voice said, "What understanding?"

"I'll pay you for the ring."

"How?"

"I can get the money from the hotel safe."

"Ha, ha. Very funny," they snorted.

"If you give me my ring back, I will promise to wait one hour before I call the police."

"Don't make me laugh," one said. "There's no police around here."

"The authorities then. I swear it, on my dead mother."

"Give her the goddam ring," a voice said.

"Like hell I will."

"She'll give us an hour's start."

"Do you believe the bitch?" They were back to bitch again.

"We got stolen property, a ring will fetch a fifth of its worth," one argued, the same voice had wanted to give her the ring back.

"Shut up."

One of them–he sounded like the leader of the three–said forcibly, "We're in charge here and we don't need to make any deals."

"We're done. Let's get out of here."

They left as quickly as they had entered.

Rita managed to rid herself of the bonds and bag over her head. She hurriedly put on a robe and ran down to the reception screaming repeatedly, "I've been robbed," and shaking the sleepy reception clerk, awaking him. He looked at the clock in the lobby which showed just past four in the morning. Rita, sobbing and crying, made a lot of noise. His first instinct had been to isolate her. No need to wake up all the guests with her ruckus. He brought her into the manager's office and closed the door. An Egyptian, like most employees, his English being adequate for short cliché-like sentences and not much more, had asked.

"How they get in? Are you hurt? What they take?"

"My jewels, my rings and necklace and some hundred dollars," Rita, breathing heavily, cried. The clerk gave her a cup of water. The manager was woken up. He spoke better English and asked her more questions. Unhurt, except for a bruise on her left hip, Rita told them what little she knew, not mentioning the shameful attempted rape. She felt too embarrassed, she did not want the sordid part to get back to her family.

"Why all those questions?" she cried hysterically. "Do something. Call the authorities!"

"We have to see your room first," the manager said. The two left, locking her in like a prisoner. They soon came back. Phone calls were made. The authorities in Sinai were but a special branch of the army located in Sharem el Shiek and the manager informed her they were on their way and would arrive sometime in the morning. The management moved her to another room. The night clerk helped her with her belongings. The activity of gathering her things did much to calm her down. She had not been hurt, thank God.

In her new room, Rita felt too overwrought to rest. They had given her the best room in the hotel. She showered, cleaning herself. Then strutted about, turning the television set on and off. There were only Arabic programs and they did not interest her. The manager sent up a basket of fruits, drinks and flowers to her room, compliments of the hotel as a disguised bribe not to make too big a fuss. Finally, lying down to rest, sleep eluded her and made her mull over what had happened.

To Rita, the overriding event of the series of past incidents had not been the burglary, but the attempted rape! Rape! She had almost been violated! She felt outraged. The actual robbery took only second place in her emotions.

She had pleaded for her mother's ring, faking a major part of the sentimentality involved, why!? There came a short period of soul searching for her. A tiny interlude of truth, revealed only because of the extremity of her experience. Her strong emotions forced her to concentrate: *There had been a compulsion to find out if, as a woman, she could make a difference in the attitude of the three toward her. Did her female self have power enough to sway them and modify their feelings?* Evidently not.

Recalling the event in detail and blushing all over while squirming uneasily between the sheets of her new comfortable bed, her thoughts continued to force themselves on her: *She grudgingly recalled to feeling some sexual excitement, together with a kind of a fearful anticipation while lying helpless in her torn nightgown.* Did that make her a slut? A whore? What did it all mean? Had she really wanted them to rape her? She would have been their victim and no one could blame her. The notion went against all her family and herself held sacred; religion, chastity, laws, compliance . . . Rita, not being of a philosophic inclination, did not analyze the situation which had been forced on her, but could search her emotions and then either accept or reject them.

Rita had a long history of refuting her feelings, even denying the denials of her repudiations and those denials too, were never or very seldom admitted. A crisis by its very acuteness can sometimes alter a used and dependable chain of dealing with controversial issues and Rita forced herself to do so and came face to face with her own private truth. *She had come to the Sinai desert not for any relaxation, but to find love and maybe companionship and of course sex . . . and if the first two of those would not be within her reach, than the sex would do.* A reality had wormed its way into her conscious and made her feel like a slut, her inner appraisal of herself sank even lower than before.

Rita's thoughts moved on; she had to think about her family and acquaintances. Why make a fuss of the sex part? Had all not best be swept under the rug? Except for the burglary, nothing had happened! Her necklace and rings were missing and would have to be accounted for. Rita felt naked and depressed without them and remained in her room all morning. The hotel management grateful for her silence, sent breakfast with flowers to her room. Rita had found a faint sense of cynical humor, 'So now I am a celebrity, flowers and breakfast brought to my room.' There came a knock on her door and the hotel manager entered.

"Is all to your liking?"

"Yes of course, thank you."

"We regret this incident, we do not know how they got in, but we hope you will not talk to the other guests."

So he meant to bribe her to keep her mouth shut . . . well why not? Being no great gossip, keeping silent caused her no problem and the less who knew the better. "I will keep quiet," she promised.

The manager nodded and left.

Authority soon arrived in the form of two army officers. They took her statement, without her mentioning the attempted rape. They asked many questions.

"Could you recognize them, if you saw them again?"

"I'm not sure, I only heard their voices."

"How do you know that there were three of them?"

"I distinctly heard them talking. There could have been more around, I wouldn't know."

"Can you specify the objects they took?"

"I have prepared a list. Is there any chance of getting my jewels back?"

"It's too soon to say."

They questioned the night clerk. How had those persons got into the hotel? Had he been sleeping on the job . . . ? The manager, with much foresight, had thoughtfully taken a few pictures of her former room before removing her things and had locked the door. All in all it had been an exhausting grilling for her and the tension of holding a part back had not been easy. Rita felt glad when the questioning finally ended.

In the afternoon after a nap, the manager of the hotel, who had become friendly, suggested a short stroll outside might release her of her tension. On the beach everything seemed changed, altered somehow . . . shifted . . . but Rita could not discern in what way. People and tourists rushed about in the mad race for gratification and pleasure. Loud music blared from places to attract tourists. A colorful scene displayed itself, but failed to engage her approval or sympathy. The clamor made her shudder and she quickly returned to her hotel. Rita had decided. She would leave, maybe today, possibly tomorrow. The manager greeted her and led her to his office, another officer waited for her.

A short introduction followed. "We have found the thieves," he informed her. "You should come and identify them."

"So soon!"

"The Bedouin turned them in. They work with us when it suits them and they seem to know everything. Those boys tried to sell the jewels."

"Have you retrieved my jewels?"

"Sorry, no, they disappeared. My guess is the Bedouin have them, they are as good as lost."

"I never saw the burglars. I only heard their voices."

"We found nothing on them, no jewels no rings and little money."

"Where are they being held?" she asked, frightened and wary, not wanting the omitted part of her testimony uncovered and talked about.

"In Ophira (the new Israeli section of Sharm el Sheikh) . . . a two-hour drive."

Rita felt reluctant to face her attackers, would the attempted rape be revealed? "How will I get back?"

"We'll take you."

On the way to Sharem el Sheikh, Rita remembered to ask her driver, "Have they admitted to anything?"

"No, at least not before I left."

Rita wanted more information. "What will happen to them if I recognize them?"

"They will be sent to Israel to face charges."

They chatted some more but nothing new came up. The trip refreshed her, in spite of her anxiety about the sex part of the burglary being exposed. The movement of the vehicle soothed her and the view flew by spectacular in its wildness. The key to her future might be in her hands. Better not to identify them. The whole situation made her feel extremely uncomfortable. Could not some kind of a deal be made?

They finally reached their destination and drove to some barracks nearby. Rita steeled herself to meet her former captors and see them for the first time. They passed through some passages and came to a kind of improvised cell-like room with bars. The three were playing cards with a guard. She did not know them, but if they recognized her, they gave no sign. The game had stopped and the guard left, not bothering to lock the bars.

Their eyes met. They stared at each other, not a word had been spoken yet. The three youths, younger than her daughter, were ragged and none too clean and they had not shaved for a week. They looked like regular kids to her, but perhaps meaner looking.

"Well are those the ones?" The officer asked after a short while.

Rita did not reply immediately. The officer repeated his question.

"Tell them to talk, to say something."

The officer turned to them, "You heard the lady, talk."

"Fuck you," one of them said.

Rita stalled. "I'm not sure."

The officer said, "We can keep you guys here indefinitely, till you talk."

"What the hell do you want us to say?"

The officer looked about, he found an old newspaper lying around which he handed to one of the three. "Read," he commanded.

The boy read, slowly and hesitating. Reading did not come easy to him. The paper was handed to the next one who read fluently and impatiently, then the last one read from the paper. Rita recognized their voices and had no doubts those were the ones. The second boy, who read aloud, sounded like the voice which had not let them rape her. Was he the one who had wanted to return her ring? She looked at them one by one. They avoided her eyes, only one made eye contact with her, number two. He looked hard at her and seemed to be conveying some kind of a silent message. She broke the contact.

"I cannot tell. You may have got the wrong persons," Rita said hesitatingly to the officer.

"Take your time?"

"I am not sure. I never saw them."

"You heard them talk."

"At the time, I felt too afraid to listen carefully."

The officer appeared suspicious, "You are definite about your statement?"

"Those may not be the voices I heard in my room."

"Come into the other room please."

When they were alone the officer said, "I have studied the photos of your room, taken by the hotel manager. I have reason to believe you are not telling us the whole truth." He looked hard at her waiting for her to speak.

"I have told you all I know."

"There is a torn nightgown, a broken chair and some ropes by the bed in the pictures. What is the meaning of those?"

Rita remained silent for a while. "I don't know. I struggled, they tied me up. I have told you the whole story."

"Did they molest you sexually in anyway?"

"No."

He did not believe her. The officer was a young person. She had no choice but to put herself in his hands. "Please, can we just talk about the burglary?"

He relented at once. "You do not want to press charges."

"I don't."

"I have to ask you again: are those the ones who robbed you?"

"I really cannot be sure. I don't know."

After her final statement, they had nothing more to say and she left. Another soldier drove her back to her hotel. Rita had a lot to think about on the way and they did not talk much. In her room, the bed and a good nap appeared very inviting, but instead Rita found herself rehashing the passing events. So much had happened since yesterday. She wanted to leave. The hotel had given her one of its best rooms for the remainder of her stay there and would go to waste. Feeling sick of the place, she intended to check out in the morning and possibly get a refund, which seemed doubtful, but perhaps a little pressure, like threatening to talk to the other guests, would get her money back. They would be glad to be rid of her and with luck, late afternoon or evening would find her at home.

She dealt with the coming night by taking a sleeping pill, which helped her to sleep fitfully. The next morning, she geared herself to face whatever might come up. Informing the reception that she would be leaving after her breakfast, asked for a refund for the days, which had already been booked. The clerk called the manager, and there arose a short argument. For once, Rita had her way and indulged in a good satisfactory feeling.

In the Sinai desert, the usual way for tourists to get from one place to another, unless one came in a car, is by taxi, which are cheap and plentiful. There is also a bus, once or twice a day, never on time and crowded with locals and takes much longer.

Rita had arranged for a taxi to take her to Eilat in Israel, a four-hour drive. In Israel, a bus would do.

Her taxi drove fast and the landscape flew by un-noticed by her. Her holiday had been cut short. She did not relish getting back to her former life, but did not want to remain in Dahab either. Rita had been a puzzled woman coming to Sinai, and felt an even more perplexed one returning home. The Bedouin taxi driver had put on loud Arabic music and irritated her, he reluctantly turned the sound down. Rita, in the backseat, passively watched the mountains roll by, busy with her ambivalent thoughts. Ashamed and disgusted with herself and regretting her trip–the sooner she got home, back to her regular life, things would straighten themselves out. She had been an idiot to take this trip.

The car sped on the desert road carrying Rita, busy with her thoughts. The sleeping pill from the night before, together with the motion of the car made her drowsy and she dozed for short periods. They arrived at a junction and Rita saw a hitchhiker trying to catch a ride. Pitying the fellow under the already hot sun, she called out to her driver to stop, as is the custom in Sinai. The hiker had only a small bag with him and he jumped in quickly and settled himself beside the driver. The car drove off.

"Thanks," he said, turning to face Rita. With a shock, they recognized each other. She saw one of the three boys who had broken into her room! He had washed and shaved somewhere.

"You!" Rita exclaimed.

"Goddam shit!" burst out of him.

What the hell now? Wanting nothing more to do with what had happened and resolved to put all behind her, she called out to the driver, "Stop the car!" The car rolled to a stop.

"Get out!" to the boy, "I never want to see any of you again."

The boy opened the car door, then he turned to her: "I'm sorry, this never should have happened. The whole thing was a mistake." He took his bag and got up wearily, a defeated look on his face. With slow motions, he got out of the car. 'He is just a young kid.' Rita thought. Had he been the one who had covered her with her nightgown? Rita felt she could not leave him stranded somewhere by the desert road, even though he well deserved it.

"Wait."

He stopped moving.

"Where are you going?"

"Eilat."

"Get in."

"You're taking me?!"

"Get in!" she repeated, "Before I regret it."

He climbed back into the car. "Thanks."

She found nothing more to say to him and turned away to look unseeing out of the window. They drove on in silence, a heavy silence, thick with hostility on her part. The Arab music on the radio made itself faintly heard as the taxi continued on its way. After a while, he turned around to face her and said, "I'm sorry for what happened back there."

She did not answer or turn to look at him. He repeated his sentence adding some embellishments. He did seem contrite.

Rita talked to her window: "So, they already let you out. You are lucky I did not inform the police." Then she remembered her jewels—her necklace and her rings. Finally, turning to him, "What happened to my jewelry?"

"The Bedouin robbed us."

The officer had already informed her. Her hopes of getting her jewels back had disappeared long before. Her jewelry had been insured, and except for her mother's ring, had little sentimental value for her. Some jewelry had been given to her on formal anniversaries by her husband and most of it she had bought herself. They drove on in silence, the view on her side of the window appeared to interest her again.

The youth again turned in his seat to face her, "I am . . . I didn't let them . . . I covered you up."

"How nice." Rita could be acrimonious.

"Thank you for not recognizing us, they had to let us go."

Rita did not answer. The view outside seemed to occupy all her attention. The car drove on.

"I've split up with them," he offered the information, "I'm going to get on with my life."

"Good for you." Then recalling the forced entrance, "How did you get into my room?"

"Easy. We climbed the wall on the outside."

"But my window was closed."

"We managed the door from the balcony."

The youth appeared to be intent on making a good impression on her, why? She could not care less about him. Those guys had robbed and sexually molested her. She continued gazing out of the moving car's window, but the boy had not finished with his former subject. "Those guys are losers. They live from day to day, from hour to hour. I cannot live like them."

"Your parents must be very proud of you," Rita mocked.

"I have no parents."

He had mentioned the information in passing, not making a big deal of the fact, but to Rita this had stuck. Her mother had been nothing to boast about and her father had never been around. The boy was an orphan and he struck a soft chord in her. She thawed somewhat and turned away from her window to face him. "I'm sorry. How old are you anyway?"

"Eighteen . . . and a half," The youth had again turned around to face her and chuckled, "Old enough to know better, right?"

A kind of morbid curiosity had set in and Rita wanted to know more, but did not have the courage to be more explicit. "Why did you . . . well, what made you do it?"

He too misunderstood and did not answer right away, taking the easy way out. "We needed the money . . ." There he had to stop.

Rita said nothing. What is there to say? "Such things are not done!" came out at last.

The boy said. "I am sorry, truly sorry . . ." and paused, "sorry," he repeated. Against her will, Rita felt their talk had gone far enough. Much too far in fact. They had become too friendly for her taste. "Enough, I don't want to hear any more," she snapped, turning back to her window.

The car drove on and the Bedouin driver, indifferent to the talk around him, hummed softly with the music from the radio. The youth talking to Rita twisted around in the front seat to face her. The night spent in custody had mostly been a sleepless one. Now turning away from her, he eventually dozed off. The car continued on its way on the never-ending desert road. They had not noticed, having being occupied with each other, but the car's engine seemed to be getting noisy. Then the motor began to reverberate periodically and as the noise grew louder a clattering background sound made itself heard. The Bedouin driver cursed and the car rocketed to a halt.

The Bedouin taxis in Sinai are a second-rate lot, many of them without the original innards and are kept with little knowledge of maintenance. Breakdowns have been known to happen. They all got out and the Bedouin opened the hood, smoke came out from somewhere. The Bedouin checked some wires and pulled a piece out.

"No good, no good. Call other taxi."

They seemed to be stuck on the desert road. They might as well stretch their legs a bit. The heat outside hit them like the blow of a hammer. The already burning sun, not yet at its zenith, made the shade of a close mountain cover a section of the road ahead. They moved there to get out of the sun and wait. The Bedouin crossed to the other side of the road and eventually flagged a south going taxi asking the other driver to send help.

He came up to them and told them, "Cousin in Dahab. Other taxi come soon, wait." Then he went to his car to have another look.

Rita and the youth stood side by side in the sudden desert silence, not knowing what to say to each other. The boy said, "Soon, over here means hours. Two hours for the taxi to get to his cousin and two more till he arrives."

"What shall we do?'

"Catch a hike maybe."

She asked the youth his name.

"Yoni."

"Rita," she replied.

"Where is your name from?" he asked, trying to start a conversation.

"I was born in Alexandria."

They were quiet for a while. Rita scrutinized the youth . . . Yoni. He had shaved and looked different from the last time she had seen him in jail; long brown hair and brown eyes. She noticed the remains of some freckles. He stood tall and slender and carried himself well. She recalled how she had lain helpless and revealed. The youth had been one of those three. A blush generated from an area in her chest and spread out to burn her face, then it tingled her spine making her shiver, however he seemed not to notice.

More to relieve herself of an embarrassing subject than anything else, she asked him curiously, "Shouldn't you be in the army?"

"I deserted, they put me in a military jail, I ran away again, till they let me go."

"Everybody does the army." For the moment, Rita had forgotten. Her early marriage had released her from army service.

"I don't like taking orders, all my goddam life I have been told what to do, I'm sick of people ordering me around."

His sentence had its echo in her, partly unacknowledged. "Where does that leave you? We all take orders one time or another."

"It leaves me alone, the way I like it."

She could understand, but not the 'being alone' part, of which Rita had her fill. She did not look forward to returning to her empty place in Tel Aviv, but what else was there for her to do? Not commenting on his last sentence, she asked, "What are you going to do when we get to Israel?"

"I might stay in Eilat, bum around, maybe find some job . . . I don't know."

A car passed them on the road.

"Maybe we can get us a hike," he said.

Every ten minutes or so, a car might come by on its way north and when one did, Yoni made the hiker motions. Many of the vehicles going to Israel had only one or no free place left, as people and especially Israelis, have a habit of sharing the expenses of the long trip northwards. There were taxis carrying passengers and they were all full. There were trucks with merchandise with no empty place beside the driver, but Yoni did not cease his activity.

At last a car stopped. The people there had one free place only. "You go," Yoni said to her.

"I have paid for the taxi, which will eventually arrive," Rita protested. "You get in."

"I can wait, I have nothing to do anyway." Rita found she did not want to leave yet and stated, "I will wait for my taxi."

Why had she insisted on remaining? Rita had never been one for analyzing her feelings, mostly preferring to ignore them. The car left with neither of them getting on.

"Why didn't you get on?" Yoni asked her, after the car had left.

"I have too much luggage with me." Rita felt her excuse feeble and not very convincing, even to herself, so she asked him, "Why didn't you get on?"

He stammered, "I don't know . . . I did not like leaving you here alone . . ."

"I'm not alone, there's the taxi driver, he's not going to . . . assault me, you know . . ." She had made a mistake, insinuating about the rape. What had got over her? 'What a fool I am,' thought Rita.

No car passed by for some time. The Bedouin sat in his car, further off and listened to music. Yoni and Rita grew tired of standing. Boulders had separated and rolled down from the mountain and some were lying near the side of the road, some were still in the shade. They sat down on them, not talking. The wild scene around pressed in on them. The Arabic music from the car came to them very faintly.

There is no bullshit or false values and pretenses in the Sinai landscape. The scene is very real. Its forceful nature tends to seep into one's feelings and indicates a pitiful waste of time and emotional resources to beat around the bush. There is no sentiment in the view, no juggling around with notions or conventions. Those two urban denizens could not but be impressed and influenced by the straightforward power of the forces of nature as depicted in the Sinai desert.

Yoni, too under the sway of the wild surroundings, said softly, "Ma'am, Mrs. Rita, you must have recognized us back there. Why did you not tell the officer?"

"Since when is it your business what I do, or don't do?" she snapped.

Her fierce answer had intimidated him, but after a while he tried again: "I am truly sorry about what happened the other night . . ."

Rita felt drawn in, but could not help being sarcastic. "Great, and for what are you not sorry for?"

"I'm not sorry we met."

"Indeed," Rita said haughtily, trying to shy away from the subject, but could not resist saying, "You had done your good deed."

"I . . . have something for you." He pulled out of his pocket a tiny article wrapped in a piece of newspaper which he gave to her.

Rita unwrapped the paper and saw her mother's ring.

"My ring! . . . How? . . . When? I thought I would never see it again!"

"I hid your ring from the Bedouins."

"Thank you, I cannot thank you enough." They had an embarrassing moment. Rita subdued an impulse to hug him. They did not speak for a time. The boys had been searched, the Israeli officer had mentioned that. "Didn't they search you?"

"I went to pee and hid the ring under a stone."

"Why did you not give the ring to me before, in the taxi?"

"I was afraid to."

"Of me?"

He shifted the subject. "I wanted to keep it for myself."

"For the money?"

"A reminder." Then he dared, "I dreamed of you last night in Sharem," he began, but had to stop.

"Go on," she said breathless.

" . . . The picture of you lying there, helpless, with your nightgown rolled up . . ."

"I don't want to hear any more," she snapped. Yoni shut up and they were silent for a while. Another car approached, seeing the taxi by the side of the road with its hood open, the driver stopped by Rita and Yoni. "Do you need help, we can make one place."

They waived it on.

Their intimacy had been interrupted and some time passed until they got back to their former mood. A sudden impulsive temptation to invite him to stay with her in Tel Aviv, until he got on his feet came over her. A ridiculous idea. . . . No . . . impossible! How could she even think of such a scandalous thing!

Yoni said, "I meant what I said before."

"No more talk. Many people have dreams." Rita remembered her own nasty ones.

He went on. "I dreamed about you! . . . I had more than a dream. . . ."

Rita breathed heavily, Yoni had dreamed of her! Her emotions surged and immobilized her mental tools. Afraid to think, to talk, she made a giant effort. "What are you saying? No good can come from your mentioning all this."

"Why not? What's to prevent us?"

"What us? There is no us!"

"To me there is."

He must be over twenty years her junior. Society and her peers would ridicule and despise her. "What do you want?" She would have liked very much to add 'from me' but did not dare.

He blurted out. "How should I know, I am drawn to you, that I do know . . ."

Rita had sensed his attraction. Yoni had been the one who had saved her from being raped, he had covered her nakedness and had wanted to return her ring and now had done so! Her heart jumped. She allowed herself to say, "What do you mean 'drawn' what can you possibly see in an older woman. A large woman too."

"What does all that matter," Yoni insisted. "Who cares!"

"You don't know me."

He dared again, "I want to get to know you."

"Come here young man."

He got up from his rock and came closer. Rita looked deep into his eyes. They were clear and without guile, undemanding. There was pain in them too. They were pleading organs. He did not shrink away from her scrutiny. She stood up to face him, her arms, as if by themselves came to rest on his shoulders, he came still closer and they kissed. Then they hugged and clove together and remained glued to each other. 'This cannot be wrong,' the thought came to her, it felt so wonderful. They kissed again and then once more.

Rita, being older and possibly the saner of the two, tore herself away, exclaiming. "Now what?" panting . . . "This is crazy."

"Whatever." Yoni seemed just as agitated.

"What are we doing! Madness. You are young enough to be my son."

"You could be my mother, so what? The mother I have never had. I want you. I want to be with you, sex and everything else too. What is so wrong?"

It certainly did not feel wrong, but Rita, conscious and only too aware of her family, friends and society, realized she would be breaking one of the major taboos.

"Let's get back," Yoni suggested.

"Back where?" Rita had not yet wholly regained her wits. "You mean back to Dahab?"

"Yes. What's to stop us?"

What indeed!? Only her whole family, uncles, cousins and all, not to mention Aliza, who would be aghast and outraged against her. One could not do what one wanted in this world. Out of the question! She had a traditional religious upbringing, how could one behave in such a manner? The thing may seem simple to him, but for her totally unattainable.

"Impossible," she said.

"Why impossible, all we have to do is to wait till the other taxi arrives and tell the man where to go."

'Of course they could do so, theoretically, the way much is possible but never gets done,' Rita thought. To change the subject, she asked Yoni to tell her about himself. "There's not much to tell. I grew up in an orphanage and I never knew my parents. Then a couple adopted me, they had a farm. At the farm, we worked and after school, more work. I do not like to talk about them. They used me. At sixteen I ran away. I slept on the streets and in empty places or parks sometimes. . . ."

As he talked on, Rita found herself listening less to the details and more to the tone and timbre of his voice, which to her appeared much more informative on an emotional basis. The boy never had a real home or any stability in his short life. A wave of strong feelings emerged in her. Could she give it to him?

A few more vehicles passed them. Yoni did not want to leave Rita and she hesitated, not sure of how to act. Finally, they ceased to give the passing cars any of their attention. The occurrences of the last few days had caused an emotional upheaval in Rita and matters could never be the same again. Swayed by her emotions and very baffled on all the levels of her being, as years of traditional habits of thought made themselves strongly felt, created a clashing conflict and caused a paralyzed inactive state of affairs in her.

External circumstances can frequently occur when issues hang on balance. Chance may step in and give a little push in one or another direction. We can call the phenomena by many names: luck, accident, destiny or providence, and opportunity may help achieve what one would have liked to get done anyway. Fate stepped in, unknown to Rita and Yoni, in the many forms and surprises which life has. The taxi driver they had met going southwards toward Dahab had been told that, on arrival at his destination, he should contact a certain cousin who owned a taxi, to come and get them. This never happened as the cousin had been away on another route.

Rita and Yoni, and their Bedouin driver waited in vain. The other taxi would not arrive. Then a southward bound taxi approached and stopped, partly empty, looking for partners to share the expenses of the trip with. The former occupants had quarreled and had decided to part. One of the two couples, changing their minds, had got off on the way to another destination–Nueba. The two empty seats they had left behind stared at Rita and Yoni invitingly. They were going to Dahab the people inside said.

"Let's go." Yoni was decisive. He had noticed Rita's wavering.

Rita, hesitating, appeared not to be able to act independently. Had a benevolent deity sent her a sign? She moved like an automaton, a drugged person. Yoni energetically pulled out her bags, from their taxi and put them in the trunk of the other car. Their own former taxi driver, relieved, as he had been paid already, feared some kind of a hitch and his cousin might not be coming, but had said nothing to his passengers, concerned they might ask for a refund.

Rita got in the car, her motions mechanic, propelled by unknown forces. Once in the car, their new acquaintances kept her from thinking too much. They chatted of many topics: 'what is happening in Israel nowadays' and 'where to stay in Dahab.' Would they pay for their part of the trip? The other couple in the taxi had taken it for granted they were mother and son.

They arrived at Dahab and the other couple got out. Rita, still irresolute, could not concentrate easily. What on heaven and earth were they doing?! Forcing and collecting herself, her mind cleared: Yes! She would . . . Yes! . . . Yes. *Yes!* The length of her scheduled holiday had not yet expired. No one would know. They were away from Israel and in a different world and place.

Telling the driver to get them to another and cheaper lodgings than the hotel from before, they got out and Yoni carried her bags. One does not register at the cheaper hotels and they quickly rented a room. The door closed behind them. They showered impatiently from their aborted trip north to Israel, wanting the moment to come, but also apprehensive and delaying a little.

Suddenly the time had arrived and was here and now. A magic and dynamic moment, fraught with terrible excitement. Suspense, terror, lust and awe of what was actually happening, chased themselves in Rita's feelings. She compelled her mind to empty and shut off all rational thought. They came together. Yoni made love to her. He worshipped her body. Rita had never been loved so before. Her husband had copulated with her, relieving himself of the sexual pressure, there had been little fondness, but it had been good, also releasing her own tensions. Yoni, here and now, exposed her to something in a different category altogether and did remind her of the two Portuguese. The basic simple wonder and amazement of two bodies touching and creating a heaven stunned them both. They could not believe their luck.

Yoni revered her from head to foot. He did her orally. At first she tried to prevent him, the act seemed too intimate and dirty, but he persisted and she felt herself swept away on an uncontrollable tide of emotions, existing in a world where there exists no right or wrong, and all was allowed and sanctioned. They were in a shabby second-rate hotel room, but for them the dingy surroundings were Paradise. There were no limitations or rules, no more guidelines, procedures or laws, and Rita let herself go and become totally immerged. In the heat of their passion nothing mattered, they existed only for each other.

The day passed euphoric and dreamlike. So did the next one and the one after. Had the desert claimed two other allies?

"We are good together," Yoni would repeat.

"You are a darling boy."

"Let's remain here for a while."

"I have a secret place. Do you want to see it?"

Rita led Yoni to her hidden cove and they bathed in the nude, being with Yoni made her feel safe. She decided to remain in Dahab as long as their incredible affair lasted. When the sex wore off, their affair would end, but for now, not capable of surrendering the bonus an erratic destiny had dealt her, she would take whatever life or fate had dished out. Come what may! Rita had thrown all her directives to the winds and for the first time in her life felt free. Her heart sang and she could not prevent herself from skipping and dancing with joy.

Not all appeared well in Paradise; Rita had her doubts. Could they have the real thing, or was she under a wishful delusion? Not being sure or caring what terms to apply, she felt happy. The two, having closed their minds to everything else but each other, lived from day to day and night to night. One more gnawing dissonant troubling her: Their affair would have to end sometime, and her former life would be waiting for her with its load of loneliness and boredom. Rita had never had a man attendant to her, or sensitive to her feelings. Yoni made her feel like a queen. She had only to hint at something and Yoni would see to it.

They ate in restaurants. Sea food is plentiful and cheap in Dahab and Yoni indulged. At first Rita felt afraid to touch the food and this induced a religious discussion. "Don't you believe in God?" Rita challenged him.

"Maybe, maybe not, but certainly not the one in the Bible . . . and some of the Ten Commandments are totally obsolete."

"Which ones?"

"The one about food and . . . the one about always wearing a cap and one or two others. Is not what we are doing against the law?"

Rita had been only too aware. "We are bad people . . ."

"The hell we are! What feels so good and right cannot be bad. Are we harming anybody?"

Those had been Rita's thoughts too. "Let me try one of that calamari." They were delicious, but she had a queasy feeling in her stomach.

"Have some more."

"Another time."

Eventually, with Yoni's encouragement she ceased making a fuss about the local food and began to enjoy herself.

The days passed happily and only too quickly. Rita had a low self-image and few delusions about herself. At first, not being able to grasp what Yoni could possibly see in an older and large woman, caused a part of her to remain skeptic, after all, her family and friends would look at the affair as more than a bit unusual, to say the least, but as the days passed, she could not help but notice that in Yoni she had the real thing. He loved her body and wallowed in her. No part of her went untouched and un-kissed. To be so adored, revealed a new experience for her. She reciprocated, giving him all of herself with no holds barred, participating in unbelievable sex acts she had never even dreamed of before and telling him about her husband sex matters which had never been mentioned aloud. Questioning him repeatedly, trying to find out what he saw in her, never came up with a definite answer.

Yoni, as many young persons, had not been aware of the more basic emotions that motivated him. Being an orphan, he had searched for some kind of stability in its various forms. All his life, even as a little boy, he had felt a stranger and not a part of any establishment. He had grown into a troublemaker, unsatisfied, unruly, criticizing and revolting against the very organizations which had tried to help him. Often being correct in his disparagements had never done him any good.

After seeing Rita helpless and exposed in her former hotel room, Yoni had been drawn to her sexually, her large form promising him some kind of a haven, but as the first few days together went by, her hunger and craving for him wormed its way into his conscious. Never having been in demand or indispensable to someone in his life before. She elevated him and gave him power and confidence. She did not pass judgment and accepted him, which in turn caused him to feel more secure and good about himself, but he too knew their affair had no future. Rita would have to get back to her home and family and leave him.

Yoni may have been a delinquent, full of anger and resentment to a world which had victimized him from the day he had been born, but in Rita he had found an anchor and felt safe and secure- emotional assets which he would never have admitted to himself. Her large person captivated him. He lusted for her flesh and in his hunger for her, found himself more than willing to take pleasure in giving to her. He could not explain, but to him she appeared a gentle and vulnerable person. A kind of fragile susceptibility in her, made him want to protect her from harm. He felt very powerful, manly and tender. Is that the love they always talked and sung about? He did not know for sure, but if anyone tried to harm her, they would have him to deal with.

"I should be thinking of getting back," Rita would mention without much conviction.

"Do you want to?"

"I don't know what to do."

"One week more won't make a difference, right?"

"Right."

Long habits of thoughts are hard to erase. The thought did come to her that he might be freeloading on her as they went from stall to shop searching clothes for him to wear. Firm with herself, she deliberately chose to ignore those suspicions, feeling happily of getting more than her fair share of the bargain, if so, she could call their lovemaking. What was money when compared to the priceless benefits which being together with him were giving her? Those would remain for the rest of her life? Having told family and friends her vacation would last for ten days or maybe two weeks or more, her time there would soon come to an end. She delayed and put her trip back off. A few more days would not matter to anyone, not having to return to a job. No one waited for her at home, Aliza was busy with her own life and family, as for the rest of them, cousins and uncles, and some acquaintances, what did she owe them? Not a thing that could not keep.

Rita and Yoni, mostly unaware, had formed an alliance, each with his or her monkey on their back, and found how being together and naturally supportive felt much stronger than being separate. They enjoyed themselves hugely and daily unimportant events became for them fraught with meaning. Ten days turned into two weeks, then three weeks. "I should be thinking about going home," she said to Yoni.

"You have said so before," he pointed out. Indeed the subject had reluctantly been mentioned every few days off and on.

"You don't want me to leave." An obvious fact, but having him say so aloud did her good.

"What is there for you in your home?" He had heard her mention the subject often enough in their conversations. "We are happy together. Why spoil anything?"

Those had been her thoughts too, but having been raised in a certain way, old habits of thought or behavior are not easy to get rid of. The three weeks had turned into a month. Rita had once again made a change in her attire. Out went her long dresses and high-necked blouse. Yoni helped her choose more revealing and sexy clothes and one of her thrills would be to see Yoni's face when she tried them on.

They had themselves tattooed, Rita had a flower on her left shoulder, and Yoni chose a snake on his arm. They had made new friends on a temporary non-obligatory basis. To all their acquaintances and contacts in Dahab, they were mother and her son and as not many questions are asked in Sinai, they had been accepted at face value. People there did not care much.

She had given some thought, more like daydreams than anything else, of taking him with her to her home. The venture would mean a definite and irreparable rift with her family and most of her friends, associates and links. No, never, impossible! Her folks would be totally flabbergasted, outraged, and despise and ridicule them and the strain of combating her family would be too great and break her.

At first, she had kept all her thoughts to herself, but as the time for leaving had neared and passed, the subject became a repeated topic discussed between her and Yoni.

"I too have nothing to go back for," Yoni would say when they talked.

"Your future is not with me," Rita would claim.

"What else is there for me to do? Be a waiter all my life? Or some other tedious job? I cannot even get a security guard job as I have had a dishonorable discharge from the army. I am probably wanted by the police for some stuff we picked up back home."

"Is that why you stick with me?" Rita always could do with some assurance.

"You know so very well why we are together."

"You cannot possibly love an older woman . . . more than twice your age?"

He had heard the same before, many times, their occasional repeated pattern had almost become a kind of pastime diversion.

"Rita, I do not know what love is, I have never had any, but I do know one thing: when I am with you I feel accepted and safe, and funny as it sounds, I feel strong. You are a vulnerable person and I can protect you. Nobody will make you feel bad when I am around . . ."

His words always brought some inside sobbing from her. Feeling his love and adoration, but finding hard to believe how anyone could her hold person at such high value, at times, a tiny part of her remained aloof to nag her suspiciously. He had never been unkind to her and had always been sensitive to her moods. Yoni would make love to her verbally too.

As Rita had often asked him what he saw in her, Yoni would come out with, "I like your body, I put my arms around those stems of legs you have and dig my nose into your pussy. I would crawl inside if I could," he said, totally uninhibited, "I love to kiss your ass and make you shiver. . . ."

At first, she tried to get him to stop the dirty talk, but as time passed, the unbelievable fact dawned on her. To him, those were not only romantic sex embellishments but were really and incredibly true! Hard as they had been for her to accept. Her breasts had become little hills to him and her eyes and lips were only too frequently the subject of his erotic musings. On entering her, he would declaim, "I'm home!" He told her that after puberty he masturbated frequently and now sometimes before their sex, would stimulate himself manually while scrutinizing her nude body. Ashamed of her body before, but now, seeing the excitement she caused in him, her body became a source of satisfaction and delight to her.

Maybe their affair would not last, but while it did, Rita could not give him up. In actual fact, they lived from day to day, but Rita had sometimes contemplated their situation. Their sex would become routine in time and boring, like with her husband. Then a younger girl might come along and he would be unfaithful to her in time, there were just too many nude and half-naked females around. A bond of real understanding, friendship, and mutual trust and reliance had been created between them. They were real buddies, lovers and close friends and a resolve arose in her: A foreign sexual encounter would not damage them. What they had was too precious. Let him have his sex with other females, but what they had together would remain intact. She would take care of their union.

One day an illuminating event occurred: Rita's forty-sixth birthday had come. In Dahab, there is an immense amount of trinkets for sale, from the very cheap ones made of plaster of Paris and ceramics, right up to metal and even gold-plated ones. Many stalls belong to Egyptians who had come to Dahab. Among the litter and many trash-like figures, they had also brought with them statuettes of their ancient Deities. Yoni, strolling by, searched for a present to give to Rita. One of the trinkets caught his eye, a naked female reminding him of Rita. He bought the figure.

In the evening he presented the figure to Rita: "Happy birthday!"

Rita, having passed a part of her childhood in Alexandria, had seen its likes before and recognized the statuette as a replica of an ancient fertility deity. Touched, she kissed him. "Yoni, you have brought me the statue of an ancient goddess!"

Yoni did not know, "She reminded me of you," he admitted.

"You are my goddess."

Rita began to shiver with emotion, and tried to control herself. "Do I look like her?"

"Let's find out." She let him undress her, feeling unable to move. When nude, he began to compare her with the deity. Their goofing had started as fun, but the similarity was really quite uncanny and excited them both. He made love to her, repeating, "You are my goddess, I worship and obey!"

Rita had metamorphosed from being a rejected housewife to a divine sex goddess and had her first taste of multiple orgasms.

Real knowing is emotional and it became clear to Rita that Yoni did worship her person. Her body, formally often a source of embarrassment to her, had now become her pride. For the first time in her life Rita dressed not to hide, but to reveal her body. A day or two later, Rita browsing idly for some sexy clothes in one of the many stalls, found a statuette with a great oversized erect penis, probably an ancient male deity. Her sense of humor had developed lately, the miniature did not really remind her of Yoni, but she purchased the figure anyway and, in their room, placed her purchase beside the one Yoni had presented her, waiting for him to notice.

Yoni noticed. "What's this, is that supposed to be me?"

"That is what you feel like to me."

"So big?"

"Even more so."

Six weeks had now passed since they had connected and she began to wonder why no one from her large family had tried to contact her. Pulling her head together, she remembered writing to Aliza after meeting Yoni and had informed her of not traveling north but to Sinai, giving her the address of her former hotel, not the one where they stayed now, as their place had no real address. They went to see if any mail had arrived. The reception clerk recognized her and wondered why she was still around. Yes, there were two letters for her.

They were both from Aliza. The first, dated three weeks after leaving her home for Sinai and among the chat and trifles asked:

'At first I thought you were up north! When are you coming back?'

The second letter, dated much later said:

'We have heard about the burglary, thank heaven you are unharmed. Albert is in the police force, remember. Are you alright? Why haven't you written? When are you coming back? Did you say two weeks or two months? Ha ha. We shall have an evening together and you can tell me all.'

Somewhere deep in her sub conscious Rita had made a decision, and her resolve slowly seeped into her awareness. She would remain in Sinai at for as long as their impossible and amazingly inconceivable liaison lasted. They had the real thing! She would hold on to what they so miraculously had, with all her power. Whatever may happen in the future, the present would be hers and would remain a part of her always.

Two months had already passed by now and she felt a deep attachment and love for Yoni, he had, perhaps unknowingly given her a priceless gift: Her self-esteem!

Two more weeks passed in a euphoria-like life style until Rita finally decided to act, but before anything practical could be done a great surprise awaited her:

Aliza arrived, totally unexpected and shocking her almost out of her wits! Rita had of course let her know that she was staying in Dahab, by the sea, but the hotel they were in had no specific name. In Dahab only the larger hotels had telephones and addresses, and her daughter had phoned to say she would be coming, but the message had not got to Rita. Aliza had inquired of the clerk at the reception, who knew where Rita lived. It only took an hour for Aliza to find where her mother lodged, the village not being a large place.

Rita walked around in brief jeans and a bikini-like brassiere revealing the upper part of her breasts, her navel had a pearl in it and one of her naked shoulders had been heavily tattooed. Aliza gaped. Was this her mother? However, there were more important issues to be discussed. Yoni had not been around, a piece of luck for Rita, as he could be dealt with later.

Their reunion turned out not to be such a happy one. Aliza, worried and angry for being made to come all the way to Dahab, felt totally baffled and tended to blame her mother. After the first surprised and happy greetings, she came quickly to the business at hand. "What is going on mom?"

"I like it here," she said defensively.

"But you have been gone for over two months now!"

"So long? The place here is good for my health."

"But you are not sick, or is there something you have not told me?"

There was much she had not told her, nor intended to. Her life should be her own business. "I want to remain here sometime longer," Rita said doggedly.

"But we want you with us, have you forgotten? Gil's birthday is coming up."

Gil . . . her grandson. Rita, longed to see him, but she had to live her own life. This had become paramount with her. "I am not yet ready to leave yet."

Aliza had noticed the change in her mother's apparel. "Mom, the way you are dressed . . . ," trying to be tactful. "Isn't it kind of revealing . . . and looks . . . cheap . . .?"

Rita, humorously but somewhat grim, faced a kind of déjà vu. As a teenager, her mom had been on her to dress properly and not reveal much skin, now Aliza was doing the same.

"People do not dress up here in the heat, I feel comfortable in my clothes."

"In your lack of them."

"Aliza dear, I am not going to ask your permission on how to dress."

"But this isn't you!"

"Dearest, it may be hard for you to understand, but I am my own person and have to live my life as I see fit."

"Mom, what is wrong with you? Your grandson needs a grandmother, like all the other children!"

While they were arguing, Yoni had returned. Seeing the two together and overhearing a part of the discussion, he grasped the situation and instinctively backed out and moved away, keeping his distance.

"Who was that?" Aliza asked.

"A friend."

Aliza could never imagine her mother having a lover, the concept being totally and completely out of her range of logical thought. "Mom, you cannot stay here all by yourself, away from everyone who loves you, away from us and your grandson."

"Aliza, you have to trust your mother. I need to live here for a while and I do have friends, I am not alone," she alluded on her situation, not daring to say more.

Her hint did not take. "But everything about you is so sudden and strange. When did all this come up?"

"Nothing is so sudden as you think. I am happy here."

"But what do you mean? I don't understand you anymore . . ."

Their discussion continued with nothing new being said, but they could not leave alone. A shift had been created in their mother and daughter relations and Aliza caught on that her mother could have a mind of her own. The concept being novel to both of them. Aliza did not relish their arguing and

Rita could not bring herself to mention Yoni, who waited outside, concerned, anxious, and not at all certain of what to do. Should he enter and make himself known? Having understood the person inside to be Aliza, Rita's daughter, he listened to their conversation. They had not mentioned him. He waited.

Rita guessed he would be nearby somewhere waiting and excused herself. "I'll be back in a moment," and went out. As suspected, Yoni stood there nearby. A hurried, shushed and short conversation in whispers ensued.

"Yoni, my daughter is here."

"I guessed that."

"I cannot tell her about us."

"Why not?"

"I just cannot, not yet. You have to understand."

"I don't like it."

"You have to find some place for the night. Aliza will stay here with me."

"Shit, fuck. . . . Okay, but I hate this."

She gave him a hurried peck and returned to Aliza. For the moment, they had exhausted their former topic and painful as it had been to them both, they ignored their differences and talked about other issues. Aliza filled her in on the current family gossip and Rita made noncommittal comments, not caring much anymore about what one of her family did or what another had said. She became aware of emotionally distancing herself from her prior life. Guilt had induced her to make a special effort to be intimate with Aliza. She filled her in on specifics about the burglary, not the sex part.

Then, in a rush of impulsive emotion, Rita asked her: "Why not remain here with me for some days? The climate will do you good." Such had not really been her intention, Yoni would have to keep hiding and she would be to blame, however, Aliza would always be her daughter.

"Mom, I cannot. Unlike you I have things to do at home."

"Aliza, no one is indispensable. They can get along without you for a few days."

"Ha, I just would like to see them. I must return tomorrow. As it is, I will find the place upside down when I get back."

"You can stay here with me for the night." Rita did not like to admit her relief to herself.

Aliza had noticed the two combined beds and mattresses. "Who is the other bed for?"

Rita never had been adept at lying; now she stammered, "I found another bed here when I rented the place."

Aliza took her words at face value and dropped the subject. As Aliza settled down, she noticed all kinds of strange objects lying around. Surely those could not be her mother's. There had been no time to hide them. Two vulgar miniature statuettes, placed side by side on a shelf, forced themselves on her attention and she grimaced in disgust. One does not need many clothes in Dahab, but there were some foreign ones hanging on hooks attached to the wall. Aliza picked up a disc player with earphones. "Whose are those?"

"Mine."

Her mom had never had such a gadget before. "What music do you like?" She put the earphones to her head and switched the player on. She heard disco, rock, pop, reggae, lyrics chanted and screamed. They could not be her mom's.

"A friend left it here," Rita said somewhat defiantly.

"But you said they were yours."

"Now they are mine."

A suspicion had wormed its way into Aliza's head. The idea of her mother having a man around seemed utterly impossible for her to believe. "Do you share the place with someone, a roommate?"

Rita had a rough time. Deceiving her own daughter was hateful to her. Did she feel ashamed of Yoni? No! Never. Having an affair with a boy twenty-seven years younger than herself, younger than Aliza, had been the real subject of her embarrassment, even so, her life should be her own business. 'Why can't they leave us alone!' Aliza saw her as a parent and as a grandmother and this used to be fine and true as far as it went. Resentment and indignation surged in her. She was a human being . . . with feelings and emotions! Did she, or did she not have a right to her own desires! Why continue lying to her own daughter about something so important to her? What she and Yoni had between them was real!

On the tide of her emotions and some anger, she answered her daughter, aggressively and challenging, "Yes, I am living with someone . . . a man."

"*You!!*"

She faced her bravely, "Yes."

Aliza broke down, crying and complained: "How could you do this to us?" she sobbed. "And there is Gil's birthday soon," she stated out of context. "You are too old. It is disgusting at your age . . ."

The last sentence had annoyed Rita beyond control and made her too burst out. "I am a human being! I'm only forty-six and I want to live my life too. Life is not yet over for me."

The argument waged on until they were both exhausted. They had different interests. Aliza wanted a grandmother figure and a regular member of the family, while Rita endeavored to be her own person with her feelings and desires. The chasm between their objectives frightened them both and might not be reconciled. At last they desisted. Rita had not even hinted at

Yoni's age, not daring to do so before, but now finding herself on a mission, a mission of revelations and truths, her intention changed. Yoni had happened–Aliza should know of him. "Do you want to meet him?"

"Where is he now?"

"Keeping his distance."

She shuddered. "No."

Despite herself Rita felt relieved. "You don't have to do anything you do not want."

"Is this where he sleeps?" Aliza pointed to the beds.

"What do you think?" Rita Countered.

"I will find a hotel."

"No, you will not. You can sleep in my bed. I will be in the other one. It will be like old times and you can help me change the sheets."

They were mother and daughter, whether they liked or not. They bickered and argued. They voiced mutual complaints and accusations and had much to talk about. They went out to eat.

Dusk had arrived outside and the night soon would follow. The breeze had totally ceased and they saw a sea, calm as a mirror. The great heat had receded. The places by the beach were being lighted, few had electricity and many others used oil lamps. Waiters were lightening candles on the tables. There were floating candles placed on the calm seashore and they were leisurely moving out into the sea. A charming scene portrayed itself. People moved about, searching for trinkets and food. Waiters were carrying trays of victuals from the restaurants to the seashore, which was dotted with diners reclining on couches, mattresses and chairs. In the background, on the other side of the red sea, a range of mountains had changed from the yellowish color of the sunset to orange and a dark red, now they were turning gray and soon they would vanish into the dark.

The scene had affected them both. They were quiet and more serene. Aliza said: "Mom, I'm not going to say anything. I believe you will come to your senses in time. We all will be waiting for you at home."

"Let's just enjoy ourselves tonight," Rita said. Privately she had given some thought of getting to Gil's birthday, she would need three days. Two days traveling back and forth and one more day for the party, it could be done with some hardship, but facing all her family there, and the questions, gruelings and suspicions would be too much for her.

The next morning Aliza departed. She would tell one and all at home that her mother needed to remain there for her health. Many questions would be asked and there would have to be some creative explaining. They promised to write and phone to each other and Rita would get her letters from her former hotel. Yoni returned to his place beside Rita.

"You did not tell her about us?"

"I did, but I did not mention your age."

"Why should my age matter so much?"

"Such is the way of the world." Rita sighed.

"We are happy together?!" Yoni insisted. Half statement and half question.

"Yes, we are, but it is strange . . ."

"Who cares."

"My family does, my daughter does."

"Are you regretting anything?"

"No, we can make this work."

Rita pulled herself together with an effort and found a bank in the town next to the village and opened an account. She wrote a letter to an uncle, a real estate agent, asking him to rent her place in Tel Aviv for the year, put some of her belongings in storage and to send the money to her bank. Not daring to explain what he would never understand, she wrote to him of her intention to remain for the time being in Sinai for her health and not caring much if he believed her.

Half a year had passed and they were still together. They had left the hotel and found a temporary place close to the sea on a monthly basis, not furnished, but cheap. They had one bed with a mattress and one mattress without a bed, which created a difference in height. They had much fun tumbling over one another. They amused themselves chasing after odds and ends, like kitchen utensils, carpets, and shelves, and other matters. A rickety table had been found somewhere, at first, they used boxes for chairs and it had all been cool and amusing fun and a part of being together and enjoying each other. The money which had finally arrived from renting Rita's place was more than ample for their needs. Sometimes, when she felt like it, Rita cooked, they lived an easy uncomplicated life.

Then they conceived an idea:

* * *

Roads in the desert are like the arteries of a huge ecosystem and are mostly found in the valleys between the many dense mountain ranges. On the way north toward Israel an intersection collects the roads to and from various places. A shack had been constructed there with a garden of stones and vegetation surrounding it. A water tank towered above the shack and a generator, placed far away, so as not to disturb the peace and quiet, fed the needed power into the place.

Tired travelers can halt there, stretch their legs and refresh themselves from the dust, heat, and the tension of a long drive. Cool drinks and hot drinks are served and even a sandwich can be had. There are sweets and chocolates for the children and an assortment of nuts, biscuits, waffles, and other goodies to nibble at on the long trip in both directions, those are displayed on the shelves. There is even ice cream. Inside the place is cool and air-conditioned. Outside are picnic tables to prepare meals on, with benches in the shade of some planted trees.

The lone desert kiosk, run by a mother and her boy, is located by the junction where they had first met. They had toiled long and hard. Rita arraigned the buying and selling of their products and saw to the many other chores. Yoni, who had never liked being told what to do, worked, inspired and enthusiastic, from morning to night. The place is theirs, Rita's and his and he intended to make the kiosk and the nearby surroundings as enticing and comfortable as possible under the desert conditions.

Yoni had constructed an enclosure with some goats, sheep, a donkey and chickens ran about underfoot. Children could ride the donkey around the compound for a fee. (They were already saving money to buy a camel.) Other attractions were the aquarium-like cages of glass which held lizards, snakes, and scorpions found in the area. Sometimes Rita had to argue and plead with Yoni to get him to stop working and get some rest. She had not returned to her dwelling in Tel Aviv. Her home now is in an air-conditioned shack, the mountains greeting them with the sunrise and parting from them in the dusk.

The desert had claimed its final victory.

THE END

LAUREL AND HARDY

The Sinai desert has opposing cultural meanings for the Bedouins and the many vacationers who had flocked to enjoy the desert. To the locals, the desert meant a rigid rule of regulations and way of life not to be disrupted. To the tourist, the vast expanses symbolized freedom of thought and behavior, a release from the pressures and inhibitions of their over populated urban backgrounds, physical, emotional and mental. This came to be termed as relaxation.

There are others too: the seekers, searching for some meaning in life, or a different lifestyle; hoping to find freedom and happiness in the desert. In our Western societies, there are many disillusioned and displaced persons in quest for something better. Often not sure of what exactly they are looking for, they travel from country to country, from one place to another, frequently seeking out the more primitive and isolated areas in hope of finding serenity: Asking consciously, or unconscious of it *'where have we gone wrong?'* little realizing that they are dragging their conflicts within them, to wherever they wander.

Such would be the fate of Lina. She came from a rural area around Nykobing Denmark. Her father, a land owner and grain merchant, was a great sticker for rules. She and her younger sister, Yana, had grown up in a normal well to do bourgeois and protestant environment, never doubting or criticizing their way of life. Lina had excellent grades and had been encouraged enthusiastically by her teachers to enlist in the university. She intended to be a history student. Thrilled, because studying meant leaving her rural home for Copenhagen, she had arrived to the university and there she had received what can only amount to a cultural shock.

Another different world confronted her. Students of all races flocked happily together under the canopy of student exchange. For the first time, Lina saw and fraternized with Africans, Indians, Asians, and students from Western countries. They had parties and gatherings almost daily and studying appeared to be only a part-time occupation. After a short while, she also found out that she was the only virgin around.

"How quaint," her roommate had said at the time. "Shall I get my boyfriend to do you?"

Lina, amazed at the turn of events, had blushed all over. She did not answer for a while. "Are you crazy? Don't you love him?"

"What does that have to do with anything?"

Lina's roommate, Helga, had come from Svendborg, which lay not too far away from Lina's home, and they had become good friends. Helga intended to take Lina in hand as her protégée, which made her feel older, more mature, and gave her a new-found confidence, which she had not had before.

A pendulum swings from one end to another, and so it is frequently with us humans. Lina and Helga had been projected into a world of parties, boys, drink and cheap drugs, all in good fun, binging and indulging with the unrestrained irresponsible and the fast passing vitality of youth. Lina had had many affairs, some short one-nighters, while others lasted for a week or two and very few had lasted over the period of some months. There were many exchange students from third world countries, and Lina, encountering black and brown colored girls and boys with different cultures from all over the world, grew more cosmopolitan and adopted a cool lifestyle. Lina and Helga did not spend too much emotional energy over their short-lasting affairs. They actually managed to do some studying too.

In her studies she had heard of and been drawn to, a new energetic young lecturer. Among her first courses had been an introduction to history. This person claimed there had never been a moment's peace on the globe since the beginning of recorded time and challenged them to find some. Lina, being reared in a quiet rural area where nothing much happened, had found that hard to believe at first. The lessons back at school had been about historic events, and, naturally, there had been wars and conflicts. She began to see her fellow men and history in a different light. Her dad had always pointed out and insisted on her world being the best of all possible worlds, and everything was as should be, with a comfortable Deity overseeing all, while in her studies, she found a world where strife and a Godless ruthless struggle for dominance were the main issues.

Then Lina had met Rick; older, with a scholarship and a permanent chip on his shoulder. Dark, handsome, mysterious and reckless, but singularly enough, they did not have sex right away which endeared Rick to her. He told her his story. He had had a hard time growing up being half Jewish and called himself a third generation Holocaust survivor. His grandparents had escaped the Germans in WW2 to Holland and friends had hidden them from the Nazis, his father had grown up in cellars and attics, always hiding, estranged from his own parents, frightened, insecure and bitter.

He made the period come alive to her: "Many of my family have been murdered by the Nazis. Only my father, grandfather and one aunt survived from a family of eight. After the war, we stuck together. Dad, often ignoring the fact that friends had hidden him, at the risk of their lives…or at the least, the possibility of a long and extremely unpleasant imprisonment under the Nazi occupation, developed a paranoia-like suspicion of everyone being anti-Semitic in one way or another, and included even his own people on occasion."

Rick told her that he had learned from his grandfather how there had been a time when Jews had desperately wanted to get out of Germany and Europe; anywhere to get away from the Nazis. Countries had closed their borders to them, only letting a totally inadequate, under the circumstances, quota in. Millions did not manage to get out of Europe and had been rounded up to concentration camps where they ended their lives. Starvation, cold and exterminations had done their jobs.

A bitterness and resentment had been passed on to Rick. He would explain to Lina, engaging her sympathy: "Can you imagine, my grandfather, who raised me after my dad died, a gentle cultured person, unlike myself?" He would cynically snicker. "Suddenly finding himself the target of unexplained hatred and discrimination amidst his own people and nation he grew up with. His countrymen and fellow citizens had abandoned those very civilized and enlightening qualities which together they had been taught from childhood. He had no tools to cope with those changes. My father too, I grew up with two subdued dead people in an atmosphere of puzzled and bewildered bitterness, till I ran away from home."

"What about your mother?" Lina asked.

"My mother, a Dutch girl, born after the war, younger than my father, she could not understand his outbursts of moodiness and lack of socializing; this is what little I know. She wanted parties, dancing and travel. She left us, my father died and my aunt and my grandfather raised me."

Lina had undergone an emphatic motherly feeling, which felt new to her. She herself had a good stable life and intended to compensate him for what life had handed out to him. They became a couple, inseparable at parties and events. Then she found out how Rick made what little money he had: Rick dealt and took drugs. She believed in her love and dedication to him; she would cure him. At the end of one of the semesters, she took him home to Nykobing to meet her parents.

Lina's parents were devout Protestants, and her alliance with Rick struck them hard. They did not have Lina's broader view of fraternization and internationality from the university. They were simple country folks. To them the aim in life justified making money under the canopy of their religion and having a family with the grace of God.

They were polite to Rick with an icy correctness which had not been lost on Lina. Yana, more flexible, seemed friendly but indifferent. Both Lina and Rick felt that her folks would never accept their liaison. Lina's dad later had taken her aside and threatened her in no uncertain terms; he would not pay for her tutorage if she continued to remain with Rick. They had a long emotional argument in which neither would budge.

For the first time in her life she criticized her folks: "All you care for is making money," she accused, "There is more to life than money ... and complacency!"

"Honest hardworking money comes first, always, and achieves the good in life," her dad had summed up for her. "We believe in the good God, your boyfriend does not, has no money and it does not look like he intends to earn any!"

"I do not care for those matters," Lina hit back. "I love Rick and he loves me. History is full of people who have come to their money dishonestly; kings, popes, lords . . . whatever, presidents, politicians . . ." she ran down.

"Is this what they teach you in Copenhagen? The scoundrels."

The gap between their perceptions and understandings of life had become very great and they were not able to bridge it, neither wanting or willing to grasp the others point of view.

The issue had remained unresolved.

For Lina, there had not been any decision to make. She would not leave Rick. Without her dad's resources, she could not live in Copenhagen and certainly not study there. Rick, his scholarship paid for, but nevertheless almost penniless, did make some money by his dubious methods, but he spent much of his cash on drugs. Lina and Rick discussed those issues between them. Lina felt that perhaps in time together with some domestic pressure from her mom, her father might relent.

Rick had seen a poster in the university, inviting the students to spend time in a kibbutz in Israel, including a short explanation of the commune-like structure. Half a day's work would pay for their keep and for the rest of the time they could do as they pleased. Not a long-term plan for them, but could be a new start. Rick would take a sabbatical from his scholarship. Communes have an attraction for idealistic young students, and would be an exciting change for them both - an adventure. He explained to her of what little he knew about communes and she had found the project to her liking.

Lina had left home with Rick without the blessings of her family, but her mother had secretly given her some money. In Copenhagen, they phoned the number they had copied from the poster and after meeting with a representative of the kibbutz movement, were accepted. Rick would have to stop taking drugs as they would be checked on arrival and he firmly promised to do so. They flew to Israel, were checked for diseases and soon after, were sent to a kibbutz. In most places, the kibbutz had set aside a separate site for the overseas students. They were called volunteers and lived in shacks. Lina and Rick were heartily welcomed by the group there. In some little way those settings appeared to remind them of the university, but minus the studying, instead they had six hours of work. There were young people from all over the Western world. They had little contact with the actual kibbutz members, but that did not matter. The volunteers had a full eventual life of their own.

Lina found herself and Rick living in a rural settlement, away from a larger city and felt pleased. Rick would be away from temptations. They ate in a communal dining hall. Lina worked in the kitchen and Rick in the orange groves. The rest of the time they spent hanging around together and swapping stories. Sex was free and couples formed and separated with a fast dynamic energy. Rick and Lina did not indulge in this.

Working in the kitchen, Lina had met Ethel, an older woman, and they had become friendly and exchanged stories and impressions. Lina learned how Ethel had lost her parents in the Holocaust and had grown up with strangers. At the age of three she and her older brother had been put on a ship and sailed from Germany. There were only children aboard, put there by desperate parents, not being able to get out themselves, but trying frantically to save their children from the Nazi regime. Her brother had died on the way. Commune life had helped her physically, but not emotionally. Ethel, on anti-depression medication, felt too timid to assert herself, and her fellow members frequently ignored her or passed her over. She had found some consolation in talking to the volunteers who often needed her advice on kibbutz issues.

Lina amazed Ethel with her knowledge of the Holocaust and they became great friends, and the two young people were frequent guests in her home were they met the rest of the family. They exchanged impressions and stories.

They had met at an opportune moment. The kibbutz had a rotation going for a paid overseas trip according to seniority and Ethel with Avi, her husband planned to fly to Denmark, hire a car and drive to Norway through Sweden and back. Then they intended to fly to Austria to a relative and take the Euro-rail to Italy. They had formulated an ambitious plan and would take them forty or more days, this being a once in a lifetime opportunity. Their children, Ilana and Rinat, would stay with friends.

Ethel, very excited, told Lina and Rick all about the forthcoming trip.

"If you are in Denmark then you must visit my home in Nykobing," Lina had insisted.

"Why not? We can try, if it is not too far out of the way," Ethel had promised. A place to rest from the privations of the trip might be useful for a few days. Lina had given her the phone number and address.

Ethel and Avi had their tour in due time and after an exhausting drive to Norway through Sweden and then back to Denmark, they found the time to visit Lina's home. Lina's parents treated them like royalty. They communicated in broken English. Lina's parents and her little sister could not do enough for them. Christina, Lina's mom, asked them what they especially liked in Danish food and would cook it for them. They had their car vacuumed, washed and cleaned. Their dirty clothes were laundered. Lina's dad, and her sister Yana, took them to an open air rural Museum. They were shown slides of family pictures and the area around in full winter snow. The real and warm hospitality had touched both of them deeply.

Then once, when they were alone with Christina, she had burst into tears and cried long and hard, revealing that she was dreadfully worried about Lina: "She is so far away and in a dangerous area. There always seems to be fighting."

Avi comforted her. "The kibbutz may be far away, but is a safe place. We rear children there. We have old people, sick people. The media always exaggerate and seek sensations. Never believe all you see and hear."

Christina sobbed and then revealed her true worry: not the kibbutz, but Rick. "When they were here I found drugs in his clothes while laundering them. He will lead her into trouble. Rick is unstable and unreliable, I don't like him or trust him."

Ethel comforted her: "Young people are headstrong, what can we do?"

She had asked a rhetorical question, but Christina chose to address the issue. "You are from the kibbutz; you must be able to get him away from her. Remove him from the kibbutz for taking drugs."

"Wouldn't she follow him to wherever he goes?" Avi pointed out. "It might only get worse."

"Please you must do something. Send Lina back to us," she implored. "Maybe go to the kibbutz office and get them to send her back."

Ethel and Avi both, were touched by her plight. They did not believe they could interfere or get anything done along the lines Christina had suggested, but of course they would try. Avi wanted to allay her fears. "We will do our best," he had promised, "but it will be over another month before we return."

"I will be eternally grateful for whatever you can do." Christina had thanked them.

A month later Avi and Ethel had returned to the kibbutz. They had many presents for their children but found them in a distressed state after being left parentless for so long and had to tend to them. Avi found the time to inquire after Lina and Rick. The kibbutz had a member who acted as a liaison and guide to the volunteers, and he informed Avi shortly: "They quarreled and left."

"Together?" Avi asked.

"No, Lina left first, then Rick." He knew no more. Volunteers come and go all the time.

Avi had a thorough nature and did not like to leave matters unfinished. He got the story out of one of the volunteer girls: "Rick cheated on her," she said shortly. Then she giggled. "He could not resist the fun."

"Did she say where she intended to go?"

"She was too upset."

Avi wrote a letter to Christina, telling her what he had found out, but he could not have known that Lina had found herself pregnant. After the initial shock, Lina had told Rick and he had shrugged it off.

"It is your child!" she had stressed. "I did not fool around. Unlike you," she had added.

"We do not want to be held back with a child," he had insisted.

"Held back from what?"

"Whatever. To be free, unhindered." They had a long argument, mutual accusations following one after another.

Then came the blaming part.

"You were on the pill," he said.

"Remember the night I told you. I had forgotten to take one, but you insisted on doing it without a condom."

"We didn't have any."

"Then we should have waited."

Lina could not stand the sight of Rick anymore. She moved out of the kibbutz to another one nearby and wired her mom for money to get home. The money had come and she occupied herself preparing for the flight back.

In Nykobing, she found her father cold at first, but mom took her 'little baby' in hand and pampered her, immensely relieved. She had Lina back. Christina had thanked Ethel and Avi profusely in a letter, erroneously thinking they had managed this and sent them gold chains with crosses for their children, in her agitation totally forgetting they were Jewish. Ethel, though not religious, would not let her girls wear those until the crosses were removed.

Eventually, Lina told her mother: "Mom, I'm pregnant."

Christina did not feel surprised, she had feared this and even had nightmares. "Rick's?"

"Of course, who else?"

"The way you have been living . . ." She left her sentence unfinished.

"I want to have it," Lina said.

"And who will take care of the baby? You?"

"Yes."

"You are too young and inexperienced. I will have to do all the work as usual."

"It is my child and I will take care of my baby. How old were you when you had me?"

The argument waged on. Lina wanted the child which would be hers to love, control and form. She would be the main person in its life; a new feeling emerged which she had never felt before, even with Rick, and she had her way. In due time a boy arrived, christened Søren. Lina lived with her parents, at first, in a kind of gloomy neutralized truce, which slowly dissolved as Søren grew older, his charm captivating one and all. Lina found work, while Christina took care of Søren.

Lina was not satisfied with her life. As we all do, she needed love and sympathy and she did not get much at home. Rick too had not loved her as she now felt she deserved. She felt a strong longing for something, but did not know what. She took the family car for long rides around the district and stopped at the local pubs, frequently returning home late at night.

"Don't you think it's time to stop fooling around?" Christina would nag at her.

"I work all day. I need to have some fun."

"Fun! You have a child now, show some responsibility."

"Let me be."

She had some affairs, and once more, two years after Søren, found herself pregnant. True she had been on a binge occasionally. Uneasily, she recognized that she would be unable to identify the father. He could be anyone of the three guys she had sex with. What would her folks say now? She deliberated long and hard, best to get rid of it. She did not confide in her mother. A human life is not so easy to get rid of, even when social and family pressures might be great. So, Oskar had been born.

Christina had wanted to be grandmother, but not full time, or even an overtime one. Lina had two children and no husband and now, as she had a day job, Christina found herself occupied during the day hours with housekeeping and babysitting while Lina was away. In the evenings, Lina often went out, and Yana reluctantly helped watch over the children. Christina resented this and quarrels became the order of the day, a state of affairs which lasted for some time due to inertia, and a once peaceful household became the center of many conflicts and disputes.

Lina, dissatisfied with her life, finally attached herself to another man and left with him taking her boys with her. They roamed around Europe at first, living from hand to mouth. They drifted to Spain, then to Italy and later to Greece. In Cypress, he had enough of being a father to her children and left her.

Lina traveled to Israel, she had been there once before and had liked it. Fellow travelers had told her about Eilat at the north tip of the Red Sea. The deserted part of the Eilat shore had become a haven for much of the human chaff drifting around. A colony had invariably sprung up, the climate being warm and hot with almost no rain. Tents and improvised shacks had appeared all over the area. There were no toilets or water to be had, except in some nearby restaurants. There she lived the life of a nomad together with a similar group of people. Sometimes they would share meals. She had a small tent together with her boys who stopped much of the free easy drugs and sex going around. Søren, at eleven, and Oskar, being nine, had learned to scavenge and even steal occasionally from the tourists nearby. They did not go to any school except for the school of life, but Lina taught them from some books she had brought with her and they could talk and write after a fashion in Danish and English and some lame Hebrew. Lina made them do homework in arithmetic, spelling and grammar, history and even basic geography. She had become a tutor to her children. They studied in their own way for an hour or two each day and for the rest of the time they ran wild.

Lina had made one friend: Ingmar, coming from Iceland; an older person, he had a beard and soft eyes. She spent some hours with him in his tiny tent.

"Where are you from again?" Lina asked him.

"Mosfellsbaer."

"And that is in Iceland?"

"An outskirt of Reykjavik."

"What brought you here?"

"The sun, the everlasting sun. I worship the sun!" He was indeed brown all over from the sun.

The area, with no toilet facilities, had slowly turned into a health hazard and had become a slum. Complaints were eventually made and the Eilat police decided to crack down on them. Those who would not move were threatened with jail. The small group dispersed.

"Where are you moving to," Lina asked Ingmar.

"Time for me to return and live a normal life.

"In Iceland?"

"With my wife and two children."

She had not known.

Lina with her boys and a few others moved south into the Sinai desert where they finally separated to different places. Lina had not wanted any of those backpacker guys around her kids anymore and found herself alone at the outskirts of a Bedouin village, once a fishing village along the coast, by the name of Dahab. With the influx of many Israelis and Western tourists the villagers had soon realized the financial advantages of tourism. They rented shacks for ready money and sold local products and others tourist items, imported or smuggled from Egypt. During the fifteen-year period of Israel's control in the Sinai desert, the small village had grown into large tourist resort with many shops, hotels and rooms to let. In Sinai, the Israeli authorities were lenient and easygoing and one could do as one pleased with few questions asked.

Lina had not wanted to live too close to civilization, meaning the nearby village turning into a town. A totally new section had sprung up with banks and municipal offices, a regular police station and Dahab City, so ambitiously called by the locals, had all the makings of an urban area while the older village remained the same; homesteads surrounded by a fence with mud paths in between and chickens or an occasional goat or donkey crossing over. Multiple palm trees dotted the area giving some shade. Lina had found a deserted, partly collapsed wreck further away by the edge of the former older village. The partly decayed and roofless ruin, probably used to keep goats or other farm animals, could be turned into a home for them.

The boys disagreed.

Søren, the older one, had questions: "Why can't we live with people?"

"People are fussy. Here we do what we please."

"Do we have to study here too?"

"Yes."

"Then why . . ."

"Søren and Oskar, dear children. We will make a real home for ourselves here and have fun." Her enthusiasm spread to her sons. "We can build this place and turn it into a palace."

At first, they slept in their tent, or in the open–the desert is warm and dry. She and the boys, working hard and enthusiastically, cleaned the place, fixed it up and moved in. In time, they scavenged additional pieces of furniture and trappings and dragged them inside and gradually the old shed became to look like a home. Things were quiet and peaceful, the way Lina liked them. No one interfered. Water had to be fetched from a nearby water tank, a ten-minute walk away, but Søren and Oskar, with a borrowed donkey, took care of it. They had dug a cesspool and fixed a toilet with an outhouse. They took turns at keeping it clean, even Oskar. Lina had learned to get groceries from the village stores which did not cater to the tourists and only the locals were customers. Cheap food could be had and she still had some money for now. Later something would come up. She might find work in one of the many stores in the village or maybe the Israelis would find work for her in one of the diving centers which had sprung up. She let herself drift with the time.

Lina had some minor contacts with the Bedouins and learned that they claim to be the most free of all tribes. Lina admired and envied them their freedom and let Søren and Oskar run wild in the mornings and afternoons, when the sun was not too hot. They were often naked, except for shorts. They found caves and hiding places and tried to make friends with the Bedouin children. Bedouins as we all, are social conscious, and a strange woman, not a tourist, with two children and no husband or family, could only be at the bottom of their social scale. To them she appeared some kind of an unexplained strange creature to be shunned and even ridiculed. The Israel army had imposed certain rules of behavior on them. They could not drive her out or harm her, and so they uneasily accepted her and the boys. Søren and Oskar, both blond and often naked, did not always have an easy time. They both had learned enough words in Arabic to get by.

Two older boys of the Bedouin group, Abd and Kamal often teased them and the result would sometimes end in stones being thrown at them, or a fight between Søren and Kamal. Characteristically of boys, they hid this from their mother.

"You have skins like women," Abd would mock, while the others laughed. Then Kamal would touch and pet Oskar.

"Leave him alone," Søren insisted, protecting his smaller brother.

Young Bedouin are lecherous, probably no more so than anyone else, but their society does not allow for any fraternization between the sexes over a certain age until they are married, and the latter is a complex social and economic procedure. Søren often kept himself and his younger brother from being molested by the older boys and there was always a price to pay. They were sometimes estranged from the group of children. Their foreign names too were a source of ridicule. Some of the tourists came with families and children, but those were kept busy with their own activities and did not have much time to spend with Lina's boys, other than getting acquainted. Children are not always aware of their needs and the boys were no exception. They were looking for kids of their own kind, age and culture to play with.

Time passed. In Sinai, time is not counted the same way as in hectic Western society. The days and nights pass evenly with only an occasional wind storm interrupting nature's routine and occurs mainly in late summer and autumn. Lina had longed for isolation from society and now she had it. Life remained peaceful with its daily recurring and reassuring routines and she sank into a relaxing state.

For us humans, nothing stays the same for very long. Lina, still young with the forces of youth stirring in her, lived a good and healthy life. However, one main feature was missing and she felt the need for some companionship and action. As the days passed by, her drives and cravings became more acute, a fire lit in her belly. She became aware of being still beautiful, having kept her figure, and being brown all over from the sun. She felt full of the juices of life. When going to the center of the little town for products, she could not but help notice the young Bedouins eyeing her lustfully.

Westerners are scantily dressed in hot tourist places. Outside the center of the town, many went about totally nude, in the water and out of it, but Lina did not have the status of one the regular tourists, the locals eyed her lewdly and joked among themselves. Lina had of course ignored those hot looks, but now she found herself, without meaning to, inadvertently acknowledging them by body language and frequently by a hot flush all over her.

Near the center of the growing town an improvised camel camp had sprung up. The camels were there for the tourists and were guarded by youths dressed in speckles shiny white galabiahs, a robe-like covering from head to foot they all seemed to wear like a uniform. Lina would pass by on her way. A youth stopped her: "Madam, a camel ride? Nice, cheap, good." She had passed by before and had never been stopped.

"No thank you." Lina made as it to continue on her way.

"Very nice view, we go to cave."

"Not today, sorry."

"I take you on my camel, no cost, free. You like?"

Lina paused, a free camel ride did sound like fun and she had not had much of that lately. Peace and quiet, yes, but fun . . . no.

"How long will it take?"

"Not long, half hour, hour maybe."

She felt excited by the prospect. "Okay."

He led her to one of the camels and helped her climb up, a real gentleman. The camel growled and complained in protest and was hit for its troubles. He climbed up behind her and grunted a command to the camel.

A camel getting up from a dormant position is like a minor earthquake. First the dromedary has to get up on its front knees and one is propelled backward, then the hind legs begin to straighten out and one is catapulted forwards, then the front legs straighten out and the rider is pushed backwards again. Lina held on to the saddle horn for dear life. The youth used the opportunity to put an arm around her, holding her steady. This felt good to both of them. The ride passed pleasantly, Lina being only too aware of the guide behind her and their bodies touching. He put an arm around her again, and Lina did not resist, she turned her head, "What is your name?"

"G'amal"

"I'm Lina."

They talked a bit. Riding on a camel, back to front is not too a good an incentive for long conversations. Neither did the language barrier help. They reached the cave and after the upheavals of the camel settling down, Lina found herself again in G'amal's arms. One thing led to another as in the way of us humans, no matter what race and creed. But . . . there are many cultural divergences and those very different strong notions and feelings give any event its meaning. To Lina, casual sex used to be an exercise of her free will. Good, healthy fun, relaxing and answering a strong need for human companionship. She had been alone too much lately.

To G'amal, raised as a Bedouin, and sex-starved since puberty, their act turned into an intense agitated event, even more so as it is strongly taboo by their sect and tribe. One can easily get killed for extra marital sex, though outsiders are fair game always, and are not considered as equals, especially loose Western women. He did not see her as a person but as a kind of prostitute, worth little human consideration. He was clever enough to disguise his notions by hiding them from her. He had occasion to study tourists, especially the ladies. He knew the power of romance and had learned how to manipulate and behave with the foreign females if he wanted to get anywhere.

Lina, amused by his intensity, gave him a great deal of slack. He did not have much foreplay and entered her. It did not take long until he began gasping. He had been too quick for her, but she found she could make herself enjoy the scene.

"Take it easy, we have time," she whispered to him, her mouth close to his ear, but he seemed too far gone. A few more gasps and he was done. They lay quietly for a while, then Lina got a tissue out of her bag and gave him one. "To wipe." She also cleaned herself. They talked a little and Lina heard from him that the Bedouins think of themselves as the most free and independent of all Arabs. G'amal boasted and Lina did not argue with him, she had once taken this at face value, but she learned otherwise; their so-called honor made them adhere to many tribal taboos and their women were little better then house slaves.

"We go back. Is late." G'amal said.

The ride back had not been totally silent. "You come . . . to . . . morrow," G'amal asked from behind her.

"Maybe," Lina replied, noncommittal.

"You come!" he insisted.

"Okay," Lina answered easily.

There had been a few occasions on which Lina had taken him up on his offer. His friends chaffed him. He had succeeded in what they all were endeavoring to get done–to get into some tourist women's pants. In due time, another youth offered his sexual services to Lina and had been accepted. Hers were the easy ways of the Copenhagen University and she did not see why not. Those short liaisons would be benefiting to both of them. In the Bedouin society, they marked her as a slut and a possible easy lay. They called her a prostitute behind her back.

Life as usual continued for a while and the word about her spread around. Nothing lasts, especially the good things. Some months after Lina had moved into her shack she noticed a telltale cloud of dust coming her way, a shabby looking taxi arrived creating a path and a local looking older Bedouin with a mustache got out. He and Lina greeted each other shortly, Lina felt uneasy and anxious. She did not like disturbances.

The greetings over, the man said, "This my land!" He seemed not to know English too well.

"Yes?" Lina inquired politely.

"My land," he repeated.

Lina kept quiet.

"My place. My house." He pointed to her shack.

"We fixed it up, we live here now," Lina stated.

"You pay."

"We found this place a total ruin, no one lived here."

"My place, no pay, you go!"

"We shall see about that," she said and closed the door angrily. The taxi drove off.

Lina had some unspecified vague connections to the few Israel authorities in the area, meaning she had once or twice talked to an officer and had been told where the water tank was located; as for the rest, they left her to her own devices. Now she sought them out in the town. A soldier guided her to an office-like room with two busy officers and she told her story. Israel is a small country and the desert is a large place, sparsely populated in some parts. The army had been thinly spread along the vast territory and all its managing resources were strained to the limit.

"We try not to interfere with the Bedouins," the officer told her after hearing her story.

"But this person could throw us out, me and the children."

"Did he threaten you?"

"No, not yet."

"It probably is his land, why not pay him?"

"That ruin did not even have a roof when we came! Besides. I have very little money. Can you not hint to him to lay off us?"

"I will do my best. I will talk to him," one officer said. "Who is he? What is his name?"

However, Lina did not know.

Things were quiet for the next two weeks, then the taxi came again and the same person stepped out, but he seemed more threatening than before to Lina.

"You pay for place."

Lina tried to pacify him. "Come in and have some coffee."

This being a known and acknowledged ceremony, he nodded and entered. She served him coffee. When this brand of ceremonial drinking ended, the Bedouin returned to his former claim. "You pay for place."

"I have talked to the Israeli officers," she said, trying to intimidate him.

He laughed harshly. "Not their land, is mine!"

"How do I know this is your land. Do you have a deed? Some proof?"

"I am Abu Salim. Land of family. You not pay, I go to officers."

He got up and left. Lina had feared there might be some unpleasantness or even violence in some way and she had sent the children out to play, but maybe it all would pass over now.

A few days later, Lina saw the telltale cloud of dust again, an army jeep came to her place. An officer and the driver stepped out and after the usual greetings the officer came to the point. "There seems to be some trouble here," he began.

"About the money for our has-been pig sty?"

"Rent must be paid everywhere in the world, even here."

"He has no proof. Does our place belong to him?"

"It seems the Bedouins confirm his claims, we have done some checking and we want no trouble with them."

"So you are on his side then."

"We are on no one's side, except for keeping the peace."

"At mine and my children's expense."

"We can provide you with army rations."

"Good. Thank you."

They did not need much there. Food and a few clothes were the only articles needing money. They led a simple and easy life, the way Lina intended.

"But you have to come to an agreement with . . . this Abu Salim."

"Done, anything in reason."

The army had kept its promise and rations were brought to them periodically, a relief for her as it made for less work. The rations had only to be prepared and not cooked, but she did buy fresh groceries and some fruits from the local market.

Abu Salim came around again. Lina let him in and accosted him aggressively. "How much money do you want?"

"Two hundred (Egyptian) pounds, you pay in shekels (Israeli money)." At the time, around sixty USA dollars.

It may not have been much, but Lina could not afford it. Life in the desert is cheap and had been one of the reasons Lina had settled down there. She had learned to haggle, the price he asked must be three or four times as much as he had in mind to get out of her.

"We have no money. Eighty is all the place is worth." She paused, "We can leave . . . find another shack, we leave your place as we found it, a dirty ruin without a roof and you will have nothing."

"Hundred fifty, is my land." So, the bargaining went on. Lina, being the more desperate, having little money saved by and no job yet, as she wanted to be at home for her children, did not relent. At last the sum came down to one hundred. He would not back down anymore.

"Too much," Lina said.

He leered, he had heard about the woman, "You pay . . . no . . . need money!"

She knew what he meant. To her, having sex had always been a normal part of her life, but sex for money or rent was prostitution, and had remained her own cultural taboo. "We'll see."

"You here six month, six hundred pounds."

"You're crazy! Where do I get the money?"

He kept quiet and stared at her, his meaning clear. His eyes burned with lust. The boys were away at some game or other. After all it meant little to her and it would be over quickly. If it would take *that* to leave her alone . . . and in peace, she could manage. Everything has a price and she found herself willing to pay for some peace and comfort.

"Come," she said and led him to her makeshift bed.

News gets around in the desert, not any less fast them in modern society and of course the arrangement Lina had with Abu Salim had somehow been transmitted by mouth to ear and even filtered down to the Bedouin children by hints and an abridged version. Lina's boys had a hard time. The Bedouin kids ridiculed them and called their mom a whore. There were many fights and bruises, which the children tried to hide from their mother.

Luckily, a much greater political event had occurred, which overshadowed all and occupied everyone's mind. An understanding had come about between Israel and Egypt. Israel had agreed to hand over the Sinai Peninsula for a signed peace treaty. Soon the Israelis, with their Western ideas of Democracy would be out. The Egyptians would be allowed only a small occupation force and the Bedouins would again be able to control the vast areas and everything would return back to 'normal.'

At the time, with the desert still in Israeli hands, Ethel and Avi had decided to take a trip to Sinai with their two girls, Ilana and Rinat. They had been there before a few times, but they felt it to be now or never. Sinai under the Egyptians would not be the same. They could get one of the kibbutz vans for four days and would take around eight hours driving to their destination. Avi, a licensed but amateur scuba diver, for once did a very unprofessional thing. He took four air compressed diving tanks with him, intending to dive alone without a partner, which was against the safety regulations and could be dangerous, but he would not let such an opportunity slip by. He had decided not to dive beneath thirty feet and if any malfunction occurred, he could swim up easily. Soon the Sinai Peninsula would be turned over to the Egyptians and getting there would be much more difficult.

The kibbutz had an organized small scuba diving set and they would get to the Sinai seashore twice a year. Avi had been to most diving locations along the Red Sea and knew Dahab to be one of the best and one of the easiest accessible, a good place for the children too, with many shops where trinkets and games were to be had. Dahab had been made into a fun place for tourists with bars and discotheques open late into the night.

He had decided on the trip which would do them all some good. Lately, Ethel and he had been having many fights. Ethel lacked confidence in herself and people walked all over them.

They had arguments. Their household had slowly ceased to be a quiet one. Ilana and Rinat were sometimes troubled. Ethel, mostly tense, frequently being too stressed and impatient to have sex, while Avi had turned more lethargic, flowing passively along day by day and hardly ever initiating a thing. On occasion, they could criticize and blame each other.

Ethel did not drive and Avi had to do all the driving. They rested every few hours on their way south, the Red Sea on their left. It turned late afternoon when Avi felt too tired to continue driving and they put up a tent for the night at a cove by the sea, protected from the strong breeze that had sprung up. They chose a wild looking spot and for Avi, it would turn out to be the first, but very minor and futile experience, of a taste in extra martial sex. Nearby a group of German tourists were also making camp amidst much fuss and noise.

Avi, eager to do some diving before dark, had scouted around for a likely place. He could not help but observe a lady tourist, nude, wearing only sneakers, had wandered off, away from the group and seemed to be going for a lone dip in the water. They were in a windswept and battered looking place, like many others in the area. The shore and sea being studied with rocks, some of them huge boulders, fragments which had broken off from the cliffs around and had rolled or gravitated to the sea. She had passed out of sight between them. His heart beat faster, instinctively he followed her between the monolith-like structures. He had taken off his swimming trunks and placed them on one of the many rocks nearby. He too had only his shoes on. She must have decided to return and suddenly they accosted each other. They were flanked by two very large boulders and had met in a narrow pass in between.

Avi stared. He saw a slim woman with small pear-shaped breasts, a tuft of pubic hair could be seen. He lusted for her.

Sex with Ethel, routine and comforting, did not create much excitement and he had not had sex for some time, but this had been too sudden and soon for Avi, and he could not get himself to make a move. He rationalized. Sex always has complications attached, he did not want to get involved, Ethel and the girls were not so far away, and maybe this female was not looking for sex. They confronted each other, face to face. He nodded to her politely, his face a frozen mask and she returned the greeting. They did not speak and passed each other, their naked bodies almost touching in the narrow passage between the rocks. A naked human male and a naked human female, yet they both went on their separate ways. Avi felt let down, he had not made the grade in his own mind and did not feel like doing any diving. Pulling on his trunks, he returned to Ethel and the girls, who were preparing a meal. "I haven't found a good spot for a dive," he told them.

They arrived in Dahab the next morning. While they were setting up a more permanent camp by the old village, the girls ran off to explore and play. They returned after a while with two almost naked sunburned younger light haired boys. "Can we play with them? They live nearby."

Ethel could tell those were well-behaved kids. They were obviously Swedish or Danish. "Yes, of course." The adults thought nothing of it. Tourists often brought their children with them. The boys could speak some Hebrew, which they had picked up during the Israeli period. Ilana and Rinat had brought some of their gadgets with them; games and toys, and they showed them to the boys. Years had passed since the boys had seen any games. Ilana, the older one, noticed their agitation. Impulsive with the natural goodwill of a yet innocent child, she offered one. "You want?" She held out a small portable game.

"Yes."

"Here." She gave him the game. He was delighted.

"Really? Mine?'

"We have more at home."

The children moved off. "Don't forget to return, we eat at one." Ethel called after them, knowing only too well that children have little sense of time. "In two hours."

The four children moved rapidly away. "Why do you live so far out?" Ilana asked.

"Our mother does not like to live too near to people."

"Why is that?"

"There is always trouble." This sounded foreign to the girls, having grown up together with a group of kibbutz children. They did not understand and left it alone.

"Where is your father?" Rinat asked.

"We don't have any." This too had been accepted at face value.

The boys could connect to the girls in a way not possible with the Bedouin children. They felt extremely grateful. The girls had accepted them unconditionally and as they came to their home, the girls were hastily introduced to their mom. Then they searched their meager treasures for some worthy object to give them in return. They found nothing as they rummaged around desperately, looking for anything which would do. Oskar had somehow managed to retain two small cheap plastic replicas of Stan Laurel and Oliver Hardy, no larger than an inch or two. Those were all they had, but Oskar parted with them gladly.

"Here . . . for you." He gave Ilana the plastic statuettes.

"Thank you."

The boys had their own private hideout places, some nearby and others further away, they showed them to the girls.

They all returned to Ethel and Avi's tent together, some hours later.

"Can they eat with us?" the girls asked.

"Sure." Avi addressed the elder of the two boys, "Don't you have to tell your folks where you are?"

"No."

"This is Søren and the smaller one is Oskar." The girls informed them. They seemed to get along very well and Avi felt thankful. It would keep them occupied with each other. While nature may be fascinating and amazing to adults, children will prefer games with other children to the wonders of the environment around them. Avi could get his diving done without too much interference.

"How long are you staying?" Avi asked them absentmindedly.

"We live here for now."

Avi did not probe. They had their meal. The kids were in a hurry to get going. "We're going with them to their place," Ilana said.

"Don't forget to come back before dark," Ethel reminded them.

"Where is your place?" Avi asked, "is it far?"

"That way," Søren pointed toward the desert. "Ten minutes, no more."

The children had left hurriedly and Avi prepared his gear and a tank for his first dive. He only had four air tanks, so no more than four dives. Ethel cleaned up and prepared for a nap. Nature did not interest her so much, but she wanted a contented family, this remained her priority.

Dahab has a reef running parallel to the seashore, stretching out for some miles, with an easy entrance from the center of the village. There were other groups of scuba divers there. Avi had his dive among a mass of underwater life and amazingly shaped corals. He had been there before, but the wonders of nature never ceased to stun him anew. Coming back from his dive he found a somewhat anxious Ethel.

"The children have not returned yet," she informed him.

"I'll go and look for them," he said. He stacked his gear and went in the direction Søren had pointed out. He came to the outskirts of the village. There were sparsely distributed small plots of land fenced in, homesteads with huts or houses in their middle and still further off he made out one lonely shack apart from the others. The children seemed nowhere near as he approached.

He could not help but notice the difference between that place and the others. Someone had created a small garden, stones had been gathered and formed rectangular shapes filled with earth and blooming flowers. Avi realized that water would have to be fetched from the army tankers. Rows of smaller stones had formed a path leading to the door. The shack seemed newly painted and had flower pots on its window. This must be the place, Avi knocked on the door.

Lina opened the door, she did seem familiar. He talked in English, which is a second language in Israel: "Hello, are you the mother of the two boys? My daughters are playing with them." He had forgotten the boy's names.

"Yes, come in, I have met your two charming girls. They are somewhere about." She too had answered in English.

Avi had not seen the children, but since the Israeli jurisdiction, the area is safe as far as people were involved and he was not worried, but there always existed the possibility of snakes, spiders, or scorpions known to be around. He showed his concern:

"They are with your boys?"

"My boys know all about the desert, your girls are safe with them."

Avi looked around pleasantly surprised; he saw a neat and tidy home. There were pictures on the walls and the room nicely furnished. On one wall, there were shelves of books. A desk with some copybooks and papers could be seen. Lina had seen him looking around.

"I teach them, I get them to study for at least two hours daily. Can I make you some coffee?"

"Yes please. I'm Avi"

"Lina."

Lina busied herself with the coffee. Avi looked at her more closely. He saw a young woman, younger then himself by maybe fifteen years. She had a white thin loose linen covering on from head to foot, it should have hidden her figure, but, as she moved about, he could not help but notice her bulges and curves.

Lina kept herself busy preparing the coffee and some pieces of homemade cake. She found herself to some extent disturbed. She had little contact with the tourists who flocked around, and her children had never brought anyone home before. She had turned herself into a loner and somewhat of a recluse, an unwanted bitter pill for her to swallow. Avi seemed familiar; he looked a family man and projected the aura of a safe civilized person. She had not been aware of how much she had missed and needed his kind. The Bedouin were harsh and distant. Suddenly she felt close to tears. She collected herself and hid this as she served them the food and drink she had prepared.

"You seem familiar," she said at last, trying to keep her voice steady.

"We are from a kibbutz," Avi replied.

"We're from Denmark, but I stayed in a kibbutz once, before the children were born."

"I visited Denmark once too, on a trip. Very nice country."

Lina did not remark. She had not been too happy there and did not want to talk about it.

"Which kibbutz were you in?" Avi asked politely.

"I don't remember, one with a long name . . . so long ago. I was a volunteer there."

"We're from . . ." he named the place: "Zik-Hadarom." (Spark of the South)

"That's it! I remember the name!" she exclaimed excited.

Then Avi made the connection, she had mentioned her name before. "Lina . . . right . . . you were there with . . . someone named Rick!"

"You remember us?!"

It was Avi's turn to be moved: "Lina, I have met your folks in Denmark! In . . . Nykobing right? Your mother, Christina, and your father. . . ." He could not remember her father's name. "Also your younger sister . . . Yana? What a coincidence."

At the mention of her mother's and her sister's name in this strange faraway place, the tears did well up in Lina's eyes, they glistened. Avi noticed . . . touched.

"What happened to Rick?"

"We separated," Lina got out. "I remember your wife . . . Ethel. We worked together in the kitchen. How is she?"

"She is well, we are here for a few days with the children." Avi did not feel like talking about Ethel at this time. He continued, "Lina . . . do you know? . . . Your mother begged us in tears, to do something, anything, to get you away from Rick and back home!"

On hearing this, the tears burst out of her in an uncontrolled torrent. She wept, sobs convulsed out of her. In her own inner self-image, Lina considered herself a failure. Her ideas of what should be and not be had been formed by her parents and upbringing. All her efforts to resist her former notions had failed on the deeper emotional level, which can sabotage or augment motivations. She had dropped out of the university. Her children had no father and she did not know who Oskar's biological father was. Her children were growing up wild and unruly, and the few hours of amatory schooling each day were certainly not adequate. To top all, she had sex to pay the rent. The latter meant little to her, but it certainly could not have been what her parents might have wanted. Meeting Avi reminded her of her past youth and hopes for the future. She wept long and hard.

Avi felt her pain and could vaguely guess at its sources. He took hold of her hand. "I'm so sorry." Her hand felt warm to the touch and, with an unexpected thrill of excitement, he became aware of her as a desirable female. To him, Lina and her children had become the symbol and epitome of freedom. Lina did what she liked unhindered, and with no restrains or holding back. He envied her this and it happened to be what he would have liked to do himself. Lina did not make up, but her face and light hair had an unruly natural beauty and reminded Avi of a wild animal. Her body called out to him from under the thin gallabiyah-like robe. He felt strongly drawn to her and quickly let go of her hand.

The scene developed into an awkward situation, as they were practically strangers. Lina got hold of herself and, breathing heavily, gasped between her fading convulsions: "I don't know what happened to me, I have not cried in years."

"It's okay, those things happen," Avi said, but Lina felt the need to explain her outburst, not being too sure herself. "Seeing your girls and you, reminded me of home. I am not doing so well with my boys. They are running wild."

"They seemed like very nice kids to me. Well behaved."

"You had no qualms in letting your girls play with my boys?"

"None whatsoever."

His simple straightforward answer and its meaning captivated her. With a strong surge of emotion Lina moved from her seat and kissed him.

"Thank you."

Lina, as always, wore her loose and light gallabiyah-like linen dress and nothing else underneath. Letting the air flow freely in and out on one's body is the best way to keep cool in the hot desert summer. Avi, drawn to her like a magnet, put his arms around her and found her lips, they kissed, then kissed again more deeply. Lina drew away.

"The children will be back soon," she said softly.

She had not repulsed him! Shaken, Avi realized what he had done, but it had come about so naturally. "I'm so sorry," he said for the second time. "I don't know what overcame me. I have never done this before."

Lina too felt an attraction toward Avi. His apologies had touched her. He appeared a civilized safe person and she had lived under the Bedouins too long. He had kind eyes and could be trusted. She smiled at him, suddenly aware of having looked for his kind all her life. "It's alright. No harm done."

However, she had not been entirely correct; they were both conscious of what had occurred, each of them trying to control and suppress their emotions according to his or her nature. Lina had learned that Avi was married and she would not trespass. She had known and liked Ethel in the kibbutz–it all had been so long ago–she recalled a lady who had suffered much in her life and she intended not to cause her any future distress.

Avi too had some fears and misgivings about what had happened and did not know how to deal with his feelings except by forcibly ignoring them. They talked about their lives and not what had inserted itself on their minds and hearts. Their talk became conventional, even mundane. Avi wanted to ask her where the father of the children is, but did not quite dare. Among other things, he recounted to her his impressions of her home in Denmark and Lina told Avi that the Bedouins were giving them a hard time. The children too were not having it easy.

"Why not go to the Israeli authorities?" Avi asked.

"They try not to interfere too much."

They were saved from any more embarrassment by the four children arriving chatting and laughing together. Rinat kissed her dad and gave him the plastic trinkets, which they had got from the boys, to hold. Ilana, not knowing what to do with them, had unloaded them on her smaller sis. Then they promptly forgot about them. When Avi and the girls got back to their tent, Avi did not tell Ethel about Lina and the whole story of their meeting. He felt uneasy and, when questioned, he told her about the boys and their mom, who lived in a nice, clean organized home, right there on the outskirts of Dahab. Ethel did not show any more interest, except for being glad that the girls had found playmates.

The following night, lying next to Ethel and the girls in their tent, sleep did not come easily to Avi. They all seemed to be sleeping heavily the good sleep of a full day of running around, being in the water, and participating in the many activities. The girls had been scurrying about with Søren and Oskar all day long and slept heavily, not moving.

Avi quietly extracted himself and went outside to mull over the main subject on his mind. Their portable picnic table, with its plastic seats, stood next to the van and Avi seated himself on one of them, deep in thought.

He took stock of the situation. He had kept his meeting with Lina to himself and did not tell Ethel. Now he allowed himself to think. Lina, a beauty, a free wild thing, uninhibited, called out to him. He had felt her nakedness under the robe she had worn. He longed for her with an almost uncontrollable passionate surge of feelings. She had not repulsed him and he had recognized a strong mutual liking. He fought this by logic; *'Where is an affair going to get me? I have a family, a wife and two dear lovely girls!'* Avi had lived in defined social structures of one kind or another all his life. He had at all times been taught, guided and induced to a certain code of behavior. First at school, then joining the army together with a group and ending up in a kibbutz.

He had consciously chosen a communal way of life, believing and trusting in his fellow men. He had feared and hated the rat race as unnecessary; the result product of a grabbing civilization and wanted none of it. He had grown up as an only child without any siblings to deal with, and was a stout believer in the dignity of men. Fighting one's way to get your snout into the common trough had never been his way. Kibbutz life has many disadvantages, but to him a communal lifestyle had always been preferable to any alternative. Marrying and raising children had been a part of a pattern too. Avi, aware of the rat race which he so abhorred, infiltrating into kibbutz life and slowly changing their lifestyle, did not like it.

Sitting by the picnic table he suddenly felt strangled. There seemed no way of resolving what had occurred over there in Lina's home. He could not leave his family or the kibbutz. He loved his daughters. He sat dejected for a long time. The sudden glow of a falling meteorite made him take notice. He lifted his head and saw the stars. On a clear night with no artificial lighting to damper the glitter of the billions of stars, the Milky Way glows luminous and amazingly radiant, highlighting the heavenly scene as if done so purposely by a divine force. 'Every one of those stars is a sun,' he thought. He had read about millions of Galaxies and knew that one can only see a tiny fragment of the Cosmos with the naked eye. 'There must be more stars than grains of sand on a beach.' The enormity of it was mind bogging. Suns have planets around them and somewhere in that entire expanse; there certainly would be life, even intelligent life. 'The Universe is not cut down to the size of our perceptions. *What do our little follies matter to the infinite universe,*' thought Avi to himself. Still consciously undecided about what to do, but somehow refreshed, he returned to the tent and forced himself to get some sleep.

Many unconscious and often conflicting forces were at work in Avi. In the morning, the family washed, brushed teeth and had breakfast. Avi found the plastic Laurel and Hardy in his pocket. He placed them on the table. "Whose are they?"

"They are a present from Søren and Oscar." The girls giggled. "We don't know what to do with them."

Avi, not an oversensitive or high-strung susceptible person, looked at those cheap trinkets. He could not help but sense the pure untainted friendly and grateful feelings of those two boys, who had given them as a present to his girls. His dormant feelings and thoughts turned to Lina. He recalled the celestial glow of last night with the infinite spaces of the Universe, and at this specific moment in time, he finally resolved to act on his feelings. Life is short and there may be no second chances. Life should be lived and experienced, not wasted.

Aloud, Avi announced: "I'm going for a dive."

"We're coming too," Ilana said. The girls and Ethel sometimes joined him, bathing in the shallow waters.

"I'm going to the far end. I want to see what's over there."

The former fishing village stretched out along the seashore and the northern entrance leading to the reef, could only be accessed by a much longer walk. The reef there consisted of sharp corals and the girls would not be able to bath nearby, also they did not want to walk so far. "Be careful!" Ethel said.

Avi arranged and gathered his gear, not intending to use it, at least not now. He did not turn north but northwest toward

Lina's place. He walked eagerly carrying the heavy air pressured tank with him on his back, having found no place to leave or effectively hide it. Luckily, the morning still felt cool, he put on parts of his diving suit not wanting to carry them, but after a few minutes he felt himself already perspiring. He took them off and packed them together with the gear in his bag

Full diving gear, including a tank of compressed air, together with some weights to keep the human body underwater, are not meant to be lugged around long distances, and Avi–unromantically sweating under his load–felt relieved as he arrived at Lina's place. The growing heat as the sun went along its way had not been the only matter causing him punishment. He had lied to the girls and Ethel, and he felt ill at ease.

Lina had not expected him at a certain specific time, but she had sensed and expected that their former meeting would not be the last one. Without being aware, she had frequently looked out of the window while going about her housework and it was not with great surprise, but with a large measure of complacency mingled with excitement, that she saw him approaching. The boys were out and would not be in until noon for dinner and then their homework, always scheduled for the hot hours of the day. She greeted Avi as if this happened to be a normal expected call:

"Come in," with a smile.

Avi trudged inside heavily, plunking down his large bag. They looked at each other, their expectations, hopes and illusions of each other in a hopeless mixed up turmoil. A long pause ensued while no one spoke. Then Avi said, "I have lied to my wife, she thinks I am diving."

Lina saw the dust and sweat on him. "We have a makeshift shower, go and sluice yourself off."

"Where do you get the water from?"

"We have a small tank here. Søren and Oscar keep it full."

"How? They are children."

"With the help of a donkey from the neighbors."

Talking of daily issues made both of them feel calmer. The real issues at hand, whatever they are, or should come to be, would be addressed later. Except for his diving suit and a pair of now, sweat soaked swimming trunks, Avi had no clothes with him. He used the water sparingly and came out of the shower draped in a tiny towel, grinning bashfully. "I didn't bring any clothes."

Suddenly, Lina felt an overpowering surge of love for this man–this kind, safe, trustworthy, handsome person. He had lied for her. Her heart beat faster.

"You won't need any," she said shakily.

Avi took hold of Lina and their bodies glued together. The towel fell down and Lina's galabiyah remained only a thin sheath separating them. They kissed deeply.

"Wait," Lina said breathing hard and extracting herself from Avi. "I have slept around some, with the Bedouins too and the one I have to pay the rent."

Avi tried to grasp what she had mentioned, but his mind tackled the more simple issue of the two. He inquired, puzzled: "What? What rent? Here?"

"We fixed the place up, we found a pigsty with no roof and now I have to pay rent to the Bedouin who owns the land."

"You have sex with him?"

"We have no money to spare."

Nothing mattered to Avi except the biological drive of male to female. Lina characterized to him an escape of all the bonds that restrict a person; she impersonated freedom, a carte blanche to life, sexual and otherwise. Strangely enough, her having sex with some of the Bedouins, only illuminated the point to him.

They stopped talking and made love. Lina found herself giving herself to him body and soul. Fleetingly she wondered what made her like him so much and then on the tide of her passions she tingled and shivered with an orgasm and then again and later once more. Sex with the Bedouin youths had been exciting and good, but quick and fast, and had left her mostly unmoved emotionally, which certainly was not the case now. She felt a strong love for this man emerging. Love with us is possessive in its nature, but does not necessarily have to be so. We want to close in, possess, and even own the object we love, be it a vase, a lampshade or a car, a house, be it a sculpture or a masterpiece of a painting, or a person we desire. Lina, being emotionally opposed to Western ways and habits, had turned to the desert for freedom and peace. She had not found the freedom she sought, but maybe she had found the second best: an illusion of independence, together with some maturity. She knew there could be no future for Avi and her and with much regret, she also knew she could not and would not estrange him from his family. She would donate herself and Avi as gift of love to Ethel and to his girls.

For Avi, Lina had been the first woman other than Ethel. Strange but heavenly at the same time, he felt a sense of unreality: '*this is really happening*?' he thought, 'life will never be the same now. Twenty years of fidelity are thrown away.' Then he caught himself: 'I am thinking too much.' He forced all thoughts from his mind and concentrated on his partner.

Between their lovemaking they talked. They talked about many matters, but mainly what they meant to each other. In time, Avi came straight to the point: "I cannot leave my wife and children."

"I will not ask you to do so."

"But I want to, very much!"

"No you don't. You think so now. It will pass."

"Lina (What a lovely name), I want to be with you. We can have so many good times together." A part of him knew the futility of his own words, but he could not help himself. Those sentences forced themselves out.

Lina put a stop to that kind of talk. "No, out of the question. Let's not talk about the future anymore."

They made love for two hours. Avi felt like being in another part of existence. He adored Lina with kisses from head to foot, but he knew their time was limited. Lina had reminded him that the boys would come soon and he had to get back to his own family. No dive took longer than two hours. "Your wife must never suspect anything," she told him. "We have a few more days, then it must be over."

He sighed. "Don't I know."

Avi managed to get to Lina three more times before he had to return home with his family. Each time, instead of scuba diving, he would drag his gear with him to Lina's place and they would spend some delicious stolen hours with each other. Lina accepted him for himself; she did not criticize or complain, as Ethel sometimes did, and he enjoyed her company as much as the fantastic lovemaking.

The situation he found himself in, seemed intolerable to him. He loved and cared for his family and would never part with them. Ethel could be grumpy at times and burst out in spurts of wounded indignation on some imagined hurt to her feelings, and he often had to tread softly, as on eggs, but she was a part of his life, he had learned to accept her and love her. Lina, to him, existed in another sphere of reality altogether; as an angel, a sex goddess, a whore, and an understanding female with a soft place for him to fall. A free soul, independent, and he envied her autonomy. He saw her as he had wanted to see her–primarily with his imagination and fantasy.

The last time they met had been in the gloomy shadow of their soon future parting. Avi had realized that Lina had no source of income and he had taken half of the family's reserve money for the trip, a handsome sum, and hid the cash in Lina's place where she would later find it, after they had left. She would not be able to return the money. He told Ethel nothing and he would somehow add the money to their expanses for the trip. Avi had strongly wished he could have given Lina more, but it would have made Ethel suspicious.

Both Lina and Avi were aware of the brief and passing nature of their affair. They would have to part and Avi seemed to have a more difficult time.

"I hate leaving you like this. At the mercy of the Bedouins," he stated

"I was here before you came and we'll be here after you leave. The Bedouins are not any better or worse than others."

"You are one hell of a brave woman."

"Am I? I do what has to be done."

"You could go back to Denmark."

"And live with my parents. No way. What would I do in Denmark, there's nothing for me there. I have no skills. Sweep the streets? Do sewing and washing or some other like job? A cashier maybe, or cleaning some offices at nights? Having a boss telling me what to do! Here at least we are free and do what we want."

"Sleeping with the Bedouins?"

"There's always a price to pay."

"What about the boys?"

"They will grow up without the so-called benefits of our civilization. They will find their own way."

"Lina, I love you, I really do. You have given me my life back. I felt my life wilting and drying up before I met you. I dearly want to remain with you."

"There is no use talking like this. You have to go your way and I mine. We both know it."

"I will remember our few days all my life. They will keep me going."

They parted with many kisses and Avi tore himself away.

A somewhat grim and silent Avi folded the family tent and packed their belongings into the van. On their way, driving back home, Avi remained quiet, claiming to be tired. Out of the four compressed air tanks he had used only one. He got the tank refilled on the way. Arriving home, he returned the gear, still common property at the time. Trying not to feel and think, he busied himself with the many tasks before him until everything had been returned to its former place.

Lina had found the money Avi had left behind with a flow of gratitude and love. However, the money would not last forever and she decided to look for some work. The restaurants, hotels and shops did not want to hire a European woman, who would have to be paid twice or three times as much as an Egyptian or a Bedouin. Finally, she found some work changing the girl who serviced the diving center, a day, or two each week. Lina took her boys with her to work at the diving center to help her with the suits and gear. They came in touch with scuba divers. Søren and Oscar were charming boys and easily took to the diving community. Lina did not earn much but enough to keep her and the boys going.

The kibbutz Zik-Hadarom had slowly changed from an agricultural community to a mechanized industrial one. At first, they had all been proud to be farmers, and transform the likeness of the weak Ghetto Jew to a strong and independent one, including the physical work this involved. Modern times had forced adjustments on the members. At this period, Ethel and Avi had money paid to them monthly for their work–not in actual cash, but in credit points, which they used in the local store and might be changed into money if so needed. Avi worked in a factory and Ethel worked in the kitchen. The girls, Ilana and Rinat, slept in a dormitory, two or three to a room, had their meals there and went to school. The afternoons were spent in their parent's home.

Suddenly it all seemed too much for Avi. He became impatient and easily irritated. He grew sick of the place. He realized this and recognized where it was coming from and tried very hard not to be short and abrupt. He twisted and turned in his sleep, both Ethel and he were tired in the mornings. They moved to separate beds. Time passed, but Avi found himself often thinking and longing for Lina. Lina, alone in Sinai, only eight hours drive away from him, but to all purposes in another world.

The Middle East is always an uneasy and troubled area, and for Israel, there had been only few short periods of peaceful existence since its creation. The Israel army consists of reserves mainly, and in those disturbed times, most able-bodied men in Israel are called up for army duty once a year. Usually for one month or up to forty days. Avi felt glad when they called him up, he would find a relief from his dreary routine. Rummaging in his shed, looking for a torch to take with him, he came upon the little plastic replica of Stan Laurel lying in a small jar. The statuette retained poignant memories for him. He searched for its partner but could not find the other anywhere. He sat down and held the tiny figure in his hand. The little knick-knack had been given in a genuine feeling of gratitude and love. Holding the tiny object in his hand, he imagined and felt the pure guileless honesty in which the boys had donated it to his girls. He sat in the shed, contemplating for a long time, reflecting. Then an idea wormed its way into his head.

He phoned his commanding officer, after the formalities he came to the point. "I can't make it this month. I need a postponement."

"What the hell is wrong with you, this is the third call I got from you guys."

"Sorry."

"Sorry is not good enough. Listen you get here on time and if we have enough men I'll release you."

"Okay," Avi said, knowing he would not be there and this might get him into trouble later, but he did not care.

He took out as much money as he dared from his account and spun a likely story to Ethel and the girls. The army was sending him deep into Sinai and he might not be able to come home on leave. Avi felt swamped in the throes of an overpowering emotion. First and foremost, he had to see Lina again and be with her. He resisted all logical thought. He had bought time, but did not feel capable of planning any further. Whatever came after . . . well he would have to deal with it some way or other, but for now, he did not have the slightest idea of what might happen later.

A puzzled but determined and eager Avi made his way impatiently on the bus southwards. He had mixed feelings. First and dominant were the excitement and joy of surprising Lina together with the strong emotions of being with her. He had brought along a lot of money and the halo of donating the cash had charmed and dazzled him, blinding him to the other issues involved. Then came the anxiety of what he had actually dared, mixed with the emotions of leaving his daughters and wife. He had not been able to make real specific plans. Overwhelmed by his own actions, he knew he could do no different. Avi faced his thoughts ironically: He had never lied to Ethel and his children before, 'except where Lina was involved.' His decision had not been an easy one and he felt those issues keenly, but he forced himself not to think about them, logical thought at the time, being beyond him. He had been swept away by the tides of forces so powerful and basic, that everything else had faded into a background. Avi felt very uneasy and the parting from Ethel and the children had been formal and awkward. He did not dare to show much emotion.

Once in Eilat, he changed busses, and in Sinai he shared a taxi with some others to Dahab. On the lengthy trip, the taxi driver, a Bedouin, found the time to complain in fairly good Hebrew: "You Israelis have cheated us. You have made a treaty with the Egyptians over our land. Many have already infiltrated here and now every second taxi is run by an Egyptian, the shops too are owned by people from Cairo."

The Bedouin in Sinai are a loose formation of tribes and their culture is a tribal one. They had no idea how to run a country. Avi did not feel like arguing, being full of what he had done, occupied himself with anticipating his meeting with a surprised and delighted Lina, but one of the other passengers answered, "You Bedouins have no police or army, you could not possibly and effectively patrol the borders of such a large place. Arms and explosives would be smuggled in, terrorists and drugs too. You guys will do the smuggling yourselves. The Egyptians can control this better."

"Sinai is our land! We live here. Our fathers and their fathers have lived here!" the driver stated. This being obviously true, stopped the discussion. The rest of the trip passed in relative silence.

The taxi let him off at the center of the village. There were almost no people about as the place would be handed over to the Egyptians soon. He walked with a fast beating heart in the direction of Lina's place. As he came nearer, he noticed a shabbier and more dilapidated view than he remembered. 'Funny how memories lead one astray,' he thought. As he approached still closer it became suspiciously clear to him, together with a sinking feeling in his gut, that the place might be deserted! The flowers which they had planted nearby, were dried husks burned from the sun. A window hung ajar on one hinge.

He entered and felt a shock of dismay. The empty walls of a bare room stared back at him. The bookshelves on the wall sagged, and the books were gone. He wandered into the other room, it too was in shambles. 'What now? Where are Lina and the boys?' Had he come so far to find them gone! Had Lina finally decided to return to Denmark? He wandered about for a short while, touching the empty shelves, the place had many happy memories for him. The authorities might know something. He made his way back to the center.

The 'authorities' consisted of two Israeli officers and some soldiers, packing and sorting out papers to be kept or burned. They were preparing for evacuation and were too busy to see him. At first, they would not let him inside the compound, but he made a nuisance of himself and an impatient officer at last agreed to talk to him shortly. "What the hell do you want, don't you know that this place is being turned over to the Egyptians?"

"There was this woman living here, with two children, where has she gone to?"

"The Danish one? I wouldn't know but I saw one of the kids around yesterday."

"Where?"

"In the old part."

"But where exactly?"

"Near the place where they keep the camels."

Avi guessed that Lina had not left as he had feared, but lived somewhere in the village, or in the new section now called Dahab

City. She might want to leave, not caring to remain under the coming Egyptians. Dahab had hundreds of shacks and places for rent. Lina could have moved to any of them. They were too many to check out. Lina did not have enough money to rent a real place in Dahab City and Avi considered his best guess would be to wander about the center of the old village or near the water tank. He might meet the boys there sooner or later.

Avi had arrived at Dahab at a strange time: a transitory period and a future change of authorities. Almost no tourists from other countries could be seen around, there were some Israelis taking leave of the place that they had taken to their hearts for one and a half decades. Avi had never seen the place so devoid of life. Wandering desperately around, he found no sign of Lina or the boys. He took a room for the night. The next day he meandered about from one place to another. They would have to buy food; he asked around in shops but got no coherent answer. Many shops were closed now; the camel camp too looked deserted.

Then a stone flew by him from one of the alleys. He looked in and saw some Bedouins boys throwing stones, but not in his direction. They were throwing them at a distant barrel and someone from behind it was flinging stones back efficiently, one boy grunted as he got hit.

"What is this? What are you doing?" Avi asserted.

They instantly recognized him as an Israeli. "We are stoning dogs. Go away, this is not your place anymore." The one that spoke, a half-grown youth, put his hand on his belt, Avi saw a curved vicious looking knife, the others snickered.

Avi did not fear them. He had been in the army, but he did not want a senseless fight on his hands. "I shall go to the Israelis with this," he threatened back. The current Israeli jurisdiction was well known for their intolerance of any harm doing. They would soon leave but were still around. The boys retreated and slunk away. Søren and Oskar came out from behind the barrel, Avi saw their blooded faces. They recognized each other.

"My God, what have they done to you!" Avi exclaimed.

"We did more to them," Søren boasted. He showed Avi a sling. "With this."

It seemed totally beside the point to Avi. He rummaged in his bag and found some toilet paper. One of the many singularities of the Sinai area is that only in the real hotels actual toilet paper is used, in most of the less expansive places they have newspapers or magazines. Most Israelis bring their own toilet paper. Avi wiped the blood off their faces. There were some bruises and cuts, nothing serious, Avi decided, but they would have to be treated with iodine.

"Where do you live now?"

"A place nearby." The boys led him to their home. They did not talk much. The boys were silently musing over the fight and Avi geared himself to meeting Lina, when Oskar asked him with the amazing intuition of children.

"Are you going to be our father?"

Søren nudged him. "Shut up," he spoke in Danish.

The question had been asked, and now would be out in the open and should not be ignored. "I have children of my own," Avi said carefully, somewhat nonplussed, this might be hard to handle. "Ilana and Rinat, you know them?"

"We can all be brothers and sisters," Oskar continued, undaunted by Søren's prodding and shoving. Avi, realizing the seriousness of the matter, became cautious. "I think your mother will have something to say on the subject."

They arrived. The Bedouins in the village and around live in family groups with rooms or shacks in the middle of a courtyard where they also keep their farm animals, all surrounded by a fence. The family where Lina had rented a room had left their place and had built tinier cubical-like rooms to let to the tourists, all empty now, except for one. Oscar ran ahead with the news.

Lina came to the door. They stared at each other silently. The boys were there and Avi, inhibited from taking her into his arms, felt himself shaking inside. She looked as beautiful and desirable as ever. Lina was surprised, but at some level she must have wanted or expected him, it seemed so natural, so in character, like the last piece of a puzzle falling into place. Lina had guessed at Avi's intention in hiding the money he had left behind. Now they would have another issue to deal with. Lina, deliriously happy at his arrival, even as she felt concerned and fearful, wanted him very much to remain with them, but she knew she would have to send him back, and she did not look forward to the task.

"Come in," she managed. Then she noticed the bruises and cuts on her children. A welcome distraction. "What happened?"

"They ganged up on us," Søren explained.

"They need some disinfection," Avi added.

"He made them go away," Oskar said.

With a thankful look to Avi, Lina busied herself with tending to her boys while they told her the story in more detail. Avi looked around; they were in a tiny room, even more so, as much of the floor space had been taken up by mattresses and some boxes stacked by the wall. A small cupboard, a table and some chairs were the basic furniture. Lina fixed them all something to eat and the boys with some intuitive knowledge of their own wandered off, leaving them alone.

Lina and Avi embraced, kissing each other repeatedly. "I have missed you so much," Avi said between kisses.

"I have dreamed of you coming," she murmured into his ear, "but you shouldn't have."

"Why not? We love each other."

The time for a discussion would be later. Lina changed the subject. "Oscar often mentioned you and the girls."

"They seem to know all about us," Avi said.

"I do not lie to them. Truth is the only thing I can give them."

"You give them your love."

"That is a part of it, certainly."

"I have lied to Ethel and the girls."

"We all do what we have to do . . . I suppose. I have found the money you left behind. Thank you. You are not a rich man, remember, I have been to the kibbutz. I know."

"I could not help myself. Why have you moved out?"

"The Israelis are leaving and the Bedouin, all of them, but especially the one who claimed to own our place, became more and more rude and insolent, insisting on more rent." She paused. "He wanted me to move in with his family and become his third wife and the boys would be raised as Bedouins." She continued, "I had a part time job at the diving center, but they closed."

Avi did not know what to say. He changed to the subject on his mind. "Lina . . ." he cleared his throat.

She stopped him. "No!"

"Lina, I have to speak. I have thought of you all the time and I brought money with me. We can leave together."

"No, Avi, let us not talk about it."

"I came back for you. You know I love you and I think you love me too. I get along fine with the boys . . ."

"And what about your girls?"

"They will have to stay with their mother."

"No! Out of the question."

"You want us to remain together as much as I do."

"What I want does not matter."

Their discussions waged on and on. They repeated themselves continuously in their agitation, passionately, intensively arguing for their happiness. Logic and emotions intermixed. Lina would not budge; she would not take Avi away from his family. They persisted desperately, persevering, but making no progress. Lina learned the details about the deception Avi had cooked up to get away. Avi found out that Lina intended to ask her folks for money to get herself and the children back to Denmark. She feared to remain there with the children under the Egyptians.

"We have the cash," he urged, knowing only too well how Lina hated to ask her folks for money. "I have my passport with me. We can all fly to Denmark from Israel."

Lina felt herself on the verge of tears. She loved this dear safe and trustworthy man. "No, Avi. We can have a month together. Let's enjoy ourselves and keep the memories for the rest of our lives."

"What about the boys?"

"I do not keep secrets from them. They will know anyway. It is best we tell them."

"Do they know about the Bedouin guy . . . and the others?"

"Generally, not explicitly."

"Those are adult issues, they should not be bothered with them."

"They live in an adult world. Ignoring a major item like us together, would only make things worse."

Avi had an idea; he liked the boys and they liked him. Maybe–through them–he could change Lina's mind. "We can afford better accommodations," he told her, "I'll rent the next room for us." Lina did not object. "I'll go now and be back soon," Lina nodded silently, she had much to think about.

He left and searched around for the boys and eventually he found them nearby. Lina, not an overprotective mom, had not kept life's lessons at bay from them. They had helped her keep the house and the courtyard tidy and clean, the outhouse too, they fetched as much water as needed and he had never heard them complain and they did their lessons daily. They were unassuming and certainly not spoiled kids, life had matured them.

"We need to talk," he told them and they found some boxes in the shade and seated themselves.

"You know why I am here," he began.

"You want to be with us, with mom." Søren said.

"Yes."

"Will you be our father?" Oskar asked again.

"Your mother has some doubts."

"Why?" Søren asked.

"She does not think I should leave Ilana and Rinat."

"Take them with you," Oskar advised.

"She does not want me to take them away from their mother, their friends and studies."

The kids were quiet, the subject being too much for them to handle. Avi said, "I need help with your mother."

"What can we do? She never listens to us," the elder brother maintained.

"She might on this one. Talk to her."

"Okay"

"Listen, whatever happens, I will stay with you for a while. We will rent the next room and you will have one to yourselves. Is that agreeable? Nothing else changes."

"Sure," Søren said. "I can hit Oskar with no one interfering." Oskar kicked him and scampered off. Søren ran after him.

Avi had tried to enlist the boys help, but nothing would change Lina's mind. A part of him felt relieved; much as he loved Lina, he could not see himself leaving his family, nor the kibbutz, he loved them and they were his home–for better and worse. He would have a month with Lina. They dragged two mattresses to the next room and had their honcymoon; not in a five-star hotel, but in a cubicle of twenty feet with pealing walls and a tiny pane-less window for air and it felt like heaven on earth for them. Strange as it may appear, a month can be a long period and a short one at the same time. On occasion, the time limit would weight on them and not always did everything seem well in paradise. They were lovers and had lovers' arguments which always ended in mutual appeasing and lovemaking.

They both knew their time would have to end and they both feared and hated the moment when they would take leave of each other. Avi sometimes wanted to throw his former life away and stick to Lina through thick and thin, and she would remind him of his family. The boys liked Avi and accepted him. They too suspected that he would have to return to his girls. Lina's way with the boys always used to be as open and transparent as she could make it and they would talk and discuss their problems at times.

The four made trips to interesting sites around the desert and as Avi had brought a great deal of money with him, they had an easy and good time. Money too had been one of the matters Lina and Avi had discussed. Lina did not have enough money for a flight back home for her and the boys. She did not want to ask her parents for money, but refused to take a cent more from Avi, while he tried to force sums on her. He could not leave her alone in the desert with the pitiful amount she had.

"Lina, my dear, if you pay for your flight you will have nothing to live on until you leave," Avi would remind her.

"Avi, darling, we have managed before and will do so again."

"But I want to help."

"How will you explain the large sums that you spent."

"I'll find something."

Their arguments were between lovers and they doted on each other. At last they decided that Lina would leave by the end of their month and Avi, after seeing them off, would return to his family. Avi insisted on paying for their flight.

Their month rolled along relentlessly with the slow rhythm of the desert. It had seemed a lengthy time to them at first, a week passed quickly and then another one. Two weeks remained. Two weeks were a long time still. They indulged in themselves and in each other. One more week passed and only too sudden they had arrived at the last few days. Those too went by, uncompromising, remorseless, not caring about the two people in love who did not want them to end. At first, Lina and Avi had counted the weeks, then the days left to them and finally the hours of the last night they would spend together. Time passed inexorably and the moment of final parting would soon come. They traveled to the main Israel airport together. Lina and Avi had exhausted themselves emotionally and their final taking leave of each other had been commonplace and formal.

Two dejected people separately made their way home, each with his or her feelings and thoughts. Their opponent and adversary had been life itself. All they had wanted was to be together. No more, no less. They were not felons or criminals. They did not steal or embezzle and they certainly had not murdered anyone. However, it could not to be.

Avi, after parting from Lina and the boys at the airport, traveled in a bus homeward, his feelings and thoughts in turmoil. He had found an additional sum of money in his trouser back pocket. Only Lina could have put it there without his noticing. The sum almost equaled the cost of their plane tickets. She had returned the money to him, *so that he would not have to explain its loss at home.* Avi, an adult, felt his eyes moisten with love and gratitude. Lina would arrive with very little cash, but her family would be waiting for her at the airport.

He had sought his freedom with Lina. To him, she had symbolized the laissez-faire of a bird flying unhindered from one place to another, while another part of him had been aware of how even birds are subject to a biological blue-print scheme; they had their life mapped out for them even before birth. Were freedom and love illusions? Then why do we need them and cling to them in the face of so many obstacles, emotional and physical ones? No! These were not illusions, Avi mused, but they were limited to a design, perhaps a master plan inside life's frame.

He had done his best, and his best had not been good enough. He could possibly have separated from Ethel, but he would not leave his girls and finally the knowledge had enabled him to concede to Lina's viewpoint and persuasions and relinquish his own wants. His affair with Lina had given him the strength to continue with his own life; whenever things got rough he would be able to reflect on this last secret month and be comforted. No one can take that away from him. Avi had not been too enthusiastic about living in Denmark, he sensed and feared to become a stranger there, even with Lina by his side . . . like transplanting a tree and transferring it with its roots to a place where the specific chemical format and climate to flourish is lacking. He might have wilted. Avi consoled himself; he was returning to his own home and to his own people. Ethel and his girls would be happy to see him. There would have to be a lot of creative explaining all around.

Lina, seated on a plane with the boys, would fly straight from Israel to Kastrup, the Copenhagen international airport. Even in her great sorrow in parting from Avi, she experienced a glow of inner satisfaction; she had managed to return the money Avi had spent on their flight tickets. She felt an overpowering flow of love for him. Lina had much to think about. Her parents and Yana would be waiting for her there to take them home. There would be a family reunion and the boys had not seen their folks since they had left, except for some pictures in an album and even Søren could not remember what his grandparents looked like. They were in for an emotional and happy event but she did not feel delighted over the prospect. Leaving Avi had torn her apart even as there had been no real alternative.

The more she thought about her dilemma the less her deliberations seemed a choice; could she have done different? Having Avi with her and a father to her boys would have made them all happy, but only for a limited period. Knowing he had left his wife and those two lovely girls would eat and worm its way into their souls and fester. Their euphoria could not last and guilt with regret would creep in. Moodiness, mutual blaming and fights might break out. Lina thought bitterly. *'Why have we arraigned the world so that one's happiness is often at the expanse of another?'*

Her affair had helped to make up her mind. No more wandering around and dragging the children with her. Time to settle down, it was not too late! Enlist in some specialized course and then find work in the same field, maybe find some nice person too, and make a so-called success of her life. She had her misgivings; after all, what is success? Doing what people expected of her? Nevertheless, she would put her mind to it. Making peace with her father came first on her list of resolutions. She would work hard to get it done!

Lina studied her boys fondly; the boys were exited, not remembering having flown before and fidgeted about. Their characters would be formed by the needs of the civilization they were going to and Lina felt not too keen about the idea. Once she had idolized the Bedouin society and she had soon learned the error of this. They too had been slaves to their taboos and inflexible ways of life, even as they had claimed to be free. 'Better to have a master one knows,' she thought wearily.

They fastened their seat belts and the plane lifted off. The boys looked out through the small round portholes as the shore of Israel receded and disappeared.

Then there was only the open sea.

THE END

www.ingramcontent.com/pod-product-compliance
Lightning Source LLC
Chambersburg PA
CBHW071530260626
47170CB00002B/582